The Seventh Generation

by Dave DiGrazie

Copyright © 2016 Dave DiGrazie
Printed in the United States of America

DiGrazie, Dave

Seventh Generation/ DiGrazie- 1st Edition

ISBN: 978-0-9984018-4-3

1. Seventh Generation. 2. Political Fiction. 3. Historcial Fiction.
4. Buffalo, New York. 5. Family Drama.
1. DiGrazie.

NFB
No Frills Buffalo/Amelia Press
119 Dorchester Road
Buffalo, New York 14213

For more information visit
nfbpublishing.com

To the hundreds of thousands – no, millions through time – who've come up through the ranks of the Thundering Herd.

Chapters

The Seventh Generation

Part I

The Mayor

1
Cesidio: A Little Backstory

The Salt of the Earth and men like him made our country great, I think. They certainly made my home town mighty. After he left us the place fell on harder times, but when he was raising my uncle Ricco out on the East Side just inside the city line, it was a place of smoke and animal stockyards; of trains and boats and steel. So much metal in the mills, in the water, in the air. So much lumber being sawed, so much grain being turned into food, or beer. So much industry that its inhabitants were oblivious that much of the place was built upon a beautiful shore.

The Salt of the Earth once stood before my cousins and me, in my Uncle Ricco's backyard in Cheektowaga, New York. He was like a surrogate grandfather then. He is part of my religion now. I believe that he came down to earth in the form of a man so that he could teach us cousins a thing or two. He held forth three or four times per year, and when he spoke to us, the sun was always shining.

Except for New Year's Day. Then when he talked, it was almost always snowing outside Uncle Ricco's living room window.

Me? My birth and baptismal papers say I am Ernesto Pronotaro. Eighteen months after those documents were drawn up, similar papers were created for my brother Tomasso. Then, our parents spent years molding us into an anglicized version of our heritage. Dad, whose name was "William," bequeathed upon me an American-sounding nickname: Ernie the Pro.

Dad died young and so did his dad; I've heard it said that on our continent, the white man destroyed the red ones with alcohol but that the red man counterpunched with tobacco. Dad's blackened lungs last grabbed oxygen a few years ago. Then he went to that place where the Old Salts go. He might have brought a pack of Pall Malls with him. He may be gone, but even today as I approach the age of sixty, I feel like he is right beside me whenever my wife or one of my smart-alecky kids calls for "Ernie the Pro" and my head turns.

The Salt of the Earth also had a given name: Cesidio Gugliuzza. You say it like this: Chee-see-dio Gool-yoot-sa. While he lived, I knew him as "Pops." That's what we were all told to call him. He was the blood grandfather of my three Gugliuzza cousins, but he loved us all, I think. He only played a cameo role in my life's story, but he's one of the reasons why I am one of the most blessed men you may ever meet.

Then one day old Cesidio and we cousins met a man that even he worshipped.

July 4, 1968

The Salt of the Earth was shrinking a bit in physical stature with each passing year, but there was no mistaking his great power. Hands big, thick, calloused. Biceps in his fingers. Shoulders, neck muscles, hips and thighs that bulged with work. His body screamed of superhuman feats of manual labor. He had raised his family in the enclave with all the other *Abbruzzesse* off of East Delevan Avenue, and to relax he coaxed tomatoes, peppers and cucumbers from the thin urban soil in his little backyard.

This particular Independence Day he sat in his usual place, a lawn chair under the shade of my Uncle Ricco's big willow, smack in the middle of the back yard. Flavor filled the air as hot dogs, burgers and spicy Italian sausages sizzled on the grill in the corner of the yard near the garage. Old Cesidio called for us cousins, nine of us in all, to gather around him.

He ran his fingers through my hair, tickling the back of my neck, inventing a new song, the melody never before heard and words in that European tongue which Dad had discouraged my brother and me from learning. But every so often I could hear that the lyrics included our real names: Ernesto; my brother Tomasso. Names of the other cousins.

His acolytes gathered together, he eased into his lesson the way he always did, by asking questions. Always the same, his questions were.

"How's-a-school?" His voice was gruff and his English words broken, but his face was kind.

"Are you good-a-boy in-a-school? Do you pass-a the tests they give in-a-school?"

"Yes, sir," answered one of the cousins.

"Be-a-good-a-boys!" the sermon started with a wagging finger of warning. That finger, and the audible exclamation point, was his signal to us that Church was in session. Anyone sitting on his lap would need to scramble to their feet, because in a moment he would start those thick arms a-gesturing.

"Stay in-a-school." Words dripping with warning. Pregnant pause.

"Get-a-good-a job."

The other adults in the yard might have been chattering, but we only heard his voice. Though we always knew what was about to come, we'd look at him as though we were about to hear something life-changing for the first time.

"Don't be like a-me!" He said it loudly, on the way up out of his lawn chair. I can still see him standing, arms extending skyward with palms open.

"Beth-a-la-hem a-Steel!" His eyes swept upward toward the white fluffy clouds floating overhead, in their sea of deep blue. The sun was shining on him and him alone.

"Open-a-hearth!" At this point, his sermon became so loud that our parents had all stopped talking. The Salt of the Earth's eyes were round and white, and wide open.

"I shovel-a-coke! Twelve hour day! A twenty year! I see man-a-killed!" If his words didn't impress his meaning upon us, we would get it from his arms and hands.

"Pops!" cut in Aunt Loretta. "They're just kids! You're scaring them."

"Good!" He wheeled around to face his daughter, who like all the ladies in *Famiglia Gugliuzza*, was quite buxom and prematurely grey.

"Good, I-a-scare them. Nineteen-a-twenty three, I work in-a-side big oven! You want them work in-a-side oven? Nineteen-a-thirty, I still in oven! Nineteen-a-forty."

He turned away from Aunt Loretta to look back at us cousins. His voice dropped back several decibels and even today, all these years later, I feel the warm summer breeze that touched our faces as he continued.

"Be a doctor. Be a smart a-man. Use-a-your head. Not-a-your muscle."

And then, on that day in 1968, a new look crossed his face. His eyes lit up like we had never seen them light up before. He pointed back behind us, toward my uncle's charcoal grill.

"It's-a Sal Frandino!"

Our hearts stopped. Our family was respectable, but we weren't wealthy or important. What would Sal Frandino be doing at our cookout on the Fourth of July? All of us cousins were years away from voting in our first election, but all of us knew who Sal Frandino was. We were all quite proud of Sal Frandino. He was one of us.

"Be like-a-him. Not like-a me." The Salt of the Earth was still pointing.

The cousins all turned toward the grill in time to see my Grandma Sara, thirty feet away, handing a paper plate that held a sausage bomber to a tall, smiling, familiar-looking man dressed in an impeccable business suit. Electricity filled my eleven-year old body. It was really him.

But what was the mayor of Buffalo doing in my uncle's back yard on July 4, 1968?

"Be like-a-him," the Salt of the Earth repeated, more softly. "Not like-a me."

2
Water from the Sky: Frozen

February 1, 2016

Tonight, I could be re-united with Raincloud. It's been what, forty-one years? I've been back in town dozens of times since moving away. I've already had a bittersweet reunion or two up here. Now, a voicemail has changed my plans for the evening. Or maybe it's the approaching snowstorm.

Nah. It's the voicemail. From the Ketchup Girl, of all people. I trust that my wife will understand if I don't come home tonight.

Lamont Raincloud. I'm not certain that I want to welcome him back into my life with open arms. An intense, challenging guy. Likes to stick his chest out. When he does, you had better be ready for it. I sometimes still imagine him standing over me. When I do, I hear his voice. "You'll never be as good as me, Pronotaro. But you'll kill yourself trying."

I'm waiting for Her Ketchupness herself – or maybe she's the Cinnamon Queen - to answer my return call. She might not have started the whole thing between Raincloud and I, but she was like lighter fluid. And I wonder how he'll react when he finds out who ended up with Esther? It occurs to me that I could still hang up. Maybe even turn my phone off so they can't call me again. Fly back home where it's safe.

My uncle Ricco always says that everything happens for a reason. I don't know if I agree. Reasons... is it really just a coincidence that today, of all days, I'd receive this last-minute invitation? I'm holding the phone away from my ear, looking at it, experiencing a flash of thoughts about my life, and this town.

June 26, 1968; North Buffalo

Just days earlier we had been released from the fifth grade and had been let out into the bright sun. This was the middle of our first full week of school vacation. Mom had already taken Tom and I, and two of our cousins, to the crowded beach at Beaver Island over the first weekend of summer vacation to celebrate. But now, just a few days later, though the sky was bright and blue and the air was hot enough to make us sweat without playing ball, the sweet state of mind called "summer" was in danger. Mom cast herself as Chief Danger Officer. I had just gotten off the phone with Raincloud, who lived a few blocks away. He and I had decided on a plan to make sure that the recent events in town did not interfere with our evening.

"I don't understand. The riots are miles away. Why can't Lamont and I sleep out in the backyard tonight?"

"No. Some other time, Ernie."

"But you can't even hear the sirens from here. Mom, there are no black people in our neighborhood. Okay, Earl and his dad are on Avery Street but he's my friend. Maybe he could sleep out with us, too. Nobody's going to try to kidnap or rob or set fire to us."

"They might have cars, Ernie. They might... they might start spreading out."

"But mom, they - "

"No means no, and Mrs. Raincloud agrees with me. No sleeping out in a tent tonight, and that's that. Come on, we've got to go to the store. Where's Tom?"

"Why do I have to come to the store? I thought you said I'm old enough to be home alone."

"Well, today's different. Those things are happening. I'll feel better if you're with me. And Tom... where's Tom?"

"Over at Esther's, I think." Esther was our neighbor from two houses down the street. She was Tom's age, a year behind me in school. Shiny long, dark hair and a pretty smile.

Mom grabbed the wall phone receiver off the cradle and was dialing.

"Hi, Miriam..." That was Esther's mom's name... "it's Dorothea. Is Tom there? Can you send him home? Yeah, thanks."

"What do we need at the store, mom?"

"Milk, bread. Eggs. Cigarettes. Essentials. What if the stores all get attacked before the police can restore order?"

"Hey, mom? Can I call Dad later on at the restaurant and see if he'll let Lamont and I have our sleep-out?"

I received an open-mouthed eye-roll of exasperation.

I had been looking forward to the ritual beginning-of-summer sleep-out with Raincloud for weeks. We had done it for two years running, and it was never a big deal. In fact, unbeknownst to any of our parents, the previous year we woke up at zero-dark-thirty and walked two blocks up to Delaware Avenue, to the all-night bakery, and split a half-dozen donuts. The warm, still nights invited kids from all over the neighborhood who were sleeping outside, to congregate at the bakery and to spend dimes and quarters on powdered sugar delicacies with jelly inside, or chocolate-covered calorie bombs stuffed with lascivious white cream. To be up and moving around in the city at 2 a.m., walking past the frame and brick houses that stood shoulder-to-shoulder on either side of us as we headed up my street to the main strip, was quite a thrill for a ten or eleven-year old.

I pondered whether to tell mom that Earl was there with all of us white kids and Lamont a year earlier, when a bunch of sleeping-out kids hooked up for donuts at Schroeder's Bakery. I'd have mentioned that all the kids, including Earl, loved on each other in the normal way that ten and eleven year old boys do. But I didn't think that admitting to the high crime of leaving the backyard during our sleep-outs would help our cause.

June 27, 1968: A Different Part of Town

Phrases explode like Molotov Cocktails being lobbed into Mayor Sal Frandino's ears as his entourage swings open the outside door and he enters the lobby of the Michigan Street YMCA. A threat against him blasts forth from an angry voice that resounds above the many other voices that boom from behind the double doors separating the lobby from the gym. One of the eight riot gear-clad cops that escort him, strides ahead of the rest and aims himself at those double doors.

"Told you mayor don't care!" Frandino hears from the other side of those doors. Then comes a stream of fresh profanities, all from the same male voice.

Frandino recognizes the next shouting voice: It is his police commissioner, Lou Lombardi. "He'll be here! Be patient!"

"Patience, my ass be patient," yells the next voice whose words Frandino could make out above the general bedlam. "We going back in the streets tonight even stronger than last night. Burn, baby, burn!"

A knot in his stomach is pinching his gut. His stride lengthens. The crowd - Frandino is always running somewhere to speak to the next gathering - they need to see him, now. The doors swing open.

"Pigs! Pigs!"

Frandino can estimate crowd size. This one might be a hundred and ten people, not counting himself and the battalion of two dozen riot-clad cops.

Tom Johnson stands behind an old wooden podium. The Reverend Doctor Thomas Johnson holds no microphone, and is raising and lowering his arms in a "calm down" gesture. Frandino's legs unlimber into a jog as he approaches the one man in town who, if anyone does, may hold the fate of the city in his hands tonight.

"Sal," says the Reverend.

Even in the midst of civil rebellion, even when they don't see all the issues eye-to-eye, they are hugging. Frandino closes his eyes and exhales over Johnson's shoulder. For just a moment, it seems like he is about to speak to the Downtown Businessmen's Association at one of those hundred-twenty dollar a plate dinners down at the Statler Hilton where he encourages and cajoles and charms the merchants and bankers into please, for God's sake, investing more into the city's core.

The hug is brief. "It'll be okay," says the Reverend, releasing arms. Frandino turns to face the mob.

"Twenty minutes late," booms a voice. "Where's your manners, mayor?" This must be the same guy he heard threatening to commit indecent acts upon him as he entered the building. Frandino sizes him up: nineteen or twenty years old, a beefy five feet, eleven inches. Brown tee shirt and dungaree jeans. Short hair, thick black glasses, hasn't shaved in a few days.

He glances a few feet to the man's left. William Snead, the city's only African-American councilman, makes eye contact, standing with the rest of the mob. Frandino has never seen Snead without a necktie before tonight.

"Well," Snead deadpans as the mob began to quiet itself, "Are you going to answer the young man?"

"Sorry," Frandino says. "Incredibly busy day today. I wanted to get here sooner -"

"Busy putting brothers in jail!" someone yells. Catcalls erupt. Frandino holds his hands out. He feels his whole body shake.

"You're here several years too late!" rings out a female voice.

"Just another white man. Stand by for more broken promises!" yells a new male voice.

"Stop it now," booms Commissioner Lombardi through a megaphone. "You wanted the mayor, you've got the mayor. Now shut up before I fill this place with tear gas."

"Lou!" Frandino wheels to his left and points at his childhood friend, who leads the city's Finest. "That's not what I want."

He turns back to the crowd. "But I'm here. I do want to talk - and to listen. So, please." Lombardi thrusts the megaphone toward him. Frandino pushes it away.

The gym becomes eerily quiet.

"All I know is the motha told us there'd be jobs a year ago," the loud young man with the thick glasses spits out. "Where's mine?"

"Randy!"

The Reverend has apparently addressed the vociferous, bespectacled man who has sworn sexual violence to Frandino, by his first name. Frandino hears unspoken things in Johnson's voice: Familiarity. Concern. Warning. Acceptance. The things he used to hear as a kid when his own mother called out to him, in the old neighborhood near the river, on Trenton Street.

Randy appears just a little bit smaller than he was a moment ago.

"Son," the Reverend continues, loud enough to be heard by all. "Straight A's for four years at East High School. Deans' list. I thought you were enrolled up at UB. You wanted to be a lawyer. But tonight, you're about to get yourself and the whole city on national TV for the wrong reasons."

Randy puts his hands into his pocket and stares at his own shoes.

"Brothers like Randy need jobs," Councilman Snead says. "They can't live on broken promises." Frandino hears measured defiance.

"Damn right!" Randy's head snaps back up. "I applied to lay down asphalt, help finish up the Kensington Expressway. Man said no. But I know they're hiring. I get a bus down to Bethlehem Steel. Do you have something, anything for me? I try Republic Steel, they take one look at me and say 'no'. I don't have money for tuition!"

The rest of the mob is starting to make noise again and Randy raises his voice to a superhuman volume.

"You and your fancy suit come telling us you wanna help us? Help us what, to die? You're just like every other white person in control. Protect the status quo is all you ever do."

Randy is still shouting but Frandino can't hear any more of his words; the rest of the crowd noise is now too intense. Reverend Johnson is calling for calm. Lou Lombardi orders the officers to raise shields.

After a couple of minutes, the crowd begins to wind down.

"Mister Snead," Frandino looks over at the councilman and extends a hand, palm up. He feels defeat. The African-American population in the city is growing, and there's talk that Snead will soon announce his candidacy for the Democratic mayoral nomination. Sal Frandino's Democratic Party. Not smart to offer Snead a bully pulpit.

Snead comes to the podium and Frandino makes room for him.

"My friends, my sisters and my brothers," the Councilman says. "This is a tough night, and these are tough times. But we can't burn the city down and expect the kind of attention we really need. And unfortunately, Mister Mayor, you've not been helpful."

The clamor swells again. Snead puts his hands up and the noise stops.

"But now, now - I want us to act with dignity," Snead continues. "Let's stay calm and show the world what it means to have true African character. Let the mayor talk and be heard."

"Well, ain't gonna make no difference anyways," says a new voice from the crowd. "We can talk now but damn, there's some nice suits inside Joseph's Men's Shop and round about 9:30 tonight, them doors gonna be wide open and I'll be grabbing some new threads, see?"

Laughter fills the air. Reverend Johnson nearly knocks over both the Councilman and the Mayor to make himself big behind the podium.

"Now, that's exactly what can't happen," he thunders. "Doctor King would be having himself a heart attack if he were here tonight, hearing you say that."

"Well, a white man in Memphis shore 'nuff took care of that possibility back in April, didn't he?" Randy shouts back.

"Only jobs they got for my sons is in Vietnam," a lady yells.

Frandino senses their complete lack of trust in authority of any kind. The whole world had been careening out of control for several months and Reverend Johnson, for all the love and respect he may engender, may not be equal to tonight's task.

"All right, that's enough!" Frandino marvels at the power of his own words.

"I know we need jobs," he continues. "We have problems, and I'm working to solve them." The people are quieting down and Frandino keeps going.

"We're just like every big American city these days. Philadelphia, they're not hiring as many workers for the ship docks. St. Louis, Cleveland, just like here, the steel plants aren't hiring as many people. Down in the harbor, layoffs. The ships aren't stopping here, they head to sea these days straight through Canada. People are leaving the city so there's not the same tax money available for me to work with. I can't balance the books without help from the state. I'm on the phone with Albany more than I'm on with my wife."

He pauses. No one even chuckles.

"Um. So we've got challenges. But there's brand new construction projects downtown that have meant jobs for some of your families. One big department store just committed to keeping their flagship location downtown open for another five years - that means jobs for you. Plus, we're getting welfare money from Albany, and - "

"Welfare, my ass! I want to be a doctor, fool!"

"This is just the same bull you fed to us in 1965!"

"Rats in my neighborhood. What you gonna do about the rats?"

The gym is in uproar. Councilman Snead appears to gloat. Reverend Johnson seems to withdraw. Commissioner Lombardi looks ready to crack some skulls.

"I can't help you if all you're gonna do is yell," Frandino tries to say over the noise.

They are chanting something about power to the people. It is deafening.

"I tried to talk with you. I'm leaving. All rioters and looters tonight will be subject to arrest and imprisonment."

"Go ahead then, leave!" William Snead raises his voice over the others. "You've been turning your back on our people for years. Why should tonight be different?"

Frandino touches Lombardi on the shoulder. "Lou, get me out of here."

Once outside the agitated YMCA, Sal Frandino speaks quietly to his police commissioner.

"If tonight goes anything like last night, I'll call the Governor.

There's two hundred men ready at the Armory. I just don't know if we can keep the whole East Side from burning down without soldiers at this point."

"You know we're ready - Guard or no Guard."

"I know. Just don't shoot to kill. Use tear gas."

A voice that sounds like Randy from inside pierces their conversation. "Damn you, Mayor Frandino. You get your ass back inside and talk to us!"

Frandino turns and there is Randy, running after them. "Goddamit, you come back and talk to us!" Huffing, puffing.

An officer in riot gear draws his night stick and prepares to smash Randy into the next week. Frandino runs to get himself between Randy and the officer. "Don't you dare!" he yells at the officer.

No one else has followed Randy out of the building. Frandino gives the riot cop a gentle shove and the mayor and Randy are face-to-face, toe to toe.

"Damn you, Mayor. Talk to us. Talk to me."

"It's Randy, is it?"

"Why you wanna leave all those angry people in there and go back to your West Side? They gonna wreck this whole city tonight, Mayor."

"But you're not in there with them, are you?" Frandino says.

Randy is not quite as tall as Frandino. Frandino sees a young, black face sopping with moisture.

"Randy, it sounds to me like you should be at university."

Randy's body jolts to hyperactivity. "And how do I do that! Ain't got no job, no money! My family got no money!"

"No scholarship? You didn't get a State Regents Scholarship with those grades I heard about from the Reverend in there?"

"I - I - didn't apply." The air leaves Randy's sails.

"Didn't apply? Because?"

"'Cause they all said it wouldn't matter. My family. My friends. Said I shouldn't even try, I'd just be disappointed like black people always get disappointed."

"Randy, do you want to go to school?"

Randy looks up with wide, red eyes and moves his lips, but there is no sound. A second later Frandino does hear a sound; muffled, unintelligible. Frandino reaches for him. Feels the young man tremble.

"I'm sorry," he says through clenched teeth. He delivers a couple of firm pats on the back. "I'm sorry, Randy."

Randy sniffles. Frandino smells stale tobacco and maybe a trace of whiskey on the kid. Sal Frandino's soul chuckles. He remembers the Italian and Irish kids he grew up with back in the 1920s on the West Side.

Then, they are not hugging anymore but standing a couple of feet apart, watching one another.

"I'm going to give you my office number. Call me tomorrow. My secretary's name is Phyllis – make sure you call her Phyllis. Tell her it's Randy, and she'll put you through."

"What for?"

"Because Randy, tomorrow I'll make some phone calls for you. If you call me tomorrow, I'll get you all signed up and paid up for school. You'll just need your transcript from East High."

The look on Randy's face registers confusion. "That's bullshit," he says.

"Reverend Johnson said all I need to hear about you. If you want to go to college, we'll take it a semester at a time. We'll keep in touch. You maintain good grades every semester, and I'll take care of the next semester for you. You dig?"

"Don't play with me, man."

"Playing, you say? I didn't get where I am by playing with people."

"I can't pay you back. You'll hold this over my head for years."

"Maybe. But you won't know what might've been unless you call."

"You ain't even a good person. Even white people don't trust you."

"Randy, I wouldn't be doing my job very well if I didn't make some white people angry."

"What's in this for you?"

"Just promise me you'll go home and stay inside tonight. And if you choose to go back in the gym - for God's sakes, Randy..."

"Mayor?"

"For God's sakes, help me keep anyone else from getting hurt. Use that great set of lungs he gave you to tell those people to go home and be safe tonight."

Frandino sees Randy's eyes focusing on him through those thick glasses, and then, the eyes shift down toward the pavement.

"Okay," Randy says. "I'll call you."

*****

Two minutes later, Sal Frandino is standing near his open car door with Lou Lombardi.

"What the hell was that all about?" the Commissioner asks.

"Do you still have to ask, after all these years?"

The police chief rolls his eyes and shakes his head. "What did you give away this time?"

"Hope, Lou. We needed to give away some hope tonight."

"Great. But the kind of hope that's spelled like 'cash' is in short supply around here. Who'll you take it from this time in order to make good on your word?"

Frandino puts his hand on his friend's shoulder. "Just do your job, Lou. And I'll do mine."

3
Negroes and Irishmen

July 4, 1968, as the cousins look on

"Mayor, it's warm! Let me take your coat," Ricco Gugliuzza says, touching the paper plate that holds the picnic food that's just been served up to Frandino.

"No, no. I'm fine - and please, call me Sal."

Five adults have already gathered around him. Frandino surveys the scene here in one of the suburban towns that is taking people and tax money from his dominion. But he's here because of the lady of the house.

"Where's my girl?" The thought of Claudia makes him happy.

"When she sees you, she'll faint." Ricco is smiling. "She never expected you'd take her invitation seriously."

Frandino then sees her emerge from around a corner of the house, heading up the driveway with a tray of something edible. "Sal. Omigosh," comes her reaction.

Everyone laughing. Now she is next to him, scolding him.

"You almost made me drop the food. You should have warned me."

"What a beautiful yard you have," Frandino says and he turns and gestures toward it. He sees a big weeping willow, fifty feet away, in the middle of the grassy expanse behind the Gugliuzza home. Two old trunks stand next to each other: a tree and an old man standing next to a lawn chair. Surrounded by eight or nine grade school-aged kids. Short, stocky and almost completely bald; the old man holds a straw hat in his hand. White shirt, red suspenders. The kids look at Frandino with the stargazing eyes he's come to recognize on so many faces since winning his first mayoral election ten years earlier.

Frandino waves and smiles. A kid waves back, and the old man beams at him. Another kid runs toward him. A moment later, they are all racing his way.

*****

Thirty minutes later, Frandino sits at a picnic table with Ricco, Claudia, and a few of their adult relatives. He has met every person and learned their names. Has kissed both of the babies; has made everyone laugh out loud with a clever joke or a funny story about Claudia, who works in City Hall. Frandino sees her on Monday mornings when she helps to set up the conference table for a weekly staff meeting. He does not want to be unfaithful to his wife this time around. Claudia's beauty and her sense of humor have always charmed him.

Frandino's career has been one of measuring people. Years behind the City Court bench have given him much practice. He considers this family: good people who teach their kids good values. Law-abiding, thoroughly American but proud of their ethnic roots; practicing Catholics.

Ricco's brother-in-law Tommy asks the question. "Sal - geez - I mean, the *Evening Star* is giving you credit for stopping the riots and everything. How'd you do it?"

"I don't know that I did all that much. I think we have to thank those thunderstorms Thursday night after I left that YMCA."

"But you went - down *there*, Sal," says Claudia. "You must have been crapping your pants!"

"Tell us about it," says another.

"It wasn't a scintillating situation," Frandino says. "I'm thankful we seem to have things under better control since last week. And I have some questions for all of you, speaking of the city."

Frandino's audience leans in.

"Obviously, Ricco and Claudia live here in Cheektowaga. But the rest of you, three other families here at the table. Where are you living now?"

"Tonawanda," says Pete. "Gosh, been out of the city for a good ten years now."

"Right down on Plymouth Avenue, where I grew up," says Tommasina. "Would love to move out, but don't have the money."

Bill Pronotaro is the last to answer as he lights a Pall Mall that dangles between his lips. "North Side now, but grew up down on Plymouth with my sister." He glances at Tommasina. "My business is out in West Seneca, and I'd love to be out there, closer to it."

Their answers drive stakes through Frandino's heart. Awkward silence.

"You know," Frandino says, "that grilled sausage is so good, I think I'll have another before I head back home to my wife. Where'd you pick it up, anyway?"

"*Maciallario* on Grant Street, of course!" Claudia exalts. "Best stuff anywhere is down on the West Side."

If nothing else, suburbanites will come into his city to shop for sausage.

*****

The next day, Frandino gets to his office a bit later than usual: 7:15 AM. Phyllis has the first part of his day laid out for him. George Barbarello, fifteen years Frandino's junior and a product of the mayor's own boyhood neighborhood of nearby St. Anthony's Parish, has an hour of Frandino's time between 8 and 9 a.m. Barbarello is the *Evening Star's* lead City Desk reporter, and new to his post - this is only the third year he's covered City Hall. Frandino smiles. Barbarello is putty in his hands.

By the time the grandfather clock in the mayor's office shows 8:10, the men have spent some time catching up on each other's holiday. Now, Frandino walks to a humidor and picks out two Panatelas. He sits behind his massive mahogany desk and cuts one end of a cigar. It is a signal. Time for business.

"Sal, all kinds of rumors and amazing stories about last Thursday night. I've got instructions to not go too easy on you but - my God! You risked your damn neck going down there. I want you alive a few years from now so I can still write about you."

Frandino looks up from his cigar-cutting. He expects a smile on his inquisitor's face. Instead, a look of concern.

"It was the right thing to do, George. Those people have suffered, just like our fathers suffered when they got here. They needed to see me. I'm the leadership symbol."

"Those people," says George, "looted and burned businesses, smashed windows and fought the police and firemen. They turned cars and taxicabs over and hurt innocent bystanders. Sal, they're not like our fathers and grandfathers."

"Really? Our dads and grand-dads killed Irishmen down in the Hooks, not to mention killing each other. Some of the old-timers still talk about all the fighting on Canal Street like it was just fine and dandy."

Frandino leans forward over the desk and George is up out of his chair, meeting him halfway to receive a gift of wrapped tobacco.

"You trust me to cut your smokes," says Frandino as he settles back into his big leather chair. "Do you trust me to run the city my way?"

George fingers the cigar, opens his mouth. Makes a noise of soft exasperation.

"I met a kid down there," Frandino says. "Smart kid, powerful public speaker. You know what this kid wanted more than anything in the world? I'll tell you, it wasn't to go out and hurt people or act like a lunatic. But last week during the violence, I guarantee you that's what he was doing."

"Okay, I give up. What did this Negro youth want more than anything?"

"This Negro youth -" Frandino stops for a moment and looks down at the cigar he's cutting for himself. "This Negro youth - and George, you ought to start calling them African-American for the same reason we don't like it when other folks call us Wops and Dagos - this kid wants more than anything else for his life to matter. He wants an opportunity to try, maybe to fail, maybe to succeed. What's wrong with that?"

"You can't save the world, Sal. Can you really? We got tens of thousands of these Negroes in the city now."

"You know why they're here? Same reason our papas and grand-papas came. They wanted to work. And damn it all, we've got to stop the jobs from leaving, George. All of our local people keep having kids, and those kids grow into men who need work. That's the real problem we need to solve."

Frandino smells his cigar. He fetches his lighter from a corner of the desk and nods to the reporter. Each man lights and puffs.

"Bible says money is a root of evil," Frandino continues. "Funny though, Bible also tells us to make wise use of it. That comes from Jesus himself. But when you have an entire group of people that you deprive money from, how can they make wise use of it?"

"There you go again, Sal. You're turning last week's riots into something biblical." Through the delicious, bluish smoke that has begun to fill the room, Frandino can see that George is now more smiling than scolding.

"Well," Frandino begins to answer, "I was talking to Al Cappello at Saint Anthony's over the weekend about the violence. He said it reminded him of the Jews in Egypt before the Exodus. Frogs, blood, flies, first born sons killed... he said when you have oppressed a minority for enough years, you should expect big trouble in your house."

"Holy crap, Sal. Now you're throwing Father Al at me."

"You want a story? Print that I'm handling the racial tension according to the teachings of the Catholic Church. That'll piss everyone off."

Honest laughter from both men.

"But Sal," George begins afresh. "You need money to fix things and the State can't help enough. What are you gonna do?"

"I'll tell you what I'm not gonna do, which is to give up. So, I keep talking with the governor about the University. They're gonna build the new campus out in Amherst, in the middle of a dairy farm. Out in the middle of a forest where guys are hunting deer! For God's sake, we need 'em to build that campus right here in the city."

"That ship has sailed, Sal. They've decided. The city loses again."

Frandino takes a long draw on his cigar, then clears his throat. "But you know, Governor Rockefeller and Mayor Lindsay down in the Big Apple don't get along. Rocky is starting to like me. I'm his favorite mayor in the whole state."

"You are an eternal optimist."

"I like that. Let's print it." Frandino puts his arms out, unfolding an imaginary newspaper and reading the headline out loud. "Frandino Eternally Optimistic About City's Future."

"So, mister Mayor. Talk to me about last week, please. I need to come up with a half-page feature on it for the B section of this Saturday's paper."

*****

If George Barbarello is Frandino's man within the Republican yet Frandino-tolerant *Evening Star*, he has no such ally at the Democratic and Conservative *Messenger*. The *Messenger* is born and bred in South Buffalo: the First Ward, where the grain mills once employed thousands, but now maybe only a couple hundred, and soon, they say, perhaps only dozens as the big mills shift operations to other places. The *Messenger* is strongest in Cazenovia and South Park, where Frandino's style of celebrity meets with the furrowed brows of the sons of German and Irish immigrants; proud, primarily blue-collar families who live in neat rows of wooden frame homes. The *Messenger* plays second fiddle to its bigger rival in this two-paper town. Its loyal following includes a few hundred thousand throughout the metropolis who soak in the viewpoint of one Finn O'Connell, Editor-in-Chief.

Ten minutes before three. At the top of the hour, two *Messenger* reporters will be escorted through the big wooden doors that separate Frandino's office from the outside world. The mayor can't resist his habit of re-reading snippets from recent Finn O'Connell editorials:

Citizens should be outraged that on the same day General Grains announced that they have indefinitely canceled plans to renovate the grain elevators at the foot of Chicago Street, their camera-seeking mayor was at the Albright-Knox Gallery, hamming it up with the University's dean of music, his make-up people fussing to get his hair just right for publicity photos that will be sent to music schools in Paris, West Berlin and Vienna. He needed to spend that time fighting for the renovation project that would preserve three hundred jobs our city needs for the longer term. Frandino remembers the title of that lead editorial, from just two months earlier: *"Mayor's Hollywood Habits Paving Road to Hollow Future."*

Frandino has saved a particularly irksome editorial from a year earlier. He fishes it from a desk drawer and re-reads underlined parts of *"Frandino's Fraternal Connections Require Review:"*

"Since his re-election in 1965, the local FBI puts the number of Mafia-related arrests within the city limits at 20% of the rate under his predecessor. The mayor's office says this statistic proves that the police, under Commissioner Lou Lombardi, are driving organized crime out of the city. But last week's discovery of Sibby the "Sure Shot" Amendola in the Niagara River off the foot of West Ferry Street, body bound and prepared gangland execution-style, flies in the face of this explanation...

"...We are not suggesting that our mayor, or anyone officially connected with the city government, actually orders the executions, launders the money, takes the bets, or manages the prostitutes. We do maintain that it is time for renewed scrutiny of Frandino and his associates. Let's get answers to the questions that this mayor has not been able to put behind him since his days as a judge."

Frandino has heard this straight from O'Connell's mouth. The men had to be broken apart from each other to prevent fisticuffs a year earlier when O'Connell, perhaps having polished off one whisky too many, made the remarks at a Democratic Party function. The editorial appeared two days later.

Frandino can't stifle a quick burst of laughter when he thinks of the near-boxing match with the big Irish lout. Ironic that the man who was most instrumental in keeping them from coming to blows was the infamous Andy the Plumber, fresh out of jail to muster one of his infrequent, unexpected encroachments into Frandino's adult life.

In four minutes, two of O'Connell's lackeys will arrive for their weekly audience with him.

Phyllis buzzes right on the hour. Frandino breathes in and out, trying to relax. Anger won't serve him. It is only City Hall beat reporters, not the big Irish lout himself, that he must deal with.

And then, enter the big Irish lout, necktie askew against a white shirt that bursts with O'Connell's big-boned, slightly overweight torso. O'Connell is three times the width of the young reporter who accompanies him. A flight-or-fight reaction propels Frandino up out of his chair.

"Finn, you're not supposed to be here."

"Tough crackers, mayor. The events on the near East Side last week weren't normal. My presence is required."

"What do you want?"

"I want you thrown out of office. But seeing as that won't happen until the candidate I support whips your butt next year, I'll settle for a cigar." He moves toward the humidor on a shelf to the right of the mayor's desk.

"Stop right there. Those are for friends."

"Yeah, sorry," O'Connell says. "You mean, friends like the Big Sieve, up in Lewiston."

"You're pathetic, Finn. I've never even met that bastard."

"Oh, really. Not even to kiss his ring?"

"Your Mafia accusations are laughable." He gestures toward the younger reporter. "You're teaching Peter yellow journalism."

"I'm teaching him to grow a pair of balls and ask the right questions."

Frandino sits and takes the phone handset to his ear. "And I'm calling security, because if you stay in this office for another ten seconds, I'm going to rip out your balls with my bare hands if I have to die doing it."

"Yeah? Can I quote you?"

Frandino glances at Peter. Puts the handset back in its cradle.

"I'm not talking to your boss," he says, smiling at Peter. "But I'll take your questions. Have a seat, and fire away."

O'Connell's voice is next. "Whose dick did you suck down there last week to shut down the riots?"

"Uh-uh," Frandino says, looking in O'Connell's direction and stroking the top of an extended index finger with the other index finger. "That's a violation. Only Peter can ask questions."

The Editor-in-Chief looks at his staffer with a plea on his face.

"So, mister mayor," Peter speaks in a thin baritone. "Whose dick did you suck to stop the riots last week?"

"Why, I did nothing of the sort. I prayed for rain. To the same God that I believe your boss says he prays to. And it rained."

"What kind of answer is that?" storms O'Connell.

"Oooh. It might rain again, Peter. Did you just hear some thunder?"

"Ah, no," the young reporter says.

"Hmm. Because I thought I just heard a dandy peal of thunder. Do you think it might have been God, or someone who thinks he's God, whispering something in your ear?"

"Uh... right." Peter's face brightens. "So, I guess some people wouldn't believe the answer you just gave me. Convince them they're wrong about you."

"Okay, my young friend. I'll level with you. I wasn't clever enough to pray for rain. I prayed for any kind of intervention. Well, the good Lord intervened all right, and a dandy intervention it was. He put those riots out with that huge storm we had blow through here."

"Bullshit," said O'Connell. "Knowing you, you promised money to someone. You committed city funds without going through the legislative process. I know all about your slush funds. How much, Sal? How many tax dollars did you divert so you can look like the movie-star hero with a big, expensive band-aid that will last for about a week and when it falls off we'll have worse problems than before?"

Frandino looks toward Peter. "Funny, isn't it? Whenever there's thunder, I can always hear it inside this office."

"Okay, enough with the silly game," O'Connell sounds more conciliatory.

Frandino turns to Peter. "You must have a loud conscience, because I think I heard it suggest what you should ask me next."

"So, uh…" the reporter starts, "some people think you… paid someone off? Made promises you aren't authorized to make? That you used money somehow?"

Frandino remembers that Randy did call Phyllis, and that Randy is going to attend the State University of New York at Buffalo in the fall.

"I went and listened," he answers. "I listened to Reverend Tom Johnson, and to Councilman Snead, and to the people. Then I left, and it rained. I can't explain why the rioting stopped, other than what I just told you."

*****

The grandfather's clock in his office now registers 6:30 in the evening. He's called Steffi at home, explaining that he needs to unwind. Won't be coming right home. Steffi is pert, devoted, admired in town, a perfect spouse for a mayor. A picture of her in her wedding train sits on his desk, second photo from the right. Portraits of his daughter and two sons flank Steffi's wedding photo. But tonight, he'll stop off at the Arkansas Lounge for a drink and a smoke, and that new lady bartender, the young thing. A Grace Kelly lookalike. What's her name, Millie?

He's in the family station wagon, his preferred vehicle, driving into the sunlight of a northern summer's early evening. The new towers that have risen downtown under his watch, some complete, some not quite; some done in black steel, some in white, reflect the orange glow of the late afternoon sun in his rear view mirror. He's thinking about the young girl who played opposite Cary Grant in "To Catch a Thief." Beautiful, inquisitive, a bit tart. Seductive. Grace Kelly.

"Just a little harmless banter," he says out loud.

4
Fat Squaw Momma

December 19, 1968

Is it frozen, Ernie?"

"I'll check tomorrow morning before school," I answered Lamont Raincloud.

We had just watched "A Charlie Brown Christmas" together for the third year in a row, in the upstairs flat shared by Lamont, his mom, and his older brother. Raincloud called watching that show our sacred ritual.

"Pussy," he said. "You don't want it to be frozen."

Raincloud was much bigger than any of the kids in our fifth grade class. I had to double step once every so often to keep up with him as we walked down snowy Shoreham Drive in the direction of my house. Kids picked on him for his size, calling him a fat Indian. I knew better than the "fat" part. A winter earlier, skates laced up and Victoriaville stick in hand, he schooled a dozen of us neighborhood guys on the little patch of ice that nestled between the railroad tracks just beyond the dead end of my street.

He could read my mind. "You think hockey is tough, try lacrosse. Hockey's nothing, Pronotaro. Come to Brantford with me some time and try my people's game."

"How come you never talk tough in school, Mont?"

"Why should I?"

"The way everyone's always picking on you. How come you don't fight back?"

"There's too many of 'em, Ernie. What difference could I make against so many white kids?"

"Kick their asses, for one thing. You gonna walk me all the way home, Mont?"

"Yeah, but not because I care about you. It's the snowflakes I want to see. Look at 'em."

Two inches of fresh snow had fallen that day, burying the sooty piles of ice on either side of the street beneath a fluffy new blanket. It was cold enough that if we stomped down hard with our black rubber boots as we walked, we could leave a bigger footprint than our actual foot size because the downdraft caused by our foot-slamming would scatter the light snow crystals out in every direction from where our feet landed. There was no wind. I looked into the halo of the streetlights as flakes floated down like oddly-shaped parachutes, illuminated by the electric light. Rows of houses on either side of us dressed in colorful patterns of Christmas glow.

"I love walking around in the snowflakes." Raincloud's voice trailed off. What a sap he could be. He could beat up all the boys in the fifth grade put together but instead, he talked about snowflakes like some sort of romantic.

WHAM! I dove down near his black rubber snow boots and wrapped my arms up around his ankles the way his big brother had been teaching us. If you want to play for the Thundering Herd one day, Jeffcoat had been coaching, you had to learn to tackle bigger guys. Jeffcoat was several years ahead of us, had played football for Riverside High, and had newspaper stories written about him. Lamont came down on top of me and suddenly, all was dark. I couldn't breathe. I heard his voice first angry, then concerned.

At some point I was standing up again, coughing at first, and then breathing hard without coughing. Freezing cold snow had gotten inside my coat and caused an ache as it melted against my throat. Lamont said something about my lack of judgment.

"Big stupid Indian. You almost killed me."

"Me? You caused it. And if it wasn't icy, you wouldn't have been able to tackle me, either."

"I... did get you down, 'Mont, didn't I?"

"Ernie. Stop comparing yourself to me. You'll never measure up."

"We'll see tomorrow, if the pond's frozen."

We discovered on the next day that the pond was frozen solid. Some guys must have already played on it, because fresh snow had been shoveled off its surface and the walls of our rink were in place: piles of snow came up over my waist around the playing surface. It wasn't a rectangle; more of an L-shape that hooked around a young tree, with the bend not exactly in the middle. The pond was as ready for us as it had ever been.

Esther was already there and was figure skating. She was the lone girl, and she started to cry when the guys showed up. We pressed her into duty so the teams would be even. She brightened when Lamont said she could play on his team and he would make sure to protect her. Esther was the prettiest girl in the neighborhood. Lamont was - well, he was Lamont. On skates, his confidence was formidable.

I was not on Lamont's team. I never was - he made sure of it. Said it was because I was fast and he needed to practice against fast skaters. Speed had little to do with his style of play. He'd park himself near the two markers that represented the goal we were defending and no one could move him. Believe me, I tried. With elbows, knees, tripping him up, whatever.

"Cut it out, Pronotaro! That's dirty play."

"Cut it out, Pronotaro!" I repeated, mocking him like I heard the kids in school mock him all the time.

But despite my efforts, he wouldn't budge. So the next time Lamont planted himself in front of our goal, I took a flying start and hit him from the side at full speed. He saw me coming and he lowered his shoulder. I was sent flying.

"Damn it, Raincloud. Go to hell!" I scrambled to my feet. He was waiting for me, no longer holding his stick.

"Come on little white boy."

The game stopped. I was going to kill Lamont. I took a swing with my stick and caught him hard on the arm, but I couldn't keep hold of the stick. I believe he punched me twice in the face, because I saw two white flashes and then all went dark. I heard yelling. I saw red drops form on a snowbank and felt myself being levitated. Then I crashed down onto the snowbank. Lamont's voice. Saying something about the Senecas getting revenge on diseased little white men and winning back the land.

I got up and faced him. I'd never seen him angrier.

"You want some more, little white boy?"

I lunged at him again and this time, he moved just so. I flew past him. I was flat on the ice again.

"Go home, you big stupid Indian," I yelled up from the fetal position.

He didn't say anything. The cheering stopped as I tried to get up again.

"Go home, Lamont. No one likes you. You big idiot Indian. Go home to your fat squaw mama."

Lamont didn't say anything.

It took me a few more seconds to get my bearings. I knew the blood on the ice was all mine. He was sitting on a snowbank near where we'd all taken our boots off to change into our skates. He was unlacing his skates.

All the other kids, and Esther, just watched wordlessly.

"Yeah," I repeated. "Go home. No one wants their day spoiled by a Raincloud. Go home to your fat squaw mother."

He looked up at me, for just a second. Then, he looked back down at his feet and continued to replace his skates with his snow boots.

The other guys started to get the idea that hockey was over for the day. One by one, they picked their snow boots out of the pile of footwear and trudged away over the snow, still on their skates. Esther returned her borrowed stick to its owner and started practicing some fancy spins, the pond once again hers.

*****

The next morning, mom and Mrs. Raincloud brought us both to the Nichols High School rink where we could watch a real hockey team practice while we ate lunch. For the first twenty minutes, Lamont and I barely acknowledged each other's presence. The moms tried to talk. I imagined that my fat squaw taunts hadn't gone over so well. I felt lousy. Mrs. Raincloud deserved better.

Lunch was hot dogs and Cokes from the rink's little grill. The four of us sat at a picnic table. It was the closest Lamont and I had come to each other all day.

"You two boys have been best friends since first grade," Mrs. Raincloud began. "You compete at everything and it makes you both the best. You're the only two boys who get A's in every subject. Both of your mothers are so proud of you. You boys are both going to be great leaders one day. We hope you'll stay friends."

For the first time that day, I looked at Lamont's face. He looked off in the direction of the rink. I grunted.

"Italians. European foreigners," he muttered, still not looking at me.

His mother put a hand on his shoulder. "Lamont. You have French blood. And Dutch."

He spat into his soft drink.

"Your father would be very saddened by your attitude."

"Dad's dead. Because he fought the white man's war."

I knew how Lamont felt about this. We were both into Second World War history. His dad went over with the Canadians to help the Allies in Europe at a place called Juno Beach, in France. He'd been involved in some pretty bad things that he never described except to say "war is gruesome" before turning away or looking down. During the summer between third and fourth grade, Mr. Raincloud passed away. Neighborhood talk chalked it up to suicide.

"Stop blaming the war for your dad," I said. "It was a long time ago."

"Mom," Lamont said, "Let's just please go home."

Mrs. Raincloud directed the slightest, quickest smile toward my mom as she rose from the table. The Rainclouds left us. In the Pronotaro family car on our way home, I got an earful of Mom's tough love.

*****

Christmas morning was sunny and cold. The sun hit the fresh snow of the last few days with such electricity that by 8:30 in the morning, it hurt my eyes to look out the window.

Dad always made sure there were plenty of gifts under the tree. This particular year was a sports theme. New footballs, shoulder pads and football pants. Bats and batting helmets. A brand new tabletop hockey game. I was crushing my brother Tom at tabletop hockey when the door buzzer sounded. Three short, familiar blasts.

"Ernie!" mom called from the other room. "Someone's here to see you."

"Who is it?" I feigned ignorance.

"Ernie!"

I declared an intermission to Tom, and walked down the hall to the side door. Mom moved so I could see Raincloud standing in the driveway.

"Hey," I offered weakly.

"Hey," he returned. We stood at the door, looking at one another.

"Well, aren't you going to invite him in?" Mom said.

"Thanks, Mrs. Pronotaro. Maybe Ernie can come take a walk with me and we can talk about things."

It was the voice Lamont used with teachers in school on the days he was getting picked on the most. Didn't sound like the right voice for anyone to use on Christmas Day.

I threw on a hooded coat, gloves and boots, and we began walking down the street. Neither of us said anything for an entire block. I was secretly glad we were walking together again, and was enjoying the bacon-and-egg smell coming from someone's house when, after five seconds of premeditation, I heard myself say, "I'm sorry I called your mom a fat squaw. That was wrong."

"Ernie, we gotta talk. Things are changing."

"Like what?"

"The world. Buffalo. The Six Nations. I've got it all figured out, see?"

"What?"

"You know all this talk about air and water pollution? They're going to close the steel mills around here and move them to Alabama. Jeffcoat heard a lecture about it at college. All the big factories are gonna leave this town."

"How can that happen?"

"Next summer, people will be walking on the moon, Humans go from Earth to the moon. Your government made a lot of Seneca go from here to Oklahoma in the 1830s. The factories go from here to Alabama. Things just move. History moves straight ahead and no one can stop it. Jeffcoat's writing a paper about it."

"I thought you were gonna tell me we can't be friends."

"Oh, we were never friends. But that's okay, because soon we're going back to Canada to the reserve, or maybe to Hamilton or Toronto. Then you won't have me to pick on anymore."

"Pick on you? Mont, you're three times my size."

We were almost all the way up to Delaware Avenue; close enough that the traffic sounds were getting louder. Then we reached the corner and headed toward the candy store a couple of blocks off to the right.

"Mont, you're moving away?"

"Mom said one day. All this stuff Jeffcoat's learning at school about how things are moving. She's trying to figure out if she wants to be in Canada or the United States. We could go to a reserve in the U.S., like Allegheny."

"What do you want?"

"I want her to find a job in Toronto. Because I like the Maple Leafs."

Sadness spread to all my extremities. Not so much that I was going to lose Lamont, but from seeing his excitement about leaving town to live in Toronto. We were outside the closed candy store, looking through the window at the holiday confection display.

"When?"

"Not right away. It's complicated. Now she's got herself a boyfriend. A white guy."

I sighed, and then so did he.

"So Ernie. We aren't really friends, but we should watch the Apollo

8 splashdown together this week."

We had watched the television coverage of almost every manned space mission since 1965 together. Another of our sacred rituals. We left the chocolate storefront and were on the move again, more than halfway to Raincloud's house.

"Why is it important to watch Apollo together, if we're not friends?"

"Mom says it's important to keep traditions alive. She says it's important to watch history being made. Man's gonna walk on the moon this coming summer, and J.J. Simpkins is gonna probably gonna get drafted to carry the ball for the Thundering Herd next year. Man, the world is changing."

"Yeah."

"Yup," Raincloud said. "Mom says we need to pay attention, because one day when we have kids of our own and people in the 21st Century try to say the earth is flat, we have to remember that we saw all the pictures of Earth from a hundred thousand miles away showing it's a globe. And Ernie – when we get upstairs, don't apologize to my mom about what you called her. She's not ready for you to apologize."

"But I'm sorry about what I said."

"But she's not ready to forgive you."

*****

Mid-morning on Christmas Day. Sal Frandino and his grandson have loaded the back of the family station wagon with presents. They are out in the driveway of the mayor's home. Burning hardwood from the Soldier's Circle neighborhood fireplaces has scented the air.

"Pipsqueak, ready to go?"

"Okay, Gramps - but it's cold."

"Only if you think about it, Pipsqueak." Frandino is in the car, turning the keys in the ignition. The young boy sits on his right.

"Seat belt, Pipsqueak."

"Why do you always call me that, Gramp-Squeak?"

"Because you're nine. If you survive to double digits, then I'll think of a more grown-up nickname for you."

"Are we making the kind of Christmas car trip you used to make with Dad when he was little?"

"Yup."

"But I already know about the trips. Can't I stay here and play my new electric football game with Stevie?"

"Plenty of time for that when we're done."

"How long do we have to be gone, Gramps?"

"As long as it takes. It's gonna be dandy - you'll see."

The car clunks backward over the patchy ice in the driveway, and onto Soldier's Circle. The skies have just clouded over after the morning's sunny start, but yellowish glows fill the windows of all the large Tudors and Victorians, the houses forming a circle of eighty yards across. White smoke drifts from brick chimneys. Frandino puts the car in gear; it leaves the circle, he drives down to Richmond Avenue, heads south, and turns left at Utica Street. Then, a red light.

"Gramps, are you taking me to breakfast again like in the summer?"

"Nope."

The signal changes and the car moves forward. Green light at Main Street. The car continues ahead. The houses are smaller. Not as many lights are on in this neighborhood as there were back in the Circle.

"Grampy, where are we going?"

"You'll see, Pipsqueak."

Frandino makes a right at Wohlers Street. Three blocks to go before he'll make his first of six planned stops. He watches out of the corner of his eye as his grandson looks out the window at things he's never seen before. Things that were always just ten thousand feet away.

"Gramps, this is a little scary."

Frandino slows the car. He's looking for house numbers. He edges over to the curb and the car stops.

"Let's go," he says. "Grab that first bag of presents. And remember, say 'Merry Christmas' when they open the door for us."

Up a short flight of crooked wooden steps onto a wooden porch that has seen better days. No doorbell. The mayor knocks on the wooden front door. Weather beaten, paint chipping and bubbling off the wood, just like the rest of the house. Just like the whole neighborhood.

"Gramps. Do we know the people who live here?"

"We will in just a few seconds, Pipsqueak."

5
Breaded Artichokes, Shared

April, 1969

Frandino sits in his office, surrounded by friends and reporters whose presence he had worked hard to secure. The *New York Times*, the *Democrat and Chronicle,* the *Times Union.* Three rags whose editorial pages shape state politics beyond his own metropolitan area. The first few minutes of the interview have gone as planned. But now, he cringes at his first stammered attempt at a response to a question.

It came from William J. Furrings, a feature story writer from the *Times* whose multi-page celebrity profiles has included many of the Big Apple's current luminaries. Furrings seems not to have a single mean bone in his body. He merely asked: "This is your second go-round as mayor of this city; you held the office from '58 to '61, then were defeated, and then came back in '65. Is it easier for you to be the mayor the second time around, or harder?"

Frandino sees honest inquisitiveness and searing intelligence in the questioner's eyes. John Klinglehaus, the young and powerful party boss who knows Frandino's back story, leans forward with expectancy. Father Al Cappello, the mayor's confessor through so much of what went wrong during that first mayoral term, looks relaxed. Furrings can move the needle for Frandino within the huge clump of humanity where half of the state's registered voters live, at its southern tip. Time to make his bid for greater celebrity. He starts again. Softly.

"It's more challenging."

He sees them all concentrating on him.

"The challenges we face today compared with ten years ago are a matter of public record. We never had to rely on the state to make up deficits and balance the city budget before now. We've got those big grain elevators sitting mostly empty, and ship traffic is down to just a trickle of what it was in the '50s. People are wondering about their futures."

He looks for a moment at Father Al. He thinks about how Furrings has written empathetically about the personal foibles of other people.

"And, I've grown as a person, I think. I made some mistakes during my first term. I was the reform candidate because the guy before me was flamboyant. I had every intention of setting a different tone. Looking back, I failed to do that in my first term."

He pauses and looks at Furrings, who smiles and nods his head.

"Yes, I made mistakes," Frandino continues, feeling righteous indignation kicking in. "But they were personal in nature. I failed at times to exercise discretion as a leader should. But I never, EVER..."

He stops himself. It will do no good to leave Furrings or anyone else with the impression that he is an angry man. He clears his throat. He must will a patrician's spirit back into his tone.

"I never took a dollar from any ring-kissing criminal. I never did any favors for them. I've never let myself be coerced by them. I've never bought a vote from the mafia. You want to know God's honest truth about why I wanted to be mayor again?"

He studies their faces. His *paesani* are smiling. The others look back at him earnestly.

"Go ahead," invites Furrings.

Sal Frandino's mind takes him back to a cold, sunny autumn day in 1932...

*****

... Men are standing in line on the sidewalk not far from downtown, on Broadway. He had heard that he might see a soup line, but Frandino didn't know there would be so many men standing in it. He's taken the streetcar to come here for a haircut at Joe's, his regular barber shop and a place where many young lawyers like himself congregate to chew the fat. The streetcar leaves him not quite one block from Joe's. The line of men extends for the entire length of his walk, and then some. He won't be able to get into Joe's without cutting through the queue.

Everything overhead is a beautiful shade of blue. The trees are at their peak of autumn glory. Stray Fords and Studebakers, uniform in their black-painted steel, clank past on the uneven pavement of Broadway. Frandino sees the faces of the men in line. Men of his age, or older. Some wear blank expressions. Some look dazed. The men in line are not talking much, but there is one snippet of conversation that Frandino has memorialized to himself through the years.

"Thees ist ein shame," says a big, German-accented man. Black wool cap pulled over his forehead down to his eyebrows. He has spoken to the man in front of him in line, who is a foot shorter than himself. The big German gestures in the direction of all the men lined up in front of them.

"*Si, si*," says the shorter guy, sporting a similar cap and a bushy dark moustache. "America is broken, all right."

"Nobody think it can here happen," says the German, shaking his head slowly. "Right here in our city it happen."

The shorter man laughs a short, sad laugh. "Maybe I send my kids back-a to Portugal," he says.

And then, just two storefronts shy of the barber shop, Frandino is arrested by a familiar face that turns beet red upon being recognized.

"Uncle - Uncle Pietro."

Pietro Rossini is not Frandino's uncle by blood. He lives in a house right next to the one on Trenton Street where Frandino had grown up. Pietro's own kids were a few years older than the crowd Frandino ran with in school, but Pietro was a fixture in the neighborhood; a well-known friend to the priests at St. Anthony's; a substitute teacher in the schools. Frandino hasn't seen him in the three years since he married Steffi and moved away from the neighborhood.

"Sallie," The older man says to Frandino in a far-off voice. Sal is a new city attorney. His very clothing communicates that he is employed. Frandino feels his own heartbeat in his face.

Frandino looks with stunned silence at one of his neighborhood's pillars. He wishes for words that don't come. Pietro draws his lips into a taut line. Frandino touches Pietro on the arm. Then he walks into the barber shop.

Frandino remembers to the men circled about him in the mayor's office how just a few minutes later, Joe the barber talked nervously of his own chances of holding onto his shop. He remembers his conversation with Steffi that same evening about how troubled he was by what he'd seen and heard down on Broadway. He recounts how, the following Sunday afternoon, he went back to Trenton Street with Steffi and a tray of meaty lasagna and fried, breaded artichokes for Pietro and his wife. The tears, the laughter, and the shared meal that followed. The Rossinis had sold most of their furniture to help them keep their house, and they had eaten that meal reclining on the bare wooden floor of a living room that was empty, save for the Victrola and a welcome mat just inside the door...

"... and I never want people to live through that again," he says in a small voice to the circle of men in the mayor's office. "My job is to stop that from happening. My job is to care for the people who live here."

*****

It is six-thirty in the evening. The interview, he thinks, went well; Furrings said the feature could be published in two or three weeks' time. It's been a good day.

It's a re-election year. Not even May, and already the Republicans are rallying around Alice Mrozinski. A well-educated councilperson-at-large, her constituency is not limited to one voting district in the city. The Republicans are looking to her as their 1969 mayoral candidate.

Today, she had been speechmaking at a noon public library event with the television cameras rolling: "The school board and the teachers don't often agree on salaries and strikes. But this year, they agree and it's no wonder! Salaries for our teachers have been stuck for three years. Meanwhile, the cost of living has gone up thirteen percent in that same time. Why would any of our best young minds want to stick around here and teach our children?"

And then, she had turned to the news cameras and had pointed a finger toward the lens. Speaking in a strong, scolding and grave crescendo she fired her salvo: "And I say, 'Where are you, Mister Mayor? Where are you, to help make sure we send our precious children to the finest schools? Schools with paint that's not chipping to poison them with lead, schools with playgrounds that are safe, schools with teachers who are paid fairly so that they will want to work and not strike, or even worse move to other cities that treat them fairly."

Frandino laughs aloud at Mrozinski's voice - that squeaky tirade. It helps him to recall her entire speeches so easily, including the precise moments at which her voice cracks. She is irritating.

Alice must be crushed, and she is crushable. Frandino thinks, whether it's true or not, that she can be painted as a racist. All is fair in love, war, and politics.

The day is winding down. It's been awhile since he's stopped by the Arkansas. It's Millie's night to work; she is always receptive to his overtures for good clean fun. All work and no play make Sal a dull boy. A cigar, a drink, some friends who never fail to make him feel important. And a beautiful woman. He'll just look at her and be refreshed by her beauty, and talk with her just enough to feed his mind with her pleasant voice. Then he'll return home to his Steffi. That's the plan. That is always the plan.

6

Driving His Pontiac Wagon. Thinking

Labor Day Weekend, 1969

Each year, local farmers entered their animals into the livestock pageants at the County Fair, but that was not what attracted us Pronotaros. Mom and Dad took us every year to what was, for two weeks each August, the best and biggest amusement park for miles around. Its roller coaster was almost as scary as the 'Comet' in Canada. Its huge Ferris wheel might well strand you for half an hour at unloading time. Other rides had names that described the resulting sensations they created. If all that wasn't enough to challenge one's sense of well-being, concession stands offered every form of concentrated, refined sugar known to man. For a twelve-year old, it was an awesome place to be.

That year, my brother and I got to each choose one friend to bring. Tom chose Esther; I chose Lamont Raincloud.

"I'm gonna kill you for this," Raincloud said in my ear when Dad pulled into the big grassy parking lot, stopped, and we all piled out.

"What?"

He pointed at Esther, striding a couple of paces ahead of us in cutoff shorts. "Stop trying to set us up," he said for only me to hear.

"It's Tom's fault," I said. "He thinks she's his girlfriend."

The Fair was the unofficial first event of the political campaign season, and people stood at the entrances and exits of the Fairgrounds to pass out buttons and literature for elections in just about every jurisdiction in the county. They'd stop people with "Hi! Do you by chance live in Hamburg? Our man Ted Hills is running for Town Supervisor, and we'd like to give you a button ..."

On our way in, a gal in a miniskirt accosted my dad. "Sir! You look like a city resident..."

"Can you tell just by looking?" Dad said, and then he recognized her. A gal just out of high school who worked for Dad as a waitress.

"Lesley!" Dad said. "Looks like they've got you working for Alice Mrozinski."

"Yes, they do. I've got buttons for the whole family, and some literature that I -"

"Well, that's great," Dad said. "But you see, the wife and the kids and I, we just want to go in, look around, hit the rides. Maybe on the way out, okay?"

Lesley was undeterred. "Mrs. Mrozinski is the candidate who stands up for kids' education and who fights to save neighborhoods from going downhill. I know you've got kids in the city schools, and well, you do live in a neighborhood, right?"

"I'll tell you what. Give me a button," Dad said. "It's great that you're interested in politics, Lesley. You take care - hey by the way, what nights are you on the schedule this coming week?"

Dad was just being nice. No way he'd pull the lever for Alice Mrozinski. He was a Frandino man, I was sure of it. Frandino was our *paesano* and besides, I had heard Mrozinski's televised speeches. She was an angry finger-pointer. She had been whining all summer on television about how "...more and more Blacks are coming across Fillmore Avenue into our fine, well-kept Polish neighborhood. And my proposal will let them continue to do just that - as long as they follow the rules about shoveling their walks, cutting their grass and maintaining their property."

As a twelve year-old, I was in favor of shoveling and grass-cutting; these activities had a prominent place in my own personal economy. But her zeal for these things was weird.

Tom and Esther went on all the rides together that day, and I could tell that Raincloud was jealous. The worst part for him was waiting for the two of them to be unloaded from that humongous Ferris wheel. "Damn you, Pronotaro," he said, jabbing me in the side. "They're holding hands up there - I can see them."

"I'm sorry, Lamont. I didn't know you liked her so much."

"You're gonna pay for this one day," he said.

*****

That autumn, Raincloud's mom took him to the Indian reserve near Brantford, Ontario one weekend each month. Used to be, during our trips with the rest of our class to the North Park Library on Thursday afternoons, that we'd sequester ourselves near the World War II books. We read stories and admired pictures of ships, planes and dogfights. But now, World War II held his interest for a couple of minutes at a time. Then, he'd switch topics.

"You know, the Senecas had to protect the whole Western Door from the tribes that lived in what you whites call Ontario, Ohio, and Michigan. Shawnees. Hurons. Miamis. The Neutrals."

"What are you talking about, 'Mont?"

"The history of America before you diseased white men came. My people used to dominate, son. We spanked people who tried to take our land. We used to raid the hell out of the Shawnees. We were the dreaded people of the long house, Pronotaro."

I know I gave him a funny look, because he continued with exasperation.

"You whites don't understand. We were five tribes all lined up from Connecticut to Ontario. We used to fight each other, but then Hiawatha came with a message from the Great Peacemaker to form us into one nation that shared the land. Hiawatha taught us to be like family to each other, so we were all side by side, from East to West. He taught families to live together in the same house, even six or seven families in a big long house. He taught us to form one big house that was several hundred miles long."

"Not a real house, 'Mont. A symbolic house, you mean."

"Yes, Sherlock Holmes, a symbolic house. And we Senecas hung onto it all the way past George Washington and Thomas Jefferson's time. We live at the Western Door of the Iroquois long house."

"Yeah, but now we just live on the North Side," I answered. Raincloud's enthusiasm for boundaries that hadn't existed for two hundred years was just as weird to me as Alice Mrozinski drawing a border at Fillmore Avenue between the Polish and the...

"You're missing the point, Pronotaro. We Seneca, we're going to take our house back. One of these generations, it'll be our turn again."

I made a face at him.

"See?" Raincloud said. "I knew you wouldn't understand. You're so white you're stinking Wonder Bread."

October 16, 1969

Frandino will not smoke a Panatela tonight; he hasn't had a cigar for a month. The polls show that he enjoys a fifteen-point lead over Alice Mrozinski in the race for mayor. Election Day is nineteen days away. Frandino will keep his breath fresh for every person he meets.

He will win, but the city is fracturing. Mrozinski and her people are shrill. William Snead complains aloud that neither Frandino nor Mrozinski is interested in helping African-Americans with jobs and programs. Snead has thrown his hat into the ring as an independent.

It won't matter. The big industrial unions are backing Frandino, and so is party boss John Klinglehaus.

Frandino figures that some of the requests for help that get funneled to his desk via Klinglehaus are likely a part of a certain equation - the "Ziggy needs two hundred bucks to keep his kid in Catholic high school this year" and "Morris needs three hundred to make rent this summer" kinds of requests that are filled in exchange for votes. But when the requests come from Klinglehaus, Frandino does not question; nor does he get personally involved. He routes them to a city department head and the details get worked out. For years, it's how political capital has been obtained.

But sometimes Frandino wants to know that he can get their votes without Klinglehaus, and he wants everyone else to know it, too. Frandino drives the old family station wagon to the biggest campaign speech of the year - a campaign dinner sponsored by the Knights of Columbus and Metropolitan Athletic Club - and he feels feisty. He parks the car and walks toward a room in which he will address union officials, political functionaries, banks who aren't making so many loans these days unless they're of the "right kind." All his supporters; all of them tools of the status quo.

He walks in a few minutes late. People stand and cheer. There may be three hundred people present. He waves and smiles. Klinglehaus arises from the head table and walks toward him. The men embrace for a moment, and flashbulbs pop.

Frandino stands behind the podium. He surveys the room as he prepares to begin his speech. Not a black person present. Only five women; four of them sitting at a round table for ten with six empty chairs.

"First, let me thank John Klinglehaus and Abraham Pincus, the current and former chairmen of the County Democratic Party - for pulling this event together. I see so many people I've known for years, people who've stuck by me through thick and thin."

He pauses, and on cue the people in the room applaud.

"It's just dandy to be surrounded by friends. You know, I did something dangerous on the way over here tonight. I was driving the old Frandino station wagon..." The room erupts in laughter. Even Klinglehaus is guffawing. The two men trade bemused facial expressions to milk the accidental gag for a bit more good feeling.

"But that wasn't the dangerous thing I meant. What I was going to say is, on the way over here tonight, I got to *thinking*."

Fresh laughter.

"I had some very powerful thoughts," he continues after they settle down, "and I want to share some of them with you tonight."

Now, there is a hush.

"I've always told people that I like to drive my own car around town because it's old, similar to the ones I see so many of our citizens drive. It reminds me that I'm not too different from the people who vote for me. But also, I drive it because I like to be in charge of my direction. I don't like being told what to do by others."

He stops, and there is a smattering of applause. They are not all clapping, but those who do, do so lustily and a few voices chant, "Sal! Sal! Sal!" He puts his hands up to quiet them.

"Now I love and appreciate all of you who are here tonight. And I can honestly say, it's not just your votes that I appreciate, it's who you are. Dandy people in this room tonight, people who care about this city as deeply as I do. People who've put their money and time where their mouth is to build upon the legacy that the area's forefathers have left to us."

Pause. Applause.

"You're all smart enough to know that as the 1970s loom, we're running into some headwinds. Our population is changing. We've never had so many people in need within our city limits. Our schools are struggling to keep pace. Our police and firemen, who put their lives on the line for us every day, deserve salary increases that keep up with the cost of living. Our teachers too, and so many others. A whole new generation of city workers will soon be eligible for retirement and pensions. That's going to be expensive. And we have a shrinking tax base."

Out of the corner of his eye, he sees Klinglehaus looking at him intently, and not smiling.

"The message I want to deliver tonight - to all of you in this room, the papers and press, and the people in the city and the whole metropolitan area - the message to the workers on the assembly lines, the men who run our great retail stores downtown, the thousands of small business owners throughout the area - I want to say that I will do everything I can to give you and your families a good life here in this city for many generations to come."

Applause. From Klinglehaus, he can almost hear the sigh of relief. But Frandino laughs inside.

"I beg you to be patient with me for the next couple of minutes while I share the thoughts your mayor had just now in that old Pontiac of his. It'll help you to see the choice Buffalo has between myself and the other candidates."

Frandino turns to Klinglehaus and Pincus, the party bosses, and smiles at them. They are staring back at him.

"Several years ago, when I decided to try politics, I thought it was a good thing that I knew some Polish, some Spanish and Italian and Yiddish and Portuguese. And even a bit of English."

They laugh at his joke, though most have heard it before.

"Because in a city like this one, I can use my languages to connect with people, to get votes. And it worked - just look at my record against Kowalski a few years back - a perfect two wins and one loss."

Applause and some laughter.

"Tonight I'm looking around, and I see two men I'm going to pick on for a moment - I hope they don't mind. Right there is Charlie Sandino. Charlie's my *paisano* - we went to Holy Angels High School together, and Charlie's become one of the best corporate attorneys this area has ever seen. Charlie and I can trade a few greetings in Italian, and Chaz - how many times have I run into you back at the old parish for St. Joseph's Day? It's a good day, isn't it?"

Charlie is smiling, and a couple of the people sitting with him pat him on the back.

"Now one table over from Chaz is Stan Bryzinowicz. He's a Polish guy, could you guess from his name?"

Laughter.

"Jak leki, Stashu. Cieszę się, że Cię widzę dziś wieczorem. Jak jest rodzina?"

"Ladny. To jest dobre widzieć was też. Moja rodzina jest dobrze. Sal," the man replies.

"Now honestly, how did it make the rest of you who don't understand Polish feel, that you paid good money to be here tonight to hear a speech and you don't understand what's being said?"

Silence.

"Go ahead, Stan, stand up and let them in on the secret."

"Sal said it's good to see me and asked how are my wife and kids. Then I told him it's good to be here and the family is fine."

"Exactly," Frandino said. "You know, we live in a city that's a lot like this room. We all come from different backgrounds. But we need to listen and understand one another, or we'll stop trusting one another and our community will start to unravel."

A smattering of polite applause.

"Now let me talk about my opponent. Have you been listening to her? In her speeches, she's been chopping us up into segments. Blacks and whites. Haves and have-nots. Workers and taskmasters. She seems to think that we need to govern according to all these divisions. And folks, that's like me having a conversation with Stan here in Polish all night. The rest of you hear noises that don't mean a thing to you. It won't work, it can't work. Not with the challenges we face today."

Some of the attendees are on their feet with shouts and applause. He gestures with his hands for them to settle down.

"It is time for us to take our party's idea of the Great Society to the next level, and I want us to try to do that right here, in our town. I am asking us to put not just our money and our votes, but also our hearts where our mouth is. I am asking that all of us, in whatever calling we have - some of us are lawyers, some of us doctors, some of us are politicians, or business owners, or union men, or educators - whatever calling we have, I'm asking us to live out the spirit of the Great Society. I am convinced that the way forward is to genuinely care about all of our people, all of our minorities. All of us will need to work together with charity toward all and with malice toward none to make sure that we can all have the good life right here in this city, that I know my papa wanted for all his children and grandchildren when he decided to settle us here many years ago. Let us go and do justice and love mercy and walk humbly. Good night! And may God bless the Democratic Party."

Frandino knows which men in the room have hardened their hearts against sentiments like the ones he's just delivered. But the overall applause is sufficient. He turns to Klinglehaus and the obligatory handshake occurs between the two men. Frandino feels one arm of the younger, shorter chairman on his upper back, coaxing Frandino to lean in closer.

"Not how we scripted it," Klinglehaus says through a broad, plastered smile as more flashbulbs fulfill the momentary purpose of their existence. "Good thing we've got a few points in the polls to play with."

"John, I hope you were listening. It's the kind of mayor I've always intended to be."

"You're already that mayor, Sal. But - ah, well. We're going to win. This is a conversation for another day."

The men turn away from one another and toward the people, Frandino's left hand clasping Klinglehaus' right. Both men smile and thrust their arms high overhead with fingers forming the victory V.

7

Storms of Life, Gathering

December 2, 1969; 7:51 A.M.

Big flakes like fluffy white eyelashes float earthward from a grey morning sky. The snowflakes add magic to the scenes of street life within a block of Frandino's sixth-floor City Hall window, and blur his vision beyond. It's been weeks since the voters have decided by a healthy margin that he will be the mayor who leads the city into the next decade. Unless, of course, an opportunity to run for a statewide office presents itself.

Frandino and top cop Lou Lombardi are mulling over the wisdom of forcing the new hockey team to stop alcohol sales at the end of the second intermission, when the phone on his desk buzzes its familiar refrain. Frandino walks to the desk and removes the handpiece from its cradle.

"Sal, it's Alice Mrozinski. Says it's urgent."

He feels his brow knit. "Is she finally calling to congratulate me?"

"Probably not," Phyllis replies.

"Put her through anyway."

"Alice. To what do I owe this courtesy?"

"Sal. I've been wanting to talk for two weeks. I must admit, it was hard to pick up the phone. I - I'm sorry."

"Okay, I'm sitting now. What's this fine business about you being sorry?"

"Well, you beat us rather soundly. I have to admit that hurts like hell. I've been soul searching. My shrink suggested that I try to talk to you about it."

"Alice. A shrink - my God!"

"Oh, I'm fine. Really. Look, you're a Democrat, I'm a Republican, but Sal, I want to grow from this. Not just as a politician. As a – as a – person."

She has stopped talking.

"Alice, are you crying?"

"No I'm not, you insensitive idiot! I'm - thinking about how to - oh, never mind." Then comes the plaintive whine of the campaign. "I shouldn't have called you, you, you -"

"No, wait. Alice. I'm not trying to pile on. Look – when Kowalski beat me in '61, it was hard for me. I understand the pain."

"Sal, I should go. I'm sorry to have bothered you."

"Alice, I'm at your service. You ran a tough campaign and you lost. But you have my respect. Now, what is it?"

He hears an unsteady breath. So, she is crying.

"Take your time." Frandino hears softness in his own voice. "I don't have an appointment 'til noon."

"You know how badly I want to sit in your chair," she starts. "To be the first woman mayor. And, I've never been one to hold anything back. I know that puts some people off. But Sal, I got hate mail delivered to my house this fall. I had threats made against my kids. All because I wanted to be the mayor."

"I'm very sorry about that."

"Well," she says. "I resolved to be bigger than all of it, to soldier on through it. And by God, I was gonna show all of you. I was gonna win! And we were going to start doing government my way around here. You must be laughing, right?"

"No. We all think those thoughts when we run for office."

"Anyways, I thought at least it would be a lot closer than it was. But I got crushed. Getting crushed, it makes a person think, doesn't it?"

"Yes, I suppose it does. What does it make you think?"

"It makes me think that I have a lot to learn. I think I can only be a better politician if I'm a better person. I've been talking with my husband, some friends, people in the Republican Party. But I've got to talk to my enemies, too."

"We're not enemies, Alice. We are competitors, and we do sell a different brand of government. But to enemies, I wish death. I don't wish that on you, Alice."

"Sal, what do you think is my big weakness? What is it about me that inspires such - such fear in so many people?"

"You're a public servant. Public servants will always inspire their share of both love and hatred. Listen, you and I don't agree on who should get how much of the gravy, but the things you stand for - transparent government, complete honesty - these are good things. Where you and I differ is on the degree of honesty and transparency that's best. If the citizens knew everything about how big deals get done - how roads and schools get built and who builds them - how grants are made and the whole thing - my God, we'd have rebellion in the streets! But it's worked this way for dozens of years before Sal Frandino, and it's going to work this way for dozens of years after me, too."

"But it doesn't have to be this way, does it?"

"Making the city tick – the job is way bigger than either of us. I'm pretty good at leadership, but you and me - we're just politicians. We talk big because we have to get voters' attention. Sometimes we can influence, but it's always the banks, the big corporations and the independently wealthy who make the big decisions. Sometimes for a politician, leadership means you just try to influence who you can, when you can."

"All I stood for during the campaign is that it doesn't have to be that way in the future. You play into their hands too easily, Sal. Don't you think?"

"Alice, underneath all the tough campaign talk I happen to think you're a good woman with a good heart. I know you care about what's right. I predict that you will live to fight another day."

"Thanks for saying that, Sal. I think I should be going now. Love to Steffi."

"And to your husband." Frandino returns the headset to the phone cradle.

"Is she okay?" Lombardi asks.

"Oh, she's fine," Sal answers. "She's one part hurt, one part naive and one part Alice. And, if she's taking her defeat anything like I did in '61, she's heartbroken."

"Yeah," Lombardi is shaking his head. "Saint Salvatore, the gracious. Did she manage to congratulate you yet?"

"Hmm. Well, maybe she meant to."

Lombardi smiles and shakes his head.

"Lou, this would be a good night to enjoy some alcoholic beverages - what are your plans for the evening?"

7:56 A.M.; that same day

Tommy Bellavia was the funniest of all the one hundred and twelve seventh graders at Public School 81. His impersonations of President Nixon, former president Johnson, the Smothers Brothers, Carole Burnett, Gilligan and the Skipper - it didn't matter who you were - if Tommy had seen you on television, you were going to be impersonated and Tommy was going to get some laughs at your expense.

On that overcast morning in early December, we congregated as always in the big, grassy playground behind the school. The first snow-flakes of the year were hitting us but that would not stop our before-school touch football game. Every seventh and eighth-grade boy who was any-body took part. Raincloud and I were regulars; this year, fewer kids were picking on him. He had learned some things about standing his ground. You might also say that was the year when he lost his baby fat. He looked like a twelve-year old professional wrestler.

Tommy played too, getting by more on good will than athletic abil-ity. His job during our games was often to count 'seven steamboats' at the line of scrimmage and then rush the passer, a job reserved for the kids who couldn't run or catch so well. But we loved Tommy; he was our guy.

That day as we chose sides, he said with uncharacteristic softness, "Guys, don't choose me today. I just want to watch."

"What're you talking about?" I asked. "You feel okay?"

"Yeah," he answered. But none were fooled.

"What's bothering you, man?" asked another guy.

"Oh ... my dad had the talk with me and mom, and the two sisters last night. We're moving."

Half a dozen of us let out a breath."

"Phoenix, Arizona," he continued, smacking his lips. "Dad got a new job and that's where it is. He showed us a picture of our new house, and my new school. Mom's very happy. I guess that's good, right?"

"You know whose land that is?" Raincloud asked. Without pause, he provided his own answer. "It's Hopi and Navajo land. Maybe Nez Perce. What part of Arizona is Phoenix?"

"Dad says we should be happy," Tommy answered. "It's a beautiful house with a built-in-pool in the back yard. I'll see if he'll let me bring the pictures to school so I can show you."

"When are you moving?"

"Over Christmas vacation."

"So, that means a class farewell party," I said.

"This'll be our homeroom's second going away party of the year," someone said. "Last year, we had three. Think we'll have three again this year?"

I recalled the names and faces of the other kids whose going-away parties I attended. Brian Thomas was out in Amherst now, just a few miles away. Gretchen Nelson, I think her family had moved to Michigan. Cindy Molino and her twin sister Candy - their dad was a college professor and they were now in Boston. Seth Chaison - I figured he was down in Orchard Park with his cousins.

Tommy changed in those last few days of his time with us. He went from being the goodwill ambassador of our homeroom, to downright surly. One of the last things I ever heard him say, just a day before the class party in his honor, was when he shouted at a kid in the cafeteria, "Well, it never snows in Phoenix! And the houses are bigger and the streets are wider - I can't wait to leave this shit hole of a town."

7:05 p.m. that evening

Father Al Cappello knows something about brandy and cigars. He is well-read both in the classics and current events. Sal Frandino loves the priest for all of this. Tonight will be a happy trio at the Arkansas - Frandino, Lombardi, Cappello. The Grace Kelly look-alike, taking care of them.

Two fresh inches of snow have fallen throughout the day but now, as they walk down Grant Street toward the Arkansas, the night sky is calm. Frandino composes a joke in his head as he reaches for the front door of the neighborhood haunt: A mayor, a priest, and a police commissioner walk into a bar.

"Oh my goodness," Millie says, placing a hand upon her forehead as they arrive. "Look at this - a Catholic priest. I am being visited by the Trinity."

Surrounded by familiar, smiling faces, Frandino feels himself on top of the world.

Millie looks at the priest. "I don't believe we've met, but can I have your boss' autograph? You know," she places her hands in front of her chest and points heavenward with her two index fingers, "the big boss."

"I'm Al Cappello. Sal and I go back years, from down at St. Anthony's."

"Well, it's very good to meet you, Al Cappello." She extends a hand of greeting. "You know," she says, leaning over and speaking softly, "I should visit you. It's been years since my last confession."

"Hmm. Good, firm handshake. A woman who can weather the storms of life," Frandino hears the priest say to her.

She laughs. "The storms of life just walked into my bar tonight - three of them. What are you gentlemen having?"

It goes like this for a little over ninety minutes and three drinks apiece. Frandino loves his occasional visits to Millie; a great and willing conversationalist. The priest seems to appreciate her as well.

The trio adjourns, and the mayor skirts Father Al back to St. Anthony's in the baby blue Frandino family wagon. The priest seems subdued.

"Everything okay, Al?"

"Yeah. I'm fine." But then, just a minute or so shy of the rectory, he speaks up.

"I'm sorry, Sal. She's um, a very impressive woman. Beautiful, and what interesting questions she asks."

Yes, she's..." Frandino stops and looks over at his friend.

"Aw, heck, Al. My fault. I knew you'd like her if you got in any kind of conversation with her and – well, you did."

"Yeah. You married guys. Don't take your wives for granted."

The priest is let off at the rectory, and Sal's thoughts now run to home. He conjures images of the big parlor with the fireplace decked out for the holidays; the room looks great. Steffi, the kids and grandchildren did most of the decorating, leaving only the tree-topper for Hizzonor.

It is about 9:35 p.m., not very late at all by Frandino standards, when he pulls into the driveway. Steffi is in the kitchen, sitting at the table, smoking a cigarette.

"Honey. I - thought you had quit."

"I thought you had, too."

"What do you mean?"

She takes a long drag and holds it in. The act of holding the smoke in her lungs serves to accentuate her trim waist. She is a shapely woman. Frandino thinks she still has the body of a gymnast. She blows smoke back at him.

"I mean," she says, as she sharpens the tip of the ashes like an arrowhead in the ashtray, "where have you been?"

"My gosh, I didn't call. Steff, I'm sorry. I should've - I - I met with Lou this morning, like we were supposed to, and we decided to stop off together for a drink or two after work."

"And where might that have been, Sal?"

"Hey - are you sore?"

"I don't know. Should I be?"

They've been down this road before. He's promised her, no more of that. He walks behind her and begins to rub her shoulders, the nape of her neck.

"So," she says, leaving the cigarette in the ashtray to burn on its own, then putting both elbows on the table and surrendering herself to the backrub. "What does the mayor have to say for himself tonight?"

"I should've called. I'm sorry."

"Hmm."

Frandino continues to rub his wife's shoulders.

"So. Who is she?"

He stops rubbing, and takes a seat at the table.

"Okay, I'll tell you. You've heard me speak of her before, and I've even offered to bring you to the Arkansas to meet her. It was Millie. We're friends, that's all. For Chrissakes, Father Al was with us! She spent more time talking to Al than to me and Lou put together. We had a couple drinks, a steak sandwich, and we just talked. That's all I ever do."

She laughed; it sounded to him like a sinister, smoky laugh.

"You introduced Father Al to your love interest? Wow, Sallie. You're going to great lengths to make it all seem innocent to yourself, aren't you?"

The spouses are looking into one another's eyes. Steffi breaks eye contact to extinguish the Viceroy in the tray though it still has a good inch and a half left to burn.

"I can't tell if you're serious or what, Steff. Tell me."

"I know you. You're a mere mortal. And pretty famous around here. I know you promised me. I believe that at least a part of you still means it. But I worry."

It's his turn to sigh. "I thought about you all the way home, how I was looking forward to seeing you."

She nods. "Maybe so. And still, I've been meaning to tell you. Sallie, I worry for you. You get distant sometimes. Like in the old days when you were –" her voice trails off and picks up again. "At least, that's what it feels like."

Frandino decides to remain quiet.

"You know," Steffi continues, "the first time I was very hurt. I don't have to remind you. But there's one person in the world I know was hurt even more than me."

"Your dad. I do know."

"No, Sallie. It was you. And it still is. You still remember what it cost you, to have scandal attached to your name. You could have been governor by now. And then the party withdrew from you... you lost one... I don't have to remind you. But sometimes, I think I do have to remind you. I think you need to hear it again."

"Let me tell you about another woman I had a conversation with today."

"And that would be whom?"

"The most esteemed Alice."

A jolt of surprise crosses her face. Then, she smiles broadly. "Ho, ho, ho. What was that about?"

"It was sweet. She called the office while Lou was there. She wanted advice. She's hurting, and I wanted to give her some encouragement."

"Hmm. My husband the humanitarian."

"You mentioned losing to Kowalski and what that did to me. And you're right, of course. Glad JFK put a job in my lap, called me and gave me that pep talk, or I'd have wasted away."

"Kennedy," she mused. "Another faithful man. God, give me strength."

"Stefania. Dammi le tue mani, per favore." He smiled.

She returned the smile and put her hands out. Her hands felt hard and calloused to him, not soft and lovely. But he did really love these hands that made their Soldier's Circle property bloom with wonderful flowers almost nine out of twelve months in the sometimes-intemperate weather.

Hands that baked and cooked for him, and when they were younger, that caressed him constantly.

"It took guts for Alice to call me and trust me with her own self-doubts. She wants to be a better person. And she's still young, got her whole life ahead of her. She sounded on the phone today like I felt in '61. Contrite."

"Oh my God, Sal. You were suicidal for a while."

"Losing hurts. But that experience is what made me want to get it right this time. I heard that same thing in Alice's voice today. I wanted to bond with her over it."

"Sallie, that's sweet. But one thing I ask, huh?"

"What's that?"

"No more bonding with other women, you big turkey."

"Okay."

"Especially the young ones."

"Got it."

"So - did she finally congratulate us on our win, or what?"

8

Queue City Blues, 1970

September 11, 1970

A crushing psychological milestone, confirmed. Frandino and his fiscal lieutenants have just gotten a pre-briefing of the 1970 U.S. Census numbers. For the first time in sixty years, fewer than half a million people officially live within the city limits. Once in the nation's top ten, the Queen City of the Lakes has lost almost twenty percent of its people over twenty years, and has fallen in rank to number twenty-eight. The census says the two-county metropolitan area is experiencing zero growth. Frandino sinks into his chair. This news, and the Republican now in the Oval Office who backs away from some of ex-president Johnson's social programs, are ankle weights to a city running a race for financial support from the State and the Feds.

Frandino looks out over the lake from his window. Noon-time sun and fair skies. He sees for miles out over the water. This was the time of year when the harbor was at its busiest; stockpiling iron ore, manganese and nickel for the steelmakers before the winter freeze. Today, he sees only one ore boat.

His third term as mayor has been a nightmare. The big department stores that were the anchors of his downtown business strategy are retreating from their previous long-term commitments to keep a presence in the central business district. Sears has just closed its big Main Street store, leaving a hulking retail building vacant in a strategic mid-town location. Two steel plants and an automobile stamping plant have just announced layoffs - all told, another fourteen hundred men out of work.

Nervous energy. Three days since he's last been to the Athletic Club to play handball. He will arrange a game for tonight.

The Club is just four blocks from City Hall; on days like this, Frandino walks there. Ironic sunshine brightens the dinginess of the older buildings downtown. Frandino feels the weight of his gym bag; notices the automobile and pedestrian traffic. Many cars and busses and many, many people. Downtown, he tries to convince himself, is still the place to be. But he can't ignore his memory. The crowds, the traffic, thinner than twenty years ago. Than even five years ago.

He will play against Sammy Toth, a guy who he often finds himself trading places with on the competitive ladder kept by the Club. Sammy, known for sartorial splendor, is general manager of the downtown flagship location of a prominent locally-owned department store chain. Sammy is Frandino's ally. Committed to the city. This stops neither man from trying to destroy each other on the handball court. Sammy is ten years younger, three inches shorter, and a hair quicker than Frandino. The mayor counters with experience. But Toth has just gone on a run of points to come from behind and win the first match in what is to be a best-of-three contest.

"Come on, Sal," Toth smiles as they prepare to begin the second game. "I know you're a betting man deep down. Five bucks says you don't get ten points on me this second game."

"Oh, no, you don't." Frandino looks without smiling into his opponent's face. "I can see the headlines in the *Messenger* tomorrow." He changes his voice and mocks. " 'Frandino Swindles Department Store Manager out of Big Bucks in Downtown Rally.' "

"You're chicken, that's all. Tell you what, let's just wager for a cocktail at the dinner tonight."

"Dinner?"

"Yeah." Toth bounces the ball off the floor and catches it as he talks. "The annual fundraiser tonight for the Athletic Club. You're coming, right?"

"Damned right, I'm coming. I'll call Steffi. It'll be fine."

Toth holds the ball in his hand. "You mean they didn't... ahh. The *Messenger* is the big sponsor. Not your fans, are they?"

"It slipped my mind, that's all," Frandino says. Then, a familiar place within his gut screams rebellion. Frandino is grimacing. He bends over from the impact of the flare-up. Why that O'Connell at the *Messenger*...

"Hey! You okay?"

"Yeah," Frandino pants slightly. Toth has come alongside with a steadying hand.

"Sal, what is it?"

The pain has already begun to subside. "It's okay," he answers.

"You don't sound or look okay."

Frandino forces himself to straighten up. "I'm fine. I get these little shooting pains occasionally. They go away, and then it could be months before it happens again."

"Mayor," Toth says. "That's not good. Have you gotten it checked?"

"Ah - yeah. It's been checked. It's nothing."

"Maybe we should stop. Call it a match."

"Oh no you don't. We're finishing the set, and I'm taking the next two games."

"Sal, I don't know if -"

"In fact, you said you've got five bucks? I'm taking it, if your money is still where your mouth is. I got five bucks and a drink after dinner tonight that says not only do I get to ten, but I take the next two games and win the match."

Toth smiles. "Three quarters of the room'll love to see you there tonight. To hell with the rest of 'em."

They are competing again. Frandino abandons himself to handball. He knows that he's making the younger man work hard; Frandino wins the second game and then, score tied at eleven in the third, notices that Toth is breathing quite hard. Frandino feels pride. Then he serves a winner and goes ahead by a point in the deciding match, and Toth looks at him with consternation.

"Damn it, Sal. You're an old man, but you're still a very tough out, you know that?"

"I do. Just ask any of my opponents."

*****

Sal Frandino feels invincible. He has taken Sammy Toth's challenge and won; the men pushed each other to their limits on the court, and in the afterglow of victory Frandino's mind is clear and calm. They've showered and changed; Toth in a wide-collared pinstriped suit with a purple shirt and a pink-and-purple paisley tie. The fundraiser will start soon; when contacted, Steffi agreed that Sal should attend. She loves any opportunity he gets to stick it in some way or other to Finn O'Connell and the *Messenger*.

At the reception, Frandino loses Toth in the crowd. There are people to greet. The Club is happy to have the mayor crash their most important annual fundraising event of the year, and the *Messenger's* people are obliged to extend their hospitality. He will not be at the head table, but he'll be announced and given a moment to take a bow. Frandino is pleased to be a fly in O'Connell's ointment.

Frandino and Toth are finally seated across from one another at a round table for eight. It is not a huge gathering; maybe a hundred men. But many are prominent in the community. Finn O'Connell is delivering his welcoming remarks. He's an imposing man with thick arms and a commanding voice. A bag of wind, Frandino thinks. But he listens. *Know thy enemy...* And then...

"We've got some unexpected company I need to acknowledge, though no doubt he's already been on the prowl and has kibitzed with many of you during the cocktail reception... I give you your mayor, Salvatore Frandino..." O'Connell jabs a hand in the mayor's direction.

Frandino rises and bows with a wordless smile. More than half the men in the room are standing, applauding, whistling.

There is surf and turf on everyone's plate. Frandino and Toth regal the other men at their table with the tale of their epic handball battle. There is food, alcohol, and laughter. Steak and lobster-tail, creamy mashed potatoes, creamed cauliflower. Dessert is some sort of pie with bananas and assorted berries, topped with cream and brown sugar. Then, one of the guys from the Athletic Club is at the podium.

"Gentlemen, tonight's keynote speaker is a guy we all know. A guy some of us have been unfortunate enough to compete against..."

Frandino wonders if perhaps, given his unexpected presence, they've changed the program and he will speak after all. He's always prepared. The emcee continues to establish the speaker's credentials. Champion of downtown business. Staunch supporter of physical fitness in the schools. Heartbeat of a winner.

"Gentlemen, I give you Mr. Samuel Toth. Come on up, Sammy!"

Toth winks at Frandino and rises a bit unsteadily. Toth appears to stumble a bit as he climbs the short stairway to the raised podium from where he'll speak. Frandino thinks the big meal has made him sluggish.

Frandino feels disappointment that the Athletic Club did not change the program so he could deliver the evening's keynote.

Toth is behind the podium. He grabs an edge of it to steady himself. "Friends of the Club," he says, a bit breathily.

No more words yet. They are waiting; Frandino recognizes the pause as a public speaking tactic meant to quiet them. Skillful guy, this Toth...

...Toth falls, hitting his head on the corner of the podium with a crack. His body lands off to one side of the podium with a thud.

"A doctor! Please!" The man who announced Toth yells and gestures with his arms.

It is not far from Frandino's chair to Toth. Frandino propels himself toward the podium and negotiates the raised platform in a single bound. He feels for a pulse in the stricken man's wrist. It is there, faint and rapid. Or is that his own pulse?

He looks up and yells. "We need a doctor!"

A background murmur of confusion in the room. Frandino's head is against Toth's chest. He is listening. He hears nothing.

"Someone help me!" He yells again. "A doctor! Or anyone!" He is opening the shirt by the buttons. He rips the white crew-cut tee-shirt. Toth's chest is hairy. Ear on Toth's chest, feeling wiry little curls. Ear over the heart, listening.

"I'm here, Sal," says a voice from very close. "What do you need?" Frandino recognizes that it is Finn O'Connell.

"A doctor, for Christ's sake! I can't hear his heart!"

"Sal! For the love of Christ! He's not breathing!"

Frandino hears panic in O'Connell's voice and then his head is clear.

"Do you know CPR, Finn..."

"I do," replies Frandino's enemy.

"No heartbeat. I'll do the breathing. You do the chest. On my signal."

"Okay, Sal. He's got - he's got a wife and kids. Sal!"

Frandino is clearing the man's air passage with his fingers. Frandino's mouth is on Toth's mouth. He breathes life into him for all he's worth. Toth's lungs expand. Frandino knows it's involuntary. Frandino does it again. A third time. He can taste Toth's dinner drink. Canadian Mist, maybe.

"Now, Finn!"

He watches O'Connell slam the palms of his hands into Toth's chest. And again. There is a groan from Toth.

"More air, Sal." O'Connell says.

Frandino sucks in as much air as he can and he's on Toth's face again. Nothing exists except himself, Toth, O'Connell. A fleeting thought that an ambulance crew needs to arrive or some heads will roll tomorrow at City Hall. In between lungs full of air he yells, "An ambulance, damn it."

O'Connell's words are softer.

"I think I can hear his heart coming back. Geez, Sal, he seemed so healthy... Come on, Sam... You gotta stay with us, buddy... Come on, Sammy..."

Sal has given him another blast of air. "Do it, Finn."

O'Connell pushes hard on Toth's chest, one hand pushing on another.

Toth is coughing weakly. The cough repeats.

"Finn. You did it."

"Sal. Oh, Sweet Jesus Christ in Heaven."

Frandino is paying rapt attention to Sammy Toth, whose eyes have opened and closed. And opened again.

"Oh, Sweet Jesus, Sal. Oh, Sammy." O'Connell exclaims under his breath.

Toth's eyes are open. His chest moving on its own, ever so slightly. Frandino takes gentle hold of Toth's hand and looks into his face. The man's eyes are open, trying to focus on Frandino. Eyes full of panic.

"Sammy. It's okay. Relax. Just relax. It's okay," O'Connell says.

"Sammy. Your friends are right here. It's going to be okay," Frandino says.

"God bless us," says O'Connell. Frandino is now aware that there are several men gathered around.

"I'm a doc," says a tall, bespectacled, younger man, who kneels over Toth's face. "They've called emergency. Ambulance is on the way."

"You're a doctor?" Frandino jerks his head toward the man.

"I was sitting in the back," the man answers. "You both were a great team. I don't have a kit with me - I couldn't have done any better."

Frandino looks back at Toth's face. He has just a bit more color, a bit more presence.

"Sammy," Frandino says. "You listen to me. Listen to us." He glances over at O'Connell. "You stay alive for us, you hear? And for your wife and kids - just breathe nice and easy, and stay with us."

The ambulance crew arrives. Only then does the mayor stand. And Finn O'Connell. Without a word, they embrace. Frandino hangs on for dear life. O'Connell's body is racked by sobs.

"Christ Almighty," O'Connell says, his face red, cheeks moistened by his eyes. "He's got a wife and kids, Sal. You saved his life, you fucking dago."

Frandino hugs O'Connell even harder. Then, he holds O'Connell's face in both his hands.

"You and me both, Finn. You and me both."

"Jesus, Sal. I... I ate at his house just two months ago. Jesus, we...

we cooked out in his yard."

Most of the men stayed on for a bit after the EMTs carted Toth off, still alive. Sal and O'Connell led them in prayers for Sammy's life, for the city, for the Athletic Club. For their own families. They stayed until they got word from Emergency Hospital that Toth was in intensive care, hanging on. It was a massive coronary event, but if they could see him through the night...

... Frandino was awakened by a phone call in his home just after six o'clock the next morning. Thirty minutes earlier Sammy Toth passed on in the presence of his wife, his oldest daughter, and his rabbi. Toth's last words were the ones he spoke from behind the podium at the Athletic Club's dinner.

Part II
The Lady

9

Water Beneath Her Feet, Churning

January 12, 1971

The DC-9 lurched and yawed as it descended. The young woman in seat 6B did not find her situation pleasant. For the past hour and twenty minutes, she had been fending off the halitosis-laden, vaguely inappropriate friendliness of the man in the next seat. Was he a harbinger of what all the men in this town would be? She comforted herself with the prospect of moving on to a bigger market after a year or two.

This business was tough, and it was remaking her in its image. She was no longer the idealistic 21-year old who graduated at the top of her journalism class back in 1966, at Creighton. She was drawn toward politics and power, and repulsed by the memory of a male classmate suggesting that she'd make a fine gossip reporter. Proud of her growing skepticism... no, maturity. After all, she was not, as her last boss in Des Moines had been fond of reminding her, getting paid to believe in Santa Claus. Or in anything the Pentagon, White House, or Iowa State Capital told her to believe.

The pilot's voice came over the PA system: flight attendants, be seated for landing. The winds on the ground, he said, were out of the northwest at eight with gusts to twenty. The local time was 7:23 p.m., the skies were partly cloudy with no precipitation, and the ground temperature was seventeen degrees. Dropping to an overnight low of ten. "Welcome to Buffalo," he concluded.

A jarring sound and an impact shook her. The plane encountered the ground and sped down the runway. From three rows behind her, some kids applauded and shouted. She felt the G-force caused by the aircraft's brakes being applied.

She could not deplane quickly enough. Reaching the cabin door, she realized that there was no jetway. The people ahead of her ambled down a set of aluminum stairs and onto a concrete tarmac which overhead electric lights revealed to be partially covered in spotty ice. She was used to the cold. Used to places where she had studied and worked. Rapid City, South Dakota; Omaha; Des Moines.

She was now inside the airport, looking for a short, bespectacled man with a pockmarked face and a nasal voice, a man who was now her boss. A pleasant meeting with him back in September. He had taken her and some others from the station to Niagara Falls where they dined in the restaurant at the top of the Seagram Tower on the Canadian side. From there, she could see the entire Niagara River; the tall buildings of downtown Buffalo not quite twenty miles to the south; the yellow and brown smoke of the enormous steel mills rising up five miles beyond those buildings; the big island splitting the river in two between the city and the Falls. Those gorgeous, churning cataracts, looming just below, white with frenzy. Water pounding the rocky bottom with such force it made clouds of its own rise out of the chasm. The sight from above was astounding. It made her feel dirty, like a sinner. She wanted that kind of power for herself. She had been replaying the frothy waters in her mind ever since.

"Darcie! Over here."

She felt her mouth form the automatic smile that comes to a person who sees a familiar face in a strange setting.

"Herschel."

Darcie quickened her pace and lengthened her stride toward her new boss.

"I was surprised that you'd be picking me up personally."

"Perks of being the News Director," Herschel replied as they shook hands. "I couldn't trust you to just anyone. Let's get your bags and get you settled into your hotel. Tomorrow my assistant will take you apartment hunting. But tonight, I've got things to tell you about. There's so much to do. It'll be exciting. I know you're ready."

They walked to the baggage carousels and Herschel began to indoctrinate her into some of the big local stories. Darcie made mental notes.

"Erie County has the elected office of County Executive, kind of analogous to the mayor," he explained at carousel number 6. "Remember, we talked about the lay of the land politically... Republicans out in the suburbs, Democrats in the city like the middle of a big donut. And big labor unions with officials being bribed to deliver votes by both parties, but especially by the Democrats."

"I remember. And the mayor is the good-looking Italian gent who speaks something like five different languages."

"Right. Well, it makes for a lot of interesting fights between the Republican county exec and the Democratic mayor. All the money's going out to the 'burbs; while the city is having problems making budget - there's union corruption making things worse - lots of good stories."

"I'm ready to stir things up."

Herschel put a finger up to his own mouth. "Let's go slowly. Gentle persistence, and I want only the truth. That's how we do things at Channel Six First Witness News."

Darcie felt her sense of having just received Herchel's first admonishment leak into her response: "Sure. The truth, because we're public trustees, and all that."

"Right. So the Democrats have this guy who's squeaky clean to run for County Exec. But he can't win. Steelworker and autoworker union bosses hate the guy because he won't do them the normal favors to get votes. We think the Democrats will see their problem sometime this spring, and ditch him for another candidate. And there's only one other Democrat around who is popular enough around the whole county to challenge this young lawyer the Republicans are running.

"Who is that?"

"Sal Frandino, the current mayor. Lots of people already see him running for Governor if he can win a county-wide election."

"I see."

"It'll be good drama, if it plays out the way we think it will."

"Great. Let's get after it."

"Darcie, there's no rush. When it's time, we'll position you to get to know Frandino. We haven't been able to prove it... shoot, people have been trying for years and he keeps weaseling out of things. But I'm convinced he's as corrupt as they come."

"Or, corruptible."

"Just keep an eye on him and the unions. And remember, we talked about the mob, too. If you can get to the honest truth about Frandino it'll be better than any fiction."

May 4, 1971

After school, the sun fought to break through the clouds and warm things up. Lamont Raincloud and I walked home from school to his place. His mom wouldn't be home from work until six-thirty. The house to ourselves for two and a half hours. Our plan was to make ham sandwiches, and to study.

Exams were coming up. Five weeks of grade school left. In the fall, we'd be high school freshman. He'd be at Bennett High, and he was convinced he'd be quarterback of the JV football team. If I survived the summer, I'd be at St. Michael's.

The conversation on the way home was the same stuff we talked about almost every day after school during the last few months of eighth grade: what signs, if any, that the girls we were crushing on reciprocated our feelings. We shared many tragedies and a few small triumphs. I never understood Lamont's reluctance to be more direct with my neighbor Esther, who had already hurt my brother Tom's feelings more often than I brushed my teeth. A certified cutie; noticeable curves in all the right places, top and bottom, to go with that smooth, long dark hair and sparkling blue eyes.

On warm days, her shorts showed off shapely legs which were no doubt a product of year-round figure skating. But a couple of years earlier, after we had eaten banana splits at my house, she upchucked all over herself and our kitchen and then dissolved into tears. Some of the vomit splashed onto me and it smelled like, well, vomit. From that day forward, whenever I saw her, I thought of barf on my arm. Thus had the prettiest girl in the neighborhood forever become chopped liver to me.

"Raincloud. Talk to her about skating. You skate, she skates. She likes you. I know she does."

"When did you become an expert on girls? Like you're doing any better with Corrie Costanzo.

"Well at least I talk to Corrie. You see Esther nowadays and get all choky."

"Anyway, I don't like Esther that much anymore. I like someone else now."

"Do not."

"I'm telling you, I'm interested in someone else."

"Well then, who?"

"I can't say." I could tell that something had been bothering him over the last couple of weeks.

We walked up to his front door. He turned his key to let us in. We climbed the long flight of stairs to the second floor flat where he lived with his mom. It always made me breathe hard, keeping up with him on that staircase.

"So, who is it?" I puffed at the top of the stairs.

We were in the kitchen now, and Lamont threw me against the refrigerator and pinned me against it.

"Drop it," he said.

"Okay. No more talk about your love life. I promise."

"That's better," he said, and let go of me.

We made our sandwiches and studied for our biology final exam. After an hour and a half, he started checking almost every two minutes to see what time it was.

"Raincloud, what's going on?"

"I want to make sure we stop in time for the six o'clock news."

"We gotta study."

"I gotta watch the news tonight."

"I'm going home then."

"Wait. Stay. If you stay, you might..." his voice trailed.

"Might what?"

"So I've got to tell someone. It's about the girl I'm in love with now. My mom knows her."

"Yeah?"

"You can see her on..." his voice cracked and he looked up at the ceiling. "TV. She always does a special report on Tuesdays."

At that moment, I knew. We both said the name together. "Darcie

Yeager."

"Raincloud. She's a grown woman."

"Well two weeks ago, she was sitting in your chair. Mom had her over."

"I'm sitting in Darcie Yeager's chair? Good God - I might have to lick it."

"She's working on a news report about Senecas who don't live on the reservation. She held my hand, Ernie. She talked to me for almost an hour about school, hockey, football, lacrosse, my dad, everything. Then she gave me her phone number and told me I could call her."

"So, do you ever call her?"

"Are you kidding me? My stomach flip-flops whenever I think of her name. She's the most perfect, beautiful female on the whole planet."

"That is some serious truth. My dad says she looks like a movie star."

"She was nice to me. She wanted to know about my life ever since Dad died. She made me cry without trying to. She was asking questions about me, and Dad, and life. All these feelings started, and then she made these eyes at me and I cried and she hugged me."

"Those Darcie eyes? And then she hugged you? I think I would have melted."

"I did melt, Ernie. I'm still melted. I know she's twenty-something. And she'll probably marry a millionaire. But she gave me a real hug, and I could feel her tits against my chest. And she told me I could call her and she would talk to me again anytime I wanted. She said I was a very interesting young man and she wanted to stay in touch with me."

"What are you gonna do, man? This is serious business. Darcie Yeager is perfect and then some."

"Yeah. She smells perfect too, and she chews Big Red chewing gum just like me. I smelled it on her and I wanted to start kissing her and never stop. Mom said I can call her if I want. But I'm a big chicken."

We sat looking at each other for several seconds before he spoke again.

"She's doing a three-part series on the Seneca Nation, and she told us she'd let us know when it would be on TV. Probably in June, after graduation. She cares about the Seneca people. I'm in love with her."

"Lamont. Man, I'm sorry. So, you want me to stick around and watch her with you?"

"Well I watched the Brady Bunch with you once because you wanted me to see the blonde chick. Fair is fair, right?"

May 5, 1971

A glorious spring day, and a late morning walk down Main Street. Maybe it wasn't New York or L.A., but the job as Channel Six's first-ever female investigative reporter was bigger than she imagined. It was taking its toll. Darcie was grateful for Herschel's 10:45 a.m. suggestion that she take some time for herself and walk the three miles down Main Street to her 12:15 lunch appointment with Thane Riley, Republican candidate for County Executive. She was tired, but Herschel convinced her that the walk would do her good.

Darcie had learned the city's geography because the job took her all over it. Down in the First Ward on St. Paddy's Day, swigging Iroquois Beer and sampling the potato farls and corned beef with the sons of millworkers, a great many of whom had lost their jobs over the last dozen years because, they said, of "the Seaway." Up at a synagogue on the North Side, hob-knobbing with the rabbis over oven-warm bagels and schmears. To the Broadway and Clinton-Bailey markets, wearing white coveralls, wielding a cleaver, learning to separate the guts of a pig from the better cuts of meat, talking with the Italian and Polish meatpackers about what went into a good kielbasa, brat, or spicy Italian sausage. On the lower West Side, she had wolfed down empanadillas with the new wave of immigrants to the city from Puerto Rico. At the little restaurant that overlooked Schiller Park on Good Friday she heard a chorus serenade diners with hymns sung in German.

She had been inside the Baptist and Pentecostal churches down in the Fruit Belt and along Jefferson Avenue and Michigan Street, watching the African-American community organize and expand. She toured attics and crawl spaces in the old churches that hid passengers on the Underground Railroad five generations earlier. Rubbed elbows whenever she could with the Anglo-Saxon bluebloods just north of Delaware Park near the Art Gallery, whose neighborhoods and standard of living were more opulent than anything she had ever seen. Always with a camera crew. Always in and out of the news cruiser. Never a moment of privacy. Buffalo was relentless.

She had learned that every so often, a couple of diet pills could go a long way to help her keep up the pace.

She walked down Main Street by herself, observing. She made up stories to herself about an abandoned storefront here, a new business there. Every so often someone said "Hi! Aren't you..." and she'd smile, and say hello, and keep walking.

Main Street was a curious mixture of old and new. This town had already taught her the human cost of a failed business. She realized that every empty window represented families and people who were out of work, or who had to start over at something else or someplace else. She knew that Big Steel was thinking hard about whether to invest in local plant modernizations that were necessary to keep the region's gargantuan steelmaking capabilities competitive with the new steel being made elsewhere. She knew because at the same Plaza Suite Restaurant where she would be meeting Thane Riley at the end of today's walk, she had interviewed officials of both Bethlehem and Republic Steel prior to their most recent negotiations with the Steelworkers' union.

She made a face and slapped herself on the butt at the corner of Main and Edward Streets because she caught herself falling in love. The place was falling apart and she understood better than any native resident that there wasn't anything anyone could do to stop its inexorable, maddening decline. She waited for the traffic signal to change, and looked around in all directions. Damn it all. The place was still so alive.

She slapped herself on the butt again as the signal turned to green and muttered under her breath. "Come on, Darse - toughen up." She tried to imagine herself one day anchoring the evening news for a national network.

The Plaza Suite Restaurant was on the top floor of one of the city's newer skyscrapers; a building, she knew, whose very existence owed much to Sal Frandino and his private dealings with bank presidents to secure the funding. She had been trying to gain an audience with the mayor, but his office was playing it coy. She was on the elevator, about to meet Riley, but contemplating why Frandino's people were shielding themselves from her. Channel Six had made it known to both parties that she'd be on point for their coverage of the unfolding race for County Executive. The Republicans appeared to welcome the idea of a female reporter; the Democrats seemed less enthusiastic.

It didn't matter. Every major labor union in the western part of the state was pouring themselves into their campaign to get the current Democratic candidate replaced. Both city daily newspapers hinted that it was a matter of time before the Democrats would draft Sal Frandino to be their man. Then, he'd have to talk to her.

The elevator door opened to a fancy dining room. Darcie glanced at her wristwatch. Perfect. Plenty of time left to freshen up in the ladies' room and make sure she looked right for her meeting with Thane Riley.

10

A Student, Involved in Her Subject

Mid-day, May 5, 1971

Frandino calls through the closed office door to his secretary. "Call John Klinglehaus and tell him I'm running late for lunch."

"He knows," Phyllis' voice crackles through the receiver. "He's out here, waiting."

"Get the Governor on the phone. He's expecting me. Tell his person it's about the school budget and they'll put me through to him."

"Sal. Beef on weck awaits." Frandino's head jerks up from an accounting ledger and he sees John's head poking through a crack. Klinglehaus has opened the door.

Frandino throws a stiff-arm in the party chairman's direction. "I need a few minutes."

"Sure. But just a few."

The door closes and Frandino shakes his head. John's a friend, politically speaking - but he sees himself as a mentor and not the mentee. Could Sal have won the last mayoral election without John Klinglehaus' help? Frandino would like to think so.

*****

Over at the Plaza Suite, an impeccably-dressed, smiling man with clear eyes and earnest countenance rose from a table adorned in white linen. He extended his right hand. "Darcie Yeager, I am charmed. It's not soon enough that we are meeting."

Darcie felt a chill go down her spine. If very first impressions meant anything, Thane Riley was a dreamboat.

He kissed her on the hand, then gestured toward the table. "Please, my love. Make yourself comfortable."

My love? Really? As instantly as something in her had responded to his appearance, something else recoiled.

*****

In the basement at Jack's Place on Franklin Street, two men are sitting back at a corner table. No one is near them. The lunch rush is over. Cigars are lit. Scraps of roast beef, salt and horseradish are left on their plates. One man is short and the other tall, so that local pundits have taken to calling them Mutt and Jeff. The shorter man speaks.

"Here you sit again, Sal. Licking your wounds after the state fails to come through with more money for your schools. We both know that you ain't in the best position to help the city 'til you're the governor. What I'm offering you is a stepping stone to get there."

"I don't understand how being County Executive helps. If I were a downstate voter I'd say, 'So what?'"

"But the voters downstate ain't who you need to impress. You need to impress the state party, Sal. You need to show them you can win the suburbs. Everyone knows you're strong in the city. You gotta show them you can win over the people with money outside the city. You win the county, and the state party can't ignore us. They'll spend the money and get you the votes downstate."

"How can I win in the suburbs, John? I've made a career chiding those folks for moving outside the city limits."

"Sal. Give me your hand."

Frandino feels himself scoffing.

"No, no, Sal. Do it. Give me your hand. Please." John Klinglehaus puts his stogie down in an ashtray, and his hand is on the table.

Frandino sighs. Klinglehaus has an amazing track record of being right about elections. His right hand finds its way into Klinglehaus' right hand.

"Sal." Klinglehaus does not grip Frandino strongly; instead, his fingers caress the mayor's hand gently. "This is a big opportunity. I've talked with Don in Syracuse. He'd get the Central New York party lined up behind you if you win. The weight of the county vote is still in the city. And Lackawanna. The unions want you, Sal. And I've got the unions. I will deliver them to you."

"Don in Syracuse would back me for governor? Keep talking."

"Sal, I love you. I ain't never gonna make a suggestion I think would hurt you and Steffi. Please. Let me make you the County Executive. Let's show the state Democratic organization that Sal Frandino can win an election that involves the rich suburbs. They see our county as a microcosm of the whole state. I will shield you from all the crappy stuff. Have I ever let you get hurt in the past?"

Frandino shakes his head.

"And I won't," Klinglehaus continues. I'm your brother Democrat, remember that. Maybe my name don't end in a vowel but we're brothers, Sal."

Frandino withdraws his hand. "Riley's not such a bad guy. He's got ideas."

"Come on, Sal! He's a goddammed Republican! He's Spiro Agnew! He's Barry Goldwater! We're losing jobs around here by the hundreds, have you noticed? I know you have. And he'll just fiddle while Rome burns and say it's okay. Just free market economics at work."

Frandino looks at his cigar. He picks it back up out of the ashtray and holds it up in front of his face. He turns it this way and that.

"Please. Sal. You can win this."

"How much of the suburban vote do I need if I get sixty percent in the city?"

"Sixty stinking percent? No, Sal. You've got to get sixty five. Sixty five in the city, and then if we can get twenty-nine or thirty in the rest of the county, you're in."

"Sixty five? I'm good, John, but that's - that's - you're dreaming."

"Okay. We go for sixty-two in the city and then you need about a third in the county. Okay, fine. I can deliver that."

Frandino and Klinglehaus look at one another. Klinglehaus puffs his cigar.

"Riley's a damn good politician," Frandino says. "Pretty boy. Plays well with the ladies."

"You too, Sal. You're still hot shit, you understand me?" Klinglehaus stabs the air with his cigar for emphasis.

"What's our message?"

"Leadership, Sal. You're the proven veteran. You have a track record of getting things done. The other guy ain't got no track record. You quelled the riots too, remember?"

"It rained buckets that night, John. I can't take credit for acts of God."

"Well, learn to start. If you want to be in charge of the whole state one day."

Frandino lets himself imagine friends and reporters gathered and Steffi at his side as he announces that he will oppose Thane Riley for the office of County Executive. He'll tell them he's doing it because times are tough, and tough times call for proven leadership. He snaps out of his day-dream, looks at John Klinglehaus, and feels a smile cross his face.

*****

Beef burgundy tips for lunch. Riley drank scotch and soda; he said he'll stop at one drink because it's still the workday. She nursed a cola, saying she'll drink a glass or two of wine at dinner - with friends, if she can ever make friends in her meager free time.

"So - Miss Yeager. Is this business only? Or can it also be social?"

"Mister Riley, you are an operator."

"No. You misunderstand." He put his silverware on the table, and dabbed at his mouth with the linen napkin. "I just think it's going to be a tough next few months 'til the election in November and if you're going to be a part of that, we should try to have a good relationship."

Darcie wanted to believe that he's a good man. He was a Republican. She belonged to a Republican family in a Republican part of the country. Her dad liked Ike. She didn't think Barry Goldwater was off his rocker in 1964. She did vote for Humphrey in '68 and was sadder than ever when Bobby Kennedy's life was cut short. But that had to do with wanting to stop the war. Besides, her boss kept telling her that the Democrat is the figurehead of a political machine whose behavior over the years has been nothing short of criminal.

"Yes," she said to the Republican sitting across from her. "A good relationship. That would be nice."

"Well, good." He took a big breath and smiled. "So, Friday night, I'm getting together with some of the party leaders out at this place called The Gardens out in Amherst. Wonderful food, and a chance for you to meet many important Riley people. May I suggest that you come as my guest?"

"Ahh. Maybe."

"I understand your reluctance. After all, you're a woman, and the world of politics is a man's world. And I have to warn you, you might be the only gal present."

"I see."

"Except, of course," he chuckled, "for the cocktail waitresses. But no one will mistake you for the -"

"That's it. Let's get something straight, Mr. Riley. I work my butt off to be the best journalist I can be. I don't like your insinuations that because I'm a woman I can't -"

"Now wait a minute. You're jumping to some conclusions that -"

"I don't think I'm jumping to conclusions. You've had a condescending attitude since you saw me. I can play as rough as anyone."

"Oh, my gosh, Darcie. I love the double-entendre, but I'll take the high road."

"See? You just did it again. You're as bad as they come."

"You're way off base. You're out to lunch."

"Maybe I was out to lunch five minutes ago, but lunch just ended for me. Thanks for the meal. I'll see you again, soon enough."

"You're leaving? With that attitude? You're getting shit for stories from my people. You understand?"

"Not if Mayor Frandino behaves with more professionalism."

"He hasn't even announced yet." Then Riley's voice went up an octave. "Hey, what do you know? What the hell are you talking about with this Frandino stuff?"

Darcie did not look back. She knew she had screwed up. She made an instant decision to trust Hersch to fix it. The elevator door closed in front of her and she remembered that busses ran up and down Main Street every few minutes. She had yet to patronize the silver-and-red Niagara

Frontier Transit vehicles that crisscrossed the city. No time like the present for her first ride.

June 14, 1971

This was Darcie and Lamont's big day on television, and I had promised that I'd be over to watch with him at his house. His mom was able to come home from work early so we could all watch together.

I was, by this time, a big Darcie Yeager fan. Not only was she luscious on camera, but in person she was the nicest, best-smelling and simply greatest person on Earth. And could she ever make bell bottom jeans into a work of art. Lamont did call her, and we had taken the bus together to meet her at a little lunch place on Main Street near the Channel Six studio. She came by herself, wearing those bell bottoms, and she treated us to hamburgers and shakes. She asked us about our upcoming graduation, and she wanted to know what we were most excited about and most afraid of as we entered high school. Before we dug into our hamburgers she prayed for peace so that Lamont and I wouldn't have to go to Vietnam and fight.

Lunch wasn't without tough moments, like when she let reality leak onto our fantasies to dissolve them.

"What an exciting day, guys! I get to have lunch with you two handsome men, and then tonight..."

"Tonight," Lamont said. "What's tonight?"

"Tonight, I'm going on a date to see a Shakespeare outdoor play over in Canada with a very nice man I met a week ago. My first night off work in three weeks. I'm looking forward to it."

I think Lamont and I were both like balloons that just got pricked by a pin. "Yeah, well we're new friends, too," I said, trying to redeem the moment for both me and my friend. "You can't have burgers and shakes together and not stay friends for awhile."

She picked up her milkshake and raised it toward us. "Absolutely, that's true. You guys are both going places in life. I want to keep hearing from you both. So..." at this point she raised her milkshake glass even higher, never taking her eyes off Lamont. "...here's to our friendship. For many years to come."

I watched Raincloud for the rest of lunch to see how he was doing. He looked like he used to look when we were younger and all our classmates were picking on him. I understood. Darcie was the essence of our best and wildest dreams and the age difference, which disqualified us from the real competition for Darcie's heart, wasn't fair.

Even Lamont's mom was in love with her. As we prepared to watch the interview, Mrs. Raincloud said Darcie was an authentic person and a role model, even for Seneca women. The televised interview did not disappoint. In three minutes of airtime, I learned things about my friend Lamont Raincloud that I had never learned in all the years I'd known him.

The interview ended with the words, "... on the North Side, for Channel Six, I'm Darcie Yeager." I looked over at him. Fresh tears were streaming down his cheeks and the red on his face was not a happy glow.

"Lamont," I said. Saying his name seemed pretty lame the moment I said it.

He got up and ran into his room. The door shut with a loud bang.

"I'm s-sorry," I stammered. I felt a wave of guilt that for the past week I had been going to sleep at night pretending that my pillow was Darcie Yeager. She belonged to Lamont.

"Don't be sorry, honey. That interview is the best thing that's happened to him since his father died. She got him to open up. I'm very proud of them both. They talked for an hour when she was here, and you got to see the best three minutes."

"Wow."

"I grew because of it too, Ernie," she continued. "I had to re-evaluate my own prejudices because of the love Darcie showed to my son that day. Do you understand what I mean?"

"I'm not sure."

"I married a man who was part white. He gave me two sons I'm very proud of. But I am Seneca. This land - all of Western New York and east to the Genesee River valley - it belonged to my people, right? They moved us with force from the Genesee Valley to these here parts, to put us in between the French and the English. The Europeans used us as human shields and then when they fought, we were forced to choose between England and France. They don't teach you that in the white history books. So I have always had very mixed feelings toward white people."

"But you don't act like you have mixed feelings toward me. You always cook me dinner. I called you names once, and you never acted angry."

"Oh, I was plenty angry. But anyways… it's been tough for him, not feeling like he could talk to anyone about his father. He won't even talk to me about how much it hurt to lose him, about what his daddy meant to him. And then this beautiful woman is sitting at our kitchen table, encouraging him. Telling him he is valuable. Holding his hand and loving him. And it all spills out. All of Lamont's agony. His longing to be with his father again. God, what a relief it was for me. What a relief it must be for Lamont. To have someone he values, valuing him in return. Listening to him say what's in his heart. Ernie, don't be sorry he's crying. He's still got to process it all. Even his feelings for Darcie. He's got to process. He will. And so will you, honey."

She paused and looked at me very intentionally.

"I'm very thankful for her, Ernie. She's a very good lady," Mrs. Raincloud got up and started walking into the kitchen. "And she's white," she tossed back at me over her shoulder. "Imagine that."

*****

Sal Frandino isn't sure why he's doing this. The gal from Channel Six is due in his office in five minutes. He should be going home; it's a quarter till seven. She is coming to him straight from the six o'clock newscast, and he's agreed to give her fifteen minutes. Tomorrow at noon, he will be on a podium with Steffi, with his police chief and with the president of a United Auto Workers' local, among others, to announce his candidacy for County Executive. Why not just meet her then? He's heard the frenzy: She's getting credit for solidifying First Witness News' ratings stranglehold. Now, she's being turned loose on the local political beat. He hasn't wanted to watch her. He does not want women reporters.

His wristwatch says she's thirty seconds late. She gets thirty more seconds, then he's leaving.

The phone. Phyllis announces Darcie's presence.

He sighs. "Send her in."

The door opens and she is wearing a business suit over a white blouse. A skirt that comes down over her knees. He rises in greeting.

"Miss Yeager. He is coming around the desk to meet her. There is a handshake.

"You smoke cigars, mayor. Perhaps this afternoon you smoked one."

"You are no stranger to tobacco."

"My dad. He was a cigar man."

"Excellent, then. Please, have a seat."

"Mayor," she says, settling into the chair as he returns behind the desk to his own leather chair. "I am honored to finally meet you. I have heard so much about you, sir. I am sorry we haven't talked sooner."

"Yes, it's a busy life I lead. But then, you're at Channel Six. You know all about keeping a busy schedule."

"God yes, Mayor Frandino. Des Moines is not Buffalo, even though it is a state capital. I've tried to make myself a student of your city."

"That's just dandy. What are you learning?"

"Lots. I um... you know it's... well, for one thing the ethnic diversity. I've never been in a place like this - well, I visited Chicago many times as a kid, but... this is like Chicago, just not quite as overwhelming."

"Tell me more. I'd love to hear your point of view on that."

"I've met all kinds of people doing all kinds of things. Young, old. From all over the world, it seems. People who want to make their fortune. Some legally, some not." She giggles. Frandino feels his eyes open wider.

"We have a crime problem, yes," he says. "We're a big city, and you're a reporter. So, you get to see the underside of things around here."

"And you, sir. We'll be at a press conference together tomorrow morning. I'll be covering your announcement. Thanks so much for meeting me first. I thought it was important since you're going to be such a big part of my life in these coming months."

"Do me a favor. Call me Sal. Everyone around here does."

"Sal," she repeats. He hears that little giggle again.

"Miss Yeager."

"You can call me Darcie. Or Darse."

"Darcie, then. You know, I've heard an awful lot about you. I know, for instance, you are very Republican in your own personal political views."

"Are you stereotyping just because I've spent my entire life in the Midwest?"

"Darcie, welcome to town. Mayors know a lot of people. I didn't get to sit in this chair without putting quite an organization in place. Now I'm sure you know a particular version of that story. Your boss, Hersch Woodstein, is a great newsman but he hasn't made his distrust of me a secret. So let's get something straight. I respect Channel Six, I certainly respect Hersch, and by extension, I respect you. But I know all about you and I'm sure I understand the instructions that Hersch has given you. So we're going to have an up-front relationship, you and me. Okay?"

"Mayor, I - yes. I would like that very much. Thank you."

"Good. Despite what some people might think, I do believe that honesty is best. So, tell me something about your background I might not already know. What kind of cigars does your dad smoke?"

"Oh, gosh. Stinky ones? Though I did become accustomed to the smell, back when he was -"

"Well, that's good. Cigar smoke and politics go together in this town. If you want to report on the real inner workings of this campaign, you may need to breathe your share of it."

"Mayor. Sal - can I really call you that?"

"Absolutely. You know, it stands for Salvatore, and I think it's a good name for me. That's what I'm trying to do. Save my city."

"Save it from?"

Frandino can't help but to laugh. They both know that she knows all the things he's trying to save the city from.

She's not laughing. She is looking at him intently.

"Exactly how are you going to turn things around, um... Sal? How will it help you to do it if you're the County Executive instead of mayor?"

"There's so much going on, Darcie. I always feel like the little Dutch boy. Running around and sticking fingers in the holes of a dike that's busting all over. You've been in town for a few months. You're smart. You know the story."

"Okay, I can't play dumb with you. But I want to hear it in the first person. How will it help the city for you to become the County Executive?"

Frandino puts his hands behind his head and leans back. "Leadership. Plain and simple. Don't get me wrong, I like the guy I'm running against. He's said some smart things. But Darcie, he's a career lawyer. He's never held an elected public office. I'm running on my track record."

"Makes sense."

"Thank you. I think it does, too."

"But I'm not buying it. There's more, isn't there? I've been studying the executive powers of the mayoralty, versus the county office. You're in a better position to help the city if you're the mayor than if you're running the county."

Frandino feels his ears open wider. This woman is good.

"Riley says that as the city goes, so the county goes and vice versa," Frandino lectures. "We're a single economic region, he says, and he's right. But the choice he's painting for voters is between whether we strengthen the core at the expense of the rest of the county, or focus on the rest of the region at the expense of the core. I don't think it needs to come at anyone's expense."

Frandino wants to see her reaction. He thinks he's stated something for public consumption that should be compelling. She smiles. He returns the smile. Neither says another word right away.

"Mayor. I can think of five responses Riley would rebut that with. Do you want to know what they are?"

"I do. I play to win. Sharpen my mind."

"How long do you have?"

"As long as it takes."

11
Working Downtown. Two Jobs

June 24, 1971

She has been with him behind the big closed door for five minutes. Neither person sits. They are touring his walls. He narrates as he shows her plaques, photos. Certificates.

It is Darcie Yeager's second visit to Frandino's office.

Phyllis rings Frandino's desk. The mayor's other guest has arrived.

"Splendid. Send him right in." Frandino walks toward the door. A young man enters, dressed in jeans and a white tee. He takes three steps toward the mayor and they are hugging.

"Mister three-point-eight GPA. I'm so proud I could kiss you."

"I ain't that kind of guy, Pops." They're holding each other at arm's length. Randy is beaming, for a moment. Then a new, serious look crosses his face.

"Pops. That's Darcie Yeager."

"Where? Really?"

"You didn't say she'd be here."

"She's a friend. But she knows that everything we say today stays in here - except if she's got your permission to make it public. Let me introduce you."

"What's up?" Randy tosses out to her. He seems unsure of whether to smile.

"I'm here because tomorrow's the three-year anniversary of the um - troubles on the near East Side," she says. I'm doing a sort of retrospective story."

"Yeah," Randy says in a plain voice.

"She's covering the election," Frandino says, resting his hand on Randy's shoulder. "She's a Republican, you know. I just want her to know who she's going to vote against." Frandino smiles at her.

"Randy, I'm honored to meet you. I won't use anything you don't give me permission to use, but Mayor Frandino thought it would be good for me to hear you talk."

"Wow," says Randy. "I mean, I'll talk about Sal and what he did that night, but look. This has been a secret. Me, the mayor, and my family. I want to keep it that way."

"Then it will be," Frandino says. "I haven't told her a thing yet, by the way. It's still just our secret, Randy. If anyone tells her anything, it'll be you."

"How will it help you, Pops? If I tell her the story, and she can't report it?"

"It'll help me understand what kind of man he is," Darcie says. "He seems to think I should know that."

They're sitting down. Frandino had sent Phyllis out for Cokes, so everyone now has a soft drink with ice and a straw in front of them. Darcie has been telling Randy about South Dakota, describing it as a different planet from Buffalo. Randy has been telling her how much he wants to get a good education so he can leave and raise a family in a place that sounds like South Dakota. Frandino's been listening with an aching heart. Another good person who longs to leave town.

"So Randy," she says, pulling out a note pad. "We're coming up to the third anniversary of the night the mayor went down to the Michigan

Street Y. The station has asked me to show how things haven't changed much since that night."

"Yeah," Randy says. "Except probably things are worse in some ways. There's more handouts now, but that's not what people want. People want jobs. People want a chance for themselves."

"But there's peace now, at least compared to then," she interjects. What did Mayor Frandino do?"

"I don't know why people aren't rebelling in the streets anymore. But he told me that night after he left the Y that he'd put me through college. Now he's putting me and my little sister through, too. Which is cool, 'cause she's the sweetest kid. Not a rabble-rouser like me."

Frandino watches the expression on the reporter's face. Her eyes open wide toward him. "City funds?" She sounds like a school principal.

"No, ma'am," Frandino replies.

"Then how? Who's paying for this?"

"Mayor won't say, but he is, ma'am. Out of his pocket. I know, because he gives me the check to give to the bursar at school every semester. I maintain my average, that's the condition. And Pops here - I mean, um, the mayor, he writes the checks against his own bank account."

Frandino watches her carefully. She looks lost, confused. Sad.

"Thing is, the night we met wasn't under the greatest of circumstances. I was cussing him out pretty strong in front of the whole crowd, blaming him for this and that, and instigating trouble. Calling him a racist. But he's the best man I ever met. He's a man of his word, he tells me inspiring stories, and he's given me and my sister a fighting chance."

Frandino does not want to say anything. He longs for Darcie to acknowledge his goodness on her own. But she wears total bewilderment. Then closes her eyes.

"If it helps you to know, I'm finally twenty-one so this is the first year I can vote. I'll be casting my vote for Mayor Frandino."

"Randy," Frandino says, "that means so very much to me. Thank you for your vote."

"Thank you, Pops."

* * * * *

"Riley wants televised debates," she says to him ten minutes later, after Randy has left. "To show how youthful and vigorous he is compared to you. He thinks he's more photogenic."

"Yes, I know," Frandino replies. "What do you think?"

He hears her little giggle again. "I don't know. He may be Clint Eastwood, but you're sort of an Italian John Wayne."

"John Wayne, then? I've seen all his films, some of them three or four times. I am flattered."

"Okay, I've just admitted that you're charming. But you said we should be honest and up front with each other. So I must tell you, I know all about John Klinglehaus and your machine politics."

"Machine, you say?"

"Yes. The kind of machine that pays for votes."

"I don't know much about that. John is the party chairman for the county. His job is to inspire people to vote for our candidates."

"And you don't want to know how he does it, do you?"

"I trust him to do what's right."

"Then tell me everything you know about money changing hands between the party and union officials."

"What?"

"You don't know or care that the union shop stewards are coercing their membership to vote a certain way in exchange for -"

"Coerce, you say? Explain that one to me. The ballot is sacred. People vote in private. Every man and his conscience."

"Or that he's paid off election officials in the past to rig the voting booths."

"Darcie. Wherever you're getting your information from, those charges have been disproven many times over."

"Sal. I've got enough dirt to bury you. And the funny thing is, I should want to. But I don't. It's not you who irks me. It's the way things are done in this town."

"Just like all the other cities in America. Shall we review some history? Engage in some comparative analysis?"

"Can we? Can you please make me understand the contradictions I see when I look at you? Because it's driving me crazy."

"What more do you want me to say, Miss Yeager?"

"Sal. I'm getting pressure from Hersch to turn up the heat. Please help me to understand you."

"You just met Randy. What is it about me you don't understand?"

"Yeah - I get that. But..." her voice trails off. Frandino knows that this woman can sway a lot of votes. Five months in town, and everyone is talking about her.

"Darcie. What is it that you want from me?"

"Time. Words. Proof. For the last several years, you've been the undisputed king of the whole town. I want - to know more about - you."

Her eyes are steadfast. Her smile is gone. She is so very formidable, he thinks.

"Okay," she starts talking again. "I've got to be somewhere now, but I'm not on the air tonight. Educate me. Convince me that you're not everything Hersch wants me to believe about you. Compare yourself to other mayors who are worse. Produce thirty more stories like Randy's. It's your chance to use whatever arguments work best for you. I can meet you at nine."

"Not a good idea, Miss Yeager."

"No. This is just professional. We'll do it in public, out in the open. There's a place up near the station called the Stuffed Mushroom. Neutral ground. Everything between us above board and in the open."

"Hmm. Nine o'clock?"

*****

Frandino spends the rest of his afternoon working through his correspondence pile, and on the phone with a city councilperson. Then, he finds his head resting on the desktop and full of Phyllis' voice on the intercom.

"Sal? Sal! Are you in there?"

"*Hola? Buon pommerigio?*" he says to Phyllis playfully, if groggily into the receiver, mixing languages.

"*Buon pommerigio* is over. It's now *buona sera*, Sal." It sounds like she is scolding him.

"Tired, that's all. Must have dozed."

"That's no small wonder. You're running a city and running for office. You've been working fifteen hour days. Would you please go home and get some sleep now, for crying out loud? I buzzed to let you know it's six. I'm going home."

"Six!" Sudden panic.

"Three minutes past, to be exact."

"I was supposed to be at that Eagle Scout thing at four-something. You let me sleep right through!"

The door opens and it's Phyllis, the curly cord stretched, receiver still to her ear.

"I thought about waking you," she says, "but you were just too cute. And snoring - oh, my gosh, Sal."

He's scrambling to his feet. "Phyllis, I missed at least two appearances this afternoon. Why shouldn't I fire you for dereliction of duty?"

"Because you won't, Sal. Look at you. I don't think you've gotten an hour of sleep since you announced your candidacy, have you? A bunch of us are concerned about you. I let you sleep because your body needed it. And I took care of it all this afternoon. No one is angry with you for resting."

He's aware that he's just made a confused noise or two.

"Sal, I'm going home to rest. Would you please do the same? Stop depriving your body, or it will fail you. And stop depriving Steffi, for crying out loud."

"Okay."

The door is closed, and he surveys the pile of papers on his desk. On top is a letter from Councilman Snead demanding an apology for the latest perceived slight to one of the community coalitions that is trying to get money to tear down blighted old properties and replace them with new housing. There will be no apology until Snead learns to behave.

Next is a set of requisitions from one of Lou Lombardi's people to upgrade radios in a few cherry-tops. Lou's troops need their radios; he signs it.

Next is a message Phyllis had taken from Lindsay down in New York. Urgent, please call; another pissing contest between he and Governor Rockefeller, the state's two leading Republicans, that only Frandino can settle. The Big Apple's mayor often works late, but Frandino decides to make him wait until tomorrow.

Next is John Klinglehaus' analysis of which major press and media outlets the mayor can count on for support as the campaign for County Executive heats up. A list of newspaper, radio and television reporters that the county Democratic Party considers to be friendly. Frandino skips the commentary about how to cultivate them, and skims for names. It was a short list; all the usual suspects. Darcie Yeager is not included in the list. That feels like a personal affront.

Pushing the envelope.

It was easier to get around town without the news crew. But Darcie's body was racked with a combination of excitement and fatigue that has become familiar this year. Coffee had not been helping lately; caffeine fogged her thinking.

She fumbled through her purse. Damn it. No pills. She was out of the car, walking down Allen Street to a restaurant known for its souvlaki. A warm, muggy night. Darcie felt fading, unfocused energy bouncing around inside her.

Inside the place was a chunky, high-school aged blonde girl behind a counter long enough for a dozen red swivel stools. Several tables for two and four; the place was half-full. A plainly-appointed place with lots of white tile. The menu was posted in black block letters on the wall behind the blonde girl.

"Hi," Darcie said to the blonde. "Randy said I could talk to him on break. Said he'd have a break about this time?"

"Uh-huh," came the reply. "Hey Randy!" The blonde stuck her head through a doorway into a back room. "Someone here to see you."

"You're that TV reporter, ain't it?" the blonde asked. Darcie wished for a disguise.

Randy was wearing the same clothes he wore when they met earlier in the day. A dish towel hung over his shoulder. It looked to Darcie like he had been sweating.

"So you're here. Let's go for a walk," he said.

They sat in the sun, surrounded by warm, sticky air, on a sidewalk bench four doors down from the restaurant.

"So you said you wanted to talk more." Randy's speech was plain and direct.

"Yeah, thanks. I mean, he's not here now. You can tell me whatever you want about him, and it'll be our secret."

"What do want me to tell you?"

"Tell me if what I heard earlier today is real. It can't be. Can it?"

"Tell me why it can't be."

Darcie laughed and then managed a sentence. "Mayor Frandino is putting you and your sister each through school with his own funds."

"You don't think so?"

"Just tell me the truth."

"I did already."

"Then why are you washing dishes in this place?"

"Because it's summer between my junior and senior year and I don't have class 'til September."

Darcie's lungs let all the air out.

"What are you, Miss Yeager - surprised that a black person wants to work?"

"No! I'm... ah, nuts. I'm sorry. So what are you going to do when you graduate?"

"Law school. I hope."

"So you expect me to believe that Sal Frandino is giving you and your sister money for tuition and all you both need to do is get good grades and listen to him philosophize about life once every so often?"

"I don't care what you believe. Yeah. He likes to philosophize. I get precious little of that elsewhere, so I appreciate it."

"What does he get in return?"

"I promised him I'd do my best. Okay, that sounds corny. So you heard me say I'm gonna vote for him. So go ahead and report that he's buying black people's votes."

"You know what I like about you, Randy? You don't like me. Everyone in this town is falling all over me, but I get the sense you wish I'd go away."

"So what makes you think you know anything about me and what I wish for?"

"Now, see that? You don't want to be my friend. You'd rather -"

A yawn was coming on. She couldn't stifle it.

"Wow, excuse me," she continued. He began a yawn of his own. "I was saying, you'd rather fight me."

"I'd rather you not yawn in front of me. Damn. Guess I'm tired, too. I been workin' my ass off." He smiled. "This job don't pay as much as it takes from me."

"Working my ass off, too," she said. That's my life. I have a big meeting tonight and I don't know how I'm gonna stay awake and be sharp for it."

"And I'm working late, closing up the shop," he said. "I got another four hours to go after this break."

Darcie was staring into a sun-kissed brick wall across the street. The evening was so golden.

"So, hey," he said in a lower volume. "Look here." She watched as he pulled a small plastic baggie out of his pocket.

"It's more than I need for tonight," he said. "You ever snort to stay awake?"

"I've used diet pills."

"Nah. This is better for you. Amphetamines will make you crazy. You can get hooked on 'em, too. See, this stuff here, they used to put it in pop. I don't even understand why it's illegal." He pointed at the bag.

"Sure, I've heard of it. But does it really work?"

"Hell yes, it works - look, let's go around to the back, and I'll show you how to do it. You can have some of mine for tonight."

"Okay," she said. "But let's just sit for a minute. It feels good to be off my feet."

They watched together as a bus stopped just a few feet away and four senior citizens disembarked.

"So Frandino - he's a good man, Darcie. But like all men, he ain't perfect."

"Aha. Tell me how he's not perfect."

"Like, sometimes I wish to hell he'd pay more than just my tuition so I didn't have to sell this shit." He opened and closed his hand to reveal the plastic bag once more.

"And -" he continued. "Some rumors that a few years ago he'd been - um, getting it on with this lady who skated on TV – you know, you ever seen the roller derby? But no one knows for sure."

"Yeah. I've heard those rumors."

12

A New Habit. Acquired

She sat in the privacy of a toilet stall with her compact open. Did everything the way she had been taught. Gave herself a moment to look at the thin white line on the compact mirror. Felt a sweep of guilt and excitement.

The deed was done. Darcie flushed the toilet so that anyone else in the room would think she was there for the normal reason. With the sound of the swirling water came the rush of a well-being that felt like a cosmic burden lifted. She was out of the stall and standing at the sink. She looked at her hands and said aloud to no one, "Aw, what the hell? They're clean." She opened the door and walked to the bar. She could feel heads turn her way.

*****

Frandino sees her coming. He puts his rock glass of amaretto on the bar and rises from his seat. They've made eye contact at a moment when a bit of breeze, perhaps from an overhead fan, has caught a wisp of her hair. Another moment, and she is with him at the bar.

Before he can open his mouth, she says "I'll have what you're having."

"I don't... I'm not usually seen with young ladies in public. Not the image of leadership church-going people crave."

"I get it. You're Sal Frandino, clean cut American hero. You kiss babies, salute the flag. You say all the right things. You don't get your hands dirty. That's for your henchmen."

His mouth opens. Nothing comes out.

"Hey," she says, as the bartender puts a rock glass of amber fluid on the bar near her. "I'm kidding. I'm - glad we're meeting away from the office. Bad attempt at humor. I'm sorry."

He continues to look away from her.

"You know, I want a do-over. I talked without thinking. Maybe we can – get out of here. Just go talk."

"Maybe we can drive around," he says. I'll show you the town through my eyes - not that there's much you already haven't seen."

"Yeah, we'll drive. But first -" she picks up her glass - "Bottoms up."

Frandino can't contain his laughter.

"What? What did I do?"

"Darcie. The entire Holy Family in heaven just had a fit. That is a dessert drink to be sipped and savored - not a shot of cheap rail whiskey."

*****

They have been driving for less than fifteen minutes, and the street lamps have come on. Darcie seems a bit less animated than at first. He figures that maybe it's because she's been concentrating on the sights, the places, the stories about the town that he's been making known to her. He has promised to take her back to the neighborhood where he was raised, and they have arrived. He stops the car in the middle of a street whose houses have been replaced by open lots. They are surrounded by bulldozers, backhoes and flashing yellow "Caution" signs. Straight ahead, the lights of downtown buildings twinkle less than a mile away.

"This is it?" The disappointment in her voice sounds deep.

He sighs. "I loved this place, Darcie. But that doesn't exempt it from progress. We need better highways to make it easy for people to get to and from downtown. We're in front of my house - or at least, where it used to be. The road will be less than a hundred feet away, right over there. And the old Frandino homestead?"

He points to the plot of empty land out the passenger window.

"Yeah?" Her voice is small and sad.

"Two years from now, luxury apartments will have replaced it. In a great location, less than five minutes to downtown on a wide, new road. I should show you the blueprints, the artist's conception, some time. The apartment complex will have commanding views of the new small boat harbor we're going to build. All according to something a city planning commission drew up back in the 1920s."

"I can't figure you out. You're putting Randy and his sister through college. You care about people. Then you show me the city block you grew up on and you're excited as hell that you've taken away their street so a highway can go through it. Sal - who are you?"

"Just a person who wants to do what's right."

She looks out the window, away from him.

"They're not easy decisions, Darcie. But these houses were all dilapidated. Our Municipal Housing Authority helped any family who needed help, to relocate. Many of them are in new high-rises."

"The projects," he hears her mutter.

The new developments he championed, and got built with Washington's help, have become a political liability. Even the friendly *Evening Star* will be running an unflattering series on life in the projects a bit later in the summer.

"Darcie. If you could have seen how rickety this part of the neigh-borhood was before we tore it down. I'm doing the best for the people and the city as I know how."

"I know you are." She sounds perturbed.

"I feel like the night is going off the tracks. What can I do? What do you want to hear about - so you and your friends at Channel Six don't crush me?"

She continues to look away, out the passenger side window. He waits; she finally turns and faces him. She is not smiling. Her eyes are big. She makes her request with little emotion.

"I'd love for you to drive me up to Niagara Falls. To see all the water."

"They don't turn it off at night. Let's go."

*****

An hour later they stand together at the place called Table Rock, on the Ontario side of a wide river that is careening over a cliff. Seven or eight feet below their toes, the waters of half a continent rush over the end of a sheet of granite and down to a pool that churns with frenzy in a deep gorge. Hundreds of people are milling about the rocks and the water. Some, in yellow raincoats, scramble down the illuminated gorge wall on a series of wooden stairways and decks that take them down the side to the churning river beneath. The waterfalls are lit up in the colors of the rainbow. Perhaps two hundred yards distant and just to their left are the "American Falls," a wide curtain of thundering liquid also illuminated in electric hues.

"I've never seen anything like this. And at night! Thank you for bringing me, Sal."

He has heard her, but his thoughts are not with her. He is leaning on the railing, resting. The water that rushes past his face, hypnotizing. He wishes the water was pure. Sad that it is not.

He feels a hand on his back. Now two hands. Massaging his shoulders. Strong hands. They feel good.

"I'm tired," he says.

The hands turn him around. Like a child being turned by his mother. He is faced away from the water and toward her.

"I didn't hear you," she says.

"I'm so tired." He needs to speak up over the water in order to be heard.

"Me, too." She matches his volume.

He thinks it's just one of those moments of brutal human honesty. They are united in weariness. She steps closer. Their bodies are touching. And wordlessly, they are embracing. She is tall enough that her face is close to his. He can see the flecks of color in her unwavering eyes. She is soft, and her breath is pleasant.

"Not here. Please." He hears his own desire and panic.

"Then where?"

"Up the road. Saint Catharines. They don't know me."

"We'll just go and rest together."

"Right," he says. "We'll rest."

The fifteen minute walk back to the car pushes him beyond fatigue. He realizes the contract he has just made with her. He is overwhelmed by the perception that every cell in his body is clamoring for something. They walk side by side, past parked cars with license plates from every state and province. He is opening the door to his family station wagon. The car he ferries Steffi around town in. The grandkids.

But then, she is kissing him deeply, and her mouth is sweet, reminiscent of cinnamon sugar.

"We'll rest together," she says in a whisper. "Maybe for a day. No one the wiser."

He is driving, and in fifteen or twenty minutes' time he is exiting the highway, into the parking lot of a place that's just a bit off the beaten track.

"You get the room," he says.

His mind works on how he will keep what he is about to do, a secret.

She comes back to the car. They drive around to the back of the place. The engine shuts off. They walk to a door, and she turns the key. They're inside.

"We'll rest," she says. "Give me a second."

She disappears into the bathroom. He sits on the end of the bed and takes his shoes off.

Two minutes later she has reappeared and they are laying on top of the bedding, undressing one another. She is soft, breathy noises, and kissing him all over: face, throat, ears, chest. Stomach. He is glad he's been faithful with handball. He knows that he is a good specimen for a man his age, yet he wonders where her enthusiasm for his body is coming from.

"Why me, Darcie?" He thinks for a moment that maybe it isn't too late to say no. He is laying on his back. She looks up. Her voice is hungry.

"Sal. Let yourself."

*****

Frandino has lost all track of everything: time, morals, elections. He does not understand the energy she has coaxed from him, the rich texture of physical and emotional stimuli. Yet he perceives in her a basic underlying innocence that makes him want to take care of her. He thinks maybe that's what their relationship can be. He will do his best to take care of her.

"Why do you think this happened, Darse?"

"That's a silly question, silly boy."

"I'm an old guy. You're a fragrant spring flower."

She kisses his nose. "You're a romantic. Like John Wayne. Or Bruce Wayne."

"I'm a -"

She's nibbling his ear. "I'm not done with you, Batman," she whispers.

*****

Some time later he is caught in the haze between barely awake and blacked out.

"What do you see in me?"

"A hero. Trying to salvage an impossible situation. An admirable man." She has whispered it tenderly.

"You admire me." It elicits a weak chuckle from him. "Like a grandfather, you admire me."

"You make love like an Italian Batman."

"And tomorrow, what then?"

"I'm no one's one night stand, Sal. Are you?"

"Next thing, you'll tell me I'm special."

"I don't have to. You know who you are."

Frandino's fingers are touching her smoothness, and his nose is full of her, earthy and floral at once. His mind is drifting, floating. He is back with his friends, out on the street in front of his house on Trenton Street, playing with a rubber sponge ball during the summer between the eighth grade and his first year of high school. The cutie from down the street stands off to the side with a watching smile he knows is meant only for him.

June 26, 1971. The Green House.

It was a festive day with food and warm sun, and a touch football game out in the middle of the street that featured the cousins against some neighborhood kids out on Harriet Avenue, off of East Delevan. The ubiquitous grilled sausage, with the customary peppers and onions, was served on rolls and washed down with grape Crush or Vernor's ginger pop.

It was the only time I remember at the house where my uncle Ricco had grown up under old Cesidio's watch.

It was past dinnertime but the sun was still shining, when my father managed to corral my brother and me. "Guys. You should see what Pops has got down in the basement. It's amazing."

Dad led us down a flight of gray-painted wooden stairs into the large, open basement. To our left: Six electric trains all running at once, creating enough of a racket that we needed to raise our voices to be heard. A third of the basement was devoted to it; a surface of plywood at counter-height; with miniature buildings, trees, cars. All laid out in a beautiful pattern, with H-O scale model trains running on tracks that interlaced the diorama.

At one end of the model city, where green land met blue water, were a number of long black buildings like oversized barns with railroad tracks running in between them. On one of the building's roofs, in yellow letters, was the word "Bethlehem."

"Whatta-you think?" The Salt of the Earth stood off to the side of his creation, near a place where he had arranged the train control boxes side by side. He wore a broad grin that seemed to me a sublime combination of pride and humility.

I glanced at Tom, and could tell that he was as dumbstruck as me, by this huge model of our home town.

"I show you me. Come see." The old man came around and led us to a place clear on the other side of his creation. Far from downtown or the steel plant, there were some plastic houses on a tree-lined street; houses of a larger scale than the rest of the model. In the backyard of one of those houses – a green one – a little plastic man wore a white shirt, overalls and a hat. Stooped over a patch that looked like a garden.

"Cool," Tom said. "What do you think about when you look at all this, Pops?"

"This," he said, turning down all the trains so we could hear him better. "This is my life."

He coughed for a second that turned into ten. Dad went over to steady him. I had noticed during the day that he was coughing despite seventy-five degrees of sun. Finally, he recovered enough that he sat in a folding chair.

"My life-a-began when I come America. Fourteen a-years old, I come America. Nineteen-a twelve. In Italia, no money. No food. We try but nothing-a-comes from the ground. My-a-father, he get sick on boat. He die on-a-boat. A-priest-a-say-a-prayer, then a-throw him overboard."

He paused for a moment.

"They throw-a-my papa overboard," he repeated. "I am a-four-teen-years old."

"Pops, I don't think I ever knew that," Dad said.

"I don't a-talk about it. My life-a-begin here. We come a-New York. Ellis Island! Stand in-a-line, doctor check to see if we can come in-a-coun-try. Me and-a momma, so nervous. Four hours, stand in-a-line. Six hours. Still in line. Then, finally." He pauses to cough, then continues a bit more softly.

"Take off-a-my shirt, doctor gonna check me. Then we stay in New York, twenty people in-a one big room."

"What happened then, Pops?" Tom urged.

"New York, hard life. Fights for work, for money. We stay only one-a-winter. Then in-a-spring, we take train. We come-a-here. I work. I sell news-a-papers. I shine-a-your shoes. Messenger boy. Carry-a-boxes. Maybe I get enough money to feed-a-myself. Bring home some pennies for mama."

He stopped to cough, and Dad had to steady him again. For a few moments, that cough of his reached a scary intensity.

Finally, he was talking again. "They build the train, it go all around-a-the-city. Mama say we come here, right on this street. She says we must a-come to this place, right here to this house. We have *cugini* here. Cousins. So we come here, we live with our cousins. Then a-my big cousin tells me, "Cesidio. You strong boy. You come with a-me. You make steel. He bring me here."

With that, he was up again, walking around the diorama, back to his wooden-painted lake. He pointed at his model steel mill.

"I telling you - they hire me to the steel. Happiest day of my life."

"But Pops," I said. "You always say not to work in the steel plant."

"You don't," he said, wagging his finger in warning. "But for me back a-then, more money in a-three week than I ever make in a-six month."

"Wooden shoes," my brother said.

"*Si*," he answered gravely. "Wooden shoes. I get-a-blisters. But if you're a man, you do it. For-a your wife. Your children and a-grandchildren. For your family, for future."

A jolt seemed to go through his body. "I show you pictures," he said.

He walked to a small wooden cabinet in one corner of the basement, not far from his miniature downtown. Opened a drawer, pulled out a manila envelope. The envelope was old and worn; it had foreign words written on it in pencil.

There was enough light in the basement to let us appreciate the four photos he retrieved from the envelope. He placed one next to another on the blue paint that stood for the Niagara River.

"My crew. Nineteen-a-forty two." He pointed to the first of the photos. It showed a lineup of a dozen or so white men, dressed in work overalls, many with shovels. They stood on a dirty floor with piles of stuff, like sand, behind them.

"Which one is you, Pops?" my brother asks.

"You can never a-guess." He laughed and pointed to a short, barrel-chested man with hair on his head. "You see. They call me Shorty."

The Salt of the Earth was the only man in the next picture, and he was sticking his arm through a window into a massive, glowing-white cauldron.

"I take temperature. To make-a-steel, it's a-science. Too hot, furnace ruined. The bosses will a-kill you. Not hot enough, bad metal. You make the temperature in furnace just-a-right."

"My friends," he said, pointing to the third picture. Four men smiled at us as they sat at a bar, each with a beer glass in front of them. One of the men had a cigarette dangling out of the side of his mouth. Another had his beer glass in hand; he might have been raising it to toast us.

"That's-a-Polish Fred. Then that's a-me. Then Jimbo. And the guy with-a-the smoke, he's Paddy." At this, the storyteller's voice faltered and shook. "My Irish friend Paddy. When we are kids, we fight. When we grow up, we save each other's life in-a-steel plant."

"Tell us about this restaurant," I said.

"Once a month, we come a-this place. Four friends. We talk about wives, kids. Drink Simon Pure beer, get a little happy. We eat good. Roast beef. Kielbasa. We brag our kids-a-gonna go to college. We save our money. We gonna tell our kids to stay in-a school. Get a-good a-job."

Then, his voice dropped an octave.

"Me and these-a-guys, we beat Hitler's ass. Steel for ships and airplanes. Work is hard, but we do it to beat Hitler."

He stopped to cough yet again. A minute later, he was able to continue.

"What a country, America! Daytime, I make steel, I kick Hitler's ass. Dinner, I come home. I have-a-my wife, my kids, my *giardino*." He pointed back across his model city, toward the little plastic man in the backyard.

"What's this picture?" my brother asked. It's the last of the four. There are no people; just an expanse of water, and a shimmering on its surface.

"Sunset," he said. "Over the lake. I watch the sun go down. Fifteen minute walk from-a the steel. Upwind. No smoke in the air. You see black and a-white but I see the colors. Blue sky turns *violetta*. Yellow sun turns orange, turns rose. Sun go down into the water. Then it's night. I bring-a my wife. We watch. Sun goes down, and I kiss-a my wife. Beautiful land, this America." He gestured back toward his model trains.

Not too many days later, I understood why we spent our Saturday at this green house with the green metal awnings and the vegetable garden in the backyard.

13

Where Are You, Batman?

July 4, 1971

The Salt of the Earth lay on his side, propped into place by pillows. Outside the hospital, the day was for jackets and long pants. The sun was bright, but it was playing a lousy trick on us. It happens that way in our neck of the woods sometimes.

It was the first year I can remember that we did not spend Independence Day picnicking under my uncle's big old willow tree in Cheektowaga. The Gugliuzza patriarch had been in this hospital room for three days, surrounded by monitors and hooked up to tubes. His body lay in lumps beneath the linen. He looked smaller than ever before.

"Pops," Dad said. "I brought the boys."

The old man in the bed did not smile, or move. His chest expanded and contracted. None of the machines around him were beeping or flat-lining. I knew from watching television that all this was good.

It was the first time I had ever in my life visited a sick person in the hospital. Should I have been crying? Was I supposed to run to his bed and tell him that I loved him? I love him now, forty-some years later, but back then, I took him for granted.

He tried to clear his throat.

"Come here," it sounded like a growl.

Dad stood behind us, and nudged us forward. The old man smelled like a damp old attic. He reached out for my brother with one of his hands. I saw Tom jump in his skin the moment the Salt of the Earth touched his arm.

"Ernesto," he said.

"No, that's Tomasso. I'm Ernesto," I said.

"Did you get-a-good grades in-a-school?" I think that's what he asked, if my lip-reading was accurate. We both said, "Yes."

"*Pomodoro*," he said. Then, with a startling burst of energy, he raised his body off the pillow and sat up straight, on his own.

"*Che bel pomodoro*," he said. He held his hands in front of his face, as if holding a precious little invisible ball up for inspection. He smiled. His eyes opened wide for a moment; they were cloudy, not real eyes. But his face beamed. For a second or two, he cherished his imaginary fruit. And then he fell back onto the bed, and the machines in the room started making noise.

"Ricco!" My father's voice yelled. I felt Dad's hand on my shoulder, pulling me away. Dad pulled and guided Tom and me out into the corridor. People dressed in white rushed past us and into the room.

Two days later, the Salt of the Earth left us. Tom and I weren't allowed to the wake or the funeral. I never had a chance to say goodbye.

*****

Raincloud and I had been riding our bicycles a lot since school let out for the summer of 1971. It was three miles from his house to the Channel Six studios, and our route often took us past the studio. "Just to make sure she's safe," Raincloud would say as we made the right turn onto Main Street off of Amherst, and I knew that we would not dismount until we were in front of the now-familiar Channel Six building. There we'd stand, looking for signs of Darcie. After a few minutes, having not seen her, we'd go riding off as though we weren't disappointed.

We went riding a day or two after Cesidio's funeral, but we decided on that day to make a left turn at Main Street instead of a right. We ended up outside a grand old building at the University, on a stately lawn with big trees. We parked our bikes near one of the big elms and sat, looking down a gently sloping hill at the bustle of the street two hundred feet away.

"Hey, quiet one," Raincloud said. "You in a bad mood?"

"What do you think happens to people when they die?"

"You sure you want to know what a Seneca thinks about that, Catholic boy?"

"You go to a Christian church too, Raincloud. The Presbyterian one, right?"

"Yeah, Mom makes me go. But I've got my own ideas."

"Here's what I think," I began. "You go to a place you love and you never leave there. Like my cousins' grandfather. He died a few days ago. I think he's still here. He had a model of the whole city in his cellar with trains and buildings and streets and the steel plants and the grain elevators right where they belong. He had little plastic people all over the place, going here and there. He loved the trains. He had a garden and he gave the vegetables to his wife to cook."

Raincloud remained silent for several seconds. Then he said, "Tell me more."

"I guess when he died, Pops went someplace where he could love all those trains again."

"Do you miss him?" Raincloud asked.

"I don't know. Didn't see him much. His English wasn't so good. He was from the old country."

"I miss my dad like hell," Raincloud said. "I wish he could watch me play sports this coming year. I like the way you think. It's how Senecas think."

"I don't know about that. It's how I think."

"The Seneca way of thinking keeps me from going crazy when I think about Dad. He's still alive, Pronotaro. He's with the Great Spirit, like what you Christians call God. He gathers all his children for a never-ending feast when they die. People from all generations are together in peace. Even half-breeds, like my dad."

"Well, I think Pops is in a place like that."

"Pops? That's a dumb name. A name is supposed to say something important about the man."

Then something clicked into place in the space between my ears. "Salt of the Earth" came from my mouth like an underhand toss.

"That should be his name," said Raincloud.

July 8, 1971; early afternoon

Sal Frandino hasn't been on this bridge since the ribbon cutting ceremony fifteen years earlier with Lackawanna's mayor. Over ten stories above a huge boat slip for lake freighters loaded down with ore, and a conundrum of smokestack industy pouring various shades and hues of stuff into the air. A bridge named for a late priest who made his reputation caring for the little guys. Frandino feels a connection.

George Barbarello from the *Evening Star* sits with Frandino in the back seat of the city-owned Lincoln Continental. Dan Spesiak, Frandino's hand-picked deputy mayor, is driving. Councilman Snead rides shotgun.

The sun is high overhead. Frandino looks to his right. The lake is blue, placid. Punctuated by white sails as far as his eye can see. Two big lake freighters are under steam in the distance, heading toward the harbor.

Spread beneath them are acres of buildings, large and small, railroad tracks running between them like capillaries. The smoke rising from the gargantuan buildings lined up against the lakeshore seems to mock all the other smokestacks he's seen on the journey thus far. Billows of burnt-orange smoke rising from the steel plant, moving across the sky from right to left. For his entire life, Lackawanna has made Frandino think of huge, metallic, fire-breathing monsters.

The bridge brings the car earthward toward the steel plant on a path similar to an aircraft landing. Frandino can see men working in the alleyways between the buildings and near the railroad tracks; can see railcars being loaded and unloaded. Acres and acres of industry. Frandino's mission is to keep it like this forever.

They clear through a security gate and park in a lot. Frandino is out of the car, and looks up. Orange and brown junk sails overhead like billows of food coloring dispersing into an agitated glass of water.

Frandino and his companions walk into a low brick building with shiny windows and a surrounding patch of well-manicured green lawn. Intense red blooms of potted geraniums grace both sides of the entrance. Frandino thinks the flowers are there to fool visitors into thinking that the air is safe for living things.

They are led into a darkly-paneled conference room with corporate furniture that rivals Frandino's office in its lavishness; a pure mahogany conference table with matching chairs. Men are sitting, smoking cigarettes, some drinking coffee. Frandino recognizes Pauly Kessler, lifelong steel man and general manager of this plant that still employs 20,000 men and has been, for three quarters of a century, the crown jewel of the area's economy.

"Mayor Frandino." Pauly is out of his chair to shake Frandino's hand. "It's been too long. We need to get a hard hat on you one day, give you the full tour."

Frandino knows Pauly from some charity boards they've served on together as a man of good will.

"Councilman Snead, I presume?" Pauly says, working his way around the room. "Good to meet you. I think you already know the Steelworkers' local president, Grady McMahon..."

*****

Ten minutes into the meeting of politicians and steel men, nothing but small talk. Then, Snead takes advantage of a pause.

"Gentlemen," he says, "they tell me management and the union can't get together on anything here, but I don't believe that. The evidence suggests that you're working together to limit the number of African-Americans you'll accept into the workforce."

"Hey, now," McMahon from the union points a finger back at Snead. "We have a great record of minority participation in our union. If you're gonna play it that way, then I suggest you take up your beef with that guy over there." He points at Pauly.

"Not to minimize, but we've got bigger problems than a few bigots," Pauly says. "They might can me for saying it, but I think we need to prepare the community for what's coming. And somehow, not start a panic."

Frandino re-focuses on Pauly Kessler. It seems that everyone has stopped breathing.

"We all know it's bad," Barbarello says. "Just tell us how bad."

"This plant loses money hand over foot," Pauly says. "Never mind overseas competition - hell, we can't even compete with the other plants in our own company."

Frandino has carried this fear in his gut ever since the last big strike, in 1959. He knew Pauly then as a foreman who stewed when the union refused to put the plant back to work. Pauly knew then that the company was losing customers they'd never win back if the union stayed out and pushed for even more concessions.

"It - won't - happen all at once," Pauly continues. "Hell, it still might not happen at all. The torture of it is that no one knows. It could be us, or it could be the plant down in Johnstown. Not even the corporate guys in Pennsylvania know yet."

"Bullshit," says Grady McMahon. "Nothing but theatre - and meant for Union consumption, I might add."

"Grady, you were with me at the new plant in Indiana last month," Pauly responded. "You know where the money's being spent. And our facility is antiquated. Grady, you're a steel man. You know it's true."

Frandino watches the union guy. Reads his posture, analyzes his face. Sees a lot of votes in McMahon's face.

McMahon clasps and unclasps his hands on the table in front of him. He shakes his head and sighs. "It's true, what Pauly says. But why not they modernize this plant? The company's poor decisions got us here and the company can make decisions to turn this place around."

"They won't, Grady," says Pauly, "and the proof is, that they haven't. No significant upgrades in years. They want to make money. They don't think they can make money here anymore."

"This is a ploy," McMahon says. "They just want to put the squeeze on labor - again."

"No one loves this place more than me," Pauly says, "but here's the reality. As long as that dirty Asian war is still going on, the plant will hum along. We've got big military contracts for certain things that we can only make here. But the need for the kinds of steel we make here won't last much longer."

"Nothing but theatre!" McMahon hits the table and begins to shake his head. "And with the *Evening Star* here! Jesus, Pauly - why don't you just make yourself some atom bombs and drop them on us?"

*****

Lamont Raincloud benefitted much from the absence of real basketball referees on the playground. Eight of us competed on that perfect July afternoon and, as usual, he refused to be my teammate. "You're the one idiot stupid enough to defend against me," he explained.

Thus the games degraded into a familiar ordeal of elbows, shoulders, and arguments between us.

" 'Mont! That's a foul. I had position."

"Don't you watch TV, son? That's not a foul. Not in college or pros."

"Raincloud," one of my teammates said. "Pro's feet were planted. You fouled him."

Raincloud answered with gruff laughter. "Maybe his feet were planted, but I sure un-planted them."

"Let's hit the Avenue Soda Bar," one of the guys suggested."

Eight of us rolled into the ice cream shop and pushed a couple of tables together. Eight guys, all heading into either our freshman or sophomore year of high school.

Our buddy Doug had an older brother who had been drafted and was in Vietnam getting his butt shot at while we played hoops and gorged on root beer floats. Doug was a tall, long-haired guy with a flower child appearance. But he was a tooth-and-nail athlete who argued basketball fouls like a trial attorney. At the Soda Bar, he goaded a couple of us into a debate over whether the guy who had recently leaked the classified history of America's involvement in Vietnam to the *New York Times*, was right in doing so. But I noticed that the smartest guy of all was not saying a word.

" 'Mont. What do you think?"

He looked around the table and shook his head.

"Dudes," he said, "You're all thinking like red-white-and-blue Americans. I'm just red. Not white, and definitely not blue."

"Well you might be an Indian, but you're an American Indian," Doug said.

"Dudes," Raincloud repeated. "You think America is this country with boundaries that expand every few years and never gets smaller. You think your country is so important, like it's going to last forever. But none of that's true."

All of us stopped. We could hear the traffic out on the avenue.

"Never mind," Raincloud sighed. You guys won't understand."

"Here we go," Doug rolled his eyes. "Raincloud believes in the old Indian tribal ways."

"Old tribal ways that got 'em all killed," someone else added.

Raincloud pointed across the table. "Listen, you little white shits. Your whole stinking country is just temporary. We're just waiting for our moment in history and then the land will be ours again."

"Never mind, Raincloud," said Doug. "You don't care about my brother in Nam. You think all our problems would go away if we passed around the peace pipe.

Raincloud looked right at Doug and kept going. "I am talking about your stinking red-white-and-blue war that might get all of your sorry asses killed."

Even old Lumpy Ed, the World War II vet who served up the ice cream, stopped what he was doing and leaned over the counter to listen.

"You stiffs are surprised that your government's been lying to you?" Raincloud went on. "Let me tell you how they've been lying to my people for three hundred years. Any of you ever heard of The Cornplanter? He was a Seneca chief, died about a hundred and thirty years ago. He was buried on Seneca land down near the Allegheny River, near Pennsylvania. That's just as sacred as any place where Christians or Jews are buried. You know what happened to Cornplanter's grave in 1965?"

He stopped and looked around. No one knew, or if they did, they weren't saying.

Then he provided an answer. "They flooded it, that's what."

"What are you talking about?" I asked.

"See? Even if the story makes the papers, which by the way it did, you little white boys don't care. You don't even want to know. Your army built a dam. Said it was for flood control. The lake that formed above the dam flooded out a huge chunk of the Allegheny Reservation. Cornplanter's grave. Guys, that land was protected by a treaty that your government signed. Damn your sorry white man's government."

"Well like, I'm sorry," said Doug, "but we're talking about the stupid war. What's this got to do with the war?"

"I'm talking about the government that got you into your war," Raincloud answered. "You Yankee stiffs have been lying and cheating ever since you got here. The true history of the country is not the crap they taught us in grade school."

"Mont," I said. "Your dad fought. You were proud of him."

"Jeffcoat told me the real reasons America fought Germany and Japan," he answered. "The Japanese were gonna kick us out of Hawaii. But we had too much money invested there. The whole war in the Pacific was over pineapples."

"Men!"

Lumpy Ed's voice was rough gravel. It startled us. We were only used to hearing it say, "Waddaya having?" and "That's a buck-forty-five, please." We all turned toward him; he was standing up straight behind the counter. Then he pointed at Raincloud.

"I'm three-quarters Tuscarora," he said, still pointing at Raincloud. "And you're a goddammed punk who's wrong about this country."

Raincloud stood up and pointed back. "What do you know?"

"Listen, you little ungrateful punk!"

"Who you calling a punk?" Raincloud was full of himself.

"I was in Germany," the ice cream man said. "Buchenwald, you ever heard of the place? That's right, 89th Infantry. We fought against evil. Those skinny, shriveled-up prisoners wanted to live. They wanted to live so bad that... when we got there..."

A sudden shriek escaped his mouth. Then he thundered at Raincloud, pointing, shaking.

"What we saw!" he yelled in a voice that the words ripped through.

My eyes went from Lumpy Ed to Raincloud and back again. Two Injuns, facing each other down.

"Two days before we got there, our commanders radioed ahead to some of the prisoners. The Nazis were low on bullets, had no gas for the ovens, so they couldn't kill all the Jews. But it was a race to get there because the prisoners told our colonels that the Nazis were gonna move them someplace where there were bullets and gas. By the time we got there, the prisoners were rioting. Our commanders told 'em by radio we were coming so they stopped following the Nazis' orders. But, but -"

It looked like Lumpy Ed was seeing ghosts. The next words came pouring out of him.

"You had to see it... they were skin and bones..." Something inside him knocked Lumpy Ed to his knees, and his big, lumpy body shook like Jell-O.

"They were running toward us... skeletons who ran up to us. Some of 'em wore nothing but a smile."

Two of our guys went over to him. "It's okay now, Ed," one of them said.

"One of them hugged me," he said from his slumped position. "A skeleton hugged me. A smelly, naked skeleton. He had three teeth left - oh, shit."

He buried his face in his hands.

"Ed, it's okay. You're in the Soda Bar now," I said.

Then Raincloud finally also came over to him. It took a couple of minutes for Ed to settle back down. Raincloud was now looking at him with wonder. "You're a Tuscarora?" he asked.

Ed glared at him. "I'm an American, goddamit."

July 8, 1971; 8:35 PM

A dot on the map labeled "Port Colborne" sits twenty miles due west of City Hall. The Canadians here have their own dreams, troubles, politics. Within this dot, anonymity for the American mayor and his lover on this, their fourth tryst.

Even in the city, no one seems to suspect. Maybe it's because he's older now, and people discount the possibility that anyone like her would tumble with him.

She has the night off after eight straight days and evenings of chasing stories and melting under studio lights. They stand together in a place called Lakeview Park, looking at the water, the boats, the old cement and grain elevators that highlight the town's meager skyline. Sunlight is fading. The weather is benign.

They stand side by side, not touching each other, watching the water and the orange setting sun. He's just given her a five-minute summary of his afternoon at the steel plant, punctuated by her questions. Now they're in a moment when neither knows what to say next.

"These boats," she finally says. "They used to be our boats. Now they go through this canal and right past us without stopping."

"Yes and it's just splendid, isn't it?" He notes the surrender in his own voice. They turn back toward one another. He's had ample occasion to study her face when she's tired. It has served to deepen his appreciation of her thoroughgoing beauty. She smiles just a little. Their eyes are locked in on each other. She brings peace and satisfaction.

"Darse. What am I going to do about the steel?"

"I don't know, but you can trust me to talk it through with. You know that."

Trust. Frandino's mind replays her voice saying the word. But she looks and smells the way a woman should, and he loves the way her scent deepens as their nights together progress. And her eyes. Holding him the way he has longed to be held by eyes such as hers.

"You're a smart cookie, Darse. What do you think the others will do with what they heard today about the steel?"

"I don't know. You said you walked with Snead out back of the restaurant - how did that go?"

The mayor's entourage had headed to Hoak's, a seafood grill on the lakeshore south of the steel plant late that afternoon, for what Frandino called an emergency meeting. Civic leaders had feared the possibility of the words Pauly Kessler had spoken for over a decade, but now the man had said it, with a sobriety that galvanized Frandino and Snead into a sad solidarity. The two politicians had walked together behind the restaurant on a rocky portion of shore after the meal: Snead had started picking up stones and throwing them, wordlessly, into the waves.

"We'll figure out a way, Mr. Snead. We'll get through this," Frandino said to him after the fourth rock was launched from Snead's hand. Frandino bent down to pick up a stone of his own, and he threw it into the lake. Then, Snead used words to communicate.

"Mayor?"

"Bill?"

"Take care of yourself. The job must be demanding your soul. Protect your soul, mayor."

*****

"Sal – hey, Batman. Where are you right now?"

"Back behind the restaurant, thinking about my conversation with Snead."

"He hates you, you know."

"Maybe so. He's human. The news hit him hard."

"He hates you. It's on his face and in his voice whenever I talk with him. I'd worry about him the most."

"He'll keep quiet. It's not the kind of information a politician wants to scoop his rival on. In politics, you try to deliver only the good news, so the voters will associate you with the good things in life."

A breeze blows strands of hair across her face. Frandino imagines, as she stands framed by a deepening red sunset, that she feels a chill. He takes off his light jacket, and puts it on her. Her face brightens toward him.

*****

Frandino has taken her to dinner and now, their ritual begins. She gets the room. He knocks a few minutes later, and she lets him in. "Tonight, we'll just rest," she says, and she excuses herself for a brief visit to the bathroom. Then she comes out and within moments they are caught up in escalating intimacy. Boundaries between them are crossed until he is beyond tired. Then, she uses strong, massaging fingertips as tools of gentle persistence. She gets answers, and eventually he manages to ask some questions of his own.

"Darse. Thane Riley - what do you think he knows about the steel plant?"

"He wouldn't have been surprised by any of what you heard today."

"What would he do if he were me?"

"Sal." She touches his nose with a finger. "You and he are not on the same page at all."

"What page is he on, then?"

"He's past the steel. He'd let them go, and start focusing now to rebuild the area around something other than heavy industry."

"Like what? Help me to understand."

"He thinks the banks and insurance. He thinks about getting university students who come from out of town to stay here when they're done with school and to open new businesses here. A total economic makeover."

"Hmm. So he believes all that."

"I think he does. What do you think?"

"Sal? What do you think about that? Hey, Batman…"

But he is unconscious, dreaming that he is back in grade school and the prettiest, smartest girl in class is helping him at the kitchen table with his homework.

*****

Three a.m. He is awake. She snores lightly, like a child. Like Steffi snores. A paralyzing thought. He won't be able to cover this much longer with stories about sleeping in the office.

His bladder tingles, and he spends a few moments working up the gumption to rise from the bed and get to the toilet. He doesn't want to wake her. He is careful.

He steals into the bathroom, closes the door, and turns on the light for himself. Glances at the sink. A round compact mirror; a thin glass tube.

He zeroes in for a closer look. Two grains of white powder on the mirror. He considers the odds that it was left there by the room's previous occupants, or maybe by the maid.

Sal Frandino straightens up and sees himself in the mirror. Naked save for his briefs. Frozen.

14
Games of Leverage: Used, Mis-used

August, 1971

Three weeks from high school. Raincloud and I reported to our respective new schools to begin football practice. The field at St. Michael's in Kenmore, was surrounded by middle and upper-middle class homes. An idyllic backdrop for the sixty or so freshman and sophomores who vied for spots on the junior varsity, or, for us rookies, relegation to the freshman team. I high-stepped through the tires, hit the blocking sleds, and practiced running on all fours like a crab, close to the ground. Learning the secret of line play: the low man wins. Encouraged to love dirt, because intentional proximity to the dirt meant leverage, and football is a game of leverage. "Good things come to those who get dirty," McCoy, our line coach, kept preaching.

Some days, after practice, Raincloud and I met at his house and then rode our bikes up to the Shoshone Pool, which was very close to Raincloud's new school. Shoshone Pool, memorable for its plethora of girls in two-piece bathing suits. Belly buttons and smooth legs. Smiling faces and long, straight hair. And this foreign-looking girl, maybe a couple of years older than me. I thought she was Mexican. She always wore green bikinis.

"Pronotaro. Stop staring at that chick."

"Can't help it. Green's my favorite color."

"Well, do you want me to introduce you to her?"

"Do you know her?"

"Hell, no," Raincloud laughed.

Two days later as football practice was ending and we freshman Marauders were running laps around the field before going in to shower, I saw two familiar figures standing with bicycles near the bleachers on the visitor's side of the field. I came around a turn, running near the front of the gaggle of JV hopefuls. I could see that it was Raincloud and her.

"Ernie!" they shouted as I ran past. Butterflies filled my stomach. I had never talked to her before. Bless that Raincloud for making this introduction happen.

But the second time I came around, they were totally lip-locked.

I felt like I couldn't run another step. Almost every single player passed me as I straggled around the track and into the locker room.

*****

Later that afternoon I rode my bike to Raincloud's house and knocked on the door. When no one answered I waited an hour before hunger got the best of me and I went home to dinner. Then I headed back. This time Mrs. Raincloud opened the door.

"Is Lamont here?"

"He's not. But I'll let him know you came."

"Do you think he met a girl?"

"Funny you should mention that. He told me about a girl named Anniselle from the pool. Why - you know her?"

Later that night, Mom was watching Johnny Carson and I couldn't sleep. I sat on the end of the couch opposite from her.

"Ernie the Pro. It's late."

"Lamont did something that I don't understand."

She turned the sound down. "What is it?"

I told her the story. "This has to mean my friendship with Lamont is over, right?" I concluded. "To stay friends with him would make me a spineless wimp, wouldn't it?"

"I don't know, Ernie. There's a saying, you only hurt the ones you love. I think you and Lamont love one another. Like brothers. Sometimes you tease Tom about Esther. Which you should stop because his feelings get hurt. But anyway, you're still brothers."

"Yeah. I guess," I answered. I'm sure that mom could tell by the look on my face that I wasn't buying her brand of baloney.

"Ernie, I know guys your age need to show each other how tough you are. But sometimes the right way to be tough is to roll with the punches and let go of it. There's lots of girls out there."

"There's other girls, but what about friendship? Trust? Raincloud betrayed me, Mom!"

"You've heard the saying, Ern. All is fair in love. Maybe he didn't mean for it to happen the way it did. Maybe they discovered by accident that they liked each other. Things happen."

"But they showed up at practice and deliberately hurt my feelings. I don't know if I ever want to trust anybody ever again."

"Trust? Ernie, don't ever trust anyone too much, especially when it comes to members of the opposite sex. When a guy and a girl have feelings for each other, it can make them do things that they swore they'd never do. One day, you might betray a friend because of a girl. And when you do, it'll seem right to you."

"So you're saying that love is awfully damn dangerous."

"You're up kind of late," she said. "Go to bed."

August 16, 1971

Sal Frandino sits at his desk, rubbing his temples. He never in his life has dreaded Monday mornings the way he does now. Life is a quagmire.

He's told the voting public his plan to work with the unions and industry to keep jobs in the area. The July meeting at Bethlehem is in his thoughts every day, but panic has given way to a hazy gloom. Another data point in a sea of unpleasant possibilities. Part of the angst that the area's economic movers and shakers have been fearing for a dozen years.

The new poll in the *Evening Star* shows that Frandino trails Thane Riley by eight percentage points in the race for County Executive. The *Messenger* has it at ten points. Two weeks ago, the gap was a little smaller than it is now.

It's been a month since Port Colborne and he's run away from Darcie. She's called him twice to arrange another evening together but he's bailed out both times, once failing to show as agreed upon, and once feigning illness. Their recent contact has been limited to playing their expected roles at campaign events and press conferences. Aides, and Steffi, tell him that her coverage is fair; she's not parroting the usual Channel Six anti-Frandino line. He imagines that she's catching hell from Hersch Woodstein and that before long, she'll lose patience with his evasiveness and let him have it with both barrels.

Every time he goes home to Steffi, smelling her roast beef, tomato sauce, barbecued chicken, or apple pies, his stomach hurts.

He'll plunge into his work. No public appearances today until the Downtown Businessmen's Association dinner at seven. A day to be the mayor, not the candidate. To stay within the comfort zone of the office and to enjoy a cigar, even if he is smoking alone.

Just before ten in the morning, Phyllis buzzes him.

"John Klinglehaus says he's on his way to see you. He'll be here in fifteen, twenty minutes. I checked your calendar. You look available."

"Guess he wants to talk about the newspaper polls. More despair."

"Come on, Sal. You're a fighter. It's still single digits. You've beaten the odds before."

"Phyllis, you're right. Beating the odds is what I do." Frandino is now smiling into the receiver. "Young John and I, we'll figure this thing out."

"I hear the county office building is very nice. You gonna hire me to work over there when you win?"

*****

Frandino has just spoken with Governor Rockefeller for ten or twelve minutes about getting some help for the city school budget; the Governor gave his personal assurance that whether Frandino wins or loses in November, the city will receive close to half a million state dollars to help pay its teachers and buy equipment for student's extracurricular activities. Rocky is a good, decent man. A cigar man. Smoke is good.

Phyllis rings to tell him that Klinglehaus is here. It reminds Frandino that the first of two televised debates with Riley is five weeks off. An opportunity for Frandino to change some minds. He feels a surge of well-being as John walks in.

"Sal, come here, please," are John's first words. He is not smiling.

"Sure. What is this?" Frandino is up from behind the desk, crossing over to the party chairman.

Klinglehaus whacks him in the arm with a fist.

"John, that wasn't a love tap. This had better be good."

"This isn't from me, Sal. It's from the County Democrats. No - the State Democrats. Let me repeat their message.

Another fist into Frandino's arm. Harder this time, almost knocking him over.

"John, you wise-ass. That's going too far."

"You're the one who's gone too far," comes a sharp answer.

"Who do think you are?"

"I'll ask the questions, Mayor. What have you done?" Klinglehaus cocks his head to one side and straightens it back, staring up at the mayor. "What did you do this time, Mayor?"

"What? We lost another point or two... I saw that. I don't know why..."

"Damn you, Sal. You and that big Catholic act of yours. Here's what the Democratic Party says to you this morning. Who rushed in and defended you when everyone put you together with the Roller Derby Queen in '58? When they tried to say you were poking Miss New York State in '65?"

"John. What's going on? Who's saying what?"

"No, no, Mayor. You tell me. You think of me as just a kid, but it's time you wake up. I am the Democratic Party around here, Mayor. You tell me who's so freaking hot that you'll jeopardize everything we've worked for to get a bullshit piece of ass. You shit scum."

"John - Settle down or I'll make some calls and you won't be County Chairman anymore. What is your problem?"

"You damn well know what the problem is, you stupid old dago. But I want to hear you say it."

"You're on thin ice, John. I'm warning you for the last time."

"All these years you had me and everyone else convinced that Steffi is so damned important to you and your behavior would be impeccable. How getting back in the mayor's chair was about coming back and doing it right this time."

"She is important to me."

"Look me in the eye and tell me you love your wife, then."

Frandino's head is spinning. "Okay, John. I love my wife. I love Steffi."

"But you slept with the whore at Channel Six. More than once! I oughta crucify you."

"You're gonna crucify me? I made you, John. And I can unmake you. You want to see it happen?" Frandino takes three steps and picks up the phone receiver.

"One phone call," Frandino seethes, "and you'll have to move so far away from here if you want a job in politics that you'll have to learn a foreign language so they'll understand you when you knock on their doors."

"You're just proving what an arrogant dago you are. You're the one who's done. Everyone knows, Sal. Whatever Democrat you think you can call to complain to about me, they've already been briefed on you and Darcie Yeager. Dates, times, places."

Frandino looks at the telephone on his desk, the receiver in his hand, and then back up at the angry young man in his office.

"You idiot," Klinglehaus adds.

"Who knows – what?"

"Don in Syracuse. And Old Man Pincus. The whole Democratic Caucus in the State Assembly could be next."

"Old Man Pincus knows?"

"They knew before me. They broke it to me last night. They sent me here and made me promise to punch you in the head. I'm hitting your arm because I'm a man of mercies. They sent me to punish you."

"Old Man Pincus?"

Klinglehaus nods. John is the commanding officer of all Democratic Party boots on the ground in the County, but Pincus is the Commander-in-Chief who turned the chairmanship over to Klinglehaus in an orderly transition a few years earlier.

"John, the fling with the reporter - that's over. I swear. It's done. I - I - okay, I made a mistake. I haven't talked to her in weeks. I never even had her phone number. I - I swear!"

"Sal, for the love-a-Mike. It's too late now."

They are looking at each other like two wounded animals.

"John. What do we do for damage control? I was careful. No one could have found out, I - I swear."

"Oh, you were careful." Klinglehaus begins to laugh like a maniac. Frandino watches silently.

"You were careful." Klinglehaus repeats through bitter laughter. "Dago mayor pokes liberated news whore - but he was careful about it. He made sure to get his rocks off over in Canada. You're a riot, Sal. What a great headline that'll make. Oh, shit."

"John, please. Let's talk about this like men."

"Like men. Like - men, Sal? You know, I've only been married to my wife for fourteen years, but I never once cheated on her. You think I ain't been tempted? But Sal, here's the thing. Your political future? And mine, by the way. Up in smoke, because you've committed the sin that most voters around here won't forgive. I've made a living going to bat for you because I thought there's nothing to any of the stuff they've ever said about you. Well, shame on me for being young and naive. Because if you slept with the news whore, who's to say you didn't sleep with Roller Derby Rosie or the Beauty Queen? This could be the end for both of us."

Frandino looks at the man standing ten feet from him and sees John Klinglehaus for the first time as an equal. Or greater.

"What do you need me to do, John?"

"Keep your dick in your pants, for starters. Sir."

Frandino listens for several seconds to the steady drone of the air conditioner.

"So anyway," Klinglehaus says, "this election is lost. The three TV stations in town are watching us Democrats like we're the mob. The Democrat-in-name-only Irishman from the First Ward who runs the Messenger? Heaven help us if he decides to pursue this, because your little news whore sang to her boss over at TV Six like a bird about the whole thing between you two. In fact, now we've got the little Jew himself to contend with. He'll be here to grill you tomorrow. That's just part of the deal I had to make."

The little Jew: Hersch Woodstein. All of five feet, five inches tall and weighing in at one-forty soaking wet, but as the anchor of the most popular television newscast most nights at six and eleven, Woodstein might as well be a seven-foot bruiser.

"Hersch is a pain in the ass," Frandino says, "but we've beat him before. Why not again?"

"Because this time, you're unambiguously guilty of something. We're one false move from the biggest scandal in the history of Buffalo. And where will that leave you and Steffi, and the voters in our very Catholic city? We're not only gonna lose, we're gonna get stomped. And on a personal note, you could lose your wife. Who you say you love."

"Why are you so sure this means we're going to get stomped, though?"

Klinglehaus shakes his head. He walks to his favorite leather chair, and plops down into it.

"Because, Sal. The deal is this – so maybe you won't lose Steffi. This stays outta the news, as we play by Woodstein's ethical rules. So we lose the unions, maybe more. There's a media pool forming. Someone's gonna be with me practically twenty-four seven, from now 'til the election. Starting this afternoon. So, we get stomped. In all likelihood."

"I guess we'll see how good you are when you play by their rules, that's all."

"Whatever, Sal. As I was saying, you owe Hersch a two-hour interview. With a camera crew, in this office, entirely on the record. Tomorrow afternoon, no matter what on your calendar has to be re-arranged. Or Channel Six goes public with everything."

Frandino feels sudden dread leaking all over his face.

"Sal, we can't win this playing by their rules, and it'll be my defeat every bit as much as it is yours. 'Cause it's me who's been on the phone with every county chairman in the state, pushing you for the governor's chair. Thanks, Sir."

*****

The Channel Six camera crew arrives to set up at the mayor's office half an hour before the scheduled two o'clock interview. Frandino and his cosmetics guy are in a room down the hall, getting camera-ready. He wears his best blue suit, a white shirt and his royal blue tie with two dozen little red stationary bison, the very symbol on the sides of the Thundering Herd's football helmets. Wearing his city love for all to see.

Frandino walks down the corridor toward his office at five before two, anticipating how Woodstein will ask leading questions, framing him as a villain whose ineptness and lack of preparation to deal with the city's current challenges is only matched by his corruptness. Frandino thinks he can walk the thin line. Too defiant, and he'll come across as defensive; voters will think something's wrong. Too relaxed, and Channel Six will portray him as Nero who fiddled while Rome burned.

He's in the office with two members of the television station's camera crew, shaking their hands. "Get some good close shots so we can show everyone how young I still am," he jokes. The camera guys yuk it up with him. It is three minutes past the hour, and Woodstein has not arrived.

"Where is he, guys? Not like him to be tardy."

The cameramen shrug.

At eleven minutes past the hour, Phyllis buzzes the phone on his desk.

"Is he here?"

"He was, Sal. He gave me a sealed envelope for you. Asked me to give it to you. Then he left."

"You don't say? Okay, bring it in."

She opens the door and turns to the television technicians.

"Mister Woodstein says you guys can pack up and leave. He's not going to do the interview today," she says to them.

She walks to the mayor's desk and reaches across, handing him the envelope. A moment of quizzical eye contact.

"Well? You going to open it?"

"Sure. A little later."

'A little later' takes twenty minutes to arrive. The camera crew has cleared out of the office. Phyllis is back on the other side of the closed door. Frandino is angry; he is not used to being toyed with. He deliberates on whether to throw the envelope away without opening it. But he can't remain ignorant of what Woodstein has to say. He opens, and reads.

Mayor Frandino:

You have gone too far. Political differences aside, your callous use of a member of my news staff for your own pleasure is a personal insult to me. I care about every person on my staff. You have hurt and confused one of those people.

I reserve the right to conduct my two hour, on-camera interview with you at any time, with no advance notice required. This includes all hours of the night, for the rest of your days on the earth. On camera. In your pajamas, if need be. Maybe more than once. If you don't grant these interviews whenever I decide to ask, I will use what I know to destroy not only your political career, but what is left of your life.

Sleep well, Mayor Frandino.

Very Sincerely,

Herschel

September 21, 1971

The Good Brothers, the tough-guy quasi-priests who ran St. Michael's Collegiate Institute, said that we were in for a big surprise at the first school assembly of my freshman year. It was held in our school's gym. I was trying to position myself to sit with what I thought was my peer group. I was engaged in a mighty struggle to get promoted from the freshman football team to JV.

I sat between Dave and Bob, fellow frosh football guys I rode the late bus home with. Today was like all the others with Dave and Bob; a mortal contest to establish our rung on the pecking order among teammates and classmates. We had discussed politics before. Our conversations tended to feature a limited understanding of the issues. We'd sit in the back of the bus so Dave could light up a smoke and hang it out the window between puffs; and we engaged in such highbrow discussions as the one we'd had the previous evening:

Bob: "Hey, you guys going to watch the big debate next Monday night between Riley and Frandino?"

Dave (with a dirty look): "Shit on that, Bob. Politics is for pussies."

Bob: "Chuck you, Farley! My dad's a union steward at the Steel. They keep laying people off, and freaking Riley don't have any ideas to save my dad's job."

Dave: "They're gonna shut down everything eventually. Your father's union is screwing up the economy of the whole area."

Bob: "You know shit. The unions are the reason most families can afford Christmas presents and vacations."

Me: "The unions aren't the biggest problem. It's the taxes. The newspapers say the state and county business taxes are too high and that's why plants are relocating."

Dave: "All people in the news business smoke dope. They don't care about truth, they just want to sell the news."

Me: "I don't know. I met Darcie Yeager earlier this summer. She doesn't strike me as a dope head. She interviewed my buddy and got him on TV with her. We had burgers with her a couple of times over the summer. I think she cares about truth."

Bob: "You know Darcie Yeager?"

Dave: "Screw Darcie Yeager. She's a piece of crap from out of town. My dad says she's only here so she can sleep her way to the top of the news business. I bet a year from now she's not even working in Buffalo anymore."

Bob: "I'd like to screw Darcie Yeager..."

I sat between Bob and Dave as the assembly began with our principal telling us how special it was to be a St. Mike's Marauder. The Good Brother announced a special guest. As he spoke, news people, some with cameras, came into the gym. There was Darcie, dressed for business. Our special guest was Thane Riley and we were told to give him a big Saint Michael's ovation.

Bob nudged me to get my attention and pointed at the news people. "So," he says, "you gonna introduce me to your Miss Darcie after the assembly, big shot?"

Thane Riley was younger and more energetic than I imagined. He took the podium with, "St. Michael's, how do you FEEEEEEEEL?" Everyone yelled their approval, clapping and stomping.

"I know you're gonna beat the stuffing out of Canisius High next week!"

If everyone in the room could vote, after that play on our emotions he'd have gotten close to 100% of the ballots cast. More noise, and lots of it.

He waited for the gym to get quiet, and then launched his talk. "You know why I'm here today? It's because all of you young men are important. Your opinions about the world matter. Today, I'm going to talk some, but I also want to listen to your ideas. The voting age is going down to eighteen soon, and some of you may even be able to vote next year."

He put his hand to his ear and smiled, and the gym erupted in more support.

"Now my opponent," Riley continued, "the way he's made decisions all his career, they're made in smoke-filled rooms and only a few men are present. But I want to be the County Executive for all the people - for you!"

The gym exploded with more happy noise, and I focused on Darcie. She was writing, head down in a pad. She was not trying to be sexy. She couldn't help it.

It went on like this for twenty minutes or so; Riley said it was time for younger men to run the government; old men of Frandino's generation were the reason we got involved in Vietnam, the whole business. Finally, he said, "Well we've got about five minutes left, so let me stop and take questions."

A senior with long hair, whom I recognized from the Kenmore Avenue bus I took to and from school every day, stood and talked. "You said this summer in the paper that you were putting together a youth commission you'd be meeting with to make sure our voices were heard in your county government. When are you going to deliver on that promise?" he asked.

"I did say that, didn't I? Yes, I remember that. What's your name?"

All eight hundred St. Michael's Marauders were staring at the longhair. He took on the appearance of a cornered animal.

"That's Mike Hutchinson," said Dave, punching me in the arm.

"The one with the hot girlfriend on the bus that you always gawk at, Pronotaro," Bob said, punching my other arm.

"It's okay, son," Riley was saying. "I want to know your name because - because I'm going to make you a charter member of the youth commission that I'll have started up by this time next week."

There could not have been more noise. Suddenly, everyone around Mike Hutchinson was congratulating him. Our principal was shaking Riley's hand and grinning. Then I understood what Mayor Frandino was up against. I had been reading about it in the papers, but now I had seen it. Riley could manipulate a crowd like nobody's business.

"Well, we don't have time for any more questions, men," said Riley when it was quiet enough for him to be heard again. But your Principal tells me your name is Michael Hutchinson. My campaign office will be getting hold of you, and thanks for your participation."

"Hutchinson's a pothead," complained Dave.

"I wonder if I can say hello to her." I said.

"His girlfriend?" asked Dave.

"Yeah. Her too," I said.

We were supposed to line up neatly and dismiss in good order. Riley was still up front, shaking hands with members of the faculty. Darcie was preparing to leave with her crew.

"Gotta go to the john really bad," I said to Bob, getting up out of my chair before anyone else in my row of seats.

"Pronotaro!" someone else said. But peer disapproval would not deter me. I had broken bread with her twice during the summer. She would remember me. She already had her jacket on and was talking with some other news people when she saw me.

"Darcie. Hi."

"Ernie - hey! How are you, my friend?"

"I'm good. Just wanted to say hi. So, how's work?"

She shrugged. "It's okay." But in that instant she looked vulnerable. I knew something was wrong and I sent up a quick prayer that I would be the person to fix it.

"Hi from Lamont. He and I are fighting now, but he'd kill me if I didn't say hi."

"Yeah. Well, look. I've gotta run to the next story but tell me, what did you think? Maybe I'll use your opinion tonight on the air."

"I guess I liked him a little better than I thought I would. Mayor Frandino is my man. He's Italian like me, and he visited our family picnic once on the Fourth of July. I've loved him since the second grade."

"Yeah," she said, with a serious look on her face. "He's a good man too, isn't he? Look, I um... Ernie. Thank you so much for coming over to say hi to me. Hang on a second, will you?"

She turned around to a guy who held a big black bag and said to him in a voice that started to break, "Hold this." The guy held her bag as she reached into it and pulled out a tissue. Whether she actually was crying at that moment, I don't know. But she turned back around to me with big, beautiful eyes overflowing with some kind of rawness, and then I was getting hugged.

"It's good to see you, Ernie," she whispered in my ear. Then she backed away just a bit and I saw emotion on her face that made no sense to me until a few months later.

"You're a good, honest kid. And I've got to go now. Take care."

I turned away, savoring the tickling warmth of her whisper and wondering why she thought I was honest. A couple of Good Brothers intercepted me and attempted to bring me to earth by giving me a week of detention for not lining up to leave the assembly with the rest of the cattle. Made me wonder what good it was to be a Marauder if it meant you couldn't step out of line to get a whisper and a hug from a goddess.

15
Retreating Footsteps, Getting Smaller

A pleasant evening later in September, 1971

Steffi wears overalls in the backyard of her Soldier's Circle home. Garden spade in one hand. Sprinkly water pail in the other.

"Sal - I'm not complaining, but it's just so strange to have you around the house so much. Especially during an election. Don't you want to win?"

"Oh, the election will be fine." He kisses her on the cheek. "You've given me three wonderful children and the best apple pie in the city. You deserve to see more of me."

"Are you okay? Both papers say Riley won the debate last night. The damned *Messenger* is all but giving the election to him."

"*Stefania*. Will you stay married to me if I - if I lose this election?"

"Oh, Sallie!" She's now hugging him, there in the back yard, on a sunny, cool late afternoon near the end of September.

"Sallie, Sallie. This is a tough race, I know. I'm sorry."

The hug ends.

"What can I do for you, Mister Mayor?"

"Listen to me. I love you. I've always loved you. I don't deserve you, but I never want to lose you."

"That's sweet," she says. "I think you're in serious need of a vacation, win or lose. Someplace warm this winter. Miami, to go see our little girl and her husband and our grandchild, okay?"

After dinner, they sit in the den and listen to a newsy radio station. The station took a straw poll throughout the county the day after the debate and is predicting that if the election were held now, Frandino would lose by nine points. He takes some courage. The first televised debate might not have helped him, but it hasn't deep-sixed him, either. In two weeks, he'll have another chance at it.

Steffi smiles. "You've made comebacks before, Sallie. But you've been more energetic before. You're not the same this time around."

"Come on, Steff. Ten nights out on the stump over the last two weeks. That's energy."

"I don't know, Sal. I'm beginning to think..." she stops long enough to shift her position on the couch next to him. Her feet are off the floor and she's turned her body toward him. She forces her feet underneath him, and wiggles her toes so that he can feel them on the backside of his legs. "I think you don't want to win this one."

He turns to face her.

"Of course I do. It's like John said - if I can win this, the state party will know I can win an election that involves wealthy suburban towns and I could still be governor one day."

"I'm not convinced. Prove it to me - that you want this."

"Prove? How?"

"Get out of the house, Sal. It's only eight o'clock. Go to the Arkansas, or to Panaro's or Sinatra's. Go where the voters are. Hell, the bars are open 'til four a.m. Go up to Riverside or down to the Ward. Go out around Bailey and Kensington - you never go there and it's time now! If you want this, go and do what you have to do. I'll stay here and hold down the fort."

"I want to be here with you tonight, though."

"There's a time and a place, Sal. Right now it's time to get out and win this election. Or I'll think you're sick and I'll call the doctor on you,

I will."

Meanwhile, a few miles away

Raincloud phoned me that night right after dinner. We hadn't spoken since he invaded football practice with the green bikini girl. My mom's counsel that evening had stopped me just short of hating him for it. So when he called, I told him I had nothing to say to him but if he really needed to talk, he could come over and I'd listen.

It was just past nine in the evening when the door buzzer rang. I could tell from those three quick bursts that it was him. We sat in the living room.

"So I came by to apologize. It was a crappy thing to do, Ernie."

"Why did you do it, then?"

"Jealousy."

"That's a load of crap. You got the girl, not me."

"So what? That's not important."

"Good. It's not important to me either."

"Right. What's important is to be friends. To trust. People have to trust."

"Oh, hey. There's that word again. Trust your teammate to make the right block. Trust your friend not to stab you in the back."

"That's why it was time for me to come talk to you, man. We had that. And now we don't anymore. I don't blame you. The price I paid to start going with Anniselle was our friendship, and the price is too high. I realize that now."

He didn't seem very contrite. I looked at him like he was dirt before answering.

"Well since you said you're jealous of me, let me give you something to be jealous about. Darcie was at our school assembly today. I said hi to her afterward and she whispered to me. Her lips may have brushed up against my ear."

"Nice try. I understand why you'd try to make me jealous. Your babe in the green bikini is a great kisser and then some."

"All right. Don't believe me. I don't care."

"Well don't believe me when I say I'm jealous, Ernie. But it's true. See, you have a dad. You have a future. I don't have either. I'm a Seneca and there's no place for me in this world. If you want, you're gonna work with your dad in his restaurant. Or your dad's gonna make sure you go to college. I don't have any of that."

"Oh, come on," I said.

"See, I've always wanted to be better than you," Raincloud said. "I always wanted to score better on tests than you. I always wanted to be better than you at everything. Because you're the best that red, white and blue America has to offer, Ernie."

"Oh, come on," I repeated.

"You know it's true. You're smarter and more fearless than anyone I know. Except me."

"Whatever."

"Cut out the false modesty, Pronotaro. And I realized the other day, I still want to beat you. I have daydreams about my Bennett Tigers lining up and smacking the snot out of you ugly Catholic Marauders. I realized that I'm still competing against you in school, even though you're not there. I came here tonight because I need you, Ernie. You make me want to live. Because I hate you more than I love you, and I need you to compete against."

"What do you want, to Indian wrestle me? Raincloud, you're so full of crap. One day, so help me God I'm going to beat your brains in so badly that no one will recognize you when I'm done."

"Yeah? Well when the day comes you want to try I'll be waiting for you. That's what I love about you, Ernie."

We sat for a few seconds, looking at each other before I spoke again.

"So does Anniselle have a friend, at least? A somewhat good-looking one who's not a prude?"

Same night, 8:15 p.m.

Frandino drives his station wagon into the night, down Richmond, toward Porter Avenue. Steffi's admonition to get out there and win one for the Gipper, hangs over him. He thinks about the steel plant, the Teachers' Union. He and John Klinglehaus on the rocks. Councilman Snead's failure to endorse his candidacy despite whatever comradeship they may have shared as they chucked stones into the lake on that sad summer afternoon.

Hersch Woodstein has not returned his four phone calls.

Frandino does not want to talk to voters.

He winds up back in the old neighborhood. The night is cool. The old station wagon is parked in front of the lot that once sprouted the house he was raised in.

He's out of the car, wearing a light coat, sitting on what's left of the curb against which he and his childhood buddies used to throw a rubber ball and make up baseball-type games, keeping score. He's thinking of three friends and himself, four eighth-graders whipping that ball against the curb, trying to bare-hand catch it on the rebound to record an out. His whole life has been about keeping score. He looks up at the progress of the road construction. The workers have poured the concrete for what will be an on-ramp to the interstate. Some of the reinforced steel is exposed; he remembers that it was shipped in from Brazil and not Lackawanna. The decision saved city money. Tough choices between keeping the local workforce busy earning salaries, or keeping their kids educated and safe from fires. One unsolvable mess after another.

He watches the twinkle of the red electric letters atop the Statler Hilton Hotel, several blocks away. The "L" in Hilton isn't lighting up with the rest of the letters, and it bothers him. He closes his eyes.

Then he feels a hand, rubbing the nape of his neck. He is aware, for a fleeting moment, that he has just been imagining incandescent blue butterflies.

"Mayor." The voice is barely above a whisper.

"Darcie."

"Sal, finally. On my eleventh visit back here -"

"What the hell, Darcie."

"Yeah." Her voice is soft.

"And your boss is acting like it's a hundred percent my fault."

"I know," she says, her voice just a bit louder.

Frandino does not look up at her. "One of us has got to get out of here," he says. "Right this minute. Why have you been staking me out here?"

"For closure. I know you come here sometimes."

"Please get the hell out of here and leave me be."

"I will, but I needed to tell you how sorry I am."

"I don't care about an apology, and I don't accept it. Just go away."

"Sal - all sorts of things happened inside me when you became in- different. I started coming apart, and Hersch could tell because I couldn't do my job. Then he started to act like my father. I wasn't trying to hurt you by talking to him. I was trying to save me."

Frandino wonders at what she's just said.

"Klinglehaus thinks my career is over. Thinks we'll get slammed on Election Day. Thinks we can't win a fair fight - whatever 'fair' means."

"Sal. I'm really, really sorry."

"Well that just doesn't cut it, Darse. Sorry doesn't put things back to where they were before you even came to this city. Sorry doesn't heal the wound or undo the damage."

"I'll be out of town soon. I promise."

"The sooner the better."

"Yeah. That was the original plan, anyway."

"That's just dandy, isn't it? You go and spread your love around to other mayors. Maybe you can end Yorty's career out in Los Angeles. Or hey, if you want to take down Lindsay in New York, I've got inside information about his sexual fantasies. Rich Daley is older and fatter and more decrepit than me, but if you want to sleep with a powerful man, he sure did show up the whole Democratic Party back in '68 at the convention, didn't he?"

"Okay, you're being really mean. But maybe I deserve it. I'll leave you alone now."

Something in him is rising, pulsing. He scrambles to his feet.

"No, I'm not done." They are facing one another, standing toe-to-toe.

"The drugs, Darcie."

"What are you -"

"Don't gimme that crap. The cocaine. You used it at the hotel in Port Colborne. So that's where your excitement for me came from."

"No, Sal, I -"

"You used sex to get information you could use in stories, and you used coke to make the sex tolerable."

"No! That's just not how it works, not how I -"

"You're nothing but a whore, Darcie. But that's not the worst of it. I - I -"

"You cared about me."

"You've got no right to say that."

"So you cared about me. You think I didn't know that? I knew that about you the minute I walked into your office, Sal. You care about everyone. It's who you are, and by the way it's what made me care about you."

"If you care about me then tell your boss to get off his high horse because I never planned to touch you. You initiated the whole thing."

"Come on, Sal. We both initiated. Who touched who first is only a technicality –"

"Stop it. Now."

"No. Call me names if it makes you feel better, but if I'm a sinner, you're a sinner too. Get over it, for Christ's sake. We cared for one another. There was chemistry between us, something that reached across generations. I'm not responsible for whatever is lacking in your marriage, and I also didn't plan to seduce you. But then we met, and you were kind, much kinder and better than I imagined you'd be. You made me feel butterflies. Yeah, you're an older guy. And a powerful man. And married. And attractive. I'm sorry!"

"Stop it," he says again. Her words are fast and getting faster, like machine gun fire directed toward him.

"No I will not stop it. So I couldn't handle you. But everything that happened between us, Sal - I saw it all happening within the first five seconds of walking into your office. So did you. And neither of us ran away from it."

She's standing there, slightly panting, slightly disheveled.

"Sal. I'm not gonna cry in front of you. I've already cried my ocean. I can't change how you feel. But I didn't intend for any of this - not the hurt I've caused you. But you hurt me, too."

"I live under constant fear of the interview from hell with Woodstein because of you." His index finger is out, shaking, almost touching her nose.

The moment dissolves into the beginning of a mutual smile.

"He's not such a bad guy. I don't understand why you two are in conflict. He cares about the underdogs, too."

"Oh? Did he tell you that before or after he ejaculated?"

A sudden white flash, and pain. Then, everything's dark. His face, hot, stinging. He opens his eyes. She's a bit more mussed in appearance.

"I think I'll leave now," she says.

"Good. This is my sacred ground, not yours."

She turns from him and starts to walk away. He starts to think about how he'll explain a bruise to Steffi. Then she turns around and walks back toward him. He starts to cower.

"Just one more thing before I go," she seethes.

Frandino lowers his arms and turns his palms out toward her.

Her speech is barely above a whisper. "You're the better man."

"Huh?"

"You'll lose the election and honestly, your city may end up the better for it. But you're a much better man than he is." Her eyes linger on his for an extra moment. He reads stubbornness and determination into the look on her face.

Frandino does not watch Darcie walk away. He looks down at his feet, and listens to her footsteps get smaller and smaller as they fade into nothingness.

16
Stop Crying and Win

Junior varsity football at St. Michael's was kicking my tail as the autumn of 1971 progressed. Practices, full of encouragement disguised as insults. Drills pitted me against bigger, faster sophomore linemen who left welts. I'm sure I sustained cracked ribs from the time we were practicing punt coverage and I blew past the first man who was supposed to block me on my way to the punter. The second man - the son of city councilman William Snead - deftly reacted from his setback position, stepped into me and flipped me high into the air. It was not a soft landing.

I nonetheless received my first starting assignment four games into the season. I was informed of this through the poetry of Coach McCoy, a tobacco-chewer from down in the First Ward who did not make his disdain of Northsiders like me a secret. It was a grey, damp day and practice was finishing up when McCoy spoke:

"You offensive linemen! Listen up for Saturday. You're gonna all need to be extra sharp, because our brilliant Kraut guards could not manage to keep their bodies healthy last week against Cardinal Dougherty. So now our brilliant Wops, Ternullo and Pronotaro, will start against Bishop Timon though neither have proven their ability to pull across center and hit anyone. So you other starters - talk to the Wops this week, and get them ready to play."

The yelling intensified over the next two days of practice.

"Pro-No-goddam-Tarro! Where are you supposed to be on thir-ty-one dive?"

"Taking the man out of the three-hole, sir!"

"So why are you tied up with the nose tackle! Are you trying to get our halfback killed?"

"Yes - I mean, no sir!"

"Yes! No! You stupid Eye-talian! What is wrong with you Eye-tal-ians, anyway?"

I hustled back to the offensive huddle.

"Pronotaro! I asked you a question!"

I was not going to win an argument with Coach McCoy, or with the guys in the locker room.

"You better step it up, Pronotaro," one guy threatened, blocking the path to my locker until I pushed past him.

"Pronotaro, you suck. You couldn't make a girls' team." It was Rid-dick, our starting JV halfback. He got right up in my grill, blocking my ac-cess to the showers, shoving me back. I didn't bother returning the shove. I punched him right in the nose. It was on. Twenty guys screaming, cheer-ing. I got Riddick down on the wet tiles, kneed him in the private parts, and punched his face again and again. Some of the varsity guys took a few seconds to yell their approval before pulling me off. I took a look down at Riddick and admired my handiwork - I was used to losing fights to Rain-cloud; so, to make someone lay sniveling in the fetal position was quite a thrill. I looked up to see Coach McCoy standing with his arms crossed and looking at me.

"Pronotaro. My office. Now."

I was screwed.

He closed the door. "Have a seat," he said, gesturing toward a fold-ing chair. His closet-sized office featured a little round cocktail table with a gray Formica top, and a black phone sitting on it. It was the most cluttered room I'd ever seen. He sat in a chair across from me, took a cigarette out of a package, put it in his mouth, and lit it. He looked at me, cigarette dangling out of his mouth. He did not smile.

"Pro-no-freaking-tarro," he mocked in a singsong voice, the Tarreyton bobbing up and down from his lips as he formed syllables. "I can't figure you out. You think you're a tough guy? I haven't seen any decent football out of you yet."

"Yes, sir." I knew from the others, that this is what you were supposed to say when a coach called you into his office.

"And now, the seniors just had to pull you off that wise-ass of a tailback."

"Yes, sir."

Coach McCoy took a long drag off his cigarette, held the smoke in, and forced it out right into my face. I coughed, which made it worse because I had to suck in his dirty air.

"Don't like that, do you?"

"No, sir."

"You'd like to hit me right now, wouldn't you, you little wop?"

"No, sir."

"Don't give me that bullshit. You North Side Eye-talians are too sweet for this game. But I got no choice - I've got to play your candy ass against Bishop Timon this week. Play angry, son. It's your only chance to come out of that game with your neck in one piece. Timon Tigers don't screw around with candy-asses like you. Understand?"

"Yes, sir."

"One more thing. I know you dago bastards vote as a block. You go home and tell your parents that Frandino is a horse's ass. Riley is going to stick it to him so hard on Election Day he'll be crying to his greasy fat dago mommy in heaven. You got that, little wop?"

"Yes, sir."

"Now get the hell out of my office and get your ass ready for Saturday."

The real challenge that day came about a half hour later, on the Kenmore Avenue bus. It was a later bus than I usually took, and crowded. There weren't two seats together, so my teammate Bob and I would have to sit separately. Bob sat first, and I made my way back to the only remaining seat. It was right next to Mike Hutchinson's hot girlfriend. I decided to stand, but she wouldn't let me off the hook.

"You can sit here." Her voice was the maple syrup that pooled in the little squares of my morning waffles and mingled with the melted butter.

I noticed the subjects of the two textbooks that rested on her lap. They clued me that she was probably two years ahead of me. She smiled. I sat.

"You date Mike Hutchinson," I blurbled, sitting with tense knees and shoulders to avoid brushing against her.

"Yeah," came her muttered one-word response. She looked out the window, away from me. When we got to her stop she said a simple "Excuse me." With that, the girl I had privately nicknamed "Miss Exquisiteness" disappeared out the side door of the bus and into the autumn twilight. It would be quite some time before we would again speak to each other.

*****

Frandino finds himself wedged between industrial neighborhoods near the city's geographic center at The Como, a restaurant known more for its food than its ambiance. It anchors one end of a commercial strip up and down South Park Avenue that features a bowling alley, pharmacies and grocery stores, dry cleaners and a coin-op laundry, a few taverns, two bank branches, and the grain scoopers' old union hall building, now quiet. The Como is a stalwart of Old Man Abraham Pincus' home turf. It is where he meets with his Democrats; which include New Dealers like Frandino, but also the more conservative ones who find their support in that other paper, the *Messenger*.

Frandino breathes in the chilly petro-smell that two nearby refineries contribute to the neighborhood's distinctive aura. This is his first face-to-face meeting with Pincus in two years, and his first visit to the Como since the first sex scandal, back in the late 1950s. This time, there are four men: Pincus, Klinglehaus, State Assemblyman Don Downing from Syracuse, who leads the state Democratic caucus; and Frandino. Four cigars. Cocktails. A fried calamari appetizer. Frandino is uncomfortable.

"Our own pollster says Sal is down twelve county-wide," Klinglehaus begins. "He's barely ahead of Riley in the city, and we have twenty-seven days to the election. Without our usual means of leverage, we almost need Riley to self-destruct."

"The worst part for you," says Downing, looking at Frandino, "is your age. Even though you look great, people know you're over sixty. We're nervous about this. For us to get you to governor, there's no tomorrow. You've got to pull this one out."

"Where's your media tail?" Pincus asks the County Chairman.

Klinglehaus glances at the door leading to the main dining room. "They're from Channel Eight tonight," he says. "As long as they know I'm just with you guys and not union people, they're okay sitting in there."

"Shoot - they're damn serious about catching you at something," Downing says.

"They're nothing. The guys from the damned *Messenger* would sit under the table to hear every word of this," Klinglehaus says.

Klinglehaus and Downing puff their cigars. Klinglehaus hasn't made eye contact with Frandino all night.

"You know what I care about the most?" Pincus says. "Healing. Right here. Right at this table."

"What do you mean?" Klinglehaus says.

"Come on, John. You're angry, and you have every right to be. Our candidate displayed a colossal lack of judgment. We finally had what we wanted - a strong upstate, liberal democrat who believes in FDR's New Deal and LBJ's Great Society, and who could have been governor of the most populous state in the union. But now we're being watched by a hostile media and we've got a tough row to hoe."

"You're all acting like we've already lost," Downing says. "I want to hear how we're going to turn this thing around. Too many people have worked too hard for too many years to get the name and face of Sal Frandino out across the entire state."

"The problem is," Klinglehaus says, "Sal can't win a county election without certain tools of influence that have been taken away from us."

Frandino wants to smash John in the mouth for saying that. He doesn't need to cheat in order to...

"I don't accept that and neither do you," Downing shoots back. "You can only buy so many votes at the state level anyway. There's too many eyes on Sal to quit now. The state party expects him to bounce back in these final weeks, because they've seen him do it before. Rocky won't run for governor again, and certainly not against a personal friend like Sal, so the door is wide open. I'm sick of governors from downstate, aren't you? Accepting defeat is not an option."

Frandino finally speaks. "Woodstein at Channel Six holds the trump card. If he gets nervous about the polls showing that we could pull it out, he busts his scoop wide open."

"Trump card?" Downing challenges. "That's like nuclear war. He plays that card, and he destroys a lot more than just your career. He's not that guy. I got fifty bucks that says no matter what happens, he's not gonna do anything to hurt his princess."

Downing's words feel like gentle rain to a thirsty plant. Frandino notices himself leaning forward and focusing on Downing. Pincus puts his hands up to get everyone's attention.

"Look all-a yous," Pincus says. "It's late in the game but we simply must stay the course. I'm a baseball guy – you know how many games are won or lost in the bottom of the ninth? So – you listen to me now."

Pincus gestures with a hand.

"I want it understood that Sal can win, even with the scrutiny we're under." Pincus looks at Frandino. "You nearly pulled it off in '61 even though you had to work against the party apparatus."

"I did. That's true."

"It's a much different climate now," objected Klinglehaus. "There's so many -"

"Stop it." Pincus looks at the county chairman. "Here's what I need from you, John. Humility. We don't need union favors and civil service job promises. Most people still vote for personalities and photos at the end of the day. Look at Sal - still very photogenic, with a reputation as being a decent, likeable, caring human being. Everyone knows he's sold himself out for his city and his constituents over his entire career. Sal, you're as lovable now as you were fifteen years ago when you decided to leave the bench for politics, understand?"

"I'm listening, Abe," says Klinglehaus.

"Don, here's what I need from you." Old Man Pincus turns to Downing. "I need a commitment of money and resources. If the State Democrats agree that Sal could get to the Governor's Mansion, then we need them to put their money and their people where their mouth is. Help us to get the vote out. And starting tomorrow morning, dig up as much dirt on Riley as possible. Constant pressure from the county and state party from now till Election Day. Riley's not squeaky clean. Don, whomever it is that you need to talk to, your hotel room has a phone. When I drive you back there tonight, I suggest you start using it."

"I can do that," Downing replies.

"And you." Pincus aims his eyebeams at Sal Frandino. Frandino's adrenaline begins to rush like it did on that day, so many years ago, when then-County Chairman Pincus first embraced City Judge Frandino's ambition of running for mayor. "Sal, listen to me and listen good. Do you want to be the Governor of New York State?"

The answer comes automatically, without thought. "Yes."

"Then, win this election. Get your Roman Catholic head out of your butt, Sal. You screwed up with the news girl. Okay, it's done. Now get up off the canvas and start running this race like you mean it. Show the state party the Sal Frandino of six or eight years ago. Or hell, even one year ago. You listen to me, Sal. You're a vote magnet. You've just got a little hill to climb. You've been here before. Get off your butt and run this race for the next twenty-seven days for all you're worth."

Frandino feels like soldiers must have felt after a speech from General Patton. "Okay, Abe. I'll do it."

"So let's end this discussion now so we can move on to more pleasant things," Pincus says. Frandino sees the old Democrat shift toward the plate of fried calamari set before them. Then, Pincus looks back up.

"Are we all gonna do whatever it takes to make Sal Frandino the next Erie County Executive, and by extension the next Governor of New York State?"

Frandino studies each of their faces in turn. There is no dissent.

17

Hugs and Hearty Backslaps

Debate venue: Pronotaro Living Room

*R*iley says laboratories such as this one, where graduate students and professors are working with their colleagues at other prominent universities to learn more about the composition of the Earth's crust so mankind can improve methods of farming - even of getting energy out of the rocks - is the best path forward for the area's economy - as traditional manufacturers find it harder to make a buck in and around Buffalo. With the Riley campaign here at the University, I'm Darcie Yeager, Channel Six News."

"Who you gonna vote for, Dad?"

"I haven't made up my mind yet."

"I thought you'd say Frandino, hands down."

"Why is that?"

"Well, why not?"

"And would you be offended if I didn't?"

"Dad. You're supposed to vote for the best guy. He's the best guy."

"Why do you think so?"

"He's the experienced leader, like he says. Riley doesn't know what he's doing. Energy out of rocks - the guy talks like a Martian."

"That's what the Frandino people want you to believe. But there's another way of looking at it."

"Which is?"

"Do you really want to have this conversation?"

"Yeah. I want to know why you'd vote for a space cadet."

"Aw, hell, Ernie. It doesn't matter who the next County Executive is. The area's going downhill either way."

"You're a defeatist! Dad. It doesn't have to be that way."

"All the big companies in the area are chomping at the bit to get out of here. We're headed for some rough times. Makes me wonder who'll be left to come eat at our restaurant."

"Dad. The addition will open in the spring. Your business is getting bigger."

That was true. Ground had been broken in the summer on a new wing to Dad's place; there'd be a new bar and twelve more dinner tables. Me, working there in the spring two days per week after school.

"The addition," he said. "Yeah, I hope so."

"So Dad. I'm starting again at left guard this week, against Bishop Turner. Can you make it?"

"Hmm. Gotta work, Ernie. I don't know."

*****

One week left until Election Day. Frandino hasn't had time for anything but the campaign. Deputy Mayor Dan Spesiak has been running the city while Frandino has been talking to whomever will listen: a convention of local Boy Scout troop leaders in the basement of a church. Three high school football coaches hunched over beer and chicken wings in a South Buffalo saloon. Ladies in Black Rock, in the Polish Cadets hall. He tries his Polish on them, talks about what a great mayor Spesiak - a Pole - will make once Frandino is promoted to County Executive. When he's done, gals thirty years his junior want to pose with him for a picture.

Frandino racks up miles in both a city limo and the family Pontiac wagon, driving or being driven all over the county, meeting and greeting. Chooses the vehicle he'll take to each event based which image the group he's visiting will most appreciate. The day shift workers at the Dunlop plant in Tonawanda present him with a set of four tires, joking with him about the condition of the ones on his blue station wagon. The managers at Fisher Price dress him up like a jack-in-the box and gave him a "Good Humor Award;" Frandino plays it to the hilt and has them in side-splitting laughter. At Republic, the area's second largest steel mill, the union stewards take him on a handshake tour of the entire plant; and then down the road at the Donner Hanna Coke Works he wears special gear and works an hour of the night shift, talking with the workers and then driving a locomotive loaded with coke back into Republic's steel operation. Hitting home runs all over the county. Cheers and well-wishes, hugs and hearty backslaps.

Frandino imagines he is a locomotive full of momentum, steaming full ahead to November 2, the day of reckoning. Taking care to stay clean-shaven, his face feels the razor twice each day. Knowing the value of good breath as he meets people, he refrains from cigars. He sucks on mints. Ducks into a restroom to brush his teeth. Understanding that mind and body are one, he keeps his handball appointments four mornings per week. New suits, new shirts, two new pair of wingtip shoes.

George Barbarello has just written an *Evening Star* column praising Frandino's boundless vigor. He is proving each day that he's still a young man, ready to breathe new fire into the community. He ends his column with this: How might Governor Sal Frandino one day bless the city and county he loves?

*****

He's on television tonight. Bright lights feel hot on his face. Thane Riley is seven feet to his left, behind a matching podium. No live studio audience to help either candidate to gauge how well they may be connecting with voters. There is a group of about two dozen reporters and there, off to left, is Darcie. Frandino avoids eye contact.

In back and to the right, are Steffi and Lou Lombardi. He looks to them; smiles are exchanged. The second and final televised debate is moments away.

For almost forty minutes, the two candidates go at it tooth and nail, articulating their positions, answering questions from the moderator, cross-examining one another. Frandino knows he must be on his game; he's already whittled the lead down to five percentage points according to the friendly *Evening Star*; six according to the *Messenger*. But time's running out. Even an overnight two-or-three point shift in his favor will not be enough. He needs a knockout victory tonight.

It is time for each candidate to make their summation speech. Riley goes first. Frandino listens to what has become a predictable patter of arguments from his opponent:

"Friends, the time is now to end the pattern of back-room politics that have resulted in paralysis. I offer a breath of fresh air..."

"The area's economy is a regional problem that will require a regional approach. I will work to strengthen all that the city and its suburbs have in common to attract new industries..."

"Mayor Frandino may have been an adequate choice for the people of our region at a different point in its history, but today's challenges demand a new breed of man with a new vision to keep our area's economy healthy. Ladies and gentlemen, I am that man, with that vision. God bless you, and I humbly ask for your vote."

He is finished, the young windbag. Frandino feels like a rodeo bull about to be let out of his pen.

"Fellow citizens," he begins. "My opponent says that we've reached a critical point in our history. I agree. Having spent ten of the last fourteen years as mayor of the largest city in all of upstate New York, I've had a front row seat to that history. I have established good working relationships with officials at the Federal, State, and County level. And of course, here in the city I have the privilege of many very rich and important friendships. With captains of industry, labor leaders, the banks who lend the money needed for us all to build our hopes and dreams. With schoolchildren, senior citizens, people in need...

"...I run on my record. Over the past few turbulent years in our country, I have worked closely with community leaders in our city's core to avoid much of the racial strife that has hit very hard in other places. I have worked with the teachers in our city's schools to help ensure that in an era of unprecedented financial challenge, we can still provide a second-to-none education to our children. Even reaching across party lines...

"...Now Mister Riley here, he wants you to believe that I represent an old guard, an old way of thinking that doesn't work anymore. He wants you to believe that somehow, we must think in a completely different way in order to secure our future...

"...He wants us to study how to bring new kinds of businesses to the area. To that, I say, 'What's wrong with the kinds of businesses we've already got?' "

He pauses, turns, and glares at Riley.

"Fellow citizens - fellow workers. My opponent - this man standing here on my left - have you been listening to him? Here is his message to the guys down at Ford; the men up at Chevy. Here's his message to the brave men in Lackawanna, Tonawanda and South Buffalo who for generations have made the steel that for two world wars and even our current conflict have kept our soldiers and sailors safe." Frandino raises his voice. "To all the working people who have carried this nation forward on their backs!" He pauses.

"You. Don't. Matter."

Riley turns to face him. Dangerous eye contact. Frandino continues.

"And to you sir, I say it's very clear that your ideas mean selling out the very fabric of our lives in favor of economic experimentalism that will hasten our ruin. You do not deserve the vote of any thinking person."

"You don't know what you're talking about," Riley interrupts. "You're not even capable of seeing the solutions I offer and you don't understand the new realities. You're showing your ignorance again."

"Oh, you want me to understand realities? I understand, all right. I understand the crushed dreams last year when Volkswagen wanted to build a new plant that will employ thousands, and they choose Tennessee over our county and its string of Republican County Executives. You say those kind of jobs aren't our future... well, the future is now for the mom and dad in Kenmore who want to save money so they can send their three kids to good colleges. The future is now for the dairy farmer down in Elma who wants to make sure there's a big, growing market locally for their products, so their sons can carry on the family business. And you sir, want to sell all of these people out in the name of new ideas you've never even given a name to."

Frandino feels joy. Riley wears his mixture of fear and anger like a bad suit. Frandino bores his eyes into him. Riley points across at him. Frandino flinches.

"The people are too smart to buy any of that talk anymore, Mayor. They can see how the city has crumbled under your watch. Your accomplishments are nothing more than moving money from one bucket to another in response to special interests and your cronies - and Mayor, you talk and act as if your old buckets aren't leaking and leaking badly."

"That's just not true. The record shows I've been very candid about our budget crisis."

"Oh, you want to talk about candid? You, the emperor who's wearing no clothes? All your talk amounts to going thirty years backwards - when I say we should be moving forward. And I understand that you have been caught with your clothes off a time or two recently."

"What?"

"You know very well what I'm talking about."

"That's a low blow, and there's nothing to what you've just insinuated."

"Oh, come on, Mayor Frandino. That cat's out of the bag."

"This is nothing but desperation."

"You know very well! Half the county knows."

"Desperation because your lead is shrinking."

"Gentlemen! Gentlemen!" yells Hersch Woodstein from the back of the room.

"Mayor Frandino, where there's smoke, there's fire. You have a history of -"

"Yeah, I've got a history of public service -"

"- taking advantage of your -"

"Check into my history."

"...women who -"

"I'm mighty damn proud of it."

Riley steps out between the two podiums, three feet from Frandino. "You can't pull the wool over our eyes anymore, you philandering -"

"Gentlemen!" Frandino recognizes an off-duty police detective, dressed in a suit, running up to intervene. Then another.

"Go to commercial!" Hersch's voice cries out.

"Mayor, you can't get away with -"

"If you've got a specific accusation - then make it."

"Easy for you to say! I'd never hurt the people involved."

"Oh, so you don't have a specific accusation. More speculation. Where have we heard this kind of garbage before?"

"From people who knew."

"From Republicans."

"From people who knew."

"Knew about what - character assassination?"

Two big, suited men have positioned themselves between the candidates.

"Stop it! Both of you." Never before has Frandino heard the nasal voice of Hersch Woodstein so loud, and so clear.

*****

The guy who covers the campaign for Channel Ten stands next to Darcie. He's been trying hard to befriend her over the last month. A week earlier he tried, unsuccessfully, to get her to meet him for drinks after a downtown campaign event.

"Finally, we see that these guys are two peas in a pod," he says to her.

"No, they're not," she answers, not bothering to look at him. There is ice in her reply.

"Well either way," the guy recovers, "that was great TV. Makes you hope they kept the cameras rolling, huh?"

Darcie begins to doodle in the margin of her blue-lined note pad.

*****

Frandino is in the back of a limo with Police Commissioner Lombardi seated across from him, and Steffi by his side.

"Well, I think that was just jim-dandy," he says as the vehicle starts to move.

"It was... rather intense," says Steffi.

"You've still got it, Sal," says Lou. "Stick and move. Jab, jab. Uppercut." Lombardi is moving his arms with clenched fists at each end.

"Our friend Mister Riley decided to play rough," Frandino says. He reaches for Steffi's hand and squeezes it, turning to her. "You okay?"

"Are you?" she replies.

"Never been better, just dandy. Hey, we're gonna win this thing." He raises his voice for the driver to hear.

"Take us over to Sinatra's," he says. "John Klinglehaus and the rest of the party folks are waiting. I think we could all use a good, stiff drink."

They arrive in less than five minutes. Frandino walks through the front door, flanked by his wife and by Lou. Cheers erupt. John Klinglehaus leaves the bar and approaches him with a big smile, and open arms.

"Come here, you big, beautiful Italian gorilla!" Klinglehaus says for all to hear.

Klinglehaus hugs Frandino without looking at him.

"How'd it look on the TV screen, John?"

"Sal, you came across great. You're a fighter. You'll fight for the little guy. And who's the little guy?"

"Just about everyone in Erie County," Frandino replies.

"You were great, Sal," Klinglehaus continues as a crowd of mostly-familiar well-wishers begins to press in on them. "Steffi," the chairman continues, "he was great, wasn't he? Tell your husband he was great. You dominated him. You goaded him. We needed you to force a fumble, and you did. Priceless!"

A Puerto Rican mother of four whose husband has been organizing the growing Latino community that nestles in the shadows just north and west of City Hall, is the first person to touch Frandino besides Klinglehaus. Frandino has met with her and her husband three times since April; she's a short, stocky bundle of energy with curly hair and a youthful, pretty face.

"Eh, Maritza! *¿Que tal?*" Frandino's diction, he's been told, is near perfect though his Spanish vocabulary is somewhat limited.

"Meestor Mayor," she says as she hugs him. "What can I speak about this? Special! You are special man. I say, all the way with Frandino in '71!"

"*Muy gracias, amiga!*" He bends and plants a kiss on her cheek. "*Mas patios del recreos nuevos por los chicos.*" He's remembering a promise he's made to her about what will happen in her neighborhood in '72, whether he is Mayor or County Executive.

"Hey! Hey!" Klinglehaus bangs a spoon on a glass, yelling for attention. "Hey, shut up all-a-yous!" His voice booms, and a spat of laughter fills the air, followed by silence.

"Hey - why don't we take a minute to raise a glass - hopefully one that's full of your favorite stuff - and let's drink a toast to our friend. And to his wife, who deserves to be the First Lady more than Pat Nixon."

More laughter, and applause. Steffi wears a big smile.

To the next County Executive and quite probably the next Governor of New York State - the mighty! The tireless! The immortal! Sal Frandino!"

A roar of approval. Frandino looks around at beer bottles and differently-shaped glasses full of red, amber and silvery liquids being raised and quaffed by people who adore him. He feels himself in the flush of victory and goodwill. He turns to Steffi, and kisses her lips. She glows back at him.

*****

Darcie and Hersch Woodstein were together in his car after the debate, heading up Main Street to the Channel Six studios. Hersch never had
the radio on when he drove. There was a light drizzle. The slow, rhythmic
pull and thump of the windshield wipers hypnotized Darcie. She noticed
that his brakes squawked a bit at traffic stops.

Halfway to the studio, Hersch spoke.

"Are you okay?"

"I think so."

After a few seconds' pause, he spoke again. "Gonna be able to go on
the air with me tonight the way we planned? If not, I understand. I have a
Plan B."

"No need, boss. I can handle it."

"Okay. If you're sure."

"I'm sure. I've got coping strategies, you know?"

"Coping strategies... Darcie. No drugs before you go on tonight.
Understand?"

"Yes, dad. Maybe just Coke."

That didn't sound right.

"Cola."

The veteran newsman chuckled just a bit.

"Hersch. Why do you care about me after all I've put everyone
through?"

"Because you make me think of my own girls, I suppose. Thinking
about my daughters makes me want to take care of you."

Darcie glances over at her boss behind the wheel. It's been a week
since the last tears, but she just might cry again. Then she looks at her
wristwatch. It has a small, oval face, a silver wristband and a jewel at
twelve o'clock. She remembers when the band was bright red, all the num-

bers were printed, and a certain cartoon mouse adorned the round face. Yes, she just might cry again. But please, not until after work, when she could do it alone.

"Hersch, less than ninety minutes to air time. How are we gonna spin this?"

"Yes," he says. "The clock is always ticking, isn't it? And we are always spinning."

"Hersch, a favor?"

"What is it?"

"It's Sal. Leave him alone. Have peace talks with him. Please?"

Hersch chuckles. "You keep asking that."

"Herschel."

"We'll see."

18

The Rockpile

I was knocked into tomorrow on the last Thursday afternoon of October, 1971. Our injured starters were healed up and I was riding the pines again that day, until Coach McCoy came by to see me early in the fourth quarter.

"Kid, get ready to play defense," he said. The score had become lopsided, and everyone eventually gets plugged somewhere into the lineup when that happens.

On my very first play I was somehow left unblocked as a big ball carrier ran straight at me. I remember being excited that I was going to make a tackle for negative yards on my first-ever defensive play.

Next thing I remember, McCoy was taking my helmet off and there were people yelling. Then, there's snippets of an ambulance ride. Then, a room with yellow walls and a metal table that I was supposed to be laying on. My arms had sprouted plastic tubes. Both my parents were there, trying to help two guys dressed in green to get me back onto a stainless steel table.

I do remember my left leg buckling under me, and intense pain that made me scream. I hadn't yet understood that my tibia was broken; they just hadn't casted me yet. They gave me a shot of something to calm me, and explained that it was Friday morning.

The doctors didn't want me to read anything, but later in the day they let my mom read me the headlines from the *Evening Star* as long as I promised to behave.

"Troop levels in Vietnam have dropped below 200,000 for the first time in three years," she said, paper in hand.

"Think they'll draft me one day, mom?"

"Hope not."

"I was talking about the football draft. 'Cause playing ball is so much fun."

"Ernie. Was that sarcasm?"

"What do you think?"

"That your sarcasm means you're going to live."

That's when Raincloud walked in.

"Ernie the Pro," Lamont said. "Would've got here sooner, but I'm suiting up with the varsity tomorrow. Practice went late."

"Varsity - you stinkin' big shot."

"Yes, I am. So, what's new?"

I made a face and pointed down at my leg.

"So, I came by to say it couldn't have happened to a nicer guy," he responded. "And oh - I broke it off with Anniselle. She's just a little too scary for me. You gonna let me sign the cast when you get out of here?"

"But I never got to meet her friend."

"Too late. I'm onto her now."

*****

Frandino has been drinking coffee morning, noon and night. Any minute, William Snead is going to walk into the sanctuary of the Michigan Street Baptist Church and meet with Reverend Tom Johnson, John Klinglehaus, and Frandino. They'll talk for a few minutes, then take the ten-minute drive together in the church minibus to the Michigan Street

YMCA. Reporters and neighborhood folks will be there for a Friday night press conference.

Frandino stands in front of a urinal because of the coffee. For an entire month, he hears Klinglehaus' voice in moments such as these. "Keep it in your pants, Sal."

Hands washed. Teeth brushed. Hair re-combed. He emerges from the restroom and rejoins the men in the sanctuary. Snead has arrived.

"Councilman. Thank you for giving up your evening." The men shake hands.

"No. Thank you, Sal. Like I said, we're competitors but it's not personal to me."

"Then why so late to the party, Bill? If it's not personal."

"Touché, Mayor. I guess if I'm honest, I do let my feelings get in the way."

They walk together into the gym, and Frandino remembers some faces from that steamy night in 1968 when they came here intending to barbecue him. Tonight's security detail is light. There is even some polite applause - and only one catcall - as he walks into the gymnasium. Tom Johnson speaks first. Warms the gathering of ninety or so to a bit more enthusiasm, telling them that they must leave this place tonight as "evangelists for Frandino" and get as many people to vote for him as possible. After five minutes, Johnson yields to William Snead. His words are few and powerful. He apologizes to Frandino for letting his personal feelings cloud his better judgment; but now there is a crisis; Thane Riley does not grasp reality and his reckless ideas spell a disaster for the city and county that will hit communities such as the one anchored by Michigan Street, especially hard. Frandino offers the only hope; Frandino could be the governor one day, and Snead could be the mayor. They've pledged to each other in that scenario, Snead says, to work together to bring prosperity right here, to Michigan and Jefferson, and East Utica and William and Sycamore Streets, and to these people who are here tonight.

Snead is winding up. "We're courageous people. We have a history of setting captives free. From this very neighborhood came the Niagara Movement, which became the NAACP. So please, for God's sake, go out on Tuesday and vote in that tradition, and get as many of your friends and neighbors as you can to vote for this man I'm introducing, the man I want to see running the whole state from Albany one day soon, Sal Frandino."

Snead and Frandino clasp hands, and some flashbulbs pop against the backdrop of a muted crowd reaction.

Frandino knows the stakes. This demographic represents over 25,000 votes. Today he's behind three percentage points, according to the Evening Star. These next few minutes can turn the tables.

He faces the crowd and they look back at him, sitting on their hands.

"Thanks for being here tonight. You know, Councilman Snead and I were chatting back at the church, and he was sharing some ideas with me about making affirmative action work. I've resisted some of those ideas - not because I don't want to end discrimination, but I've always been hopeful that we could end it by changing hearts instead of laws. But anyways, experience may show that our hearts may need a little legal help to change for the better."

Frandino pauses, hoping for some positive reaction. There is none. There's a lump in his throat. He looks over at Klinglehaus. Klinglehaus flashes a quick thumbs-up.

"So. I think it's time for us to look carefully - deliberately - at whether minority hiring quotas for all government jobs makes sense for the city and county. This isn't a promise to do anything specific right now - but a promise to examine it and to identify a plan that makes sense for all citizens of our city and county."

He pauses. A smattering of polite applause.

"Some of you might have seen my opponent on TV the other night. He has a much different vision of the area's future than I do. His ideas are reckless for all of us..."

After three minutes of explaining the difference between himself and Riley, Frandino senses that the crowd is still uninspired.

"I know I haven't always connected with many of you the way I would've liked in the past. But as God looks down on us, I can say I've always tried to do what is best and truest for you, and for everyone. So tonight, I ask for your charity as you consider how to vote on Tuesday and whether to convince someone you know to vote for me. Because I think that this time around, your charity toward me is also charity toward yourselves."

A few people clap. Then, there is a pause.

"Mayor Frandino." A woman seated directly in front of him is up out of her chair, speaking. "I been listening very carefully. I been observing this whole campaign. Here's what I think. It don't matter who we vote for. You don't care about us any more than that other man does. You just here tonight trying to win an election."

Murmurs from the crowd. Frandino can detect a few "right ons" and "tell it, sisters."

"Then if you won't believe me, believe Councilman Snead. You heard what he had to say."

"The system won't let me vote for Councilman Snead in this election," comes a male voice from the rear. "We got to choose between Tweedle-Dee and Tweedle-Dum."

The murmuring in the gym picks up steam.

"People!" yells Snead. "It's not like that. It's the difference between night and day."

The crowd is all talking to one another.

Frandino sees a familiar figure dressed in slacks and a button-down shirt, striding to the front. It is Randy. He now stands by Frandino's side.

"Pops, let me talk to them."

"Are you sure?"

"It's time they knew."

Frandino hands him the mic.

"Brothers and sisters! People! Please!"

Sal knows it is time to take two steps back.

"Hey now!" Randy is louder. "I've got something important to say, y'all."

"Listen up," someone shouts. Slowly, the gym quiets.

"I've been going to school. Up at UB. This is my senior year. We always hear men like Rev Johnson say education is the key - knowledge and information are the biggest things we lack. That's what DuBois taught us, too."

Frandino realizes that Randy's raw talent at commanding an audience is now a polished skill. Some voices in the crowd begin to encourage the young orator.

"Now, I've always heard my own friends, and parents of my friends - they say the white man has a conspiracy against us. They will deny us information. They will deny us education. And that's what will keep us enslaved."

Frandino sees Randy finding a way with the crowd, many of whom respond with vocalizations of agreement as though Randy is their pastor.

"Now, I can't see into the minds of men," he continues. "I can't look at a man and know his thoughts. You feel me? But I can see what a man does, and that tells me who the man is. You understanding me? Now my family, we're no better off than your family, most likely. My dad, he's been busting his butt for years doing whatever comes along, see? My family could not afford to send me to college. I want everyone to know that I'm able to go to school because of this man." He points at Sal. Someone gasps.

"Back in those summers when we carried our struggle into the streets - the night the Mayor came right here and stood in this very place... some of you who were here that night remember me. I was right there with you all - expressing my anger, my disappointment, my frustration... in some very strong ways, toward this man right here."

Randy pauses again. Sweet noise, positive crowd noise.

"We chased him out of here that night with our angry voices, and I chased right after him. I cussed him up and down right outside of this building. And he responded by asking what I want to do with my life. Ain't never before that a white man asked me a question like that. And the next day, this man right here, he wrote me a check. He got my high school grades and called his friends at the school and got me enrolled. This man put his reputation on the line for me. And he's still paying for my education, right out of his own pocket. Now in a few months I'll have a degree and I'll be going to law school. This man - he is not part of any conspiracy against us."

There's that polite smattering of applause again. It sounds to Frandino like failure.

The applause stops and then a man yells out, "You ain't goin' to school 'cause of no mayor. It's them drugs you sell me every weekend puttin' money in your pocket." There is laughter as though half the people in the gym have just heard an inside joke.

"No. Mayor writes checks with his name on them. It's his own money. And for my sister, too."

"Who is making you say these things about the mayor?" a woman shouts her question.

"Shut up and let him talk," scolds a man at the woman.

"Cocaine-dealing liar," sounds another voice.

Frandino is focused on Randy. The panic on the kid's face.

Frandino can't help but to glance at the reporters. Their heads are down in their pads, pens moving furiously. Darcie is right there with the rest of them, head down, pen scribbling away.

Frandino will not watch Channel Six's eleven o'clock evening news. He cannot bring himself to watch Hersch and Darcie on the air. He is resigned to hearing about it from Steffi.

He wants to ask Randy questions, but he's not sure he wants to hear the answers.

*****

It is Saturday morning. Frandino has propped his head on his pillow so he can look out through the bedroom window at Soldier's Circle. The morning sun enhances the red and yellow leaves on the still-proud elms. The *Messenger* must be waiting on the front porch. He is down the staircase in his bedclothes. Steffi is making his favorite eggs; sunny side up. The radio is on; that newsy station. He kisses her at the stove.

"Did you catch any of the TV coverage last night?"

"Yes, I watched Six and Ten. Straight reporting that Snead endorsed you. No color commentary."

"So, television ignored us. What's the radio saying this morning?"

"Pretty straight reporting. Not much editorializing."

"Did they mention anything about Randy?"

"Should they have? Was he there?"

Frandino doesn't answer. Instead, he goes to the front porch to retrieve the newspaper. His eyes go right to the headline. It's about a three-alarm fire. He scans the front page. Nothing about the election.

Finally on page three, below the fold: *Snead's Late Frandino Endorsement Raises Questions*. It takes him less than two minutes to read the article. It doesn't say much to either help or damage him. Damn the *Messenger*. Later in the day, the *Evening Star* will hit people's doorsteps. George Barbarello will take better care of him.

Sal drives the family station wagon to a noon rendezvous with what he hopes will be a sizeable crowd at a high school in Clarence, where suburban housing developments are fast-replacing farmland. It is the richest and fastest-growing part of the county, one of Thane Riley's strongholds. A high school band. Grilled food. Don Downing from Syracuse to represent the state party. Lindsay, the mayor of New York City, who's just switched from Republican to Democrat.

Frandino arrives twenty minutes early. Pretty girls, legs exposed to the sunny chill, pass out campaign paraphernalia and welcome the gathering crowd that files into the school auditorium. Men and women tend charcoal grills, offering free hot dogs and hamburgers. Hundreds of red, white and blue balloons, saying 'Frandino in '71.' A big crowd is gathering.

He parks far from the building. He wants to talk with people in the parking lot and work his way to the auditorium slowly.

"Hi, I'm Sal Frandino." Smiles for everyone. Most everyone smiles back and stops to chat. He asks: What should I do in the first ninety days after being sworn in as the County Executive? Do you think people out in the little suburban towns should have to pay for their police and fire departments on their own? Can I count on your support this Tuesday? I hope you'll listen to me thoughtfully when I speak, and may God bless you as you decide how to vote.

He's close to the front steps of the school building, stooping to talk with gorgeous twin girls, all of seven years old, and their mom. He is laughing. The girls tell him how lucky their daddy says they are to have just moved from Bailey and Lovejoy in the city to a huge new home here in Clarence. He tells them to please congratulate their daddy on all the hard work that must have gone into his success. He rises to smile and shake their mother's hand, and she returns the smile. Suddenly, an all-too-familiar personality is standing next to the mom, and a cameraman is shooting him.

"Mayor Frandino, time for a question?"

"Why, yes. Look, girls, it's the lady from Channel Six."

Frandino sees that the girls' mother is now uncomfortable.

"Mayor, Thane Riley says that you've been avoiding places like Clarence, Hamburg, and East Aurora because you know your message and your track record don't hold any promise for these people. Do you have a message for Mister Riley and the Republicans today as you get ready to speak to this crowd?"

Frandino straightens up and allows himself, for the first time in several weeks, to make eye contact with Darcie. Did she just wink?

"Well yes, I sure do. Look around you, at all the people out here who want to come and hear me. Let's let them judge whether my message of veteran leadership and my deep love for the people of this area is the right one. Look at this family - look at these beautiful girls. Public service is a sacred trust of doing right by all the people - I want to do right for these girls and their mom."

"Thank you, Mayor Frandino."

"Thank you, Channel Six. I've got to run inside." He smiles his best campaign smile.

*****

Sunday morning before Election Day. Sal Frandino will spend the day with his two favorite men of the cloth - Father Al Cappello, and Reverend Tom Johnson. After attending the early Mass at Saint Anthony's, he speaks in the church auditorium about the history of the Italians in the city, and then he drives with Father Al to Michigan Street Baptist, where Tom has invited him to speak during the service about the historic contributions that the area's native sons have made to the national civil rights movement. This is much better than Friday's presser with Snead. Frandino speaks about history he knows well. People are respectful in church. He tells them that Jesus wants his church to promote freedom and justice for all. Loud "amens" rise from the congregation. Afterward, people want to pose with him for pictures. They tell him that the story has gotten around about how he helped that boy and his sister go to college and it means a lot to them.

Then, after Father Al sheds his vestments in favor of jeans and a long-sleeved football jersey, it is off to see the fans of the woebegone local team. The loyal supporters are already streaming into the gates of the Old Rockpile by the time the three men arrive; the day has warmed up nicely. Frandino thinks the pretty girls must be more comfortable in their short skirts than they were yesterday in Clarence, as they hand out Frandino literature outside the stadium. The conversations are equal parts sport and politics.

"Think they'll finally win one today, Sal?"

"Absolutely! I've got a priest and a minister with me."

"And I'm praying hard for 'em," one or the other holy man would say.

"Good, because nothing else they've tried this year is working!"

*****

It sure was nice of Mrs. Raincloud to take Lamont and me to a game as our Halloween present. Before my injury she had called in some favors with her boss and secured tickets right behind the home team's bench, just high enough so that we could see what was going on pretty well at either end of the field, and low enough so that when the action was closer to midfield we could hear the shoulder pads pop and the players yell at each other. The Rockpile was the happiest place I knew, even when the team was bad. I was grateful for the sun, which felt warm in between breezes that called for a light jacket. My newly-casted leg throbbed, but that beautiful sun and the way it bounced so sharply off the green grass, the white-and blue clad Herd, the red-and-white clad Redbirds - the Rockpile was intimate and electric, and being there was twenty times better than watching on a big color television.

The game itself was better than expected. The home team hung tough against their heavily favored guests - but that day was memorable for other reasons. During one of the breaks in the action during the second quarter, the public address system announced that Sal Frandino was in attendance with a Catholic priest and a Baptist minister. The entourage got up to acknowledge the applause - two rows below us and about a dozen seats to our right. For the rest of the first half I watched the mayor almost as much as I did the game. I made up my mind to say hello at halftime, and to wish him luck in the election. Lots of people came by to see him after that announcement, to the slight consternation of those who were seated just behind them. The mayor was gracious, his smiling words disarming the people around him; and he moved out into the aisle so that people behind him could see the game. I had heard that he was now within three points of Riley in the polls, so I imagined that he would win. I heard the talk that if he won this election he could be governor within another two years. My heart was proud for us Italians.

Then I saw Coach McCoy with a couple of other big guys, wearing their Thundering Herd jerseys. I laughed out loud to see McCoy wearing number 32; during practices he often dispensed obscene critiques of our J.J. Simpkins, who wore that number. McCoy wouldn't even say the guy's name to us. But there he was, decked out in number 32 with "SIMPKINS" spelled out across the back, and also waiting in line to say hello and shake hands with that horse's ass, Sal Frandino.

"Get a load of this, Lamont," I pointed. "That's my line coach. The guy who hates Italians? The guy who hates the Simp?"

"Wow. That's Coach McCoy?"

I watched McCoy as he shook the mayor's hand. I was trying to read lips. Looked like Coach was being asked for his vote. With a big smile and a slap of the back, the conversation concluded. McCoy bounded up the concrete steps like a big, goofy kid who had just met the real Santa Claus.

I wondered if this meant that all the people who had told the pollsters they would vote for Riley were lying. Maybe Frandino would win in a landslide.

I had to beg Mrs. Raincloud to let me get up at halftime - she wanted me to sit because of my leg - but I gave her a song about how moving around took my mind off the throbbing pain. A total lie, by the way. So Raincloud and I got in line for hot dogs and sodas at halftime and there was McCoy again, three places ahead of us in line.

"Aren't you gonna say hi to your coach?" Raincloud said.

"I don't know. He don't like me a lot and it's mutual."

"He's a fat bastard. He owes you a civil greeting."

"I don't know."

"Wait here - I've got a plan."

With that, Raincloud went up to McCoy and his two friends. I heard him say, "Hey, don't you coach JV at St. Mike's? I think I've seen you on the sidelines at some of their games."

"Yeah, that's right." McCoy was pleased to be recognized. "Hey, you're a big boy - what's your story? You playing somewhere?"

"Nah, I'm just in eighth grade. Trying to decide where to go for high school. Hey, can I introduce you to a friend of mine?"

"If he's in eighth grade and as big as you, a friend of yours is a friend of mine," I heard McCoy say.

Raincloud then led McCoy back to me.

"Oh, maybe you know my friend already," Raincloud said to him.

McCoy got this blank look on his face. "Ternull - I mean, Pronotaro."

"Coach."

"Hey, kid, I'm real sorry about your leg. Hey, good to see you." Then he turned to Raincloud. "So kid, you're still in the eighth grade? Have you thought about where to play in high school?"

"So, Coach!" I cut him off loudly. I was always a little braver when Raincloud was around. McCoy turned to me.

"Yeah, kid?"

I pointed at his jersey, feeling my smirk. "Miami's got the Idiots, but Buffalo's got who?"

"Miami's got the Idiots, but Buffalo's got the Simp," he said, reciting the popular Thundering Herd slogan. Then came that goofy look he wore after he exchanged backslaps with Mayor Frandino. He went back to his place in line.

The food lines were slow. It was three minutes later, in that same line, as McCoy and his friends were being served, when fingers that smelled of ketchup covered my eyes from behind.

"You guys just won't leave me alone, will you?" said a woman's voice from behind me.

I was so excited I could have re-injured my leg as I turned around.

I think Darcie didn't know whether to laugh or cry as she beheld my cast. Lamont, being healthier than me, beat me to the first hug. Hersch Woodstein from Channel Six was with her. I'd never met him in person but I recognized him right away from television. I never realized until that day, how short he was.

Darcie stepped away from Raincloud and looked at me. "And you! What happened? My heart hurts for you!"

"It's nothing," I lied.

"Come here, baby! Oh, Ernie!" I enjoyed her physical expression of sympathy immensely.

"Did you score a touchdown at least?" she said.

"I was on defense."

"Oh." She let the syllable drag out.

"Hey, kid!" I recognized McCoy's voice. Obviously, Coach had been watching her on the tube, fantasizing over her just like any red-blooded male.

"This is one of my players - Pronotaro. They call him Ernie the Pro in the locker room." McCoy smiled. I was not aware he knew that about me.

McCoy turned in the direction of his companions. "Hey, guys! It's the news girl and Herschel Woodstein!"

McCoy's breath smelled strangely like a hospital, even from a few feet away. "So you know Ernie, huh?" he said, addressing Darcie. "That's cool. He was having a great season up until Thursday, and then..." he pointed overdramatically at my cast.

"Look," stepped in Mr. Woodstein. "Here's my card, Coach - um -"

"McCoy. Sean McCoy." That goofy look again. I always had wondered about his first name.

"Coach Sean. Very good. I've got a great idea." It was funny to hear Hersch Woodstein's overly-nasal voice anywhere but on television. It didn't sound nearly as authoritative in person as it did when he was on the air. "Why don't you give me a call during the week, and we'll plan a story. You can tell how you respond when one of your star players gets a major injury. A story about how football coaches care about all the kids and their character development. Call me Wednesday, okay?"

"Umm... sure. We can do that."

"Talk to you then. Excuse us while Darcie catches up with her friends, okay?"

Darcie waited until McCoy was out of earshot and said, "Thanks, Hersch." I understood how much she meant it.

"Guys," she turned back to Raincloud and I. She brightened. "Have you ever sat in the press box before? It's awesome. And you don't have to wait in line for the food. Come on!"

"My mom's out in the stands," Raincloud said. "Can she come, too?"

"Absolutely. I always love talking with her. Go get her. Hersch, you'll wait for Lamont and his mom and bring 'em up to us, right? Come on, Ernie. You need a head start, so you and I can go up now."

That sounded like a plan. I couldn't resist throwing a smile in Raincloud's direction before she and I began to make our way to the press box.

But I was still a little clumsy on my one crutch.

"Ernie, this will never do. Lean on me for support."

Raincloud tried to murder me with his eyes, but his death-stare made me feel more alive. Darcie and I walked arm in arm, her denim-covered leg brushing softly against my own good leg. I noticed that she and I were the same height.

"So, how's life, Ernie the Pro? Other than the leg?" she asked as we negotiated the crowd.

"Interesting. Really kinda good." Which, at that precise moment, was very true.

"I've never been to a pro football game before," Darcie said as if she were confiding some deep, dark secret to me. "Went to a few college games in Iowa, but usually I studied on weekends."

"How do you like it so far?"

"The first half was great! So Ernie, that coach of yours. Are you close with him?"

I couldn't help but laugh. She began to laugh with me. Just like that, we were both laughing hysterically.

"He'd be a lot closer to me if he thought it would help his chances with you," I said in an even voice. And our laughter started again.

There was much more laughter between us the rest of the afternoon. The press box was like a party in heaven. Darcie and Hersch knew all of the important people, and we shared in their fourth-quarter excitement as the game got tight and it began to look like the Thundering Herd just might win one. And the autographs my cast collected! Van and Stan, the announcers who had done the radio play-by-play of the games all the way back to the team's origins. A smart young guy named Costas up from St. Louis to cover the Redbirds. Larry, Jim, Phil and Milt, local sports writers I had idolized from the time I could read. Hersch Woodstein, the most important news anchor in town - and Darcie, who wrote, inside a heart, "Darse Yeager Chan. 6 - Bright Hopes. P.S. You're funny!" Good thing I could cover that part of the cast with clothing. It could've caused problems with the Marauders at school.

Just before the end of the third quarter, Mayor Frandino and his two holy companions came up to the press box because the local radio was giving him thirty seconds between quarters to greet the listeners.

"I know you want to say hi to him," Darcie said to me. "Hersch and I can arrange it. Wait here."

I don't know what they said to him, but he and his heavenly escorts came back with her about five minutes later. He was as wonderful as I knew he'd be. He had a big hug for Mrs. Raincloud and all the right words for Lamont, who talked about being a citizen not of the city or county, but of the Seneca Nation. Frandino seemed so on top of himself that I couldn't see how he'd lose. He could charm an aggravated cobra. The way he found common ground with Lamont, who told him that all the land had been stolen by the Europeans from his ancestors, is something I still think about today when I need to charm the snakes in my life. Then, he was about to sign my cast.

"Mayor, I met you once before. You came to my aunt's picnic on the Fourth of July in 1968."

"You're Claudia Gugliuzza's nephew? Oh, gosh I remember that day! How is she? I haven't seen her since she got promoted."

"She's great. Can you write on my cast, 'Frandino all the way in 71?"

"You bet your life I can. And if I write it here on your cast, I have to make sure it happens that way, don't I?"

19

Here Comes the Wind Off the Lake

The room is packed. Frandino guesses that most of them have eaten dinner. Now they are working on dessert. Steffi has been laboring at it all day. It is warm for this time of year, and dry. Frandino smiles at George Barbarello, who has camera in hand.

The polls will open in thirty-six hours. It's time for the mayor to kick off one of his long-standing rituals. "It is so wonderful to see you all," he beams. "First things first - do you like my wife's apple pie?"

The Frandino's den fills with appreciative noise.

"Well, that's great. Let's get started. I've got this book here, and I'm going to read you a Halloween story. Some people these things really happened, down in another part of New York State, in the Hudson Valley. Raise your hand if you know where that is."

Five, seven, and ten-year-old arms shoot up.

"Let's begin then." Frandino begins to read; he notices that his hands, inexplicably, are shaking as he holds the book. He reads dramatically, wanting to help the kids guess the meaning of unfamiliar words from his tone:

"In the bosom of one of those spacious coves which indent the eastern shore of the Hudson, at that broad expansion of the river denominated by the ancient Dutch navigators the Tappan Zee, and where they always prudently shortened sail, and implored the protection of St. Nicholas when

they crossed..."

He pauses and looks out at his audience, sitting on couches, chairs, pillows on the floor in the den of his residence. Honest love for the neighbor's kids pulses through him.

*****

Monday morning. Warm weather expected right through Election Day. The pundits in this morning's *Messenger* are predicting one of the highest turnouts ever across the entire county. Even this Frandino-bashing paper says that if turnout is as high as expected and Frandino pulls it out, the state Democratic Party may need to look no further for its next gubernatorial candidate. Frandino realizes that his late stretch run has changed the political landscape from Buffalo to Albany to Staten Island and Brooklyn. He has worked too hard over the last three weeks; he's come too far. One more day to run the race for all he's worth.

John Klinglehaus and two Democratic Party volunteers are with him in a rented black sedan, crisscrossing the county. At ten a.m., he meets with the State Parks Commission at a ribbon-cutting ceremony for new facilities in Akron. He must be in Lancaster by eleven for a machinist's union rally. Then, for lunch, it is off to a pumpkin pie eating contest down on the Lakeshore, near Angola. One of Steffi's old high school chums, whose husband moved the family out of the city three years earlier, has become a Lakeshore social scion and has convinced some of her friends that they must meet him, have a chance to sit with him, to understand how good he is. At least the story goes, per Steffi.

One-forty five has him at the Ford plant, just south of the city, a stone's throw from Bethlehem Steel. Eight hundred workers crowd around to hear him thank them for their hard work and pledge that he'll do everything in his power to work with Ford and the banks to keep the plant modern, and relevant, and always there for their families. But he can't stay long; at two-forty-five he is slated to appear in the city, at the Central Park Plaza, to reassure merchants and neighborhood leaders that whatever the election's outcome, he will continue to provide funds as best as he can, from whichever seat of power, to reverse the trend of the plaza's vacancy rate and hints of decay.

Four o'clock finds him in Kenmore, at the village's municipal building and library. Out on a V-shaped lawn with Kenmore's mayor and two of the villages' four trustees, all the Democrats elected to village government. A temporary grandstand has been set up; it is perhaps two-thirds full as the mayor speaks. Then he walks with his entourage, meeting and greeting up and down the busy main thoroughfare.

The last public event of the campaign is within the friendly confines of the Arkansas, back on the West Side. It is billed as the pre-victory celebration dinner. Friends from the neighborhood, friends from City Hall, friends from his childhood. The black sedan stops on the way at Soldier's Circle, and Steffi joins the group. The car stops in front of the familiar restaurant at the corner of Grant and Arkansas. Frandino glances down at his wrist. It is 6:20 p.m.

Millie is at the bar. Smiling, pouring drinks. Wearing a "Frandino in '71" button. Father Al sits at the bar, watching over her. The neighborhood guys are ready to party. A gaggle of Democratic volunteers, many of whom Frandino recognizes, sit at some tables to his left.

The minutes fly past. Conversations are heartfelt, cheerful, warm. In the background, Frandino hears Millie tell this person or that, that they must find a way to get Sal to make a speech. He hopes the occasion will pass him by. After all, he has all of these votes whether he speaks or not.

But now Millie is clanging a wineglass with a fork, and then Al Cappello and others join her. "Speech! Speech!" they chant. He tries to ignore it.

"Sallie." Steffi's elbow makes gentle contact with his side. Her eyes search his face.

He leans over and whispers into her ear. "I'm shot, honey. I just want to enjoy this."

Darts come from her eyes and find their mark in his. Her mouth looks is taut, and small. "See, I knew it all along. You don't want this. You never did."

"Speech! Speech!" It is loud, unified clamor and he knows he can no longer ignore it. He looks toward the bar and finds Millie. Their eyes, and a jerk of her head, communicate an entire series of questions and answers. He gives a tug to Steffi's hand. "Come with me, then," he tells her.

He puts a hand high into the air, and the throng applauds. They clear a path. He and Steffi are behind the bar. Millie shouts, "Ladies and gentlemen - I give you the man and his lady - it's time to hear from Sal!"

The bar glass behind him shakes as the place erupts in cheers. Sal's hands are raised, and he forms a V with his fingers. They settle down, and he talks for six minutes. He is interrupted by applause several times. He thanks his friends for their loyalty over the years. He ends by saying that because of the love they've shown him, whatever the outcome, he has already won. He ends with the words he used to end each session of his court before he became the mayor: "And now friends, what does our Lord require of us but to do justice, and to love kindness, and to walk humbly with our God?"

They know he has finished. He has run the race to the end. He is cut from their cloth, and they love him so very, very much. The Arkansas Lounge is tumultuous with noise. Sal Frandino is a good man who will win, and who will soon be governor of the entire state.

*****

It was fun to be excused from school those first two weeks after my injury. It was Election Day. I was full of excitement for what the evening would bring. The local TV stations would broadcast the election returns beginning at about eight o'clock, shortly after the polls closed. I was listening to my favorite radio station during the afternoon, and every half hour the news brought the same reports of high voter turnout in every precinct in every city and town but giving no clue as to what it might portend.

The preliminary reports came in starting at about 8:15 that night, and in the beginning it wasn't quite as good as I'd hoped. The first tallies were coming in from the Lakeshore suburbs south of Lackawanna, and as expected, Thane Riley did very well there. No reason to panic. Everyone knew it would go that way, and besides, the uber-wealthy Lakeshore was home to less than five percent of the voters.

By 8:30, some of the city and inner suburbs were being added to the tally. Frandino was pulling even. Channel Six showed people downtown at the Statler Hilton, all set to celebrate the mayor's victory, jumping and cheering with excitement. Then they cut away to the Riley camp at a new hotel up in Amherst. Those people were jumping and cheering, too. Darcie held a mic and was asking someone about the mood.

"We feel very, very good," the man said. "The big turnout today helped us. We note some softness in the city for Mayor Frandino and while it's still early, we expect to have a big night..."

I couldn't stand that kind of talk, so I flipped the channel and watched a sitcom for ten minutes before they cut in with an election update. Numbers flashed; with about thirteen percent of the vote counted, Riley had a nine-percentage point lead over Frandino and the commentator talked about how surprised he was to see this. "But it's still early in the night. Let's go to Riley headquarters and get a sense of the mood..."

"No, let's not," I said out loud. I got up off the couch and hobbled to the television, and flipped back to Channel Six. Darcie wouldn't lie to me.

It was about five minutes before nine when Hersch Woodstein appeared for an election update, behind his anchor desk. "With just over thirty percent of the vote in, Republican Thane Riley appears headed for a big victory tonight..."

I'm not sure what he said next. I felt just as crushed as if I was the candidate who was losing. I did what I often did when my team was on TV, playing poorly. Turned it off and did something else for a while. I'd check in later and see if my team was coming back.

I was working a crossword puzzle about twenty minutes after shutting down the tube, when I heard the phone ring. Then, mom's voice.

"Ernie, it's Lamont. Think you can make it over to the phone, honey?"

"Hey, Pronotaro. You watching TV tonight? Your candidate is really something, huh?"

"Yeah." I sounded dejected to myself. "I was watching earlier." There was a pause.

"You mean you stopped watching? Ernie! Turn it back on." Raincloud sounded excited; it wasn't like him to be excited about politics. "Put it on Six. They've got the best coverage, you know. And there's a big story in the making I know you don't want to miss."

It took me a couple of minutes after hanging up to get back over to our big color TV, turn it on, and watch a smiling Thane Riley volunteer answer one of Darcie's interview questions.

"... we were never too concerned," was the first thing I heard him say as the set came on. "We felt we needed to stick with our message that new solutions are needed, and the citizens of the county deserve better than the same old politics. That's what we Republicans represent, and what we're seeing tonight proves that most people in the county agree with us."

I was watching an airplane crash. Could this be? And damn it, that Darcie Yeager was all smiling and acting happy about it. I felt like she was cheating on me.

I decided to watch long enough to see the updated vote count, which they gave at about 9:25. With over one-half the votes counted, including roughly the same number of city as suburban votes included, Riley led with fifty-seven percent to forty-one for Frandino, and two percent for other candidates. I realized at that moment that Sal Frandino would never become the governor of New York State.

"Darse, we've got breaking news from the Statler downtown," Woodstein cut in on her reporting. "Apparently, Mayor Frandino is about to make a speech. Let's switch our viewers to the Statler..."

It was very quiet at the Statler. The mayor came out with a guy I figured was John Klinglehaus, whom I'd never seen before but whom I'd heard of and had seen caricatured in editorial cartoons. And a slim and attractive, if older, woman. The reporter said it was the mayor's wife. Frandino stood behind a podium flanked by his wife and Klinglehaus. All three of them looked tired. I had never seen Sal Frandino look so old before. He'd aged fifteen years since he signed my cast at the Rockpile just two days earlier.

"Tonight, I'm happy to report that I'm the mayor of this, the greatest city on earth. Tomorrow, I will still be the mayor of this wonderful place," he said. "True to my calling, I will be in the office sometime between seven and seven-thirty A.M., and I expect to see my many partners in city government there with me, doing the will of the people who elected me to that office."

The people applauded him.

"I want to congratulate my opponent on a job well done. It has been a tough and sometimes emotional campaign, but in the end he is a good man who also wants what's best for us. We will not always agree on how to make it happen, but I pledge tonight that I will work for cooperation between the city and county governments in the future so that we may all prosper."

I got up from the sofa and worked my way over to the phone. I dialed a familiar number. I delivered my message the moment I heard Lamont's voice.

"Raincloud, you suck."

"Oh, Ernie," he said, in a falsetto. "You poor thing, you need a head start. Let's walk arm in arm so I can help you up to the press box and then I'll draw a heart and a smiley face on your cast."

"So, how many votes did the Seneca candidate get tonight?" I said.

"Seneca don't play these bullshit Republican and Democrat games, Ernie."

20
St. Anthony's Parish. Waiting

December 6, 1971

Frandino looks over the lake through the sixth-floor picture window in the mayor's office. The view is gray. Wind gusts are trying to maul him through the large window pane. The glass utters a humming objection against the buffeting blasts of near-freezing cold that are sweeping in from across the entire length of Lake Erie. The bright autumn warmth that people call "Indian Summer" in these parts, is gone. Sal Frandino is just another working stiff who will be tortured in winter's icy embrace.

Embrace. Steffi has grown distant since the election. Feels as if they are just going through the motions of life together. She must have found out. Damn it, he was supposed to get everything right this time around as mayor.

He has cancelled an appointment. No energy this morning to deal with a school superintendent who is angry about the lack of promised money. Instead, he broods over the churning lake. Any day now, the waters will condense into massive snow clouds. It will happen when the next blast of sub-freezing air pushes in from the west. All will be buried in white. Six inches, a foot, sometimes eighteen inches at a time. He remembers a snippet from a psalm he studied as a boy in his Catechism classes:

Cleanse me with hyssop, make me whiter than snow...

God will bring snow, but it will not cleanse. Year after year the whiteness does not last. Plows turn it into snow banks, churning up dirt that will mix into the mounds. Soot from the cars and the factories will settle atop the piles and turn them grayer still. Weeks of cold whiteness fading to cold grayness; virgin December becoming icy January grime as people soil the air in their striving to get ahead. Frandino thinks about his soul. Shakes his head.

It is not just that he was bombed by an electoral margin of fourteen percentage points and that his political career is at its dead end. The money promised from the governor for the schools is being blocked in the State Legislature. What a horrible message to have to deliver to the city.

He walks back to his desk and sinks into his chair. He scans the papers on his desk; there are three stacks. He fears for the hidden booby traps that may turn up in those stacks.

He props his elbows on the desk and rests his face in his hands. The voices start again. Voices of his daughter when she was seven years old, the center of his universe. Now she lives far away, with a husband and child of her own. Steffi's voice, asking, "Sallie, how could you do this to me!" John Klinglehaus stands by her side: "I want to know too, you stupid old dago!" William Snead, urging him to be a man of his word and to make hiring quotas in city government a reality.

Darcie's voice. Always trying to redeem herself. He gives yet more attention to it until it is nearly real, and then he catches himself being swallowed up in an imaginary conversation with her at the Rockpile on that day he was there with the holy men and she and Hersch hinted that it would be a good idea to say hello to that kid with the cast who turned out to be Claudia Gugliuzza's nephew.

He is due at the Knights of Columbus social hall this evening. A

Democratic fundraiser, nominally in his honor. A lot of the promised State party money never materialized after the defeat. A modest $50 a plate with more contributions asked after the meal, will help.

He arrives after the rest of the head table has already been seated. Hasn't seen John Klinglehaus since election night, and he dreads the reunion. He spies the empty chair - his chair - between Klinglehaus and Pincus. There is a stir as the men at the head table become aware that Frandino has walked into the room. Frandino forces a smile. Pulls his chair out and sits.

Klinglehaus turns to him. "Sal," he says, and puts a hand on Frandino's shoulder.

Frandino looks back, wordlessly.

"You son of a gun," Klinglehaus says, hand still on Frandino's shoulder. "You're one lucky man."

Frandino can feel the puzzlement on his face.

"Yeah. Ain't you heard, Sal?" The party chairman's voice is low, and serious. "Steffi loves you. She's crazy about you."

*****

Just past 5 p.m. the next day, Father Al sits in his study at St. Anthony's, wearing his workweek uniform: black button-down shirt and trousers, black patent leather shoes, and a collar that features a near-perfect square of exposed white fabric under his throat. Frandino looks across the coffee table at his friend. They sit, sipping Frangelico. Behind the priest is a wall covered in bookshelves that are full.

"The serious personal stuff stays in the room, right?" Frandino asks.

"It's a holy sacrament," the priest answers. "The Lord zaps me if I rat you out to anyone."

"So. Getting creamed back on Election Day. It took the starch out of me. City Hall is as high as I ever get."

"Puts you in touch with your - what, mortality? Limitations?"

"Everything since 8 p.m. on November 2 feels like a repudiation of my life."

Father Al looks back at him.

"The days are hard," Frandino continues. "There's no joy in my work, nothing to look forward to. The problems we face. Always knowing about bad news a few days before everyone else. Al, I never thought I'd say this but ... I want out."

"Out of what?"

Frandino squirms in his chair.

"I don't want my job anymore. I want to escape, to go far away. I can't deal with it all."

"Deal with all of what?"

Frandino takes a sip of Frangelico and holds it in his mouth before swallowing.

"Time. Getting older. Getting pushed to my limit and I still haven't done enough. Demands of other people. Trying to buck history. It feels like we're being sucked forward into a black hole and it's too powerful for any of us."

"Who's 'we?' Am I getting sucked into the black hole too?" the priest asks.

Frandino raises his voice. "I can't save the city. I'm scared that I'm just making things worse. Crap, Al, I tore down the whole neighborhood – my neighborhood – west of Niagara Street. It was supposed to get re-developed but now it's time for the developers to make proposals and no-body's stepping up. I'll be forever known as the guy who tore it down and replaced it with nothing but weeds and piles of leftover road construction materials. My soul aches over it."

The two men exchange silence. Father Al grew up in that neighborhood, too.

"Not to say that isn't important," the priest says. "But if there's anything else you need to get off your chest, this is as good a night as any."

"My marriage," Frandino spits out of his mouth.

"Now we're getting somewhere. What about it?"

"I screwed up again this year."

"The lady bartender?"

"No, no. Not her."

"Good." Father Al seems relieved.

"Well? Who, then? Or maybe it doesn't matter?"

"That girl at Channel Six."

"Um hmm."

Frandino feels a weird mixture of pride and shame. He knows that both are bad for him.

"She swore to secrecy, and it seems everyone in the city knows."

"Mmm... rumors, Sal. That's all most people know, and from where I sit I think a good many people who are loyal to you don't buy it. But your enemies? Yeah, there's been talk since sometime around the first of August."

"Did it cost me the election?"

"Might've swayed some votes, but I think you lost for other reasons."

"Such as?"

Father Al rises. "Oh, no you don't. Don't make this about politics or public policy. Your sexual excursion cost you something far more valuable than the election, and that's what we're here to talk about."

"Yeah. Steffi must believe the rumors. She's so cold toward me nowadays. Guess during the campaign she decided to ignore it and stand by me, just to see if I could win."

"I'm talking about something bigger than your marriage, Sal." Father Al is standing at his office window, his backside framed by the flood-light-illuminated winter garden of pansies and evergreen shrubbery just outside the window. A church garden, enclosed by a brick wall that keeps the rest of the city out of view.

"Then, what?" Frandino is still sitting as he asks.

"Your manhood, Sal. You've become the old guy who doesn't think life's worth living. You're acting like a shadow of yourself."

The priest turns away from his garden and continues to talk as he re-seats himself facing Frandino.

"You're in a tailspin. It's not because your sin made you a different man. It's because you've let yourself become haunted by your sin. And when a man is seeing ghosts -"

"I see her ghost. I hear her voice. Darcie, I mean."

"Well, that's got to stop."

"How?"

"Saint Augustine said that sin happens when we desire something less than our greatest good. He said a man stops being haunted by his sins when he begins to desire something even better than sin. And for you, Sal, that something better is Steffi. That something better is a restored marriage."

Frandino sighs.

"Sal, you've made a pretty good confession for now. But your work is just beginning. I'll say the absolution prayer for you, and then for your penance you must start paying more attention to Steffi and figure out how to fix what's wrong between the two of you."

"Can't I just say prayers for my penance?"

Father Al smiles, and takes a fresh mouthful of Frangelico and swallows. "No, because you're not ten years old anymore. Besides, Holy Cross Church is right down the street," he says. "If you don't like the way I hear your confession, maybe you can go try one of their priests."

"Scintillating. They'll put me in the clammy little booth, draw the curtain, and I'll be sitting in the pitch dark. The whole nine yards."

"That, they will. But before you run out on me to go visit the church up the street, let me say the absolution prayer now, okay? Oh, and one other thing I think you need to hear. About tearing down our neighborhood."

"Oh, boy. Here it comes. Alright, I'm bracing myself."

"Worrying about your place in history isn't about your soul. It's about your ego."

Frandino's mouth opens slightly, but there are no words.

21
Feast of St. Valentine and Other Songs

February, 1972

Sundays after church and Thursdays after school, I rode shotgun in our big Buick. Dad drove down Elmwood, beyond the tree-framed Albright-Knox Art Gallery to the Scajacquada Expressway. There, he'd steer us onto a pothole-laced ramp - exposing our car tires to bare metal girders every thirty feet or so - and we'd bounce our way down onto the expressway. Passing the state college and the Mentholatum Deep Heating Rub plant, we'd reach the river. Ramps could carry us left toward downtown, or right toward Grand Island and Niagara Falls. We'd go left, pay the fifteen-cent toll, and follow the river toward the clump of taller buildings.

We had a birds-eye view of what was going up and coming down in the city's core. Swing east on the 190 and survey the industry of the First Ward and the Valley, where the refinery towers were always blazing - even at night, never failing to cast an orange-yellow glow on the industrial panorama. Ponder the sunlight echoing off the windows of the hulking, abandoned Larkin Soap Company warehouse. Consider the old, gray tower of the Central Terminal, rising above the surrounding neighborhoods like an uncircumcised hose nozzle about to shoot liquid straight up. Slice through the aging residential neighborhoods of Kaisertown and Cazenovia, and finally, the city limits now in sight, exit the highway and cut through a tight-knit neighborhood of frame houses with postage-stamp lawns.

Work our way toward Clinton Street and then into West Seneca, where the road took on a vaguely rural feel. Five or six minutes later came a bend in the road, a warning sign to reduce our speed. Ease in among the several dozen homes, taverns, gas stations and little stores that constituted the older village of Gardenville, nestled amidst newer suburban sprawl. In the heart of the village sat our restaurant.

"How's business?" I might ask.

"You're there twice a week now. What do you think, Ernie?"

"I think we're holding our own. Still nervous about opening the addition?"

"Too late for nerves. It'll be ready in April. We'll do okay with it for a few years, I suppose."

"The food is good. People will come."

"Hey Ernie. It's almost Valentine's Day. How come you never talk about girls with me?"

"We do, Dad. You tell me to be confident and always positive."

"And?"

"I'm only a freshman in high school, Dad. Most high school girls want an older guy."

"What about Esther? You're a year older than her. I've seen you and her talking."

"We're just friends, Dad. No sparks there."

"What's wrong with her? Not a thing, if you ask me."

"She's nuts over her figure skating partner. Besides, your other son burns a candle for her."

"One of you guys better do something about her before it's too late."

"It already is. This summer she's gonna move with her parents someplace down near New York City."

Détente

Two city blocks from the Arkansas, the Roseland stands a world away. No mere local gin joint. Impress, and be impressed. Sal Frandino made his reservations weeks in advance. The feast of St. Valentine.

The Frandino's table affords them privacy save for the ubiquitous dining room staff. They have given their drink orders and have received warm bread and oil. Sal looks at his wife. She shrugs. Gestures with both hands.

"Sal. Would you say something?"

"Me? Would you?"

"Sallie, you've been like a tortoise since the election. You never talk. I was shocked you brought me here. What do you want?"

"Do you love me, Steff?"

Her laughter feels like shrapnel hitting him in the face, arms, and chest. "Oh, you," she points at him for a moment with an index finger. A few more dribbles of laughter.

"Don't make this about me, Sal. This is all about you, and you know it. So out with it."

"Happy St. Valentine's Day, Steffi." He reaches down into a trouser pocket, takes out a small gift box, and puts it on the table between them.

"I don't want a box from you, Sal. I want words. I want to know what's going on with you. I want you to see the doctor. Lately, you're half dead. You go into the office late and come home early. You don't talk to me. There's a stack of notes piling up from friends and well-wishers that you haven't touched. You had your daughter and son-in-law concerned about you at Christmastime."

Frandino remains silent.

"I think whatever it is that's bugging you is not just that you lost an election. You're keeping a secret from me. That's what I think."

"Steff, I don't have any secrets."

"Oh, shush." Her finger is suddenly across the table, over his mouth. "I wasn't born yesterday."

He gently takes hold of her hand and moves it away from his mouth. He guides it back to her side of the table and lets it go.

"So," he says. Feels himself like a child about to dive off the high board for the first time. "You must know what's bothering me."

"I've got ears. I hear things. You were out late a lot, slept at City Hall a lot last year. So, who were you busy with?"

"Do you believe them?"

"You just admitted it. What does it matter now if I did or didn't believe them?"

"I didn't admit anything. I just asked if you knew what's been eating at me."

"Oh, I didn't just hear an admission? Okay then. Tell me."

"You want to know what's wrong. The job itself - it's terrible these days. This city - there's just too much going against us now. And the rumors about me sleeping around? Sure, they're hard to hear."

Sal watches as Steffi sips her drink and replaces the glass on the table with an inordinate amount of fuss.

"Must uh, must have been hard for you to hear, too," he offers. She looks up at him.

"Sal. I'm gonna ask you one time. Point blank, yes or no. Did you get intimate with Darcie Yeager? Or anyone else for that matter?"

"No. We met each other through our jobs. After all she was covering the election. We talked a bunch, even in my office. But, I never touched her."

Frandino watches his wife exhale as though she's exhaling fifty pounds of grief. He admires how she's made up her eyes for the evening.

"Okay, then," she says. "*Basta* with all of this. We're done talking about it. And I don't ever want her name mentioned in my presence."

He feels himself brighten a bit. She returns a hint of a smile.

April, 1972: Egg Laid. Bird Hatched

Even the music on the radio was beginning to make Randy's Michigan Street neighborhood brighter. The sun was shining more and the snow on the ground had disappeared, but for the grimy remains of the plow-piles in some parking lots. His wool cap and heavy winter coat: no longer needed. Randy even imagined that today, once he got into this, his first car - a red 1965 Chevy Impala purchased just a week earlier - that he'd drive to school with the windows rolled down. But first, he had an errand.

It would take him only ten minutes to run the stuff over to Shantelle, who waited at a bus stop at the corner of Ferry and Grider Streets. She was a good kid; a friend of his sister's, modest and well-mannered. Had just turned eighteen and had scored a job downtown at a department store. Always dressed nice. Always applied just the right touch of makeup. The last couple of years had been kind to her, transforming her from girl to woman. A smooth voice from Philly was on the radio as the car began to roll: *Betcha by golly wow - you're the one that I've been waiting for, forever...*

Just around the corner from graduation. Then, grad school in a different part of the state, maybe Syracuse. Maybe even take a year off first, to make a little more money and put himself in better position to take care of himself in a new town. But grad school - law school! He'd studied too hard for it not to happen.

There she was, at the bus stop in front of the corner tavern just as she had waited there for him there on those past occasions.

"Hey, young lady." He smiled through the open passenger-side window. "Going my way? I could take you to Main Street."

"Thanks, but I want to ride the bus this morning," she said as she let herself into the car. "So. What have you got for me?"

"Um, uh..." He reached down into a pocket and removed a plastic baggie. "Here. Same stuff as you got from me last time. Quality high for a quality girl."

"Um... thanks," she said, taking the baggie. "Seven?"

"Seven," he said. She handed him some crisp new singles. "Count 'em if you want."

"I'll count 'em later." He couldn't help but to smile at her. "I trust you."

"That's um... nice, Randy. Well look, bus is coming, and you got class, so..." She opened the car door for herself.

"Let me know about next time, now," he said, feeling himself glow toward her.

"Yeah. I'll call the house," she replied, turning to leave.

Randy was driving back down East Ferry Street. He planned to make a right on Fillmore and hook up with Main Street two miles south of the University. He'd be to class on time. Grateful, as he put the money on the seat next to him, that he now could buy lunch. Cash was always at a premium, what with a car payment and insurance.

He had just turned onto Fillmore Avenue when he heard the siren from behind. He looked into the rear view mirror and saw the flashing lights. He thought about the gas pedal for a moment. Too much traffic. He pulled to the curb.

*****

Hersch Woodstein sat in his office holding the letter that he'd just read. Its contents felt to him like a knife wound. People don't come to this town just to use it as a stepping stone to a bigger market, do they? Wasn't this the kind of place where a gal like Darcie Yeager could make a great career for herself?

He put the piece of paper down on the desk, and re-read the words it contained. It was not a long letter. Then he picked up the phone and dialed.

"Darse? Yeah, it's me. I've read your letter. First, let me say that I'm sad..."

"...Sure, I will help. I will say nothing but positive things when WRC calls me. I just wish you'd make your future here with us..."

"...You're welcome, Darcie. I'm glad you feel that way about our time together. How soon do you think they'll want you..."

"...Well look, between now and then there's an important story down at City Hall I think it would be good for you to break. You'll still be here for a few weeks, and this one'll look real good on your resume. Can we meet to discuss later this morning, say in my office at eleven?"

*****

Sal Frandino thinks, as he sits in his chair behind the big desk in his office, lit cigar in hand, that maybe he's reached a time in his life when it is appropriate to relax more and worry less. He has started a habit of being home before 6 p.m. and to take walks with Steffi. She has been a willing, if not effervescent, participant. He's not played handball in weeks; and that's okay. Doctor Bumbalo always touted walking as a great form of exercise. Here it is, mid-April, and while the tree limbs are still a couple of weeks away from greening up, the mornings are earlier; the evenings longer; and the daytimes warmer.

Frandino thinks his marriage is a long way from healthy, but they are together, walking and talking, taking turns in the kitchen at home making each other a bite to eat or perhaps trundling over to Elmwood and Bidwell, where a number of restaurants await and a mixture of locals and kids from the state college a mile up the avenue come to eat, drink and play.

He has begun, over the past month, to shift more responsibilities of city government to deputy mayor Spesiak. For the first time in years, Frandino isn't letting the job, or guilt, kill him slowly.

The telephone brings his focus back to today.

"Yes, Phyllis..."

"Oh, I see. Well, where is he now?"

"...Oh, he is. And you say Lou wants to fill me in first?"

"...Well, okay then. Tell Lou I'll be there in fifteen, twenty minutes."

Frandino walks three city blocks to Central Booking. It is sunny and pleasant - light jacket weather. He is no longer thinking about walks with Steffi or dinners with new friends out on Elmwood. He thinks like a father.

Frandino sees Lombardi waiting for him outside the building. "Let me brief you on what we know," Lombardi says.

Having been briefed, Sal Frandino is led into a room with mirrors and a conference table with plain wooden chairs. A young man sits, hands cuffed to one another behind him, ankle cuffs further restricting him.

Frandino says nothing. He chooses the chair on the young man's left and sits. Neither man says a word. The prisoner looks frightened, perhaps even more so now that he has recognized Frandino.

"Do you want an attorney?" Frandino deadpans.

"Mayor," the prisoner answers and droops his shoulders. Frandino recognizes that this gesture is not flip; it is one of hopelessness.

"Do you want an attorney?" the mayor repeats. "Because this is very serious."

The prisoner turns his head to face Frandino.

"Do we need an attorney present so I can talk to you?" says the mayor. "You've been studying. You know it's your choice."

"No, sir."

"Well, then. Do you want to sell me some cocaine?"

"Sir?"

Frandino sounds less calm to himself this time. "Do you - want to sell me - some cocaine?"

"No, sir."

Frandino nods.

"You know," Frandino says, "I'm no angel. A man lives his life long enough, and if he truly lives he'll have his share of regrets. Randy, I took a chance on you several years ago. Maybe that night, I needed you as much as you needed me but still, I took a chance. Reverend's words told me the sky's the limit for you."

The prisoner's face is toward the floor.

"You're supposed to be different from the guys we see down here in this building - thieves, rapists, drug dealers, mafia wannabes."

Frandino studies the prisoner for long, silent moments.

"I thought you were different," Frandino says.

With that, Frandino slides the chair out from beneath himself and gets to his feet. He walks to the door.

"Mayor, sir."

Frandino stops and turns back toward the prisoner.

"You've got something to say to me?"

"Yes. That I'm really sorry."

"Oh. You're sorry. Okay." Frandino turns back toward the door.

"Mayor." Frandino turns again, and Randy's face appears wild with fear.

"Mayor Frandino. Please."

"Please what?"

"Please. I want to be different. I don't use it. Much... I don't ... I don't like that I sell it. I want to stop. My problem is not drugs. It's money. It's the easiest way for me to have a few bucks in my pocket."

"Oh. I suppose that makes it okay. Let me think about it. Hmm. So, I've given it some thought. It's not okay."

"Mayor, I would never ask you to do more than you've done. I know this is my fault. I - I just wanted some better clothes to fit in with everyone at school. Sometimes I just want a hamburger. My dad... he just don't have that kind of coin. Mayor, that's my explanation."

Frandino knows the prisoner is being honest. These topics have come up between them before, except for the cocaine. Frandino walks back to the prisoner and re-seats himself.

"Here's the deal. I'm finished giving you money."

"I understand."

"But you can work for it. I can get you a job that pays some. With the city, maybe with Streets and Sanitation."

"Mayor. Yes, sir. But..." The prisoner moves his hands and feet. Metallic noises. "I'm under arrest."

Frandino raises up off his seat and slides it so that it touches the prisoner's chair. Then, he sits so that his knees are touching Randy's knees.

"Do you want to make this situation right with me?"

"Yes, I do."

Frandino has the collar of the prisoner's shirt in his right fist and he jerks the prisoner right up into his own face. The prisoner cries out. Frandino talks fast.

"Then here's what I need from you. I'm gonna leave this room, and you're gonna sit and wait about thirty minutes for a detective to come in and ask you to identify who you've been getting your cocaine from. And then, he will release you into your own custody. During these next thirty minutes, you're going to think long and hard about your life and the opportunities that you've been given and what you want to do with them. Do I make myself clear?"

"Yes. Yes, sir."

"If you lie to us about who you're getting your drugs from, I will accompany the officers who re-arrest you. And I will have your ass thrown in jail for a very long time. *Capisci?*"

"I *capisci*."

"Good. And by the way, you say *'capisco'* when want to tell me in Dante's Italian that *you* understand something *I* said."

"I *capisco*."

"Good. Then, after about a week, you're going to get a call at your house from Phyllis, and she will get you going on the paperwork you need to get a part-time job with the city. And you will show up for that job, and you will work your ass off in that job, and in exchange for that hard work we will pay you. Got it?"

"I do."

"So you're going to go free today, son. And then you're never going to sell an illegal substance again. Not in my city, not in this county, not in New York State, not anywhere at any time. Or so help me God, I will make an example out of you and you'll rot in jail. Even if I'm dead I will come back and make your life as miserable as possible. Do I make myself clear?"

"Yes."

Frandino lets Randy's collar go.

"Aaah!"

Frandino is through the door. He walks up a flight of stairs and into an office, where Lou Lombardi sits, waiting. Frandino leans on a window sill and looks at his chief of police.

"How'd it go, Sal?"

"As expected. Let him sit for an hour or two, then send in a detective and he'll sing."

May 20, 1972

Over the last ten days, Hersch Woodstein had been hinting at his dissatisfaction over Darcie's failure to break a story that he told her she should own before leaving town. Yes, she had made a few calls. Yes, she checked out some places where men allegedly involved were said to congregate. But she had not followed up aggressively. Couldn't the whole thing please go away?

It had been a day and a half since John Falzarini returned one of her half-hearted calls. Maybe he was half-hearted, too. She had placed a call into his office over two weeks earlier, and never once followed up. Just like the other ten or so calls she made from the list Hersch had provided.

She looked at the little yellow note from a Channel Six secretary that said, "J. Falzarini – returned call." Just beneath those words, seven digits beginning with the now-familiar "88" combination which meant the caller's phone was located on the West Side.

She dialed. Braced herself like someone about to open a door that is bound to have a stinking dead animal - or human - on the other side.

"Yeah. This is the Falz," a gruff voice said after three rings.

"Mr. Falzarini, Darcie Yeager of Channel Six News. Sir, is this a good time to talk?"

"Oh." The man's voice softened. "Miss Darcie Yeager."

"Yes sir. If you have time I'd like to ask you some questions about the city payroll."

"Yes, to you I'll talk. Can we meet somewhere? I'll behave myself, ma'am. Honest. I could um… I could meet you in fifteen minutes if you'd like."

She was in the car, heading towards Darone's Fargo Grill on Niagara Street. Hersch has told her this is something that can propel her into a long and successful career: Breaking a brand new story so big for her audience that people would talk about it for years. A story that would re-make some villains into heroes, and re-cast heroes as villains.

22
La Cosa Nostra

May 22, 1972

Forty-eight hours interviewing underworld figures, talking with disaffected city employees who took their work seriously. Consulting with cub reporters from the city's two newspapers. Piecing together a jigsaw puzzle of on-and-off-the-record statements, circumstances, events that don't seem random anymore.

Over her last forty-eight hours, Darcie had managed six hours of sleep.

Over the last forty-eight hours, whether sleeping or awake, she was trying to convince herself that Sal Frandino did not matter to her anymore.

She had been up to Lewiston, on a posh residential street known to some as the Den of the Dons, talking with men whom others referred to as bosses. She had been in hardware stores, bowling alleys, public parks. A diverse sampling of men. Some cooperative; others not so much. Her personal safety, should she ever come back to ask these kinds of questions again, had been twice threatened.

Now she sat with her boss, in his office. Her wristwatch is less than a week old. Mickey's big arm is pointing straight up, and his little arm points to the nine. It's a serious conversation, yet it is as peaceful as it had been for her since she first talked to The Falz that previous Saturday evening.

"So," Woodstein said with a tone that indicates that he's heard enough. "Given what we know and who's agreed to be on camera, we do two things."

"Right. One, we go public. How soon?"

"No later than mid-week is best for something like this. I think we plan for the Wednesday six o'clock show."

"Okay. Falzarini is expecting our call," Darcie said. "He's so ready to talk – gosh, he must be ticked off. He's putting himself in the crosshairs of a lot of people's anger to help us get this story out."

"Yeah. I expect he'll be physically harmed. He's mad, courageous, stupid, or some combination."

"So – what's the second thing we do?"

"The U.S. District Attorney is a friend of mine," Hersch said. "You get ready to break it on Wednesday's show at six. Wednesday morning, I'll brief the D.A. and soon after, I'd expect the subpoenas to start flying."

May 26, 1972

Dan Spesiak has just come in from the rain, has hung up his coat. Straightens his tie after having just sat down in a chair to face the mayor. He is the last arrival. Nine other men – Lou Lombardi of the police, and his counterparts who represent the firefighters, Departments of Education, Streets and Sanitation, and a half dozen more – sit in leather chairs, a semi-circle, facing the mayor. Occasional rumbles from the storm outside are heard in the office.

Everyone knows why they've been summoned and what their mayor needs from them.

"Okay," Frandino begins. "Dan, please take notes. No songs or dances, gentlemen. The count and the amount will do just dandy."

He turns to the man seated farthest to his left. "Perry, how many people in your department's payroll are part of this, and what does the annual payroll with benefits amount to for them?"

"Three dozen, from what I can tell, sir. Total payroll with benefits and overhead is seven hundred and six thousand a year."

"Three dozen. Doctor Pankovitz, how many in Education?"

"Zero, sir. No one."

"Zero. Okay, I'm sure no teachers. But bus drivers? Janitorial? Security? How many are we talking?"

"Zero," Doctor Pankovitz repeats. "Too many people have been watching Education too closely for any of this to go on."

"Gentlemen," Frandino says. "This is not a time to tell me what you think I want to hear. We're under attack, damn it, and it's just started. It's going to get worse. We've got to play defense, and we've got to understand how much turf we're defending. If any one of us goes down, the rest will end up going down, too."

"My brother-in law," Pankovitz confesses. "The man is sick, used to work at the coke plant. Down near Republic Steel. Got hurt on the job, they denied his claim. Union didn't take care of him. Sixteen thousand a year, plus benefits. Shit."

Lou Lombardi, seated next to the educator, puts a hand on his shoulder.

"Okay. So with benefits let's call it twenty-eight thousand. Lou, you're next."

He continues the inquiry, left to right, and then asks Deputy Mayor Spesiak to tally the total for all departments.

"Two hundred and thirty-six people," Spesiak announces. "Total damages are five million, a hundred and ninety two thousand a year."

"Out of a payroll of over four thousand people," Frandino barks. "And for this, the media wants to crucify us? I want every single one of you to hear this loud and clear. We're going to stick together, and we're going to beat this."

The men say nothing. Frandino looks at Spesiak. "Do you doubt me, Dan?"

"How do we deny charges that even we know are true?" the deputy mayor responds. "Now that Channel Six has started the feeding frenzy the pressure is gonna go up."

Frandino gets up and walks over to his humidor, talking as he walks.

"First thing, we've got this big payroll to keep track of, and mistakes can be made. I'm a bit of a mathematician, see? Two-thirty-six out of, I believe last week it was forty-one-oh-three, that's maybe five and a half percent of the total city payroll. They've got to give us a margin of error. Just like the steel companies. Do you know that Pauly Kessler down at Bethlehem once told me that on any given day at the plant, thirty to fifty, maybe fifty-five percent of the workforce who shows up do actual work to earn their pay?"

"That's great, Sal," says Lou Lombardi as Frandino returns to his chair, cigar in hand. "We just gotta get the facts out."

"Exactly. And there's more. Lou, who is Miss Yeager's star tattle-snitch in all of this?"

"Ha! Good point, Sal. The notorious little rattlesnake, John Falzarini."

"Splendid. You know something about the law, Lou. What would you say about his unassailability as a witness in court?"

"Let's just say the slimy little rat is not exactly a stranger to either the city or county jail. Burglary, larceny, racketeering."

"Yessir." Frandino has cut the tip of his cigar and is brandishing a big metal lighter with his initials etched into it. "Gentlemen, if Channel Six and the rest of the media want a fight, then a fight is what they'll get."

One end of his cigar is igniting, and Frandino begins to puff on the end in his mouth.

*****

Ten minutes later he dismisses them with a smile and a few words that they've grown used to hearing over the years as staff meetings end: "Lou. Can you stay behind for a second?"

The two boyhood friends are alone. "Lou, help with Education, will you? Find out how bad it is. Pankovitz doesn't have the stomach for this."

"Saint Salvatore the Gentle," Lombardi smiles. "Yeah, I'm on it, boss."

Business as usual. What would that look like today? There's a Chamber of Commerce luncheon at noon, and a stack of mail that can occupy him between now and then. Frandino extinguishes the cigar and settles in. The letters and notices are the usual things that cross his desk except for a post card from John Klinglehaus, vacationing in Mexico with his wife. Their first vacation in years. He wonders, just for a moment and without malice, how many of these alleged city jobs that don't require the job-holder's performance of actual duties, were a product of Klinglehaus' years of wheeling and dealing.

Frandino's stomach. Sharp stinging hurting fire. Raw, powerful, hell. He must not cry out, must not let others know. It gets worse and worse. He whimpers, doubled over in his chair.

Oh, God! Please no more!

I am finished! Just take me!

He hears the clock ticking in his office. And then, it seems to leave him. He opens his eyes. He is still in his office. Beads of sweat on his forehead. Dizziness. Fear. Sal Frandino feels his eyes full of tears. A single, spasmotic sob. He will not give in to tears. Instead he puts his hands on the desktop and slowly, tentatively, sits up straight in his chair.

Lunchtime he is at the Chamber of Commerce event, but decides not to eat. More reporters than usual are present. Frandino knows why they have come. He surmises, as he takes the podium to talk about more plans and progress downtown, that Darcie is not among them. He emits a sardonic grunt. All she needed was to light the match, and now all the firebugs in the city have come to grill him.

Frandino talks for five minutes. His audience treats him with the same polite, lame-duck disaffection he's gotten from almost every group in the city since losing the County Executive race. Then, he is finished.

"Mayor Frandino," comes a voice from the back of the room. It's that pesky city desk guy from the *Messenger*. "A lot of people would like to hear your comments on the recent reports that a number of city employees are on the payroll without being required to do any work, and that in some cases senior city officials are receiving part of these salaries as kickbacks."

"Now, Marty," Frandino replies. "That's not the kind of stuff I would condone. We are aware of those reports and we'll be looking into them."

"Mayor," one of the radio station guys follows up, "witnesses have come forward saying that top city officials have been complicit in granting these no-show payroll checks. Can you tell us what you know?"

"Lance, I heard these reports for the first time this week, along with the rest of you. Obviously I'm very concerned."

"Mayor," the investigative reporter for Channel Eight pipes in. "A lower-level city employee named John Falzarini has gone on record saying that he's overheard from others in City Hall that you have had personal knowledge of this situation dating back to at least a month before last November's election."

"Blatant balderdash, Tim. I'm familiar with Mr. Falzarini's police record and the circumstances of his hire. I was personally involved and I'll admit his father is a friend of mine. We tried to give him a chance. We gave him a job so he could walk the straight and narrow. I'm very saddened to learn of the charge he's made."

"So you're admitting that you do – at least in some cases – give city jobs to people based on favors or personal relationships."

"Tim, let's live in reality. Does it happen? Yes, and I just gave you a situation. I was involved in that one so if you're going to demonize anyone over the circumstances of Mr. Falzarini's hire to the Recreation Department, look no further than right here." Frandino points a finger to his ear, pulls an imaginary trigger, and chuckles. "Like I said, I was familiar with the case of this man, who came to us humbly and told us he wanted a chance to make good as a law-abiding citizen. And yes, since I knew the family I got involved and did what anyone in this room who's human would've done. I helped a friend."

"Mayor, what about the reports that perhaps as many as four hundred people have been given -"

"I'm sorry, gentlemen," Frandino cut off his last inquisitor. "I understand that this topic has everyone's interest, and I'm sure that as I continue my own inquiry which in fact I've already begun this morning, we'll have more to say."

"Mayor, can you tell us today beyond the shadow of any doubt that you have never been aware of…"

"Mayor Frandino, do you think it's possible that the Democratic Party and John Klinglehaus in particular, have arranged for…"

"Sir, does it make you nervous that your political power base has eroded, and that the Democratic Party may not be willing or able to protect you from this latest…"

The mayor reaches the exit, then turns back to his inquisitors with a smile.

"I know these sensational reports make for good theater and your job is to report on any theatrical charges, but I assure you there's nothing sinister going on in City Hall."

He is out the door. Echoes of the pain in his gut.

Frandino declares his workday over at 5:45 p.m. The rain has stopped but the city is damp from a morning and afternoon of spring showers. Frandino is driving his beat up station wagon. He wonders if it might soon be time to trade up at least for a Buick, if not a Caddy or a Lincoln. If his days on earth are nearly over, at least give Steffi a nice car for the funeral.

He is stopped for a signal at Elmwood and West Utica. In his rear view mirror, the same truck that was behind him back near City Hall. That crazy, maniacal, smiling face. A big guy with one gargantuan hand on the steering wheel, and the other hand on a huge pipe wrench. Grinning.

Andy the Plumber. A real plumber who was even, for a brief time, employed by the city as a building inspector - and that was on Kowalski's watch, Frandino reminds himself with a measure of self-righteousness. A ring-kissing Wise Guy who has twice been assigned by his higher-ups to carry out hits against his bosses' rivals. Never served enough time. The ring-kissers employ skillful lawyers. The lead pipe is his preferred weapon of violence, according to folklore.

Frandino turns left onto Utica and then onto a quiet side street. Andy is behind him, still clutching the pipe wrench and grinning insanely. Frandino parallel-parks, and gets out of the car. Andy stops behind him. Frandino walks up to the passenger door of the plumber's truck. The driver puts down the wrench, and rolls down the window.

"Mayor! Good to see you again, sir. Go for a ride with me?"

"Been a long time, Andrew. Where are we going?"

"Sal. I just been asked to explain a thing or two to you, maybe ask a favor. Ten minutes of your time, then I'll drop you off right here nice and safe. I promise."

Frandino pulls the door open. "So, what is this?" he asks as he climbs in. The truck begins to move.

"The Big Sieve himself expressed his heartfelt desire that I should have a conversation with you. Pass along some info, so to speak. Sallie, he needs you. And I think we've got you, Sal. He thinks – we thinks - you need us."

"Nothing's changed in twenty years for me, Andrew. Not in '52 as a judge, not in '72 as a mayor. No deals with you guys."

"Yeah, I know," the Plumber singsongs. "But we think you oughta start seein' it different. You see, the thing is, the black dude you had rat out his cocaine connection – you know, we think it's real keen you're help-ing him go to school and all that – but Sallie, the little rat made it so the dominos are startin' to fall, tell you the truth. His singing started a chain reaction of busts that are hurtin' some guys in the pocketbook. Makin' guys nervous. Reshuffling the business."

"Andrew, you know I have no pity over that. I'd rather the Big Sieve and all the rest of you make your living legally."

The Plumber begins to laugh. "You're funny, Mayor Sal. I mean, you're right – so to speak. Maybe you could put us all on the city payroll so we could sit in the bar all day and play Canasta!"

"I don't think you know the whole story."

"You're right, Mayor Sal. Is it three hundred guys? Six hundred? I don't know. Make our livings legally? You know what I spent seven and a half hours doing today? Fixing leaky stinking toilets and sinks. Oh, I did put in a bathtub for some people over on Stanislaus Street. I played Lincoln Logs with this dame's three year old kid while she went to the corner store for ten minutes! Whaddya you think, all I do is go around busting people's heads? Ain't that common an occurrence. And, Sal. Sometimes strangers whose houses I go into - they leave their valuables laying around. Easy pickins! But I don't just take people's stuff – I'm just as good a guy as you. But look, Mayor, I'm here to help you, so to speak."

"Then say something helpful."

"Well the thing is Sal, some pretty high people on the totem pole got busted, and so you've got others rushing to claim their spot, to fill in the proverbial power vacuum. And some of us, well yes, some of us are on the city payroll when our real jobs involve other things like makin' pizzas, repairin' sidewalks - why, we even do plumbing work, some of us. So our livelihoods are being threatened now like never before. And you know, Sal. Guys like these weenies, when they feel threatened – bada-bing. Violence. You see?"

"No. I don't see. Spell it out for me."

"Shootings, Mayor Sal. On your streets. In your city, which we all know is already bleeding people so fast the Titanic went down more slowly than this freaking place. Sal, look. I don't have any specific information, I swear. But I can predict in what we call general terms, right? I'm tryin' to be straight with you here, without sayin' too much. There's a bunch of guys looking for an opportunity. And these guys, Sal – they're not nice guys, not the kinda guys a smooth cat like you would want to sit down and watch a Yankees game with, you know?"

"What's your point, Andrew?"

"The point, mister mayor sir, is this: that you need to drop the charges on three key guys that have been arrested. You know who these three John Does are. See, that keeps the city streets safer, keeps the business more stable. 'Cause mayor, I live in the city too, and I don't want to live in a violent town where people are shot and law-abiding citizens have even more incentive to flee to the suburbs. Or to the freakin' South where they'd have to make do with stinkin' grits and butter instead-a pasta and red sauce, you know?"

"Andrew, take me back to my car now. No deal. I've got enough hot water, real or imagined, to deal with these days. I'm in no position to start cutting deals with your bosses."

"Hot water? Hey, you trying to make a plumbing joke?"

"Take me back to my car, Andrew."

The plumber sighs.

"Okay, mayor Sal. You and me go back a long, long ways. You know I love you, Sallie. They're always wanting me to talk to you and sometimes at great personal risk, I've told 'em no, leave Sal alone. Let him play the choir boy so to speak, I tell 'em. 'Cause I'll always remember what you have done for me. So, please understand. What I'm about to say is nothing personal. It's coming from the boss. From the Big Sieve, up in Lewiston."

"*Dimmi*, Andrew. Tell me what he says, though it's not going to matter."

"Sal. The kid who ratted out his connection and started the whole chain reaction of arrests. Yeah, they know who the kid is, Sal. Randy Loring, he's a marked man, see? Because they know you care about him. So you see, mister mayor, we have you on this."

"Tell the Big Sieve my message is not to touch him, or I'll have so many FBI agents camped out in his yard he'll think he's living in the middle of a Federal Law Enforcement Convention."

"Ha! That's funny, Sal. I hear those cats are comin' after you! You always have been a barrel of laughs, though. Mayor, he ain't playin'. He's as serious as a heart attack. He makes a phone call, and your friend is dead within twelve hours. Yeah, they've been tailing him. Got this guy who's insanely prejudiced against the coloreds, a guy with a hyperactive trigger finger. Sal, ask yourself this – it's been twenty years since you and me talked like this. You know I'd rather stay out of your way – except for maybe stopping newspaper editors from smashing your face every so often - while you do your mayor thing. So you think the Big Sieve ain't serious?"

The truck has circled a couple of city blocks and is stopped back at the Frandino station wagon.

"He's got no leverage, Andrew. You're offering to spare one life in exchange for putting a serious crimp in the kind of criminal activity I deplore. The way I see it, there's no guarantee that your buddies won't kill each other on the streets on any given day whether our informant lives or dies. If they do all kill each other, it's just dandy to me. So the young man's life doesn't enter into my equation."

"Mayor. I tried talking to you. I understand your position. I'll communicate it back up my chain."

"What if my answer to the Sieve is that I need a little time to think about it? How much time can you buy me?"

The Plumber scratches his head thoughtfully. "I don't know, Sal. Maybe twenty four hours?"

"Okay. My boys at Precinct Seven know how to get hold of you. You'll be hearing from them. 'Yes' for I agree and we'll get the three men out of jail, and 'no' for no deal. I'll have one of 'em let you know tomorrow before 5 p.m."

"I'll try to stall for you, Sal. What the hell, maybe we just collaborated to save a life, huh?"

Frandino does not answer as he climbs down from the truck.

"Hey Sal, I'll just wait here till I know you're safe in the car. Make sure there's no muggers or nothin, y'know?"

"With friends like you…" Frandino says above the truck engine's idle.

"Hey, Sal!" Andy the Plumber raises his voice above the idle of his truck's engine. "I was wondering. About the news babe. I mean, would you recommend her? To a lonely sailor?" Frandino sees Andy's grin.

"I'm going to ignore that," he responds, loudly enough that he thinks Andy can hear.

"Hey, Sal!" The plumber yells out his open window. "Honest to God. Give my fondest regards to *Stefania*, huh?"

*****

The next few days are a whirlwind. And now, Sal Frandino enters police commissioner Lou Lombardi's office. And hears something that shocks him.

"Lou! I can't believe you guys lost Randy."

23

Her Beloved Ketchup. On the Table

May 24, 1972

Sal Frandino scrutinizes the face of his police commissioner. It is
a look that he does not know how to read. If he didn't know any
better, Lombardi is upset with Frandino himself.

"Talk to me, Lou. What the hell is going on?"

"Last we knew he was at Rev Johnson's eleven o'clock service on
Sunday."

"So – you have talked to Tom Johnson."

"Can't find him either. Left messages, knocked on the door. No one
home. Not the wife, not the kids. Janitor and secretary at the church, say he
might be on a personal retreat this week. Don't know where."

"We've got to find Randy. We could do something pre-emptive,"
Frandino says. "Bust the people most likely to pull the trigger, keep 'em in
the slammer overnight, just to buy time."

Lou Lombardi's next breath out comes through his teeth like steam
escaping from a boiler. Frandino studies his friend's face for some reassur-
ance that the worst has not already happened.

"What is it, Lou? What are you thinking?"

"You really want to know?" Frandino takes a step back; Lou's voice
is suddenly loud, and he looks ready to pounce.

"You wanna know something about yourself, Sal?" Lombardi's

head moves from side to side as he talks. "You're ready to finally give me permission – after all these years – to haul in every ring-kisser in the city. You selfish son of a bitch."

"Selfish?"

"Yeah, selfish. 'Cause I've been waiting for a chance like this for years. For years! And it pisses me off that what it takes to get your permission to launch a pre-emptive crackdown on the mob is when the life of someone you love is on the line."

"I don't love Randy," Frandino hears himself stutter.

May 27, 1972

It was a perfect springtime Saturday. Light breeze, lots of sun, temperature in the high sixties. Best of all, the start of a three-day Memorial Day weekend from school. We played pickup basketball that morning. Then I rolled into the house around noon.

"Ernie. You got a rather interesting phone call this morning." Mom wore not quite a smile.

"Okay," I replied.

"Darcie from Channel Six."

"Really. Why?" I felt my heart quicken.

"That's what I'd like to know, Ernie the Pro. What's going on?"

"I haven't seen her or talked to her or anything since that football game in the fall."

"She left a number for you to call. Her home number. Says she wants to see you."

"No kidding."

"If this happens," her first word was loud, "I will chaperone. She didn't sound right. What's going on with you and her?"

"Mom! Nothing! What would she want with a not-quite fifteen year old kid like me?"

"That's what I want to know. If you're going to see her, I'm coming along."

"Mom! I can handle it."

"That's what I'm afraid of."

For the next three days I was on pins and needles because that's how long it took to connect - how did we live before answering machines and text messaging? She finally caught me on Monday evening while I was studying for my geometry final. Tom called me to the phone.

"Ernie the Pro," she started. "How are you, my friend?"

"I'm – surprised to hear from you. What's up?"

"I've got a lot going on, Ernie. I need to slow down and have a cheeseburger and a milkshake with a friend who can help me think through it all. I choose you as that friend."

"Me?"

"There's a place on Main Street not far from where I work called the Copper Kettle. Great place for burgers and shakes. Maybe tomorrow or the next day after school. Can you get there?"

"I know the place. Tomorrow?"

"You bet. And Ernie. Promise not to tell anyone?"

May 31, 1972

Randy was walking about his neighborhood with a peace that surpassed all understanding. Just returned from four days at Reverend Tom Johnson's three quarters of an acre down in Colden, A place he'd not seen since he was eight years old and his family had gone to take part in a church revival. Tom Johnson listened, talked, and listened some more. Randy thought he had discovered something to found the rest of his life upon, and a plan for making his dreams come true. In Syracuse, where

Mayor Frandino had arranged for friends in the Democratic Party to get him an internship with a prominent law office and where, Frandino had told him, the skids were greased to get him into post-graduate law studies at the university.

The plan was on his mind, whether walking to the corner store for a pack of cigarettes and a little bottle of schnapps – habits on the decline but still present in his day-to-day doings – or taking the family's laundry to the coin-operated dryers two blocks away.

Tuesday evening, his mother asked him to walk to the corner store before it closed for a dozen eggs and bread for toast the next morning. He had walked two hundred feet when he felt a sudden sting in his leg and heard a jarring blast. Something invisible had knocked him to the ground. His left leg below the knee hurt like hell. He tried to scramble to his feet but stumbled and fell. Flashing red and blue lights now reflected off of everything.

"HELP!!"

Men ran toward him from two different directions. Still trying to get upright. They took hold of him. How many were there – Five? Seven?

"Okay. Okay. I give!"

"Randy, I'm Detective Stokovsky of the Buffalo P.D. Relax. You're being taken into protective custody." The man who spoke held a badge in front of Randy's face.

"Protective – what. What have I done?"

"Take it easy," said the Stokovsky guy. "We've gotta cuff you but it's just protocol. You haven't done anything. Trust me, it's best for you."

"What the hell is this. I ain't done nothing, I'm telling you!"

"It's okay," said a uniformed cop. "Give us twenty minutes and it'll make sense."

Ten guys surrounding him, nine in uniform and Stokovsky, the plainclothes guy. Randy's leg stung so much he couldn't have run anyway.

He sat in the back of a police cruiser, cuffed and nonplussed. Would a white guy being taken into protective custody get a rubber bullet to the leg? And normally, he'd be in the back seat by himself but the plainclothes guy was sitting in the back, next to him. And why, if this was done to protect him, didn't they just knock on the front door of the house? The driver was telling someone over the radio something about a manhunt being over.

"Manhunt?" Randy felt his eyes grow large as he searched for answers from the man seated next to him.

"You're gonna be okay," said the man. "We're going to see a good friend of yours."

"What the hell's going on?"

"Mister, the mob's had a contract out on your life for almost a week now. How you're still alive is a mystery to all of us. Just be glad we got to you first."

*****

Mom and Dad had a conversation over my upcoming date with Darcie. I know, because I overheard it from my bedroom at about one o'clock in the morning. It might also have woken the neighbors.

"She sounded unstable. He's barely fifteen. He'll be sexualized too early." Mom's voice, stuck in my memory.

"He'll be fine. Let him grow up, for Christ's sake. Neither of us were angels, Dot." My father's refrain. I lay awake in bed, rooting for him and feeling misunderstood by him all at once.

I didn't think I was on the eve of losing my virginity, though if I told you the possibility didn't cross my mind, I'd be lying. I took Darcie at face value. I theorized that I was like a brother she never had. She just needed to talk.

Mom finally agreed to drop me off at the place and then pick me up ninety minutes later. I was supposed to meet Darcie at six o'clock. I swung mom's passenger side door open in front of the Copper Kettle at 5:58, ears ringing from her admonitions that even though she trusted me, I'd better be careful.

The place was a nest for high school kids. I didn't see anyone I recognized. I went to the one remaining empty booth and sat. When she came through the door a few minutes later, it was not the television version of Darcie. Denim head to toe and her hair pulled back into a ponytail. I'd never seen her wear it like that before. I waved; she smiled, came, and sat.

"Oooooh," she said, settling into the booth across from me. "So tired." She was almost whispering. She wore no makeup. She didn't need any.

She directed the flow of the initial small talk. All the typical questions a grown-up would ask a high school freshman, except that she made every question seem fresh and important. She wanted real answers. Not that I minded. Her eyes held mine in thrall, and I would have given her the secret combination to the safe at Fort Knox if I had it.

We ate and talked some more about inconsequential things. The last of her cheeseburger had just vanished when I asserted myself.

"So, Darse. What's really going on with you?"

She made a scrunchy face. "I feel like you and me, we're friends. You have to promise that whatever we say stays just between us."

"Yeah. I'd never –"

Her eyes were darting about the room as though she were a wanted woman and the cops were closing in.

"It's no good, Ernie. Too many people here. Let's go to my place. It's only a few blocks away and I'd like privacy."

I heard a siren that sounded like it was coming from a few blocks away. I remember thinking that maybe it was God's way of warning me not to go to Darcie's place. Then I felt excitement.

Inside the Warning

The squad car's siren came on as it approached the intersection of Delaware and North Streets. Randy could tell that the driver switched the flashers on, because he saw alternating red and blue light thrown onto the surrounding buildings as though he were inside a space ship as it sped through the neighborhood. How ironic. Seemed like yesterday when these same eerie sirens meant an escalating battle, when Randy felt a different excitement.

The car continued straight through the intersection and the lights and siren stayed on until they had crossed Elmwood. When the car turned right onto Richmond Avenue, he figured that he was being driven to the mayor's house. He didn't know whether to be relieved or to prepare for the butt-chewing of his life.

Five more minutes and they were in a park-like circle, and then in the driveway of a large home. Detective Stokovsky walked him to the side door. The detective knocked.

A well-preserved older woman with dark hair answered and smiled.

"Thank God," she said. "You must be Randy. I've heard much about you."

She led the two men up a flight of wooden stairs, through a kitchen that was several times larger and better-equipped than anything Randy had ever seen in his own neighborhood, and then into a room that was full of books, bric-a-brac, pretty lamps, nice oriental rugs and furniture. There, wearing striped cotton pajamas, was the mayor. He was already on his feet as Randy and the detective entered the room.

"Sir," Randy said reflexively.

The mayor walked toward him. "Am I ever glad to see you," Randy heard the mayor say. The mayor embraced him.

"Agh!"

"Jesus, Mary and Joseph, detective. Uncuff the young man!" The words were music to Randy.

*****

Frandino wants to communicate urgency, hopefulness, and affection. "How much have they told you on your way over here?" he begins.

"The mob has a contract out on me. Probably for snitching on my connection."

"Superb," says Frandino. "That's right. And we're working on putting the people responsible behind bars for conspiracy to murder. But it's no easy process. These people are tricky and it could take us months to line up our ducks to make convictions stick. Meanwhile there's an assassin looking for you, and more where he came from. So we've got to get you out of here."

"Well, I could get set up in Syracuse a few weeks sooner than we were planning, right?"

"Maybe eventually. Right now we've got to get you out of the geographic range of this group. They have people in Syracuse. But I've got a plan."

"Which is?"

Frandino senses Randy's fear and confusion. "I know it's happening fast," he says, but the plan is Miami. I've got people there. People I've known for years, people I trust who can help you and who can keep me posted on how you're doing. Besides, the winters in Syracuse are – more snow than we get here, on average."

"Miami? But what about the connections you had in Syracuse for law school and everything?"

"I know, son. But first, let's keep you alive. The FBI will help. You're going to sleep here tonight. Tomorrow, you'll get to go back home but you'll have bodyguards. The plan is this – you get your things, you say your goodbyes, and we get you out of town."

"Pops." Randy looks glum. He goes from standing to sitting, almost melting into a chair.

"I wish it were different, but your safety is important to me and to all the other people who care about you. So we're paying for two plane tickets. One for you, one for Pastor Johnson. He'll go with you for the first few days, help you get set up down there. Then in about a week, he'll come back home."

Randy's voice is small. "When do I get to come back?"

"Please understand, son. You got yourself mixed up in a nasty business. Unfortunately, sometimes there's consequences that follow you around for a while."

Frandino watches the expression on Randy's face as they look into one another's eyes.

"But the story is still being written," Frandino says, "and I'm going to do everything I can to make sure it comes out right. If the police and the FBI can get people arrested soon and cooler heads prevail, it might be safe for you to come back in a jiffy, maybe a few weeks. Though I can't promise it right now."

Lilacs and Cinnamon

The inside of Darcie's car smelled like cinnamon chewing gum. It was awesome that she was listening to the FM rock station I liked best. We pulled to the curb on Linwood Avenue in front of a big house among large trees. She cut the engine.

"Home, sweet home," she said. It sounded sad. She turned to me. "Come on, let's go in."

I followed her up a long flight of wooden stairs, feeling like a big jackpot winner. Keys jingled, a lock turned, and we were alone in her apartment.

"Let's go to the living room," she said.

We had to go through her kitchen first - it was small but it made me think of love and family because her table and chairs, done in pink with chrome trim, were exactly like the kitchen set in my grandmother's kitchen, where I'd eaten many a comfort meal. A half-full bottle of ketchup stood in the middle of the table. I knew from our burger dates and the football game that Darcie craved the stuff. The living room was small. She turned a light switch on – the walls were painted green. She had a grey couch and loveseat, and lots of family pictures on the wall. Looked to me like she had two brothers and a sister. The rug on the hardwood floor was a bit threadbare. A modest color television set on a wooden table, and a stereo with a turntable. Two bookshelves built into the wall. They were quite bare, save for a stack of magazines and three books leaning against each other. One of the books was "Valley of the Dolls," which I had never cracked open, but which mom had told me a few months earlier, was positively evil.

"Get you a pop? I'm having one." She gestured that I should sit on the loveseat, so I did. She came back with soft drinks. Then, in one dramatic flop, she threw herself on the couch and landed on her back, looking up at the ceiling.

"Tonight, you're my therapist," she began. "But only for about the next hour and twenty because I've got to be in the studio to do a few things for the eleven o'clock show. Ernie, you're going to analyze me."

"Sure, I'm Doctor Ernie the Pro. No, really, Darse. I'm not qualified for that."

She turned her eyes from the ceiling, to me. "I think you're as qualified as they come," she said with a compelling matter-of-factness. "I'm
going to tell you a story. And all you've got to do is tell me what you think
about it. You can do this, Ernie."

I may have squirmed a bit in response. But within seconds, I was
lost in her story.

Except for Raincloud, I had never before had another person tell
me the kinds of things that Darcie told me about herself that night. She'd
look at me, then look back at the ceiling, and then look at me again as she
talked. More than once I thought she was about to cry but she held it together. About fifteen minutes into it, she got up from the couch, went into
her bedroom, and brought out a big stuffed brown bear. She began to take
turns talking first to me, then to the stuffed bear, then to me again. She also
addressed Mickey Mouse, who sat perched on her wrist, more than once.

Looking back at that night as I occasionally do through the years,
the thought I always have about Darcie's apartment is that it was the first
time I ever knew what it could feel like to love someone so much I wanted
to be joined to them - and not just physically. I experienced her in deep and
unforgettable ways. I didn't like everything she revealed about herself, yet
I had overwhelming feelings of wanting to protect her. Under her beautiful
and successful exterior was a hurt and confused human being who needed
to heal. By the time I started to talk to her in sentences, I was so captivated
by the potent combination of her glory and ruin that I had the actual physical sensation of not knowing where she stopped and I began.

Then I found myself wanting to hear her next sentence and there
was none.

"I'm sorry about you and the mayor," I said.

At that point, she stirred herself from lying on her back, to a sitting position. She faced me, hands folded in front of her, and both feet on the floor. She looked glum. I saw her head shake ever so slightly from side to side.

"It was cool to hear about you and your dad. He loved you so much and he sounds like such a great man."

"The greatest, Ernie. I wish he could've lived longer."

"I hope you don't leave town."

She shook her head more noticably. "I don't know how to feel about that one. But I do know that I want music." She got up and walked over to her stereo setup, and put the needle on whatever vinyl was already in place. She sat back down to a musical backdrop; the opening guitar riff of Van Morrison's *Wild Nights*.

"Love this album," she said. "Anyway, when I came here I thought I'd be here for a year or two, make my mark, and then it would be easy for me to go on to a bigger city. But it's not easy. Hersch is the closest to my father I've ever met. Genuine, caring, courageous man. The city's lucky to have him as one of its news anchors. And it's such an interesting place. Leaving's hard, but if I don't go to Washington now I'll always be kicking myself if the door isn't open for me later on. The national news has been my dream since I was six or seven years old."

"People here are gonna miss you a lot, Darse."

"I'm gonna miss some of the people here, too. But remember, my leaving has got to be our secret. We're not announcing that until the week or even the day before I go. That's how it works in our business. So here's the other part… Ernie, it's Lamont. He's scaring the hell out of me."

"What?"

"He started calling the station a month ago. I talked to him once. He's got a romantic notion for me and he won't put it down. If I knew I was going to hurt him by doing that interview I'd have never done it."

"So he's obsessing over you?"

She nodded emphatically. "Ernie, you've got to talk some sense into him. I can't. He said some things to me about his feelings he shouldn't have said. And honestly, that's another reason why I should leave town. I never meant to hurt anyone and it seems like I've hurt everyone. Women don't trust me. Men all have agendas and the one man in town I care about most – my job involves ruining his life, so now he hates me." Then came a short burst of bitterness, poorly disguised as laughter, which betrayed to me how much she was hating on herself.

"I came here thinking I was too cool for school, but this town has kicked my ass. I screwed it all up. Now I need a new start and Lamont does, too."

She sniffled, and I saw the first and only tear of the evening stream down a cheek. She took in an unsteady breath and gathered herself.

"Darse. I don't think you're a screw-up."

"Ernie the Pro," she was shaking her head, almost whispering. "You have no idea."

I felt like such an adult as we sat across from each other, our eyes as serious as they could be.

"Well, I don't talk to Raincloud much anymore. Over the last few months we've mainly gone our separate ways."

"But you could. He talked about you the last time he talked to me. Just last week. He respects you. Maybe it's time he hears from you again."

Her phone rang and she got up from her couch to pick the receiver off the wall. "Hello?"

"Hersch. Omigosh. What time is it?" She glanced at her wristwatch.

"My God, Hersch. Mickey's short arm is pointing a little past the ten. Oh, no. I'm so sorry…"

"Yeah, I know it's not like me. I don't feel well. Gosh, I must've dozed." She stood, holding the phone, winking at me.

"His mother? She did? Oh, crap, I'm busted. No, no. He's here with me..."

"We're talking. Yeah, we've been talking. He's a good person to talk to. Remember the fun we all had at the game? No dad, I wasn't laying down with him..."

"You will? You're kidding!" She smiled and gave me the thumbs up sign.

"I do need a night off, don't I? Yes, dad... I will. Yes, I promise..."

"Yes, I screwed up with Ernie. I'll take care of it..."

"Okay, see you tomorrow, then."

She put the earpiece back on its hook, and motioned me with a single finger to come to the phone. "You need to call your mother right now and tell her you're still a virgin," she said. "She called the station and wants to put out an APB for us."

We both laughed, like we did at the Rockpile.

"I'll call my dad at the restaurant and tell him where I am," I said. "He'll call my mom and deal with her."

Dad didn't disappoint. His concern for my disobedience was overshadowed, I could tell, by unspoken pride that his teenage son had befriended the hottest woman to hit town in maybe forever. Having enlisted his cooperation, Darcie and I drank another soda and listened to some more music, and shared some laughs at Coach McCoy's expense. Then she drove me most of the way home in her cinnamon-mobile, leaving me only the final block to walk. She stopped the car and put it into park. Our heads turned toward one another.

"This might be the last time we talk, Ernie. Thanks for being my buddy. I know I can trust you."

I nodded. She smiled broadly.

"Let's open the windows, Darse, and smell." I knew that lilacs grew at this street corner, and it was their time of year to be in bloom.

"Pretty flower smells," she said, and smiled big. "You're the best, Ernie the Pro. Some girl is gonna get a real prize when they get you."

For some reason, that made me think of something I had heard Coach McCoy say to a teammate once.

"Darse? Your screw-ups here are behind you now. Learn from 'em. You're gonna win next time."

I floated home above the sidewalk through the lilac evening, brain full of a haunting love song from that Van Morrison album. As I drew closer to the hell I was about to catch from my mother, I was unaware that the capacity for empathy that Darcie had begun to unlock in me that night was just a foretaste of what would become the most memorable summer of my youth.

24

The Game, Changing

I planned to use summer vacation between my freshman and sophomore year of high school to make as much money as I could. I wanted to buy a used car of my own when I turned sixteen. My ambition led me to a job as a bicycle courier two days per week, running envelopes and small packages between businesses in Black Rock, Riverside, and parts of Tonawanda and North Buffalo. Two days doing that, plus two nights working in dad's restaurant, and I was doing okay.

The very first week of summer vacation, I had to run some envelopes to an auto body shop in Black Rock. There was a gal behind the counter in the body shop with her head down so that I couldn't see her face. I heard a male employee yelling at her.

I watched as the girl buried her face in some sort of accounting book and the male voice kept yelling. "Yes, Mike, I'm trying to find it!" she said; and then, "Sorry, Mike, I don't know what happened to it."

"Idiot!" exclaimed the male voice. "You're gonna get us both fired!"

She looked up and I recognized her. She smiled.

"You rode the Kenmore bus to school this year," I said.

She nodded in the affirmative. "Shh, he's so jealous, I swear." She gestured in the direction of the voice, which must have been coming from a back room.

"You're Michelle, right?"

Her face radiated something warm and vaguely red. "Michelle Delancey. And you're Ernie."

"You know me?"

"Ernie," she shrugged, scrunched her nose and rolled her eyes. "He's so possessive."

I leaned over the counter. "Michelle, I can't help myself - you and me gotta go and see a movie sometime." My own words startled me.

"Are you kidding me? He might try to kill you."

I smiled and gave her a shoulder shrug of my own.

She shrugged back, and our smiles turned to soft laughter. I felt her blush enter into my bloodstream.

"Ernie," she whispered. "I'll write my name address and phone number on this page for you and by the way have you seen *Deliverance* yet because I want to see it."

By week's end I had learned to call her Shelly, and we were becoming inseparable. She was going into her senior year at an all-girl's school out in Snyder. She introduced me to her parents right away and for some reason they took a liking to me, telling me to come around whenever I'd like. We started watching a lot of television together at her house on the days I wasn't cooking with Dad. We did go to see *Deliverance* together, and after the movie we stayed up late on her family's front porch swing, talking.

"Was it too much of a guy movie for you, Shelly?"

"It was a guy movie, wasn't it? But I thought it was about courage and when breaking the rules is the right thing and those themes are interesting to me. What did you think the movie was about?"

"Self-discovery. Burt Reynolds and all his group, they all learned something new about themselves because they were forced into situations."

"That's insightful. You're a very smart guy, Ernie so who do you think learned the biggest lesson and what did they learn?"

"Burt Reynolds learned that no matter how good you think you are, don't take a single day for granted. Or a single person."

"I like that, Ernie. And by the way, I've been dating a guy who I think has been taking me for granted."

"Yeah. Guess I sort of forgot that you're Mike's girlfriend."

That's when she swung herself sideways and put her legs over mine, and put her arms around me.

"Think you can convince me to date this new boy I've met? He doesn't seem to have that same problem." That first kiss, which commenced about five seconds after this interesting question of hers, stood as the highlight of my life up to that point.

When it ended, she smiled. "You need lessons but I don't charge tuition," she said.

*****

At dinnertime on the eve of July 4, Shelly and I sat on the Delancey's living room couch watching the Channel Six news. Hersch Woodstein came on and announced the top news: more damning information come to light in the big payroll scandal at City Hall; two hundred more layoffs at Bethlehem Steel. News, weather and sports with a healthy dose of Michelle's bright eyes and beautiful cheekbones. And then Hersch back on camera, speaking at the end of his show:

"A final note tonight, and a sad announcement that we're losing a very special person from our Channel Six news crew. Darcie Yeager, who has touched all our lives in such a powerful way during her nearly eighteen months with us, will be moving on to WRC television news in Washington, D.C. We at First Witness News wish her nothing but the best. Her last broadcast with us will be tonight at eleven; so tune in because she has a great piece prepared that you won't want to miss about what her experiences here in the Queen City have meant to her."

Michelle sighed. "Shame because lots of girls were jealous of her but I liked watching her and she's a role model you know?"

I turned to her and touched her face with my fingertips. Shelly and her run-on sentences were like Novocain as the dentist's drill of Darcie's departure hit me.

*****

Sal Frandino has been thinking about handball. He hasn't played in a long time, but maybe he should get back in shape. He must continue to lead, to stay strong. Though he knows that he will never again run for political office, he feels a moral obligation to lead his men through the present scandal. Many of them have a track record of sticking with him through thick and thin. Frandino has been on the offensive, and an *Evening Star* poll conducted just a week before Independence Day revealed that despite the media blitz of coverage, a majority of the city's residents who vote do not believe the mayor is guilty of any serious wrongdoing.

Even as it has recharged him, it has required a lot of his energy. Independence Day must be a respite. Family and very close friends have gathered in the mayor's backyard. Steffi has worked with a caterer; there is New York strip steak, Carolina barbecue, New Orleans gumbo. Forty or fifty guests. Frandino's daughter and her husband are in town from Miami, and have brought grandchildren with them. And Randy. Randy's parents and sister have come from the East Side. Father Al will be around later, and Millie from the Arkansas. Frandino is aware that Lou Lombardi, John Klinglehaus and Randy have been sitting together near the food, talking for close to an hour. Frandino is happy that they are finding common ground. All of the people who matter most to him, gathered.

Time for bocce ball. Frandino chalks his name onto the blackboard to challenge the winner of the current match. He and Klinglehaus will team up again. Not against the Republicans but against Frandino's daughter and son-in-law, who are destroying their current opponents. No breeze, just sun and warmth. A touch humid.

"You're in trouble now, Bethany!" he crows at his daughter as the preceding bocce match ends. He has partaken of gumbo and barbecue; he's been sipping from a clear plastic cup of burgundy wine that one of the caterer's assistants has been refilling for him every so often. The little square of cornbread was delicious. The cream puff, to die for.

But he is not eating now; he is focused on defeating his daughter and her husband. He's aware of a little sweat under his arms; just a little lightheadedness as he continues to bait and cajole his opponents, as he congratulates Klinglehaus on a *boccia* that nestles within half an inch of the *pallina*.

The score is twelve to eleven, advantage Sal and John, as he bends over to pick up the balls and prepares to take his turn. He straightens up and feels just a bit of vertigo. He smiles at his daughter, who stands next to him.

"Love you, Dad," she says, smiling with a hint of mischief.

"Ha! You always tell me that when you need something from me. Well I know you need mercy right now and you'll get none."

"Oh, Dad," she is laughing as he focuses, *boccia* in hand, puts a foot out in front, bends a knee, and bowls, extending an arm, aiming... the ball leaving his hand and suddenly, his stomach hollers out in pain.

"Aaaa."

"Dad. What is it?"

He is doubled over, prone, on the grass. "Aaaa," he repeats. He hears rapid footsteps that get louder. John Klinglehaus is there, bending over. He hears Bethany's panicked voice. "Mom. Mom."

"Take it easy, Sal," Klinglehaus says. "Just take it easy."

He hears his wife's voice. "Sallie."

Someone has brought a folding lawn chair and they guide him into it. He is sitting.

"I feel - nauseous," he says. It is hard for him to breathe and he feels like he's panting.

He knows he will throw up. He puts a hand up over his head in an attempt to warn them, and then he leans forward as far as he can and the contents of his stomach are ejected onto the lawn.

"Aaaa. Oh, that hurt."

"Daddy."

"Sal."

Feels like something in his gut just ripped open.

*****

I was on top of the world as my life sailed into the Fourth of July. I had freedom, for the first time ever, to spend the holiday apart from my parents. They gave me twenty dollars for the day on top of the thirty or so of my own I planned to spend. And a real sweetheart of my own to take to a holiday carnival. She drove her family's second car to my house, and from there we walked through the field at the end of my street, following the tracks for a hundred yards or so, and then exited the field through a hole in the fence that opened to the back of a shopping center. In front of the shopping center, taking up half of the large parking lot, the carnival had been set up.

We made each other laugh, Shelly telling me she expected me to be her hero and win a prize for her. We analyzed all the games and prizes and then discussed which one to play, and what prize we would win.

We settled on the horse race. It seemed to involve a bit more skill than the other games; and we both liked the prizes; once you won some races, you could trade in little stuffed animal horses for bigger metal horses that Michelle thought would look cool in her room, stationed on one of her bookshelves. We started to walk back through the carnival to the horses, when she grabbed onto my arm with both hands.

"Ernie oh no."

"What?"

She pointed to a group of five big guys that were walking straight toward us. Twenty feet away. Twelve feet.

"Michelle." Husky, man voice. "Long time no see."

"Old friend," she said to me under her breath. "I don't want..."

One of the guys in the group was Lamont Raincloud. Bigger than ever.

"Mont!" I said. "What's going on?"

"Dude. Looks like you've been lifting weights," he said to me. His voice had gotten deeper since we had last talked.

"Looks like you've been eating metal," I replied.

"You know this suckhead?" the guy who greeted Shelly said to Raincloud.

"He ain't no suckhead," Raincloud said to him. "This is my boy, Ernie Pronotaro. Ernie, these guys are the Bennett High School defensive line. They're switching me over to defense, see?"

"Cool."

It was clear that despite our having not talked recently, Raincloud was not going to turn on me. He was every bit as big as the guys he was with, and it didn't seem that anyone wanted to cross him.

"Gents," Raincloud said to his mates. "I'll catch up with you. Ernie,

Ernie's friend..." he gestured toward Shelly. "Wanna grab a hot dog or something and let me and my boy catch up?"

A few minutes later, the three of us were sitting. It seemed like Raincloud was into Shelly and I wondered how it was going to end. Then we sat.

"So Ern. You know, yesterday my heart was double ripped out, man."

"What do you mean?"

"Didn't you hear the news? There was even a little article in the *Messenger* this morning. Darcie's leaving town."

"Yeah, I saw that."

Shelly touched me on the arm. "You mean, Darcie the news girl?"

"Man, you gotta get over it," I said to him. "Look at you, Mont! You've got a great life."

"Wait," Shelly said to him, in a not-very-nice tone of voice. "So you're all strung out over a news reporter on TV?"

"Yeah, well it's more than that. Ernie knows. We have a relationship. Okay, not in the normal way but maybe you saw when she interviewed me on TV about a year ago. We talked. She said she cared about me." Raincloud was breathing hard.

"Yeah, but -" I sensed that Shelly was about to rip into him. I looked at her with pleading eyes for a moment, and put a finger to her lips. Which she bit.

"Ouch!"

"Well let me know when I can say something about this stupid nonsense," Shelly hissed.

"Mont, I know she's special. But dude, I gotta be honest. She called me about you. You were starting to freak her out."

"She called you - to complain about me?" Raincloud was a big, powerful mountain about to cave in on itself.

"You know her?" Shelly poked an elbow into my side.

"Mont. She did care about you. She still does. But she's older than us, man. She's been though college. We're not even through high school. She's scared for you. She's sorry she hurt you. She wants you to have a good life and she said if she realized she was gonna end up hurting you, she wouldn't have done the interview."

"I don't understand," he said. "Just like at the Rockpile last fall, she goes for you and not me. Why did you get to be friends with her, and I didn't?"

I didn't know how to answer. And Shelly had suddenly become an angry lioness.

"Ernie. Was she your girlfriend or something? Is that why you never tried to talk to me on the bus?"

"No. You were dating someone, Shelly! And I'm just a kid I mean I'm young I mean... come on, Michelle."

Raincloud was sitting across from me, reeling. This big, smart, strong-as-an-ox kid who seemed destined for greatness. In a flash, I remembered all we'd been through, growing up together.

"She said she'd never forget you," I told him. "But she was afraid if she told you that in person before she left town you'd never be able to let go of her the way we all know you need to."

They just looked at me with big, hurt eyes. He and Shelly both.

"Mont. Man, I miss you. We haven't talked in a few weeks. We need to stay in touch. I think your grown-up Seneca name should be "Mountain." I want you to know that every day I'm in the weight room at school you're in my brain, yelling at me to do another rep."

"Seriously?" He brightened just a bit.

"Dude. Seriously."

He spoke the next words like the second-grade Lamont who used to crumble when the other kids at school made fun of him.

"Esther's leaving, too. Next weekend. Shit, Ernie."

"I heard about that."

"I've liked her since I was five years old. The neighborhood will seem empty without the chance I could run into her at the store or something."

"Yeah."

"Can I - can I just sit with you guys for a minute and pull myself together before I find my buddies?"

"Hey," Shelly said to him. "It really hurts when people you care about leave town, doesn't it?"

He shot her a wounded look.

"I'm so sorry, Ernie's friend."

"It's okay," he said. "I guess this summer I need to grow up some."

*****

Sal Frandino is sitting in the parlor, not far from a window air conditioning unit. Randy is standing near him, and Steffi, and his daughter Bethany. And John Klinglehaus.

Frandino wonders if this is what it feels like to be ninety or a hundred years old.

"I don't understand why you won't let me take you to the hospital," Steffi says.

"No hospital. No publicity."

"But you can't even move without it hurting."

"Just let me sit here. I'll be okay in a few minutes."

"That's what you said almost an hour ago. Sal - you're sick. Let's at least figure out what's wrong."

"I don't want to."

"Why not!" Steffi pleads.

"Dad," says daughter Bethany. "For God's sake. Let's get you the attention you need."

He just looks back at her. He can't tell them why not. It's because he does not want to know what's wrong, and never has.

John Klinglehaus speaks next. "Randy - what do you think Mayor Frandino should do?"

"Honest?"

"Mayor brags a lot about how smart you are. So - what do you think he should do?"

"I uh - I think he ought to get his butt over to the hospital and get checked out."

"Yeah?"

"Um hmm."

"So, Randy. Would you please tell him that?"

Randy put a hand on the mayor's shoulder. "Pops," he says. "I'm asking you, sir, to please take care of yourself and let them get you to the hospital."

Frandino feels Randy's hand as though it were a hot towel around his neck after a long, hard workout. It makes him feel cared for. He thinks about how much pain he's in, and he thinks that maybe, just maybe, he is as small as he feels. Then he hears the voice of his three year old grand-daughter, from another room.

He winces and says through clenched teeth, "Okay. But no reporters."

*****

We had just left Raincloud and were heading back toward the horse game. Shelly was very quiet. I wondered if meeting Raincloud, or seeing an old boyfriend, was giving her second thoughts about being my girl. That's when she grabbed me by the wrist and swung me around to face her.

"You care about Lamont a lot," she said.

"Yeah."

"Do you care as much about me?"

"Yeah."

"So I never want to hear Darcie's name mentioned. Okay?"

"Um... no problem."

"And," she smiled, "I want you to win me a big metal horse for my bookshelf."

It took about an hour, which was about fifteen races at fifty cents a pop, but we traded up to the big metal horses and finally, I held a bronze stallion, at least one adult hand tall, replete with fancy saddle and stirrups.

"Now we have no choice," she said as I handed it to her. "We have to go to Riverside Park for the fireworks tonight."

"Yeah. We have no choice."

Then she fell quiet again, for long minutes.

"Shelly. Everything okay?"

"I'm trying to decide whether to tell you something because I told someone once before and it didn't work out too well."

We stopped walking.

"I'm falling in love with you. Too sudden, right? But I always liked you on the bus so maybe not."

"You love me?"

"Yeah." She was blushing, so beautiful. Like being in Darcie Yeager's living room, times about five. You know what I said in return and how the rest of my day went.

*****

It is 9:30 a.m. the day after the big holiday. Sal Frandino feels a little better. He's in a bed at Millard Fillmore Hospital. The hospital doctors want to do more tests. His personal physician will be there to see him at eleven. John Klinglehaus and Phyllis, his secretary, are cooperating with the hospital to ensure that his whereabouts and medical condition are, for now, carefully-guarded secrets. He closes his eyes; his next important visitor isn't due for another half an hour.

He is awakened; it is five past ten and Dan Spesiak, deputy mayor, is in the room along with Lou Lombardi.

"Sal. Hey, they tell me they'll have you out of here in a couple of days."

"That's just dandy, Dan. Just great, yes sir."

"I'm so sorry, Sal. That you're not feeling top shape. But don't worry, I've got a handle on things while you're here."

"I know you do. But I've been thinking about something more long term."

"Yeah?"

"Yes, sir. Dan, I want you to be the next mayor."

"Thanks, Sal. I know that. I've got to be elected of course, but I'm sure John can help with that."

"Dan. It'll help you if you've already got experience as mayor when you head into your first election."

"Well, but Sal. You're the mayor until 1973."

"Dan, that's what I want to talk to you about this morning. Let's put a plan in place to make you the mayor before then."

"Yes, sir."

25
Porches, Late Summer

Inevitable. The word has confiscated a big chunk of Sal Frandino's conscience as July progresses.

Benign. It describes how many of the days feel. He is still being diagnosed, but already getting medicine.

Malignant. His intuition.

"Is this a terminal illness?" he asks the oncologist.

"Hmm. How hard you want to fight it?" the doctor replies.

In some moments he wants to be a warrior. He wants a long retirement. He and Steffi could become snowbirds. A few months each winter in Florida, closer to his daughter and grandchildren. The rest of the time, here near his sons. Elder statesman for the Party.

Other moments. The city's fortunes continue a slow, downward spiral and the forecasted deficit for the year has risen steeply from the last forecast. Channel Six and the *Messenger* have shown the city's no-show payroll problem to be much bigger than what the city's department heads reported to Frandino on that stormy day in June. The U.S. District Attorney is investigating. Rumors that the Feds want to talk to Frandino. These other moments, death seems less cruel.

For the first time in two weeks, he drives to City Hall. Rides the elevator to the sixth floor. Now, he stands with Phyllis Romanello inside the mayor's office as she briefs him on the day's schedule.

Lunchtime. Sandwiches and *empanadillas* have been brought in. He is playing lunchtime host to Maritza, to whom he had promised money for playgrounds, and to her husband. George Barbarello photographs the smiling mayor as he presents to them a ceremonial check for seventy-five thousand bucks. That will put two new kid-spaces in commission by October. The paper won't chronicle the wrangle it took to scrape the money together. Fifteen thousand bucks diverted from needed repairs to two classrooms at a city high school. Twenty-four thousand taken from a plan to contribute to a facelift of one of the city's historic theater houses on Main Street. The rest? Well, the groundskeepers at a city-owned golf course will be furloughed for a week toward the end of September. They will be angry; so too, the duffers. All Frandino can do to remain a man of his word to Maritza, is to take things away from other people.

Maritza leaves smiling. He looks at his wristwatch. Ten minutes of quiet before Dan Spesiak comes to brief him. The window is a canvas of blue. The lake, the sky, the sunlight. Reminders of childhood. He could stand on a bluff two blocks from his house on a summer's day and look out over the lake. The breeze felt good. If only it were 1920 again, when Sal Frandino was a boy and his neighborhood still teemed with Sicilians, Calabrians and Neapolitans and he had the world by the tail as a full participant in summer days of ice cream and fishing poles. Back when there where ships and coal, timber and trains; organ grinders and fruit vendors, and all the rest of the characters that made up his lower West Side and his life stretched before him. When people smiled and knew that the city would yield a still better life for their kids. Back when it was unthinkable that the neighborhood should ever be torn down. Back when Sal Frandino's body knew no sickness.

Spesiak interrupts the memories. "Dan, give me the five top issues you're working this week," Frandino says with no greeting or fanfare.

"Number One, sir. The payroll. Woodstein's going on the air at six tonight and telling everyone that it's nearly six hundred workers and twelve million bucks a year. He's going to say that the dollar amount we're giving away is twice the forecasted city deficit for the year."

"That's bull. What're they basing this on – overactive imaginations, that's what."

"Sal, take it easy. It's just your first day back."

"Take it easy? They're making it up as they go, aren't they? They want to – to bury us, that's all. I want to know who or what they're basing these numbers on."

"Mmm. Are you sure?"

"What do you mean, am I sure? Of course I am."

Frandino is alarmed by the look on Spesiak's face.

"Dan? What?"

Quiet words. "I think – between you and me – it's not all that much of an exaggeration."

"Dan. How?"

"We haven't done a good job of minding the store. We've always just chalked it up to the price of staying in power. It's – taken a lot over the years, Sal. And it builds up. Once you put people on the books, it's hard to take them off. Because then you run the risk that they talk."

"What are we doing to get them working at something?"

"Lots of 'em have jobs outside of city government, Sal. They don't have time to work for the city."

"Well, that's just dandy, isn't it?"

"No, sir."

"You know something?" Frandino says. "I just nipped and tucked to find seventy five grand for new playgrounds on the lower West Side. Seventy-five grand, and I had to take it away from a high school, from Shea's

Theatre, from the parks. This is wrong, Dan. I didn't know –"

There is a long pause.

"Sal, you didn't know?"

"Didn't know it was this big."

*****

My entire life was now work, sleep, and Shelly. The cream of the summer was the two days I spent as the Delancey's guest at their beach cottage in Angola-on-the-Lake. Shelly had begun lobbying her parents, right after the Fourth of July, to allow my visit. The Pronotaro and Delancey parents convened. Predictably, mom had reservations. Dad's perspective held sway. Fortunate me.

Shelly was an excellent swimmer. The Delanceys had a big rubber raft, and she and I paddled it fifty yards offshore before diving into the water. Her father had two rules: don't swim more than twenty feet away from the raft, and don't do anything with each other that we wouldn't do if he and his wife were watching us. Rolling waves. Me on one end of the raft and she on the other. We could have been kids on a teeter-totter. We sang Top 40 to each other that entire afternoon.

That first evening, we made a campfire on the beach and cooked over it. Shelly's parents asked me what I hoped to accomplish in school in the coming year. After sunset, her parents walked to the cottage leaving Shelly and I to tend the fire, and each other.

I sat near the fire, leaning back against a big metal cooler. Shelly sat with her back relaxing on my chest and her legs fitting comfortably inside mine. She let loose with three hundred word sentences about sunsets over the water and what they always made her think of; movies that made her feel alive; ecstasy when she and her dad jumped out of their seats at Memorial Auditorium to celebrate a goal by the Swordsmen; and I'd be able to go to some of the games with her in the coming season. How hard it was to find a guy who wouldn't take advantage of her because of her tendency to give her heart away. Then she turned around and faced me, and brought her forehead to touch mine, and talked very softly.

"Ernie I never want this to end I don't know what it is about you but please this never has to end."

"Yeah. I don't either."

Her body shook and then I felt the wetness of her tears.

"No, sweetheart. Why? Why are you crying?"

"Because I'm too happy right now," she whispered. "I'm so happy and it's like I can't handle it or something and I'll burst. My friends think I'm crazy Ernie, I'm not though am I?"

I massaged her back as our foreheads seemed to merge into one. We clung to each other for a half hour before we headed to the cottage to rejoin her parents.

*****

Football kicked back in during the first week of August and there was less time for Shelly. I hoped she would understand. The first week went okay, but then I noticed a change. She was at little cranky at first, and then very quiet. Then one night on her porch ten days before school was to begin, I mentioned something about going to the St. Michael's homecoming dance in October and she snapped at me.

"Nothing's guaranteed, Ernie. October's too far out to plan for."

"Okay." I'm sure there was hurt in my voice. "What's going on with you, anyway?"

"I don't want to talk about it."

"Shelly. Whatever it is, you can tell me."

"No I can't."

I tried to be playful. "Come on." I made a goofy face that always made her laugh. "It's me. Ernie the Pro."

"Look, maybe you should go."

"Hey. Did you meet another guy?"

"No."

"Then, what?"

"Ernie please can you leave?"

"Why? What did I do?" Panic. I searched her face.

"Okay it is another guy all right? Yes our relationship has to end okay?"

"Michelle."

In the next moment, before she looked down, I glimpsed her face. It looked like she was watching her best friend being slaughtered. "Go, Ernie," came a small voice that didn't even sound like her. "Go, and maybe I'll call you tomorrow or sometime. I just don't know right now, okay?"

I touched her on the arm.

"Ernie don't. Just please let me be by myself."

"Is it because of football?"

"No. You're making this hard." She sounded frantic. "Do you have to make this so hard?"

I felt like a puppy that had been picked up by its tail and whipped against a wall by his owner. I wished for the universe to turn its entire clock back ten days, or even ten minutes.

"You're just making it worse for both of us sitting there Ernie, go home. Please."

"But you drove me here."

"Walk, Ernie. Call for a ride. Whatever. Go, I'm begging you."

"Okay. But you're not very good at breaking up."

"No I'm not."

I had told her before. A lot, actually. But this time, it sounded pathetic. "I love you, Shelly."

"Dammit you can't love me Ernie. Goodbye."

Forlorn. Seven thirty in the evening. I went down the Delancey's front porch steps for the last time. A thirty-five minute walk home if I went straight and walked at a normal pace. I meandered all over the North Side. Head down. In no shape to be alive. I didn't want to see my parents or my brother. It was late when I made it to Shoreham Drive and rang the buzzer. Mrs. Raincloud's voice came through the intercom. "Yes?"

"It's Ernie. I'm in big trouble. Can I please come in?"

"Yes. Lamont's still up." She buzzed me in and I climbed the stairs. The top door was open. I entered the familiar living room to see that the television was on. Lamont was sprawled on a couch in a tee shirt and shorts, watching a detective show.

"Dude," he looked up. "Whoa. Ern. What's wrong?"

"I don't know. I don't even know who I am anymore."

"Huh?" Then a look crossed his face. "Okay, either a death in the family or a girl. Or you got cut from football. Which is it?"

"Girl."

"Oh, shit." He jumped off the couch and turned the television set off. "Sit," he said, pointing to a place on the couch. I obeyed, and he sat and turned toward me.

"The girl from the Fourth of July?"

I nodded.

"Dude. What a fox. Crap, that blows. I'm sorry, Ernie."

"Yeah."

"It's the worst," Raincloud said. "I'm still recovering from... well this is stupid, but from Darcie."

"I don't think that's stupid anymore."

"Yeah." He sounded bitter. "Mom says I got to come to grips with my testosterone and all this. Because we're men now."

"We're men," I repeated. We were sitting a few feet apart from each other on the Raincloud's old couch, the one his mom kept a blue sheet over so that the holes in the upholstery wouldn't be visible.

I don't know which one of us started crying first. There we were, two fifteen year-old guys. Trying to convince our football coaches and teammates – and the rest of the world – of our toughness. We held each other. Cried for a full minute.

"Dude, we're bigger than this testosterone shit," Raincloud said as we held on to each other. "What don't kill us makes us stronger."

"Stronger," I echoed softly.

Raincloud balled up his hands into fists and started punching me in the chest.

"We're eventual winners, you and me. We just gotta toughen up."

*****

My hurt turned to anger. The guys at football bore the brunt of it as I channeled it into aggression the way Raincloud had taught me over the years. I had seen him get picked on when we were little. I had heard him talk about the lack of status for his Seneca Nation. I had seen him respond by going deep inside himself and finding a certain toughness that allowed him to steamroll through challenges. It wasn't surprising during the fall that our friendship enjoyed a renaissance of sorts. We were talking a couple of times every week on the phone. Meeting at the ice cream parlor.

"How you holding up this week, Mont?"

"Kicking tail, dude. We go to Burgard High for our second game this Saturday and I'm suiting up with the varsity. Coaches say I'll get fifteen or twenty snaps at nose tackle. How about you?"

"Still Jayvee, man. But playing more. They moved me over to defense, too."

"Still thinking about her?"

"Yeah, and it makes me as mad as hell. Another guy, she said. Well, we play Bishop Neumann next, and whoever's lined up across from me is that guy. He will pay."

"That's what I love to hear, dude. That's what I love about you, Ernie. You never cry."

But I wasn't getting over her. I dreamt of her, and I'd catch myself doodling her name in my notebook during classes. Then I'd realize what I'd just written, and a fresh wave of anger would wash over me.

September 25, 1972

Sal Frandino's body doesn't feel different from the way it felt a week ago, but this is the first full day of carrying around the awareness that no matter what treatment he decides on, he is, without a medical doubt, a terminal cancer patient. The oncologist had 'the talk' with him a day earlier.

He calls Al Cappello.

"Sal. How's my favorite mayor in the world?"

"Got some tough news from the docs yesterday. Can we talk tonight?"

"Oh. Okay then, with Steffi too, right?"

"No. Just us."

"I insist. Steffi too. Did they give you a timeline?"

"They gave me a range. A scintillating smorgasbord of possibilities."

"Aw, Sal. Sallie. Okay, look. You and Steffi both. I'll come to the house. We can sit on the porch. It's supposed to be a nice night. Seven o'clock, huh?"

*****

I got home that day at the usual time: six p.m. I was feeling more alive, like I was healing. I had a good practice that day. I was now one of the major participants in the locker room debate over which actress we'd make it with if we had our choice. In the locker room I was as crude and insensitive as they came. Most freshmen were in awe of me, and there were whispers that I could move up to varsity toward the end of the year. Coach McCoy had started calling me Ernie the Pro. Much better than "Number seventy-eight!" or "Hey, stupid Eye-talian!"

I found my mom and brother in the kitchen. Tom said, "You're going to the Delancey's for dinner."

"Shut up about them!" I said. Damn, that kid could ruin my mood.

"Shelly called for you," Mom said. "She said her dad would come pick you up."

"What the hell for?"

"I had quite a talk with her dad. You should go there for dinner tonight, Ernie."

"What? No. I'm over her."

"No, you're not," mom said calmly. "And tonight you should go see her. Do yourself a favor. Please."

"Mom…"

"Call right now and let them know you're ready to be picked up. Please."

Mom had a way of letting some of the emotion still show through when she was trying to hide it all. This was important to her.

Mr. Delancey was the kind of man that you wanted on your side. I got into his car and felt as welcomed by him as ever. Shelly was his only child, he explained to me again as he drove. He loved her like he loved himself and he knew that she was very unhappy. That's how the conversation started. Then, about halfway to her house, our talk turned on this:

"Ernie, she told you a lie, and tonight you're going to learn the truth."

"What was the lie?"

"There's no other boy, Ernie. There never was."

"What, then? Was it because of you?"

He smiled. "You'll figure it out. Michelle wants to have dinner with you, Ernie. We all do."

We turned onto their street. I saw a "For Sale" sign on the lawn.

We parked in the driveway and went up the porch stairs. The porch swing and most of the flower pots were missing.

Mr. Delancey opened the front door. There were boxes stacked against the walls. The furniture and rugs were missing.

Shelly walked into the room and stopped in her tracks at the sight of me.

"You're moving," bounced my voice off the bare walls. "Where to?"

"Ernie." She flew across the room and hugged me. She started to cry. That was all it took to strip away the toughness I had cultivated since last seeing her.

"Baby, baby," My fingers on her silken hair. "Where are you going?"

"Seattle," she whispered.

A noise came from me like I had just been punched in the chest.

"I'm sorry, Ernie."

"I'll let you be alone for a few," said her dad. "But then we do have lasagna in the kitchen, Ernie. Your favorite."

We stood in the packed-up room, pressing our foreheads together. Feeling one another's sweat pores. She was weepy.

"You're a senior in high school," I said. "What a crappy time for this."

"Yeah I've lived here all my life but Dad's new job well he starts Monday and he didn't want to go and well he thought he had it worked out to stay here." Her voice cracked on the word, "stay."

She had good musculature in her arms and I could feel it as she held me.

"Let's eat," she whispered. "Then can we go walk. The vans come tomorrow and then mom and I catch a flight and I want my last walk through my neighborhood to be with you."

After dinner we walked. Shelly's world was falling apart, and she invited me in to see it through her own heart. We passed houses where her friends lived, and she told me stories. We must've covered every square inch and storefront of Kenmore Avenue between Colvin and Niagara Falls Boulevard, and she had a story for all of it. Some of them, I'd already heard. It didn't matter. Some guys told me their girls talked too much, but Shelly's vocal cords made amazing sounds and I savored every syllable.

Every so often we'd stand in front of a house and she'd tell me about the family who lived there. "Well, let's knock," I said once.

"I already said goodbye to them. I've been saying goodbye for weeks to cousins and aunts and uncles and all my best friends. You're my last goodbye, Ernie the Pro."

We got back to her house and sat, side by side, on the porch steps until her dad came to check on us in his pajamas. Our last embrace was at two-thirty in the morning. I didn't fall asleep until third period American Literature class several hours later.

Same night; on the Frandino's veranda

"You know what stinks about this, Al?" Sal Frandino sips Irish coffee with his priest and his wife on the porch of his Soldier's Circle mansion. "When I die, the city loses one more body – and it's harder to get Federal funding every time that happens."

Frandino doesn't have to force the smile. He feels no panic. He reaches for Steffi's hand and squeezes it. "It's a beautiful night," he says to her. "On nights like these, I close my eyes and imagine lovers walking together, planning their futures. We were that couple once, *Stefania*."

She chuckles. "Yes, we were all so innocent once."

"Yes, we were. But not anymore. I think I'd like to take my journey into the next world with as clear a conscience as possible."

"You're not going anywhere tomorrow or the next day, Sal," says Al Cappello. "You've still got a year, maybe longer."

"Yes, and I want to enjoy it. So tonight, I want to get a couple of monkeys off my back. Steff, my priest is here so I'm going to confess a few things. First of all –"

"Sal," the priest cuts in.

"No, no. It's okay. Steffi, I have to confess that the rose-scented perfume you've been wearing to church these last few Sundays is driving me crazy. I hate it."

"You told me you like it."

"Well, I was trying to be a good soldier. But really, what's the point now? Next order of business. Steff, I've never understood your brothers. Charlie is as bright a man as God can make, and he spent all those years driving a taxi cab?"

"Some confession. I already know how you feel about my brothers."

"There's some smart cab drivers who attend St. Anthony's," says Father Al.

"Okay, that wasn't a very risky confession. I'll make another one. You know what I wish? That I didn't get so hooked on cigars. They're quite nasty, smelly objects, aren't they?"

"Hey, I like my occasional cigar," says Father Al. "You better be careful with all this confessing."

"We don't need more confessions, Sal," his wife says.

He turns to her. "Well, maybe you don't need any more of them. But there's one more I need to make, honey."

"No," she says.

"Last year, I –"

"Stop," his wife says.

"But I –"

"I already told you how I feel about that."

"About what?"

"About – you know what."

"But I don't. There's this wall between us. Well now, I'm going to die. But first I want to knock down that wall. Before I leave you, so we can truly enjoy what's left."

"Sal, don't. I can't afford it. Yes, there's a wall but a part of me still wants to believe in a different reality about you. Don't take that away from me. Please."

"I want to be unburdened, though. I want –"

"Oh, you want. You want! You've always gotten what you wanted from me, Sal. A dutiful wife? Loyalty in exchange for disloyalty? Well this time I want. I want you to shut up now, and stop confessing. I want you to take whatever it is that's eating at you to your grave. Because whatever you've done, whatever sins you've committed, whatever dishonor you've brought upon yourself – I don't want you to barf it up on me. It's your problem. Your responsibility. So now you just keep your crap to yourself."

There is silence on the porch. Frandino and his priest are exchanging glances.

"Okay," Frandino says. He turns to his wife, who sits with her arms crossed.

"I want to be your friend, Steff," he says. "For the rest of our lives together."

"Okay. We're friends, already."

"We were friends an hour ago. It doesn't seem like we're friends now."

"Friends know to let sleeping dogs lie," she answers.

Changes in Latitude

Randy sat with a young couple in lawn chairs on the couple's backyard patio. Drinking wine. Counting stars. Randy was not in school yet, but had a good-paying job through a connection of Bethany's husband Jerry, in a big Miami Beach hotel. Law school would happen soon enough.

"Can I ask you to tell me a story?" Randy looked at Bethany.

"What do you have in mind?"

"What was it like, growing up and having him for a dad? He seems too good to be true."

Bethany and Jerry rolled their eyes and laughed.

"What? Is it that funny?"

"Yes," the married couple replied in unison. Then, Bethany collected herself.

"Dad. Oh, geez, where to begin. I think it's great that you're one of his fans. And I love him dearly. He's been a good father to me and my brothers. But so very busy. Dad has always been a very ambitious, egotistical man. And - he's the real storyteller of the family. I know better than to believe the half of them."

"You don't believe half his stories?"

"He's – complicated. Much more so than most."

"Hmm, complicated," Randy said. "Well, does he – does he care about me?"

"Yes," Bethany replied. "But here's the thing – he cares about baby robins that fall out of their nests. He cares about zoo animals that aren't eating enough. He cares about every single person who might not be getting a fair shake. And he hates to say no. Hates not making a difference. And now, I'm afraid it's all caught up to him."

"Yeah. He was very sick back on the Fourth."

Bethany looks at Randy. "He wired you something. Let me go in the house for it."

She took her leave of the two men, and Randy took a gulp of wine.

Bethany returned with a white envelope. She handed it to her guest.

Randy opened it; there were bills inside. He felt a rush.

"Count it," she said to him. "Dad said it's spending money. Something about for when you want a burger."

There is serious eye contact between them across the table.

"He's given me and my sis an awful lot," Randy said. "You don't think that he took from the city to…"

Bethany shrugged her shoulders and clasped and unclasped her hands. "I have no idea," she answered. "Like I said, he's complicated."

October 9, 1972

Sal Frandino has strung together a few good weeks. The whole thing with Steffi seems to be working itself out. Since that night on the porch she's been cheerful, and he realizes that nothing more needs to be said of his final infidelity.

He's decided against the most aggressive cancer treatment, which the doctors think could give him eighteen to thirty-six months longer. He does not want to lose his hair, to lose all kinds of weight, to be seen as a vegetable. He wants to treat the symptoms and be comfortable until the end.

He's been spending several hours per week with Dan Spesiak. Now, the second Monday in October, it is time to move forward. Spesiak is due to his office at eleven o'clock. At 11:04, Phyllis rings. The deputy has arrived.

The men are sitting in the big leather chairs, and have just caught one another up on their weekends. Spesiak is no patrician; he participated in a bowling tournament and took his boys to see the Thundering Herd play against New England in the Rockpile. A blue collar guy for a blue collar town.

The pleasantries are out of the way.

"Dan, are you ready to be mayor?"

"I'd be stepping into very big shoes, mayor."

"You'll do just dandy. The thing of it is, it's your turn now."

"When?"

"Let's plan to announce by mid-month. Let's shoot for me to resign by Thanksgiving."

"Sal, are you okay? I mean, health-wise?"

"Oh, yeah. Fine. Look, you're the Democratic candidate next year, and it's just time to give you a running start. That's all."

26
We Graduate. All of Us

June, 1975

The rest of high school was a whirlwind: Dances on Saturday nights in the St. Mike's gym, crowded with boys and girls and rest rooms thick with illicit tobacco smoke. Football bumps, bruises and locker room drama. The Thundering Herd, stampeding back to the thick of contention after some down years. Our Swordsmen, banging their way to the Stanley Cup finals.

Parties and drinking and girls, some of whom had fewer qualms than others, and everything that comes with all of that.

A nagging realization that we weren't little kids anymore, and that soon we'd have to give an account of ourselves. Choices beckoned that might determine the course of our lives. Our guidance counselor tried to get us to think about college. I was not one of the two or three guys in my graduating class who would go on to play big time college football. St. Mike's was the beginning and the end of my gridiron wars.

Business in the restaurant was brisk during my senior year of high school. A new mill opened at the steel plant in Lackawanna, partially reversing the long string of layoffs and unemployment which undoubtedly had spurred many a family decision to dine at home instead of coming out for steak or savory lasagna at our place. And, it was on the television set in the restaurant's bar room where I watched the last American diplomats and Marines being evacuated from the roof of the U.S. Embassy in Saigon. I was sad that so many of our older brothers fought and died in vain, but relieved to know that there was now no way I'd go there to be shot at. In the spring of 1975, it seemed that things just might turn out okay.

Children's Letters to God

The Salt of the Earth was kneeling in his backyard garden, using a weeding tool. His back didn't hurt like it had in the old days; the vegetables flourished like never before in his garden; and the weeds never took a very firm root. Every day for thousands of days in a row, the ground had yielded beautiful, delicious vegetables.

On some days he rode the train to work. Once there, he socialized while others performed the hardest labor. At home, there were always two dozen beefsteak tomatoes in the kitchen. He and his wife would boil them. Rinse them under cool water. Peel the skins. Smush them into Ball's preserve jars with fresh sprigs of basil and oregano, and thyme.

When he and his wife weren't guests in someone else's home, people came to his house. He did not know some of them, but they would become friends over a glass of Chianti, share meals that always included fresh meat or fish, cement new friendships over a bottle of Strega. They would leave with gifts from his garden.

After dinner, the Salt of the Earth often went into the basement to play with his trains. These were times of tremendous joy. Now, he shrank to scale. Joined the diorama he had built, as a participant. He could walk the streets, ride the trains and busses, fish in the river, and, wife at his side, watch velvet summer sunsets paint the open sky over the lake.

Every so often when he played with his trains, life turned into a winter day. A train whose existence he did not remember from the old, hard days, would take him to Ellicottville in the hills south of the city; he and his wife, and his children. They would ski. He never remembered downhill skiing before; each time it was a new experience for him and he found it exhilarating. Each time, his skill on the slopes surprised him. But the next day was unfailingly sunny and warm.

It was on one of these evenings of his new, endless summer - whether he was playing inside his diorama or living outside of it he was not entirely certain - as he disembarked from the train that took him home from work, he recognized a man who got off the train at his station near East Delevan Avenue. It was Sal Frandino.

*****

Frandino holds a piece of paper with an address written on it; the address is on Harriet Street. He recognizes the handwriting: John Klinglehaus. He has followed the written instructions to get off the train at East Delevan. He walks, feeling a glow of friendship. Recalling his most recent conversation with the party boss: "I love you, Sal, you hear me? I've always loved you, and I always will. You can let go now, Sal. God willing, I'll catch up with you later."

"I screwed it all up. Why does anyone love me?" Frandino had asked as he looked up at John from his sick bed, using what was left of his voice. Father Al had stood on one side of John, and Steffi on the other. She was holding Frandino's hand, caressing it in her fingers.

"Do justice. Love kindness. Walk humbly," he heard John say. Then something took his sight away and send him flying, accelerating through space. Then, he woke up on the train as if from a nap. In his hand was that note in John's handwriting. In his being was a sense that something new was about to begin.

*****

"*Salvatore! Signore Sindicato!*" The Salt of the Earth has addressed Frandino as "mister mayor" in his native tongue.

Frandino realizes that for the first time in what seems to him like many weeks, he is looking forward to having a meal. The pain in his gut is gone, as is the unpleasant, cancerous taste of his own saliva. Thinks he understands what has happened to him.

Frandino turns around and waits for the Salt of the Earth to catch up. He shows him Klinglehaus' handwriting. Says to the Salt of the Earth, "This is your address, isn't it?"

*****

The front page of both local papers had chronicled Sal Frandino's failing health for the last couple of weeks, so I wasn't surprised when they announced his death during the week before my high school graduation. He had resigned during my sophomore year of high school for health reasons. Then he slipped out of public life. Some guy Spesiak was the mayor now.

I hadn't heard from Raincloud in almost a year. We were going separate ways. I kept tabs on his athletic career through the newspapers; he would soon go to Syracuse on a football and lacrosse scholarship. He had set a city record in the discus throw. He came off the bench to average ten points per game in his senior year for his school's basketball team. He didn't have time anymore for a mere mortal like me.

Then one day in June he called me out of the blue.

"Dude. You going down to the cathedral for the funeral tomorrow?"

"You mean, Frandino's? I wasn't planning on it… why, are you?"

"Ernie. A great tribal chief of the area is passing on to be with the Great Spirit. He lived quite a life, so… he could have some Iroquois in him after all."

"I think he was pure Italian, Mont."

"This is Seneca land, and the Great Spirit allowed him to lead the people for many years. It's important for us to be there, to witness history."

"What time should I pick you up?" I said.

*****

As if I needed a reason to skip a meaningless half day of school a couple of days before graduation. I picked him up in my Bonneville convertible, and we headed down Delaware Avenue to the Cathedral. We knew it might be crowded, so we were early. Hundreds of people, more than could get inside. The front pews held a who's who of politicians, media, bankers and businesspeople.

We got in line to file past the coffin, kneel for a few moments, and offer a prayer before the Mass. Raincloud burst with excitement.

"I want to offer my own special prayer," he said.

"What's gotten into you? You of all people, don't pray in Catholic churches."

"I pray to the Great Spirit," he answered. "It's just a different name and different stories about the same God you Catholics pray to. He answers the prayers of all his children. He's the father of all, Ernie. Even of Italians."

"Wow, what's got into you?" was all I could muster.

The line moved fast; two priests were stationed at the coffin to make sure people didn't kneel and linger for too long. After a few minutes in line, I could get a good look at my first-ever cadaver. Smaller than the man I had seen at the Rockpile a few years earlier. They had him dressed in a fine suit. His face was made up so he looked like a wax model of his former self. His hands, folded together over his heart, held a rosary that was cleverly arranged so that a horizontal version of gravity pulled the black beads toward his feet.

Everyone paid their respects with hands folded in the traditional Catholic pose, and prayed in silence. But not Raincloud. He kneeled in the appointed place, but then reached out and touched the coffin. If his arms were longer, I'm sure he would have touched the body. And then he prayed out loud.

"God of Abraham and Jacob, of Hiawatha and the Peacemaker and all living creatures, please receive Sal Frandino to your feast. And please help our leaders to abide by the great law of selfless service you have given to all leaders. Help them in every decision, in every deliberation, to think about how it will affect their children and their grandchildren and great grandchildren, even seven generations into the future. Please prosper our land and give our leaders the courage and wisdom to do what is right for all of their people's children."

I had never heard a prayer like that before. Neither did the priests who were stationed there. I think if the elderly priest on our right had a hatchet, he'd have taken my buddy's scalp right then and there.

"I am Raincloud," Lamont volunteered to him in a clear, measured tone as he stood back up.

"You are something of a cloud, indeed," muttered the priest, looking up at Lamont from a considerable height disadvantage.

"Well, I think those were just lovely sentiments," a lady's voice scolded the priest from behind us. I turned to look, and recognized Alice Mrozinski, who had tried twice over the last decade to unseat Frandino. She smiled and winked at Raincloud.

The service proceeded and after the official Mass portion, several people were allowed to speak. We heard about little bits and pieces of Frandino's life from his wife; then from the powerful upstate Democratic boss John Klinglehaus, who broke down and cried twice; then from his parish priest Father Al, and then from current mayor Spesiak. Newspaper editor Finn O'Connell, who often editorialized against Frandino in the *Messenger*, offered a moving, funny and emotional tribute that got to all of us. Everyone credited Sal Frandino with dedicating his life to helping the little guy. Everyone agreed that he loved the city, and said his death marked the end of an era.

"I wish they'd let me talk about him," muttered the heavyset adult male with curly dark hair who sat just to my right. Every so often he had been dabbing beads of sweat off his forehead and temples. I knew that this guy couldn't wait to change out of his suit into something more casual.

"What would you say?" I whispered to him.

"We go way back, Sallie and me," the guy said, not really whispering. "Name's Andrew, by the way." He grabbed my hand and shook it. Killer grip.

"So as I was sayin', when he used to babysit me, he put out a kitchen fire and probably saved my life and my sisters, too. When I was five. Sal Frandino? He was a saint amongst sinners, so to speak, my friend."

"That's a great story," I said. A lady in front of us turned with a scowl.

But the guy continued. "That ain't the half. He and I saved a guy's life once, just a couple-a-years back. And we coulda both got in a lot of trouble for it but God watched over us."

"What a story," I said.

"Yeah. And I've already said too much, my friend."

I felt Raincloud's elbow. "Dudes!" he scolded. Conversation ended.

When the speakers were finished, Raincloud and I walked outside into a gorgeous day. People milled about the Cathedral grounds among trees, benches and shrubbery. People reconnecting in small groups. Within a minute or two, our attention was drawn to a young black man in a black suit. Distraught.

"Randy. It'll be okay." A couple of older black men were saying. I recognized that one of them was politician William Snead, the very Snead whose son had waylaid me nearly four years earlier in football practice.

"What're we gonna do now?" The young man named Randy seemed more in shock than in mourning. I didn't think his upset could be related to Frandino's passing. But the next thing we heard caused Raincloud and I to turn to one another: Something about Frandino putting him and his sister through school, and giving him tough love at a time when he needed it to keep his life from going off the rails.

Just beyond this Randy fellow was Hersch Woodstein and a camera crew. He was on the air.

"Let's get closer," Raincloud said. We tried, but the crowd was too much for us to negotiate. By the time we were close enough to hear, he was saying:

"... truly a favorite son of our great city, and a friend to so many in need. Salvatore Bernardo Frandino: nineteen-oh-eight. Nineteen seventy-five."

Woodstein was finished.

"Let's go back inside," Raincloud instructed.

"Lamont, you're going to church twice in one day?"

Inside, there were still gaggles of people talking to each other. Even the occasional chuckle. But the church-echoes of it all underscored the sobriety of the occasion.

"Hey, there's his wife," Raincloud said. He pointed to one corner of the cathedral where a small line of people had formed to talk with Mrs. Frandino.

"Let's go thank her," Raincloud said.

"For what?"

"Are you dense, Pronotaro? For sacrificing her marriage for the people of this city. Because he was the mayor for so many years. How much time do you think she ever had with him?"

She stood with Frandino's parish priest. A young blonde woman – a real head-turner, by the way – stood with the priest and I'll be darned if she wasn't holding his hand. There were four people ahead of us in the line, which moved more slowly than the one we had waited in to kneel at the coffin before the Mass. We could overhear her conversations. Mrs. Frandino was a small woman with dark features, very petite, aging gracefully. Apparently her name was Stephanie – I never had known that. Seemed to me that she was being patient through what must have been quite an ordeal.

It was our turn. Mrs. Frandino smiled and the priest said, "Guys, I'm Father Al. Thanks for being here today."

"Thank you, ma'am," I said to Stephanie Frandino, wanting to please Raincloud.

"Thank me? For what?"

"For being the mayor's wife," Raincloud cut in. He spoke slowly and enunciated each syllable with care. "I've been studying leadership and what happens to leaders. I think it's always the spouses who suffer. He must have been very busy a lot of the time and you must have been hurt by that. You have sacrificed for us."

She did a double take. "My," she said. "Who taught you to – to speak like this?"

"My name is Raincloud," he replied, continuing to speak as though narrating a documentary on public television. "I am a Seneca. My own people don't study the ways of leadership in my nation, but I study them. I want to be a great leader for all people. I will study the life of your husband."

"Oh, my. What a – precious thought. How old are you, my son?"

"I'm graduating Bennett High this weekend. I was a leader at my school in sports and now I'm off to Syracuse University. Maybe one day I'll be a leader in business or politics. I'm not sure yet."

"Oh, Lord," she said, grabbing his hand and holding it. "If Sal could hear you talk like that, he would be so happy. Thank you both, thank you for stopping by."

I shook her hand, and we turned to leave. Then I saw her. Way back as far from the front of the church as she could sit. Alone. Black scarf over her hair and sunglasses with big lenses. But I had spent a night at her place, listening as she and Van Morrison poured out their hearts.

"Wait outside," I said to Raincloud. "I think I see my cousin."

"Okay, I'll be right outside."

I sighed relief as he complied. Then, I went into the pew and sat next to her.

"Darse?"

She turned to me. "Ernie the Pro."

"Still on TV?"

She sighed. "I'm working on it." Then she put a hand on my arm. "Ernie, you've gotten so big. And was that Lamont?"

"It was."

"Unbelievable, you two - so big and handsome. Ernie my friend, it's good to see you. I debated about flying up here. It might be wrong, but he's such a part of my life."

"Yeah. You still in Washington?"

"Yeah, when I'm not flying somewhere. Quebec, Montevideo, Houston, Atlanta. And that's just so far this month. Tomorrow, I go to Caracas. I worked for the local station down in Washington for a few months and then the network picked me up to cover stories all over North and South

America. Sometimes a few of the network affiliates pick up my stories. Sometimes not. It's a tough business."

"Is it still your dream?"

"Yeah. My crazy dream. Following it means I won't be able to settle down and have a husband and kids till I'm an old maid. But I love it even when it doesn't love me. How about you?"

"I don't know. Four years of football was quite a meat grinder. I graduate in three days, and..."

"You graduate! Where are you going to college?"

"Staying local. Gonna go to UB and help my dad in the restaurant, you know?"

"Yeah. Okay. What about Lamont?"

"That dude is going to be a Syracuse Orangeman with a football scholarship. He's doing great, Darcie. Just missed being class valedictorian. You should have heard what he just told Mrs. Frandino up there a minute ago about how he wants to be a leader. He almost made her cry. I wish I had it together like he does."

"You do, Ernie. You're both gonna be just fine. You guys have always pushed each other to be the best."

"How long are you in town?"

Darcie looked at her watch. I noticed that Mickey Mouse still lived on her wrist. "My flight leaves in two hours. I should start back to the airport now."

We sat side by side for the next few seconds, looking up toward the front. I felt a knot in my stomach. I knew what I had to do.

"Darcie. You told me that night at your place I should ask if I ever saw you again. The cocaine and the pills."

She turned to me without smiling. Looked like she was beholding a ghost.

"Well?"

"I'm getting help," she said, not using her vocal cords but instead forcing air out from between her lips. "Thank you for asking."

"I'm on your side," came my automatic reaction.

"Yeah. Lots of people are. I've been clean for six months. It hurts like hell."

I grabbed her hand and squeezed three times. "I just gave you a triple shot of St. Mike's Maurader positivity. Got us to nine wins and one loss this past year. So now you'll be fine."

"You are so silly."

"Maybe, my sister. But I got you to smile."

"Yes, you did. You're sweet, Ernie."

Silence overtook us once more. I turned my whole body toward her and felt myself smiling broadly. But she didn't even return my gaze. She was watching the people at the front of the church.

"She's so in control up there," Darcie said. "Like royalty."

"Mrs. Frandino?"

"She's probably a great woman. And... shit. She probably hates me."

"Darse. Don't think about it anymore. He's gone, you know? But you're still here."

"Ernie. I'm so grateful you've kept my secrets. My time here was the worst eighteen months of my life. But I think one day I'll be able to handle the memories. Does that make any sense? And, hey Ernie?"

"Yeah."

"Say hello to Lamont for me, huh? But wait at least a month."

My left hand reached and moved her scarf just a little, and I leaned in and kissed her on the cheek.

"Get out of here, Ernie," she said. Then she smiled, and grabbed my hand and gave it a quick squeeze. And then, I was up and headed back outside to rejoin Raincloud.

Part III
Generations

27
Struggles: Nickel City Montage

I've only seen Lamont Raincloud once after Sal Frandino's funeral Mass, not counting the two or three times I caught the Orangemen on TV when he played college football. A month after the mayor's funeral, some friends who were enrolled as freshman at a local college invited me to a party in one of the dorms. I met a gal from Long Island who convinced me to share her sloe gin fizz from a gallon jug. An art major. We sat on a couch together, mildly aware of the surrounding celebration, when she invited me to go someplace where she'd paint my portrait with my own brush. I was intrigued. I heard his voice from out of nowhere.

"Pronotaro. Dude, on your feet."

I looked up. "Lamont... uh, Theresa, this is my friend Lamont. Lamont, Theresa."

"On your feet, Pronotaro," he repeated.

"Excuse me for just a sec," I was up off the couch.

"Ernie. Out in the hall with me. Now."

"Gimme a minute," I said to the lass.

"Dude," he said to me out in the hall. "You're making a big mistake." That same documentary narrator delivery he had used with Mrs. Frandino. "If you're planning to be with her tonight, then you can't even see what you're shooting at."

"She looks okay to me. And she feels -"

"Listen to me," Lamont said. "You're going to regret her. She'll transmit something that will last a lot longer than a cheap thrill. Look at her. Look at you. What are you doing with a tramp like that?"

"If I gotta tell you, I'm not sure you'd understand."

He looked up at the ceiling. "Ernie, that is the difference between me and you. I am out to bust every Native American stereotype I can bust. No alcohol, no tobacco. No tramps. Just a lean, shit-kicking, fighting machine. Eventually, I'm going to win big. What are you winning tonight?"

"'Mont. You know I love you, man. But right now, you're a downer."

"Come on, I'm driving. Let's go on Hertel Avenue and get some pizza and tacos. Sober you up."

"You go. Leave me be, huh?"

He lost his bravado and his face morphed into that hurt second grader.

"Okay, have it your way." I watched him walk down the dormitory hall, and disappear behind a closed door.

Haven't seen him since. A lot has happened leading up to our reunion this evening. Wonder what the years have done to him. Shoot, I wonder what he'll say the years have done to me.

February 20, 1977

Four people in the restaurant: Dad and I, and two idle servers. Seven o'clock on a Sunday evening. Sundays weren't the busiest restaurant night, but we should have had some tables seated, some phone calls for carryout orders. We had zilch.

For several months, business had been tapering off. During the big blizzard at the end of January and into February, every business in the metropolis was closed for multiple days. The first week we reopened, we experienced a rush that reminded me of the expression "pent up demand."

Then the whole thing died again.

Dad was in the back tinkering with our dish machine. I watched him for a minute. He was focused on the contraption. Finally, he straightened up. Sighed. Shook his head. I still see him in his stained white apron and checkered chef pants.

"Nights like this give a man time to think," I said. If he tried to smile back, he failed.

"Dad, should I tell Liz and Sandy to go home? There's nothing for them to do."

"Let 'em off the clock at nine, if there's still nothing happening."

"Okay." We just stood there, looking at one another. The quiet in the kitchen had become way too familiar.

"Dad. What's gonna happen?"

"When the weather gets better, we'll start picking up, I suppose."

"Yeah. It always does in the springtime."

"Well then, here's to an early spring, huh?"

"Early spring, then," I said as he turned back toward the dish machine.

He talked to the machine. "We put everything we had into this place. Everything. End of this week, and I gotta borrow again to make payroll. Four of the last five weeks. Ten of the last fourteen. But, who's counting."

"Well, that's what a line of credit's for, right? For the little slumps."

"Little slump," he echoed.

"But it'll be better in the spring, right?"

He straightened up and turned to face me. I had never seen my father quite that way before.

"Ern, you're almost twenty years old. Two more years, and you'll be done with college."

"Yeah. I'll have that degree. We'll start building the franchise."

"Ernie, graduate and get out of town."

"What?"

"There's nothing here for you now. And by the time you graduate, there's gonna be less than nothing."

"There's the restaurant."

He answered with a slow head shake.

Then it dawned on me that I didn't have the first idea of what I wanted to be when I grew up.

One night shortly thereafter, I found my mom where I often had found her over the years when I needed her counsel: on the couch, watching late night television. She used the remote control to turn the sound down without getting up from the couch. A cool trick in 1977.

"What's up, Pronotaro?" she asked.

"What's Dad been telling you about the business these days?"

"That it's slow."

"I always thought Tom and I would inherit it. Our dream was we'd open a couple more. He'd run one place, and I'd run one."

"Ernie, don't."

"Don't what?"

"Don't keep hoping for that. Expand your dreams beyond the restaurant. Beyond this city. Or you might be disappointed."

During the spring semester my computer lab mate was an exotic gal from Iran or Pakistan or one of those countries where she could get stoned to death for dressing in tight jeans the way she did at school. Friendly gal, good English. Never got past lunch with her in the student union. I did hyper-focus on the computer class to impress her. And got so wrapped up in it that I scheduled an appointment with the professor shortly before the semester ended.

"Yeah, you definitely could merge business and computer science into a career," the prof told me. "Lots of our business school alums are doing that. We see 'em getting jobs in Atlanta. Washington D.C. Houston, maybe. California, and Boston, Mass."

"Well… what about right here?" I asked.

The teacher laughed. "Not so much, Ernie."

Great. One more authority figure telling me that to get a decent career off the ground, I had to leave family and friends, the teams I rooted for, and the streets and sights and flavors that contained my life.

Christmastime, 1977

Not only would Randy eat multiple holiday dinners at Bethany and Jerry's place. The Frandino estate flew his parents in to be reunited with him. The estate was also supporting half the cost of law school at the University of Miami.

Steffi came to Florida, too. Randy loved her. She spoke wisely. Was kind. Cared about Randy because Pops had cared.

It was just he and Jerry, for a time, in the kitchen on Christmas Eve as the women folk ran last minute errands before the stores closed. Randy's dad was upstairs, asleep. On the twenty-fifth there'd be turkey and ham; but on Christmas Eve, a big, traditional Italian meal. Jerry was teaching Randy how to prepare the meat for the *bracciole*; Randy was about to tenderize the escalloped cuts of beef.

"Before the first blow falls upon these cutlets," Randy picked up his wineglass and raised it toward Jerry. "I was thinking. Tonight when we toast, I want to toast this whole family. My folks – to be treated like this, they would never have dreamed."

"Yeah," Jerry said. "But first…" he raised his own glass. "Here's to you, man."

"I'll drink to me, sure." They partook.

"But why? I still can't figure it out. Why do you all love me?"

"Because of what you did."

"Sold drugs and got a contract put out on me?"

"Not that, man. You stopped a riot."

"Oh, no I didn't. I was powerless that night. It was because of the rainstorm, I guess."

"But you went back into the Y that night. And talked to them. Didn't you?"

Randy's mouth opened. He stuttered something unintelligible, even to himself. Then he said, "Yeah."

During Christmas Eve dinner, Randy did not make the toast. He did not feel like a hero. He sat opposite his father at the dinner table so he could look at the old guy and appreciate him. Dad was not walking well; he was a little stooped over, and quiet. Dad moved north from Mississippi during the Second World War to get a decent wage in the Curtiss-Wright airplane factory helping to make P-39 Aircobra fighter jets. When the aircraft industry started to leave town after the war and through the '60s, Dad bounced from one job to another. Lots of men did. It wasn't a character thing. They were Black. Nevertheless, the old man sitting across from Randy at the dinner table had persevered. Tried to live clean. Wanted the family in church, even after he said he stopped believing. Expressed his heartbreak to the 19-year old Randy about the conditions that brought about the civil unrest in the '60s, but also heartbreak that Randy was so gung-ho to join the violence.

Randy smiled at him across the dinner table. The smile was returned, even amplified. No words needed.

Bethany didn't allow anyone to smoke inside the house. The house rule brought mother and son together after dessert, on the patio. Mom spoke first.

"Baby. It's good to see you. We all miss you."

"Good to see you too, mom."

"Yeah. So, you know baby, your sister looks like she's gonna take that job in Chicago she's been talkin' bout."

"Yeah, yeah. Mom, you got yourself two college grads with office jobs and some damn good meals out of this. Not bad."

"Well son, two college grads, and neither one of them will be at home."

Randy considered his cigarette for a moment, then looked up at his mother. She smiled, then the smile faded.

"I'm not feeling quite so young as I used to, boy. And your daddy, he's -"

Randy sighed. "Dad looks so broken down."

"Umm hmm."

Mother took son by the hand.

"Well son, I'm just wondering that it's got to be safe for you to come home now."

A breath rushed out of his mouth.

"Please, Randy."

He bit the inside of his cheeks and looked up at the Florida stars.

"Daddy and I – we could use your help, son."

"Yeah." He dropped what was left of his smoke on the patio, and crushed it with his foot. The South Florida air was clammy and still.

"I – I don't know, Mom."

"The detectives think maybe in another year, son. Maybe even now. Those people that wanted to hurt you have other things to occupy themselves. Some of them are already gone to meet their maker."

"Those people don't let go of grudges, Mom. That's what makes them who they are."

"But it's home, son. It's where you're from, where your family is. And I – I miss you. Please."

"I love you, but I got a job here. School. A girlfriend. My life is here now."

She cried. He held her.

*****

"Some damn present," Dad spit out the words at the kitchen table. He held the first section of the morning *Messenger* in his hand. It was the day after Christmas.

Dad had managed to keep the restaurant open during the year; the springtime business rally we hoped for did materialize. Then, summer was beautiful, and people came out to eat. Restaurants did close, but enough people chose our place over the others and did so often enough, that we almost broke even for the year. Dad was proud to be one of the survivors.

But the front page of the December 26 *Messenger* caused a wounded animal bark. He tossed the paper and shot a look my way. I read the headline: *Bethlehem Announces Huge Layoffs*.

The first sentence of the first paragraph of the lead story was a haymaker to the temple. Over the first few weeks of the new year, the plant would implement a permanent reduction of its workforce from 14,300 to just under 8,000 employees.

I searched his face. He looked away and up. Like his eyes were searching for God someplace near the kitchen ceiling.

28
New York City: 1983

Nights here were never kind to me. I had been awake until two in the morning, getting talking points ready for the next day's meeting. Then the thin, dry air kept waking me. Directing me to the sink for another glass of water. Five hours of *sleepus interruptus*.

I was in Denver in late August. It was not home, nor was Dallas, or Minneapolis, or Houston. Four cities where Ernesto Pronotaro, consultant, had spent most of the year. Three side trips to California.

Home, when I was there, was the Brownstone apartment in Chelsea I shared with two guys I had graduated college with. One small bathroom out in the hall for the three men who lived in my apartment. And for the married couple who lived across the hall. The lower west side of Manhattan: people living on top of one another; the rich and the ragged vying on equal terms for square inches of space on the A, C or E trains. Chelsea was friendly dope peddlers on every street corner. Chelsea was four stops from 23rd Street to the World Trade Center. Outrageous rents.

Chelsea was Donna, with curly dark hair and a flawless body, who lived in our building. Four years my senior, and seemed to know every good, affordable place to eat from the Battery all the way up past Hunter College on the East Side. A good Italian girl, my grandmother would have said.

I looked out the window of my eighth-floor hotel room at the cranes.

They were building a new downtown Denver, just like I had seen in Houston and Dallas, and on my trips south from San Francisco to the giant suburb that people out near the Bay were calling "the Valley." Cranes, buildings, new houses and schools. From sea to shining sea; a ridiculous amount of new construction.

I turned on the television to use one of the morning network shows as background noise. Shower, shave, suit up. Be at First Mountain Bank headquarters, along with my partner, by eight.

Having showered and shaved, I exited the bathroom and grabbed clothes from the closet. Then the woman on the news show caught my eye. It was Darcie. Finally, after all these years, on network television. Interviewing President Reagan's wife. I laughed aloud. Darcie was living out her dream in my hotel room as I stood naked before her.

I waxed nostalgic that day.

I was getting home to see Mom and Dad at least once each year, and when I went back I always saw guys from the neighborhood. I'd tell them about the places I had seen. I had lost track of Raincloud. Last I knew about him, I saw in the *Daily News* sports section a couple of years earlier that he'd been cut by pro football's Detroit Cats.

I loved going home, but it was sad that nothing was changing. No cranes, no new buildings. Things kept getting older. One big company or another was always in the midst of leaving town.

I was next due back home to see the Thundering Herd play the Fish, whose annual visit to our neck of the woods was the highlight of the football season. I was making more money than Dad, though miraculously he had kept the restaurant open. I bought tickets for myself and my brother Tom, for Dad, and a couple of my friends.

We tailgated in supurb weather. Dad was in high spirits; I was thrilled that he fit in so well with my friends. After the game we drove to a pasta-and-wine place just a stone's throw from the Niagara River. Then, when my buddies took off, Dad, Tom and I went across the bridge into Canada. Just for the hell of it.

We went to the park in Fort Erie where the water rushes by one's toes as the lake empties into the Niagara. The view across the water and back at the city, setting sun reflecting off the buildings, was exactly the way it had looked when I was in high school.

Tom was looking down into the current.

"Cleanest it's been in my whole lifetime," he mused. It was true; I looked down as the current swept into the river and I could see the bottom, four feet deep right at the shoreline, very clearly. The water sparkled.

"Well, sure," Dad said. "And it'll get even cleaner, now that the steel is gone."

"What?" I looked at Dad.

"Yeah, Ernie. Guess you didn't hear. The whole thing shut down earlier this year. Now Republic's in big trouble. Lackawanna and South Buffalo remind people of the Great Depression. You look around, there's men lining up to..." his voice trailed off.

*****

Donna had moved into our Brownstone just a few months after I moved in with my buddies. Our relationship began at the intersection of her initiative and my fearlessness. Worked for a Wall Street brokerage. To hear her tell it, the trading floor on the Exchange was a boy's club. She was being worked in as an industry analyst instead of as a securities trader. We talked shop. Too much, probably. Sometimes she'd say "Love you babe," when we parted company. "Yeah, you too," I'd say.

Halloween night of 1983. Donna knew about a costume party in the neighborhood. We went as gorillas in full, hairy suits. We were there twenty minutes and this elaborate E.T. costume – from the movie of the same name – started following me around. E.T. was telling clever jokes and stories. A device distorted his or her voice.

I had to pee. E.T. followed me into the men's room.

"What the hell?" I turned to the creature. "Who are you? And what do you want with me?"

"Off with your head. So I can see you. I know much about you, Mister Gorilla."

"Who are you?"

"I will not let you out of here until I see your face. Come on, Ernie. Be a sport."

"How do you know me?"

I lifted the ape head, and heard hysterical, distorted laughter from the alien. The creature's arms were clutching at itself and its whole body wretched with laughter.

I turned to the bathroom mirror and saw why E.T. was laughing. I had perspired mightily in that costume. My somewhat-longish hair stood straight up. I was a drenched, unkempt, uncool mess.

"You are a courageous man to bare yourself to me, Ernie Pronotaro."

"Who are you?"

The thing took its head off. "It" was suddenly a very attractive "her." I was mortified.

"I am Sarah," said she, in her non-alien voice.

"Donna's sister," staggered from my mouth.

"Hey. I've seen nice pictures of you. Go for a walk? I mean, after you take care of your business in here. I won't look. Well – maybe I won't." She smiled.

"You're quite a bad-ass," I said to her.

"Want to borrow a comb?"

Donna had mentioned Sarah to me. Three years younger than Donna, a year older than me. Lived near her parents on Long Island. We snuck away and walked to my apartment. I showered off while she listened to my stereo. Then we walked for hours, lost in sailboats, baseball, old flames, anything but business. We were walking over a stone bridge near a duck pond in Central Park when we stopped to watch the sun rise. She told me stories of her life, happy and sad; and I found myself wanting to tell her my stories, too. From that first walk, a part of me that was killed off during my sophomore year of high school was alive again.

Donna spent the next six months steamed at us. A year after that costume party, Sarah and I were married in the neighborhood church where she grew up. Donna, by that time, had found enough forgiveness in her heart to make her mark as a swell maid of honor.

Charlie the Pro came along just a year later, right around the time I bought our very first house, across the Hudson in Paramus. Then came Ernie the Coach, and Jennifer, whom Sarah and Donna both loved to call "Cotton Jenny."

While Sarah was carrying Charlie, my brother Tom announced that he was marrying our neighborhood sweetheart Esther. His torch burned through years of letter writing. Weekend visits of being told he was only a friend. Two years of stoically enduring her college fling with a guy named Roger. Relocating when she found work in Tennessee. They settled in Nashville and got down to the business of giving my children cousins of their own.

Dad was so proud of them. I think the toast he gave to Tom and Esther at their wedding reception was the highlight of Dad's life.

But the angels had put their call in for Dad's soul.

29

"The hell He don't punish cities."

It was a party. Dad had carried on for as long as he could but on Labor Day evening, 1990, it was time to let go. A new generation of six cousins - three each from Sarah and Esther - helped to fill the place. The girls nursed their youngest in the original dining room, now unused.

Some of the old timers who frequented the place in the '60s and '70s came to join us on that final night. We laughed and hugged, felt happy and sad, and remarked to one another on all the ways in which we'd changed or stayed the same.

Emphysema.

In January 1991, just a few months after the restaurant's swan song, the Thundering Herd had earned the right to appear in their first championship game in a generation. Dad's prognosis was worsening and the part of me that wants God to exist knew that he would allow Dad to see his Herd be crowned champs before he passed into the next world. Tom and I had already agreed, when we spoke on Christmas Day, that if the Herd made it to the championship game we'd be back in the homeland to watch it with our parents, our wives, and each other.

Dad was frail that weekend of the Big Game, but his mind was sharp. With Sarah and the kids safe in the hotel, I went to my parents' place and sat up with Mom, Dad and Tom late into Friday night. Dad talked about everything and anything. We already had heard all the stories, but

I listened carefully. We might never hear them from his raspy voice again.

*****

Two weeks later, he was gone. Sarah and I, Tom and Esther, and all our kids were re-united in Buffalo for the third time in just a few weeks. Esther was the most torn up of all of us; Dad had favored her from the time we were all very small, and she had grown to love him like her own father. But she was able to compose herself for stretches at a time. During the grace meal after the burial service, as I walked around the buffet room greeting friends and relatives, she grabbed hold of my arm.

"Where is Lamont Raincloud? Why isn't he here?"

"Why should he be here?"

"Because he was your best friend. Do you even know where he lives now?"

"Should I?"

"Didn't you even try to find him? When someone dies, you're supposed to get everyone important from your life together. And you know stuff like this matters to Lamont. You jerk."

January, 1993

Randy went into the office on Saturday mornings just to catch up, because the weekdays were madness. After passing the Florida bar, he got a job as an associate at a firm on Biscayne Boulevard where he toiled at workplace and religious discrimination issues. Married a beach jewel. Had a young daughter. Life was pleasant. But on this particular Saturday morning, he sat in his office reading and re-reading the same e-mail. Nothing like this was ever supposed to happen. An offer. He owed it to himself and maybe to his mom, who was struggling on her own with no family close by, and possibly down to her last few years.

On the following Monday he had a thirty minute conversation with a woman named Sylvia, who just might become his next boss. He hung up. Took a deep breath. How he would explain to Bermuda born and bred Melanye, whom he had plucked from the sands of Miami Beach and with whom he had conceived his child; that the perfect job was calling him to return north?

A month later, he wore his best suit to the interview. Flew in the day before, stayed in the house he grew up in with his mom. Lamented to her the condition of the house, the street, the neighborhood.

"Pops wouldn't have let this happen," he told his mother at breakfast that morning. "Pops wasn't perfect, but he gave a damn about this town."

"Your Pops Frandino wasn't big enough to stop this, son," she replied. "It's a curse. God's own hand against the city. He's punishing us for something. Gotta be."

"God doesn't punish cities like that," Randy said.

"The hell he don't!" she countered. "You go look it up in Genesis, what he done did to Sodom and Gomorrah. Or Jonah, what he was gonna do to Nineveh if them Ninevites didn't repent. He even swallered up Babylon. I tell you, son, some real bad stuff must've been going down in lots of bedrooms and back rooms 'round here. The Lord was just savin' up his vengeance. So now we see all his wrath poured out upon us."

"Mom, you sound all wound up like a preacher-woman!" Randy smiled at her, got up from his chair and put his arms around her from behind.

"Mom, if I get this job, you come live with me someplace nice. Like Snyder or East Aurora."

"Now how you expect me to fit in with all them rich people out in Snyder! I'm a Michigan Street Daisy, is what I am. You get that job, and then you come visit me right here in the evenings before you go driving off home to Snyder, hear me? I'm gonna stay right here 'til the day I die, you see?"

"Mom, you're a trip. I love you."

"I love you too, son. But don't be telling me I got to leave my neighborhood." She slapped his hand. "You hear me? Damn."

Randy was still warm inside, smiling at the thought of his mother's speech, as he drove the rental car down Michigan and toward his downtown interview. Yes, the old neighborhood looked ragged, worse with every passing visit, which was about once per year. He wanted her out of this place. He still could spot, nowadays with more detachment, where the drugs were being sold and who was selling them, in these places.

He arrived ten minutes early. Told the receptionist who he was, and sat down.

Two minutes later, a woman in business attire, perhaps a few years his senior, came for him. "You're early. I'm Sylvia Snead."

Randy rose and extended a hand in greeting.

"You might remember my father, William," she said as they shook. "He speaks of you. But I'm the person you will need to impress in order to join the firm."

"Well, Ms. Snead, you've already impressed me."

"Of course I have. Oh, and there's one other person you need to impress. You'll meet him now. He's not a member of our firm but we asked him to come in this morning because we think you'd be working closely with him. You'll see."

Through a door that led to a room full of cubicles and back toward a corner office. Randy saw a short white man with a shock of silver hair. Rising from a chair. A suit and a smile.

"Hey, there he is." The short man extended a hand.

"Good to meet you," Randy said in the midst of the handshake.

The short old man took a step back. Mild consternation.

"You forgot me," the man said. "Don't tell me this, Randy. You forgot me, ain't it?"

"Um. You do look sort of familiar."

"Sal Frandino's house. Had to be what, twenty – what? Twenty one years ago, almost. I'm John. I've always remembered you and your family and that talk we had on that Fourth of July."

"Klinglehaus! John Klinglehaus!"

They hugged.

"Randy. Look at you, all grown up. Aw, man. We've been following you. Sal's daughter Bethany and me - we talk. Good things are gonna happen up here. We want you to be a part of it."

30
Every Purpose Under Heaven

June 13, 2000

Darcie's voice filled our bedroom and called for my attention, but it was 6:45 a.m. and I needed to get dressed and leave the house. Boy, could she talk. Every so often, I paid attention to a sentence:

"On some days, deer are seen grazing the vegetation that grows in the ever-widening cracks in the pavement of the old roads and parking lots..."

"A person could imagine that eventually, the Iroquois who once fished here will return for their morning catch..."

"Today on the shores of the eastern end of Lake Erie, all that's left of a bygone era are these rusty railroad tracks, these huge, abandoned brick shells that housed the ovens and mills..."

I realized that she was talking about my hometown. I stopped knotting my necktie and turned to the bedroom television set to see her on the air, standing outside on a bright, breezy day in an abandoned rail yard with the lake behind her. Sarah was downstairs, helping the kids be on time for their school bus.

"Some say the future of the area's flailing economy is tied to acres of underused waterfront property like this, potentially beautiful and scenic, that could be de-contaminated and repurposed as a prime destination for tourism. Here at the abandoned steel plant in Lackawanna New York, I'm

Darcie Yeager for *America in the Morning*."

Darcie had become a regular on the network's morning show, and the substitute anchor for the network's evening news broadcast. She had dined with heads of state and had given speeches at college commencement ceremonies. I didn't go out of my way to watch her but when I did see her on the air, I was proud of her. The talking head in the studio asked her to share some reminiscences about her time as a young journalist in my home town, but I could watch no more. I was needed on the very next PATH train into Manhattan.

*****

It was easy for Randy to become discouraged. Sometimes, he spoke to groups of fewer than ten people in venues that were built for hundreds. Attracting two dozen area residents to any one event, represented a triumph.

The money, the lifestyle. Not what he had in Miami. His title sounded impressive. He had easy access to all the area's political leaders. But the personal costs were high. His marriage, over. His little girl Helena, back with Melanye in Bermuda. They tried to make it work. She came north and he accommodated her choice of neighborhood: a five-bedroom Victorian home on a wooded three quarters of an acre in Hamburg. Melanye substituted Toronto for Coconut Grove when she wanted high-end shopping; and when she longed for the World Beat of South Beach, she gave the artsy feel of Allentown a whirl. But she complained about the differences, especially of the cold. "Choose your lady," she told him in her lilting English one night during a cold snap in March. "Your family, or your damned city." Something about her ultimatum made him angry. Something about her materialism disaffected him. He chose his damned city, his Michigan Street Daisy, and her sworn lifelong allegiance to her neighborhood.

Within a year of the separation came the divorce. He sold the spread in Hamburg and downsized to the second-floor flat of a turn-of-the-century house in the Parkside Crescent not far from the city zoo. Ten minute drive from his mother. Told the octogenarian German landlord couple who lived on the first floor that he'd paint the house in the colors of their choice, and put in new flowerbeds. Followed through on all of it during that very first summer. Some with his own sweat, and some by neighborhood high school kids that he paid – sometimes in cash, sometimes with a communal meal of the thing he cooked best: chili con carne. September came and a local magazine came to take pictures. The pictures made it into a feature about how older city properties could become charming with tender loving care.

His living arrangement reaped a tremendous savings in rent, and the landlords – Winkler was their name – began to trust him like family. Neighbors came to see what he'd done, and began adding similar touches to their own properties. Randy knew that barriers were coming down, that something more significant was happening between himself, the neighborhood, and the Winklers.

Then, January. A tremendous storm. Parts of the city under five feet of snow. Old Man Winkler, possessing a stout soul that disdained the frailty of his old body, clawing his way to the snow blower in the garage. He later admitted that the chest pains had begun when he was about halfway to his goal. He also said that a Buffalo guy should never let pain interfere with life. So he resolved to push through it. Randy found him and carried him inside. Called friends in the city government to send a snowplow and a team of medics. They could not get him to a hospital; so they brought the hospital to his bedroom. While it was still touch-and-go for the old man's life, Randy sat with Mrs. Winkler in the kitchen, and they prayed.

"You are the most important person to come into his life since our own kids," she said to him when the praying was over.

Randy gave her quizzical eyes. A slight head shake.

"It's true," she continued. She then had reached for Randy's hand. "For years and years, Hans was so prejudiced against black people. I think you've helped my husband to grow up more in the last three years of his life, than he managed his first eighty-two years."

When the old man recovered, Randy began to spend a little more time with him than before the heart attack.

But the Winklers did not fill the void in his heart. Neither did the five times per year when he would see Melanye and his daughter. Four times per year he flew to Bermuda; the cheap rent he paid made the trips affordable. Once per year, always in July or August, he would fly the ladies in his life to Buffalo for a week. She told him she would not remarry; she'd rather play the field. It made the separation from her worse, as though she was hinting that he could have her back if he would only return to warmer climes. So he ached.

He frequented the little jazz clubs downtown on Friday and Saturday nights, clubs that scuffled to stay open even as he scuffled to keep going. He ached as he worked to provide legal representation and leadership to the city's neighborhood and community associations who sought funds to fix up their city one property, one street corner, at a time. He ached as he often perceived that, more than funds and more than political and legal clout, encouragement and inspiration were in shortest supply. He tried to provide it to the city's people even as his own tank seemed to always be just a drop or two from empty.

Randy ached as he sat, on Saturday mornings, in the same little café to read newspapers. On Fillmore Avenue near Main Street, a few blocks from home. The same woman had been serving him coffee for two years. A white woman, close to his own age. Looked intriguing. Always very businesslike toward him, and he didn't have the emotional energy to say much. He knew that her name was Millie.

December 24, 2000

I had just purchased our family's second home computer, and the whole crew clamored for me to set it up in time for the little Christmas Eve get-together with friends and neighbors that we always hosted. The kids wanted it for the games; Sarah wanted it for – well, to be honest, for the games.

I always become nostalgic as the end of a year approaches, and 2000 was no exception. I reflected on my career, but mostly on the family Sarah and I had created. I remembered some of the endearing things the kids did when they were smaller. Sarah had become more beautiful to me with every passing year: her physical charms, her wise parenting of our children, her warm friendship. By so many measures, I was a blessed man.

There was a big hole in my soul.

The guests had left, the kids were in bed, and Sarah sensed, at half-past midnight, that I was pooped. "I'll finish up in here," she told me in the kitchen. I started upstairs to bed. But first, I couldn't help but to spend a few minutes with our new computer. I wanted to use the Internet to look for Lamont Raincloud. I wouldn't rest until I found a way to get back in touch with him.

I typed in his name and received many results. None of them pertained to the person I was trying to reconnect with. After a few minutes, I started to lose focus and I put in other names from my past. Christmas Eve, 2000 was still a few years before people had put so much information about themselves online, that almost everyone would be easy to find. I shut down the machine and dragged myself to bed.

*****

Randy had tried, during the fall of 2000, to arrange Christmas with Melanye and Helena. But his ex had met a man that was causing her to re-evaluate her stance against remarriage. This holiday season, the new guy was whisking them to Lake Tahoe for winter holiday fun. Randy had then suggested himself and Byrncliff, a resort several miles east of his own hometown, as alternatives. But Melanye dismissed him as if he was pathetic.

He headed to his favorite downtown tap room to drink rum, hear jazz, make the best of Christmas Eve. Busy night at the bar. He recognized a few regulars. Many of them regarded this holiday only as an excuse to stay out late because there was no work the next day.

Just past eleven some of the stools to his right vacated. Three women swooped in and sat. The older one, who sat between the other two, looked familiar. The rum inside Randy propelled his words.

"I've never seen you here before. It's Millie, right?"

Her eyes flashed recognition and her mouth opened so he could see her teeth. "You come into the Perfect Drip on Saturdays," she said.

"You're my faithful barista."

She laughed. "You mean, faithless. Faith left me years ago."

It was not that she described herself as faithless, for he considered himself to be a man of faith. He sensed hurt and disappointment. He felt a connection.

"Well, it's good to see you here," he said.

"You, too."

"Uh-oh," said the younger woman sitting between them. Randy saw the woman smile.

*****

Two a.m. The tap room was closing. Randy and his new friends had made a dinner of alcohol, shrimp cocktail, garlic bread, and a piano-bass-drum trio that rendered seasonal favorites as a compliment to the strings of multi-colored lights whose soft glows adorned the bar like iridescent gum balls. A female soloist doing a creditable Ella Fitzgerald on some of the numbers. Why did it have to end.

"But I have to go," she said. "Got to drive my friends home. Look, let's have dinner tomorrow. My place. I'm off of Massachusetts Street, and I'm volunteering to cook for a homeless shelter. But that ends at three in the afternoon, so…"

He took her hand and kissed it. He waited at his mom's house for the appointed time on Christmas Day, but the early afternoon passed like an entire week. At last, he was parking his car in front of an unfamiliar house in a West Side neighborhood that had seen better days, and he walked to her door. Bottle of wine in hand.

She looked beaten down, but the light in her eyes made her noble. Her speech was seasoned with modesty. She was a cancer survivor; a vegetarian who couldn't help but cheat if there was a good steak in front of her. Had lived in town once. Worked at a popular neighborhood hangout just a few blocks away that had been closed for years. There was an affair with a priest.

"Snuck around with him for almost five years. I thought he'd leave the priesthood and give me children. I was young enough to be a mom, then."

"So, what happened?"

"I gave him an ultimatum. After all, my so-called friends said I was making him commit adultery against God. Talk about laying a guilt trip down on someone. He chose his collar over me. So I left town. Figured I could get a job at anyone's bar. I was pretty, once."

"Still are," Randy said.

She frowned at him for a moment. "Anyway," she said, "I went to Toronto, tended bar up there. Met a guy, thought I'd marry him... he wanted me to become a Canadian citizen. I might've done it for him but then I discovered he was sleeping with another gal. So I went to Ypsilanti. Place was falling apart. So I took a bus to Dallas, just to check out Texas. That's where I found out I was sick. Mechanical bulls, faith healers, my boss wrestling me away from the faith healers and getting me to the doctors and paying my deductibles. Fake boobs. Another breakup. That sums up Texas."

"I love how fast you talk once you get all wound up," Randy said.

"Whatever. So it took four years of medical stink but I got better. Went to the desert in Arizona and studied Tai Chi to try and get clean and that whole Eastern mysticism thing is bullshit too, if you ask me, and... I don't know, Randy. I'm from near here, from Olean. Went to college at Buff State. My happiest times were here. So I came back to work six days a week, ten hours a day in the Perfect Drip 'cause it's better for me than working in a bar. And I never met this guy who came in on Saturdays but acted afraid of me. And now we're having Christmas dinner together."

Randy smiled at her. She looked up at the ceiling and sighed.

"So, that's my story. And yours?"

*****

Ten-thirty at night. They had eaten and talked. Not much alcohol. Now, she invited him to leave because it was late.

He got up from his chair – they had spent the whole time at the round, wooden table, sitting across from one another, dirty dishes and silverware between them. He walked behind her and started to massage her shoulders.

"I could help you clean the kitchen. And then –"

She went from a sitting to a standing position like a rocket launch. Turned around to face him.

"No," she said, pointing with one hand at the table, "and no," she repeated, using her hand to alternately point first at Randy, then at herself, and then Randy again. "I don't date. This isn't a date."

"Last night, downtown? Talking today? Saturday mornings? Millie, we're into each other."

Her face softened and hinted sweetness. "Okay. Here's the deal, mister. This is not, first of all, about you. This is about me being healthy."

"It's not healthy for people to go through life alone, Mildred." He had heard her friends call her that the night before at the bar a time or two; it seemed to be their special term of endearment for her. He loved the effect it had on her. She smiled more broadly, and it made her glow. She took his hand and cupped it in both of hers.

"I've wanted to meet you for a long time," she said. I've often wondered which Saturday morning we'd break down and talk to each other. And this connection we have through Sal Frandino – it's interesting, isn't it?"

"We could just let it happen between us."

"Yes," she said. "Just let go for now, and let's see what happens."

31
No Illusions

June, 2005

I wanted to test my mettle as a leader. I took everything I had ever learned from my Dad, from my bosses, and from various books I had read on the topic and I poured it into my own niche of the software industry: "EP;" Earnest Professionals. The name of my startup company was a constant source of amusement to those who knew me well, and Sarah loved sending me text messages that read, "EP phone home."

It was a beautiful summer in so many respects, this summer when I returned to New York State to live. We bought a house not far from the river, one of the most scenic places my eyes had ever beheld. The view of the bridge on clear, sunny days from our little picnic area and boat landing just across the road from the house, was stunning. Looking across the water at the opposite shore, no matter what time of year, was like having our very own, ever-changing postcard. Our two youngest, one fourteen and one sixteen years of age, would now benefit from one of the most highly-regarded public school districts in the country.

But it was not the Niagara whose banks we inhabited, nor was it the Peace Bridge up the river that we admired. Nor were those Canadian hardwoods that loomed across the water. No; the Hudson, the Tappan Zee, and Westchester County defined these features of the surrounding topography. We had come north about twenty miles from our old New Jersey stomping grounds to move into our dream house.

We had been in our new digs for about four months, and it was the middle of the football season, when I made a Saturday grocery store trip. On the next day I would be sitting with other ex-pats from the Buffalo area, in the stadium down at the Meadowlands to see the Thundering Herd take on the New York Airplanes. I was buying my share of the tailgate food. Coming around a corner at the end of a food aisle, I stepped right into her path. Or at least did the shopping cart I was pushing.

"I'm sorry!"

"No, you're good," she replied. "Don't apologize." I took a second look.

"Darcie. It's Ernie. Pronotaro."

Her mouth formed a big "O" and within three seconds, we were hugging.

"Ernie! Look at you. What are you doing with yourself? Do you live here now?"

"Yeah. I'm three miles away. Right on the river, Upper Nyack."

Her eyes opened wide. "We're practically neighbors. Well, when I'm around, that is. We've got a spread south of Monsey and every so often, I actually get to live there for a few days at a time. So, you're married? Kids? Tell me the story."

We chatted for ten minutes. Exchanged phone numbers and e-mail addresses. Promised that when we had more time, we'd get together and talk more. I sent her e-mail a few days later, but she never returned it. I called her once the following spring to see if she was interested in coming for a cookout, meeting the family. My voicemail message went unanswered. I didn't take it personally. She was busy. Married to a network news executive. Lead anchor for the national six o'clock news. Interviewing everyone from international terrorists in hiding, to U.S. Presidents.

Ketchup Girl, helping to shape America's opinions about the world's unfolding events.

October, 2005

Randy was about to give the biggest speech of his life. He had spoken in this same place years earlier. The neighborhood had changed much since he had first addressed an audience in this YMCA. Half of the buildings had been removed, and the other half looked stark. Some of what had been removed had unattractive cinderblock replacements. The neighborhood where he had grown up was now riddled with empty lots where houses had once stood.

Randy and Millie had gained a reputation for do-gooding. He was a lawyer who knew how to get money and encourage people. He often told people how his painting and gardening work in the Parkside Crescent sparked the neighbors to follow suit; and how they lit up an entire city block. She embodied the spirit of volunteerism. Had empathy for the downtrodden. Touched them with her life, her hands. The couple drew off of each other's energy. Not married but of one spirit. Theirs was a gospel of doing small things to make little differences in their neighborhoods. Keep the grass cut in vacant lots. Place a park bench here or there. Plant a garden. Look out for the weak and the elderly. Fix up salvageable buildings and open new stores that improved the quality of life for people who lived nearby.

Then an idea came from John Klinglehaus, now almost an octogenarian.

"Randy, you can be mayor," he told him in a little Hertel Avenue pub, Millie seated next to him." You've got quite a following. You're clean as a whistle. What does anyone have on you?"

"I sold cocaine for a few years," Randy answered.

"Yeah, and what was that, thirty-some years ago? Youthful indiscretion, very explainable. It's a different day. People ain't concerned with that."

"I guess I just don't want to be mayor."

"You don't want to be mayor, or you don't want the hassle of running for mayor?"

Randy didn't answer.

"Think about it this way," Klinglehaus shifted in his seat. "You owe it to us. What Sal did, putting you and your sister through school. He took his failures as a mayor to the grave with him. He had to reckon with a lot on his deathbed. He thought he made mistakes and let the city down. He wanted to leave a positive legacy, and he felt like he did the opposite."

"I'm sorry he felt that way. But not my problem."

"Maybe not. But I know people, and I know you. I never took my eyes off you, because the man you call Pops, he made me promise I wouldn't. You were groomed for this. He loved this city, and he wanted to die believing that somehow, some way, all the mistakes he made would be corrected."

"So?" Randy said. He and Millie looked at one another.

"You are his legacy, my friend. And my legacy too, if you don't mind my saying. But what you do with it, it's up to you. Because you're a good man, and the people in this town – they'll vote for you."

Randy felt his head wag its negative reply.

"Randy, you also owe it to yourself. You coulda stayed in Florida, coulda stayed married, coulda raised your daughter. But you didn't make that choice. You counted the cost, and you planted yourself here."

"No," Randy replied. "John, look -"

"No, you look. Sylvia Snead and I, when we called you with this opportunity ten years ago? This was the plan. Believe it or not. We didn't know if you are who we thought you are, who Sal thought you were. But you are. You've proven it over a decade back here. You're a leader. It's your time, Randy."

Overwhelmed with a sense that his entire life had just reached a watershed moment.

"I – didn't expect a conversation like this," he said.

"I'm not above begging, Randy. I'm a very old man now." Klinglehaus wrung his hands. "So I'm begging. There's nothing in it for me, other than the joy of seeing something good happen for this town. I go home to my nice street here in North Park after this, and I'm not gonna live long enough to see this neighborhood decay. But I promised Sal on his deathbed that if I ever thought you were ready for this, I'd step in and do what I could to make it happen."

"That's crazy," Randy said. "I don't believe you. That Sal Frandino told you all those years ago he wanted me to be the mayor. Shoot."

"You didn't believe him when he first told you he'd pay for your college, either. How'd that turn out?"

Randy turned to the woman seated next to him with hopes of rescue. "What do you think?" he asked.

Millie smiled. "I say, do it. For me and Sal."

He continued to look at her, and after a few seconds he began to feel his head nodding up and down. He did not smile. He felt solemn.

*****

So it followed that tonight, Randy Loring would speak to his supporters and to the media. Three weeks until the election. He had learned politics quickly; Klinglehaus said Randy was a natural. Sylvia Snead and her dad, politician emeritus, were the face of the Loring campaign to the city of 280,000 people; over half of whom were now people of color.

William Snead introduced him to the over five hundred who had gathered. The embattled residents who stood their ground inside the city limits were ready for something new. Perhaps it had been there, latent for years, but now had come a palpable tipping point. A throng of those who remained in the city were becoming a tribe. In search of a worthy chief.

Eighty-six year old William Snead was still an active voice. Beloved of his community. He craved speechmaking, and he gave them often. He had learned to infuse his delivery with emotion since the earlier years. Now, he employed everything he had learned to whip the overflow crowd into a frenzy for a candidate they had already embraced. Randy sat behind him, between Sylvia Snead and Millie, on folding chairs. Holding a hand of each lady, waiting his turn. And then he heard the elder Snead shout his name. Thunderous acclaim. He walked to the dias.

He recited to himself a mantra that John Klinglehaus had given to him; a mantra that had guided their joint formulation of his prepared and rehearsed speech: "Be honest."

He could only be honest. It was what the city demanded; what his soul demanded. He stepped onto the podium filled with a sense of wholeness that far exceeded anything else that life had ever provided. Basking in adoration. Knowing that hundreds of others who were not present that night would be adoring him along with those present. He said "thank you," a dozen times. He smiled, he floated above the ground. Finally they settled down enough that he could make a start.

"Ladies, and gentlemen, brothers and sisters of all races and creeds. To be honest with you, I am not a politician."

They screamed again and he could not continue. He grasped the contradiction. He was not a politician, yet now, he most fully and certainly was. He had just told his first campaign lie. All the while, being as honest as he could.

He told them next that they were the City of No Illusions, and that meant they all knew they needed to help one another. They knew they needed help from outside the city, too, but having no illusions meant they knew that no one would care about them if they wallowed in self-defeat. The citizens needed to find ways to do whatever they could, even the smallest of things, to remake the place into everything it could be. They must promise to never quit on each other. He promised that as mayor, he'd fight to give more funds directly to each neighborhood group that presented a sensible plan to improve their streets, start a business or provide a needed service.

Fifteen minutes after he started, it was time to wrap up. He belted out his concluding points:

"And so, when you're voting for me, you're voting for the guy who says to Albany, to Washington, and to the world! Do you hear me, to the world!"

The fervor in the gym was now was deafening.

"That we are taking care of ourselves! That we are getting our city ready for a good, solid future. That when you invest here you are investing in a people and a place that will not ever quit, that will keep getting up and answering the bell, that will eventually succeed. I have a feeling tonight that none of you are quitters. I have that feeling 'cause you're here with me. See you at the polls. God bless all-a-yous!"

*****

The *Star*, now the City's only daily, was full of news about Randy's speech the next morning. Columnists were split; some praising him as a breath of fresh air; others decrying his call to neighborhood self-help as naïve, small-minded and doomed to hasten the city's demise. But a week before the election, the *Star* as well as three of the city's four television stations and a prominent local political Web site, endorsed him.

It was after midnight on the night of the election tally. Randy retired to the privacy of his suite downtown in the Hyatt Regency. Exhausted. In the excitement of the evening, he'd forgotten his cell phone in the room and now, before collapsing on the bed, he checked his voicemail. He hit the button to see what he had missed, and his eyes went straight to the one from Melanye. They hadn't spoken in nearly two months. He listened to her island-accented voice.

"Congratulations, mayor-elect. We been following tonight on the Internet. Your daughter is interested in learning about how government works. Can she be an intern in your City Hall next summer?"

November 13, 2005

Five days had passed since the election. Randy has been invited to watch the Thundering Herd's contest against the Kansas City Arrowheads from the owner's box at The Ralph in suburban Orchard Park. A tradition the team's owner has extended to the winners of every mayoral election since Kowalski took the honors in 1961.

Randy and Millie drove that morning with Sylvia Snead and one of few dentists who still maintained an office on the Michigan Street corridor – Sylvia's husband. They began with breakfast at the Perfect Drip where Millie had toiled for so many years. Then they drove the waterfront as it stretched south and west from City Hall. It was partly cloudy and windy, the chameleon lake blue or gray depending on whether the sun was veiled behind the white, puffy clouds that pushed from west to east. No boats in view save for those docked in the small boat harbor. Even a warm November day was not quite warm enough for most pleasure craft owners; and the freighters - well, they had disappeared over a decade earlier.

"It's beautiful," said Sylvia's husband.

"It's as empty as hell. Hulls of empty buildings. Just emptiness," said Sylvia.

"It's haunting," said Millie.

Randy thought they all saw it correctly. It made him remember what a college philosophy class taught about raw potential. It was ruin, chaos, the absence of direction. It was the waterfront. It could become anything.

On this Sunday morning headed into Lackawanna along the water there were no cars, no people, and nothing that looked like it had been built in the past fifty years. To the right were stretches of a couple hundred yards at a time with an unobstructed view to the lake; some of the plant's old buildings had been leveled. Other buildings remained, brick and metal containers of loneliness awaiting their inevitable fate.

Randy thought the quiet which had descended upon this sector of the metropolis was more profound than that of Sabbath rest.

Not far inland from the lakeshore, the terrain gives way to gentle rolling hills alive with suburbia. Approaching the stadium, the mayor-elect's Caddy fell in line with game traffic. Once the 74,000-seat outpost of professional football was in view, dads and sons, blue-clad men and women with names and numbers on their backs congregated everywhere. Footballs cut spiraling paths through the sausage, burger and rib-scented air. Randy rolled down the window so he could breathe in the life of it.

So it happened that Randy Loring attended his first football game since his life in Miami and rooting for his adopted Fish. He would soon be sworn in as the mayor of the city that cheered for the Royal Blue, White and Red no matter what misfortune befell the town or the team. He squeezed Millie's hand and silently resolved that he would rebuild his emotional bridge to the Thundering Herd.

The game was almost over. The Herd was going to send the throng home happy. He engaged eye contact with the very old man who had extended the invitation, and who sat next to him.

"Mister Wilson, thank you."

"What for?" returned the elderly man's unsteady voice. "I didn't make any tackles today. Didn't gain a yard."

"Thank you, sir, for never quitting on our town."

All afternoon, Randy had perceived the frailty of the man who owned the team. And then, Mr. Wilson put surprising strength into his grip on the new mayor's hand.

32
The Thundering Herd, Re-gathered

July 4, 2010: Morning

Sarah and I often timed our visits to Uncle Ricco and Aunt Claudia to coincide with the summer months. My parents were both gone, but the Gugliuzzas had the gift of longevity and good health. The kids knew their mother's relatives on Long Island well, and crazy Aunt Donna had become a favorite. But I wanted my children to also know my side of the family tree. There was a new generation of cousins in Buffalo.

During many visits I would plan on half a day at a time to drive around town, alone. Check out what was going on in all of its nooks and crannies. So it wasn't unusual that I was driving alone at half past eight in the morning on a sunny Independence Day. I decided to sit in an Elmwood Avenue cafe with a cappuccino and a biscotti.

The barista asked what name to call when my drink was ready. Another Ernie had just ordered. She wanted my last initial.

"Ernie P," I said.

Five minutes later I was sitting down at a table with my drink, head buried in the latest edition of the *Star*. A woman cleared her throat. I looked up at her. She held a cup of Joe.

"Anyone sitting across from you?"

"No." I was a little confused. There were a few empty tables in the place.

"Well, I might need that outlet to charge my phone," she explained, pointing to one close by.

"Oh, sure."

She smiled and sat. Pretty smile, pretty eyes behind wire-rimmed frames. I went back to my paper. For about thirty seconds.

"You're Ernie P."

I looked up at her. "Uh. Yeah. I am."

Her eyes grew bigger. "Ernie the Pro."

I allowed myself a good look at her. I felt my eyes grow bigger too.

An Old Man and His River

The President of the Seneca Nation of Indians thought ahead to the council meeting scheduled for the very next day. Black and white leaders would participate along with the red ones. There was money at stake, and jobs. Many people had very strong reactions to his proposals. He was touted as a savior. He was hung in effigy. Lamont Raincloud.

He was a self-confident man, but even so, every precaution must be taken. Today, he must prepare himself spiritually.

Raincloud readied his canoe. The river that snaked its way through the city of the same name, awaited. He would start at the lighthouse by the Coast Guard Station, where the river emptied into the lake. He would paddle upstream all the way to Ebenezer where the ancestral leader Red Jacket, a thorny acquaintance to Jefferson, Franklin and Washington, had once lay buried - before his grave was relocated by the white man to Forest Lawn Cemetery among other deceased city luminaries.

The day, pleasant. The current, easy. The water, clear. Gulls called overhead. Some game fish the white men had stocked the river with, flashed silver off the starboard side. Raincloud imagined sportsmen coming to enjoy this place.

Inner laughter commenced with the first stroke. He contemplated the new arena, a flying saucer that landed near the Skyway Bridge. He had never dreamed, when he learned the game as a boy, the possibility of a professional lacrosse league and how white people would clamor to watch and to play. A spaceship of concrete. A temple of hockey and lacrosse.

It would take Raincloud until past noon to make Ebenezer. Fine. The white man's Independence Day was a day to relax. The empty grain elevators monitored his trek up the river in grand silence.

He carried songs in his heart. Part of him wished that they were the songs of the *Haudenosaunee*, the Iroquois, from which he had mostly descended. But he had grown fond of Pitbull. He grew in happiness with each stroke of the oars. Something old and something new; Latin rap, the grain elevators – a smallmouth bass.

He passed by the place on the banks of the river where he wanted his casino built. If all went well, the parcel would be designated as traditional Seneca land, giving him the right to build on it.

He understood the controversy. Did a casino belong in the city? He understood the moralists' concerns that it would feed addictions and end up as an economic drain on the region it was purported to help. He was a moralist himself.

He reached the place called Riverbend, once dominated by heavy industry. Now, it was nothing more than an overgrown flood plain. He spotted a lone beaver, and he smiled. One beaver meant there were other small mammals.

He recalled a conversation about history after a recent Sunday School class. His pastor, a Princeton grad with one of the sharpest minds Raincloud had ever encountered, made a convincing case during a Starbucks debate that history ultimately is linear, not circular. Raincloud laughed out loud. He embraced the essential truths of Christianity just as certainly as he revered the stories of Handsome Lake and Hiawatha. Was he a walking contradiction? An enigma? A lost soul? He rehearsed to himself his simple formulas for reconciling his beliefs into a coherent whole. Handsome Lake and Hiawatha were like Old Testament saints. Raincloud smiled to himself.

Finally, at the place where the stream passed alongside a road intersection, Chief Raincloud emerged from the ravine, canoe on his back, an anomaly to vehicular passers-by. Ebenezer. Dressed in khaki shorts, a Syracuse University t-shirt and a Bisons baseball cap, a big man with a canoe hoisted upon his back needed no feathers on his head to look odd to passers-by. He laughed aloud.

He sat on a metal guardrail that kept errant drivers from spilling over into the ravine he just had emerged from. Retrieved his cell phone from a waterproof bag in which he had also packed a roast beef and bacon submarine sandwich for his mid-day meal. Punched a few keys. A familiar name synonymous with "love" appeared on the screen. He pressed "talk."

Three rings. Then she answered.

"Hey. What's cooking?"

"Hey, Darse. How's things on your end of the state?"

"Busy. But I can get away this weekend. The usual disguise. The flight I always get on Saturday mornings."

"The lake was so beautiful today. It's a holiday for you European Americans. Wish you were here to share it with me."

"Ha! That proves what I've been telling you for years."

"And what would that be?"

"You actually do like the Fourth of July."

*****

"Ernie. Oh my God."

"Shelly Delancey?"

"Shelly Kelleher now, but yeah," she answered me.

"You look great."

"I've put on a few pounds, but thank you. And you..." With that, her voice cracked.

"Shelly."

"Ernie the Pro. Oh, my God." Our hands reached across the table.

"Shelly," I repeated. Like a dummy.

"My aunt passed away," she said. "My husband flew back a couple days ago to Seattle, we live there you know though we had a few years in L.A. thrown in during the nineties."

"Yeah."

"I stayed here a few extra days to take care of my aunt's estate. Ernie let's go for a walk. Can you?"

I thought for a moment about Sarah. Then we were up out of our chairs.

The wire-rimmed glasses she now wore did nothing to spoil her appearance. A touch of gray mixed in. We walked outside. Corner of Elmwood and Bidwell Parkway. And then we were holding one another. I felt her sobbing. Saw her red face.

"No, Shelly. Don't."

"Ernie oh my God my life has come full circle."

"Okay, but stop it. Please." Me, feeling such happiness.

"Yeah," she said, her face filling my field of vision. "No tears because we both married good people and we have good lives, right?"

"Whatever you say."

"Ernie, let's walk."

"Whatever you say."

This was crazy. I had friends in the area and someone might see me walking with another woman, holding her hand.

We ended up on a bench in a nearby park, sitting beside each other. I looked straight ahead. Her face, her eyes. Too familiar. Too much for me to handle, like looking directly at the sun.

"I'm sorry it's so awkward," she finally said. "I couldn't help myself when I knew it was you because I've never forgotten you."

"Awkward, but I'm glad. Glad you're here and alive and..."

"Yeah me too Ernie turn and look at me please."

"I want to, but I can't."

"But I'm looking at you. You're not so scary to look at you know."

That made me laugh. I turned my face toward her.

"There. That wasn't so bad. Ernie, I don't want to get you in trouble. But how much time can we spend? To talk?"

"A couple hours? My wife and kids are hanging out at the hotel."

"Do you know the way to Angola? I want to see the beach again. I spent all my summers there as a kid and I'm not good with directions."

Looking at one another with intent.

"Your car, then. I'll drive," I said.

We put an oldies station on her rental car's satellite radio, and we headed off. I knew it was wrong to get in the car and go with her. To trade soft laughter with her once again; the same laughter we shared when my appointed rounds as a bike courier brought her into my life so many years earlier and I stole her from Mike.

I did it anyway.

We discovered the many things that, had fate kept us together, would have united us. Saturday Night Live. The E Street Band; the Graceland album. U.S. women's soccer. Harry Potter teaching our kids to read. A special person taken from us on September 11. Shelly's struggles during a difficult first pregnancy. The agonies Sarah and I faced as our oldest son experimented with club drugs during high school.

She said she was used to the cold Pacific at Coos Bay; or to clear mountain lakes in Idaho, or to the times she and her husband took their kids down to the Baja. But her earliest beach memories were of our lake, which warms nicely in the summer. We looked for the cottage her parents had once owned. We couldn't find it. So we parked. Hiked a trail over a grassy dune and through a stand of trees, and then down a long wooden stairway to the beach where her dad had taught her to swim so well.

We set off on a walk along the sand. When she reached for my hand, I didn't pull mine away.

"Thank you Ernie for bringing me here these last few days have been so meaningful and now I'm with you again and this is the icing on the cake."

"Weddings and funerals," I responded. "You know what they say."

"Remember our campfire, Ernie? I told you all my crazy thoughts, and you listened and you loved me despite how crazy I was."

"You weren't crazy. You were beautiful. You were exquisite."

We stopped walking, and faced one another.

"You - you um, still are, Michelle."

"Am I really?" She didn't say it to tease. More like a scientist. A skeptical one.

"I'm not afraid of you, Ernie," she said. "Let's just sit together and look at the water."

But we didn't look at the water. We sat cross-legged in the sand facing each other, holding hands and smiling. Squeezing fingers and not saying much. Faces drawing closer. Conflict rising within me. Then, six inches from what might have ended in a kiss, her soft words.

"Sarah sounds like an awesome wife and a great gal. I mean, she stole you from her big sister. She's got lady stones."

"Cleo sounds like a great husband. You did really good, Shelly."

All around, people thirty-five years younger than us played out their own beach stories.

"Shelly," I finally said. What do we do now?"

"We simply declare victory, Ernie."

I felt the confusion on my face.

"We declare victory," she repeated, "and we agree to friend each other and stay in touch and we'd better get you back now because from what you tell me of Sarah if I don't have you back to her on time she'll kick both of our asses."

Laughter.

"You know what's great?" she said.

"Tell me."

"History moves forward in a straight line to a destination, right? But these days we have all this great technology to rediscover people from our past. We can make little circles of history for ourselves."

"Little circles," I repeated.

"Yeah. Little circles that make the forward line of our histories more beautiful."

"Circles. Lines. Shelly, I'm lost."

"Don't play with me," she was still smiling. "You know what I mean with my lines and circles."

"Yes, I do."

She kissed me. A sudden little peck on my unsuspecting mouth. Then she scrambled to her feet, a strong hand pulling me up with her.

July 4, 2010: Evening

Darcie and Raincloud lay in each other's arms. A room at a bed-and-breakfast outside the city whose owners claimed Seneca blood. Her crow's feet and moderate wrinkles combined with the light from her eyes to make hers the most interesting face he'd ever seen. Her body trim and solid, forged by thousands of hours in a yoga studio over many years. Her hair had lost its sheen, but was as stylish as the day his mother introduced them to each other in the kitchen on Shoreham Boulevard so many years earlier. He had loved her every day since. He hated that she was living a sham with a rich old guy down in Rockland County.

It happened between them twenty years earlier during a congressional hearing on the plight of Native Americans on reservations. She, the nationally-famous news personality covering the story. He, a rising voice of advocacy in the prime of his life. Dinner and wine became a night of sexual frenzy. All-consuming. By the end of the second night, he knew her story. She was finished trying to be the good wife. Her husband didn't want kids the way she did; didn't even want to spend time with her. Her marriage would reshape itself to accommodate the reappearance of Raincloud.

In the beginning he build his entire life around her visits like an addict. But she became afraid. Blamed him for making her risk her career. For six months they fought over it. Nearly broke things off. Decided to try again.

Sometimes, her guilt over their unsanctioned relationship would still trouble her. Though their day and evening together had been pleasant, he sensed that as they lay together, she was fighting this battle again.

He began to massage from the center of her forehead back to her temples along her hairline. He knew that she loved this. It soothed her.

"You're doing it again," he said.

"What're you talking about?"

"You're questioning us. You're thinking we're wrong. You feel like a sneak again."

She sighed. "I'm busted."

"What tapes are playing inside you?"

"The dad tapes. You know, that my Dad wanted something better for me."

He readjusted himself so that he could kiss her gently on the forehead. Then she turned her body to face away from him, and she lay spooned against him. He draped one arm around her waist, and used his other hand to rub the nape of her neck.

"Our dads loved us," Raincloud said. "They wanted us happy. They've arranged this whole thing from their place at God's feast table."

"Yeah," she said. She broke free of his embrace so that she could lay on her back and turn her face toward him. She broke out into a grin.

"That's the best explanation I can come up with," she said.

"Yesterday, today and for always," he said.

"Hey, chief. Important question."

"Ask me."

"I want to know your biggest regret in life."

"Got no regrets."

"Come on, Monty. I'm a reporter." She stroked his chest with her hand. "There must be something. Tell me."

"Why?"

"Because you've never told me, and I've never asked. But if I die tonight, I want to die knowing one more thing about you than I do now."

"Okay, you remember Ernie Pronotaro? Ernie the Pro?"

"Ernie Pronotaro —" her voice trailed.

"Don't give me that. You remember him."

"Okay, I remember him. So —"

"I don't have regrets. But, I sort of wish I knew whatever happened to him."

"Well. Why don't you Google him?"

"Because I want him to Google me first."

She stuck a finger into the side of his face. "You're a turd," she said.

September, 2011

Monday morning and Randy is in Albany. Summoned by the governor. Another opportunity to grovel. He hated this part of the job. A day-old hatchling in the nest, his desperate peeps for food barely audible because his voice was so small. It seemed like years had passed since anyone from outside of Buffalo had cared for it. He would beg and hope the mother bird would drop some regurgitated nourishment into his city's coffers. He straightened his tie and heard a voice from the television set in his hotel room remind viewers that it was September 19, 2011.

A limousine will spirit him off to the Governor's Mansion. He, Sylvia Snead, and John Klinglehaus. The night before they had dined together in one of Albany's better steak houses; Klinglehaus, a hearty eighty-something years old, ate more red meat than either of his dinner companions and held forth with stories about the old days, making his younger companions laugh despite themselves. Gallows humor about how meetings with the Governor went for political leaders from Western New York.

The meeting was scheduled for nine a.m. The Governor did not keep them waiting. The chancellor and provost of the State University system were in the office with the Governor. Handshakes and hugs. The normal Bee-Ess that happens at the start of these meetings.

The Governor settled into his chair. "Randy, Sylvia, John." The Governor beamed a campaign-ish smile in their direction. He was a young man; some would say handsome. "I know the things you want to ask for. But this will be a little different. I get to go first."

Randy squirmed. *What will we get blasted for this time…*

"I've asked the scholars to sit in because I want to tell you about a plan of mine that involves them," the Governor continued. Randy, first off, you've succeeded. I've seen it in your neighborhoods on my last few visits. Since we turned control of the city budget back to you and your people, we see a continued trend of improvement…"

Randy entered a trance-like state as the Governor continued.

"…the responsibility your citizens are taking for beautification. We've got people from out of state asking about the garden walks your communities have organized…"

"…cities like Detroit who have the same or worse levels of distress are studying what you've done. Why just last month, the Michigan Department of Public Works inquired about…"

"…Enough talk about the new Medical Campus. It's time to put our money where our mouth is. That's why Marv and Mary are here. Mary, let them know our vision for the city's core."

Mary from the University system took command of the room for the next ten minutes as the Governor rose to dim the lights for a PowerPoint show. A huge new urban campus, and money to draw new businesses and development to the sections of the city with the biggest needs. A dollar figure ending in so many zeros, that Randy wondered aloud if a mistake has been made on one of the slides.

"It's no mistake," the governor said.

When the Governor turned the lights back up, Randy noticed that John Klinglehaus was drying his eyes with a hanky. Randy turned to face the Governor.

"Why all this, now? All this money, all this sudden attention. This… help."

"Reason one – it's the right thing. Right for you, right for the state. And right for me. Which leads to reason one-A."

"Which is?"

"I'm a professional politician. I make no bones about it. I've not only got to get re-elected, but I also have ambitions beyond the state. I need success stories. Powerful ones. The national party says I need to be seen a guy who steps in and fixes problems that are bigger than any one state. So I need to be perceived as a big hero. And you need a hero. Here I am."

"Nothing's free," said Klinglehaus. "What will this cost us?"

The Governor smiled. "An understandable reaction."

Klinglehaus chuckled. "Yes, now that you've succeeded in making us feel like we've just heard the Vienna Boys Choir sing the Hallelujah Chorus. What do you need from us?"

The governor put his hands out in front of him, palms up.

"Loyalty. Just let me take credit. Sing my praises. I will make it happen in the Legislature. In fact, that process has already begun. And in return, Mayor Randy Loring, you're my guy and I'm your guy. From this day forward when you walk out of here, the public face we put on our relationship is that we each have indisputable proof that the other guy is a freaking genius who knows how to turn around the fortune of an entire region and we're sweet, moral people to boot."

"This," said Klinglehaus, "is too good to be true. If you can get the money voted for all these projects."

"This, my friend," said the Governor, "is pragmatic politics. And, on a non-pragmatic note, I do know in my bones it's right."

Later that afternoon, the threesome cleared security at Albany's airport with an hour to kill before the charter flight back home would be ready to board. They sat in a semi-private VIP lounge. Randy sipped a glass of white rum, and Klinglehaus peered down into scotch on the rocks that he had hardly touched. Sylvia, the teetotaler in the group, chewed gum.

"New construction like we haven't seen in my whole lifetime," Randy said. "Sustainable industry. Thousands of jobs if it all pans out. I wish Pops were here today."

"He is," said Klinglehaus. He paused, and then pointed a finger across the table at Randy. "He's living inside you."

"The Governor's words today mean nothing without action," Sylvia Snead said. "It sounds fine, but as of this moment, nothing has happened."

"You sound skeptical, counselor," Randy said.

"Only one way to find out," Klinglehaus said. "I suggest we get on board. Because if we don't, history ain't gonna be kind to us."

33
Water From the Sky: Reprise

February 1, 2016

Mayor Randy Loring watched the clouds increase as the morning continued. Storms this time of year often came disguised as a flock of white sheep, only to soon become a horde of black goats that marched out of the lake in a long line and vomited ice and snow upon everything in their path.

Sal Frandino was on the wall. Frozen in two black and white dimensions, frozen in 1960. From time to time, Millie would visit. She'd point at the likeness of her former Arkansas Lounge patron. "Good old Saint Salvatore, eh? Looks just like a movie star, don't he?"

Millie's visits were now almost certainly of the past. After the holidays, she was hospitalized for shortness of breath and chest pains. January was a time of hospital visits and doctor talk. An emergency surgery to clear Millie's blocked artery; medication to save her once when her heart stopped. Over the past weekend, a coma. The latest doctor talk: she had days left.

Randy knew that her legacy was secure. Throughout the city, as cold and snowy as the rest of winter might be, spring would come and when it did there would be flowers and fresh paint, neighborhood fairs and food festivals, local microbrewers contributing craft beer; urban farms that had begun operating in the city where abandoned slums once stood, contributing food. Millie had poured herself into encouraging all of it.

Thank God for Helena. Randy's daughter took care of the business Phyllis Romanello had once handled. Taking care of her "old man," she called it. Helena had three years' tenure as her dad's administrative chief of staff. Some saw nepotism. Randy viewed it as sanity.

The downtown skyline was changing. The new additions were not titanic towers but rather, structures of modest height that housed much of the new life that was being breathed into an old metropolis. Blocks of buildings devoted to biotechnology and medical research. A new complex of ice rinks that hosted amateur hockey tournaments the year round. On the banks of the snaking river that shared its name with the city, new industries that helped equip America to solve the energy challenges of the new century blending with nightly laser shows that celebrated the city's industrial heritage. New hotels and restaurants to accommodate visitors and patrons of all that was now happening in what many called the New Buffalo.

Yet the lingering scars of industrial decline presented themselves to Randy every time he visited his mother, who clung to her neighborhood and to her life. Her grand-daughter's permanent residence in the city invigorated her like the right plant food brings the bloom to a daisy.

Randy looked at the clouds once more before his 10:30 a.m. appointment, and then at Pops.

"Hey, bud," he said to the silent portrait. "They say we could get a blizzard tonight. Not the best news… hey, man. We need some help from Albany, just like when you were here. We got ourselves a strange new governor, different priorities, he says. The state portion of the public investment might not come through this year and that means one of the green manufacturers might pull out. Two thousand jobs in the balance."

He still had four minutes to kill until the 10:30 appointment. He was grateful that occasionally, small businessmen from out of town wanted to come talk about what they can do to help sustain the area's resurgence. But he was not in the mood to meet a stranger. To face 2016 without Millie.

He looked at the resume of the out-of-towner he was about to meet. They shared the same undergraduate alma mater. A local one.

Helena buzzed. "Send him in," Randy said. The door opened and a balding fellow walked into the office. "Mayor Loring," the man said, a hand extended. "It is truly a pleasure to meet you." Firm handshake.

*****

I was never going to be wildly rich and successful. Many of the people I hired to staff Earnest Professionals were smarter and more ambitious than I was. As we grew to over a hundred people, I knew I had reached my capacity to lead. It was no longer about getting bigger or richer. It was increasingly, as Sarah often reminded me, about staying healthy and finding personal fulfillment.

The idea for this business trip had been germinating in me for two years. If it happened as planned, it would bring fulfillment. Much of my thinking, I can't explain. Except to say, the idea was woven into the fabric of who I have always been.

On this cold Monday morning, I landed in Buffalo for a mid-morning meeting with Mayor Randy Loring.

We shook hands. He looked tired and worried. I hadn't been in the City Hall building since I was eleven years old and went down to get the physical exam the city administered back then to kids who applied for newspaper delivery routes.

I settled into my chair and the mayor started.

"Mr. Pronotaro, I've looked through your resume and the literature you sent on your company. But I'd like to hear in your own words, what you'd like to do and how I can help you."

"Sure, mayor, thanks," I said. "The three main points are, number one, I have a profitable business that the new industries who have located here can benefit from; number two, I was born and raised here and my heart's desire is to see the area grow and prosper, and number three, a 100% waiver of city and county taxes in years one and two, and a 50% waiver in year three, will allow me to immediately create at least forty high-paying jobs, providing services in the information technology sector that are needed and that will make it even more attractive for other businesses in the new economy to operate here. If it goes well, future expansion beyond the first forty jobs is not just possible, but likely."

"Wow. I love a man who doesn't mince his words. You say you were born and raised here? Where? Was it right inside the city?"

"Played in the Delaware-Hertel Little League, if that helps you."

"I played Pop Warner football for the Central Park Eagles," he replied. I felt myself smile and lean forward. Chances were good that we'd be doing business together.

*****

It was Seneca Nation President Lamont Raincloud's 60th birthday. Despite the forecast of a snowstorm, there would be parties at both the Western Door club in his casino, and at the new Marriott at Canalside. Darcie was seeing to it. Her divorce, retirement and relocation back to the city had long since run the cycle of newsworthiness. Now in her seventies, she was seen as a grand old dame of the local scene. She appeared at grade schools and neighborhood libraries to help with literacy programs. Lectured as an adjunct professor in the University's school of media and journalism.

Darcie had orchestrated everything. She had assembled people from Lamont's past and present to roast him, to toast him, to love him.

Raincloud didn't care so much about the party. He wanted to go on a driving and walking tour. He started in the morning while the sun was still mostly shining and the temperature was rather moderate, in the high thirties, Fahrenheit. Started from the casino and walked along the river, past the new commercial and dining enclave of Larkinville. Crossed a new footbridge over the river and decided to do a slow jog south, toward the Tifft Farm nature preserve. Saw foxes and deer as he walked and jogged the trails. The Seneca had won the land back after all.

He ended his walk an hour later at the Basilica of Our Lady of Victory, in Lackawanna. He smelled something in the air that reminded him of the smelting that took place in his childhood neighborhood on the North Side. He remembered having just read that a specialty steel mill had just opened not far from the Basilica. Metal being made again in this town for the first time in over thirty years. Maybe this time, on a more sustainable scale.

He went inside the Basilica and sat, kneeled and prayed in thanksgiving for the history that had been handed to him.

He'd make it back to his room downtown soon enough. This was a time for sitting. For his ancestors, it would have been a time to smoke.

Frandino watching...

We were forty minutes over the planned time. Mayor Loring's first gut-burst of laughter came ten minutes into the meeting. I had agreed that if the deal went through, my company's employees would spend some time in the still-struggling city schools as volunteers, teaching kids entrepreneurial skills because, as the Mayor impressed on me, it would help to save the city from ever again experiencing a downturn like it had in the second half of the twentieth century.

"You feel me?" he asked as he pushed for that condition.

"I feel you loud and clear," I said. "I think it's a great idea and I say, yes."

He agreed to introduce special legislation to give me the city tax relief I needed to get my local venture started. He walked me out and rode the elevator to street level with me.

When I got back to my rental car, I checked my phone messages. There was only one.

"Ernie, my friend. This is your old acquaintance, Darcie. Yes, that Darcie. I know this is last minute, and I'm a bad person for not returning your calls way back when, but is there any way in the world you can get up to Buffalo tonight? And hurry, 'cause it's supposed to snow! I just had a sudden inspiration, but it's a great one. I want to spring a big surprise on an old, stubborn friend of yours who is having his big six-zero up here today. Please find a way to get here, Ernie. Life is short. Call me back."

Damn that Darcie Yeager. Here I sit in my rental car, head full of childhood memories of February birthday parties for Raincloud, and his talk of being the eventual winner. How in the world has he managed to have Darcie in town, involved in his sixtieth birthday celebration?

I'm pressing the callback option now. I'm already in town. The coming snowstorm might cancel my flight home in the evening anyway. I guess I'm stuck for the night in this infuriatingly fast and slow, big and small, warm and cold, cutting-edge and old relic hometown of mine. Aunt Claudia and Uncle Ricco are still alive and kicking. Though the old willow is gone now, they still have the same backyard where the Salt of the Earth used to warn us cousins not to stand too close to open hearth furnaces. I know they would love to see me for a couple of hours while I wait for whatever Darcie is cooking up for Raincloud here, in the homeland. I'm waiting for her to answer her phone and wondering if any of us have ever left this place.

Also by Dave DiGrazie

Dave's first two novels are both **available on Amazon.com:**

Von Lagerhaus

Two women with very different lives become too careless to stay alive. In a flash, they are together. Out in the woods. With others joining, and a mystery person who seems to know where they're going. Can these people handle the possibility that they're all heading toward their wildest dreams? Could you handle it if it were you?

Clarion Foreword: *"A combination of Lost, Fantasy Island, and The Twilight Zone that's been sprinkled with a pinch of The Wizard of Oz… there is much of value in this odd tale."*

See John Play

Connie Kaminski's considerable charms have earned her frustration – in the person of her golfing, gambling, gallivanting husband. A woman with attractive options – and then, he starts winning big money. A trite forumula? Not the way Connie deals with her situation.

Kirkus: *"A rousing tale of character interplay. DiGrazie succeeds … Humor helps: It's funny to watch a golfer who's just won almost a million dollars ask someone to pay for his gas."*